Of course, there was plenty of money now – and always so many things to spend it on. So how had it come to this? Living a life that seemed so perfect – a life in which they talked but never communicated, had sex but never made love, argued but never reached agreement. Was this, as she asked herself so often, how things were meant to be? Was she foolish to hope for more? After all, they were married, living together as husband and wife, a normal middle-class couple with friends and family of whom few suspected they were anything other than blissfully happy.

In these disturbing moments of truth, she could not deny that they were deceiving everyone. And worst of all, she realised, with a sick jolt, she was deceiving herself.

Jane Elizabeth Varley studied at Oxford and went on to qualify as as barrister. She became a law lecturer and taught at Kingston University before going to live in France and write full time. She now divides her time between Surrey and Normandy. She has one son. *Wives and Lovers* is her first novel.

WIVES *and* LOVERS

June Elizabeth Varley

ORION

An Orion paperback

First published in Great Britain in 2003
by Orion
This paperback edition published in 2004
by Orion Books Ltd
Orion House, 5 Upper St Martin's Lane,
London WC2H 9EA

3 5 7 9 10 8 6 4 2

A CIP catalogue record for this book is
available from the British Library.

ISBN 0 75285 884 X

Typeset by Deltatype Ltd, Birkenhead, Merseyside

Printed and bound in Great Britain by
Clays Ltd, St Ives plc

For my mother

CHAPTER I

Victoria Stratford considered that her husband's fortieth birthday party was going as well as could be expected. The drawing room hummed with animated conversation, smokers had taken her gentle hint and drifted into the garden and she had so far managed to avoid prolonged conversation with any of her guests. However, the continued absence of her husband was increasingly irritating. She did not fear an accident – or worse: David could be relied upon to be late – only to burst in upon the room – and, with tales of awkward judges and London traffic, apologise for his absence in a way that suggested he was not terribly sorry at all but expected to be forgiven his lateness.

He would be forgiven, by the friends, family and neighbours who had gathered to celebrate his birthday but more especially to gaze upon his Wimbledon house, which after a year of renovations over three floors and thousands of pounds, was now theirs to occupy again. It was *his* house: although he had been married to Victoria for fifteen years, and they had two children, David was at heart a lawyer and had thus omitted to place the house in their joint names.

There was, moreover, as their guests were to be told in good time, another event to celebrate.

Victoria heard more people arriving. Her daily, Consuela, was stationed by the front door to take coats and point new arrivals in the direction of the drawing room. Six guests had arrived together and were bunched dangerously in the hallway beside two waitresses bearing trays of hot sausages coated with marmalade. Victoria had been unsure of this last concoction but Panda had assured her it would be a certain hit and guests, after initial reservations, seemed to bear this out.

In truth, Victoria found Panda rather intimidating, but she had been highly recommended by one of the mothers at school and she certainly looked the part – slightly porky, nudging forty, and always dressed in a man's blue-and-white-striped shirt, navy pedal-pushers and those flat blue pumps with gilt chains across the front that Victoria thought they'd stopped making years ago. One of the last surviving Sloane Rangers still at large in the King's Road, Panda had made it clear over the telephone that she normally only catered for central London parties but, as it was a quiet time, would on this occasion venture south of the river. Of course, at their first meeting, Panda had rumbled Victoria within seconds – guessed that she had never used caterers before, breezily substituted champagne for white wine and smiled patronisingly at Victoria's enquiry about serviettes before assuring her that *paper napkins* would be provided.

But David had been insistent: influential people would be coming to this party, senior barristers, well-connected friends, and the neighbours. Neighbours from their side of the street – the Edwardian semis – but more especially from the double-fronted Victorian houses opposite, on bigger plots, with basements, four reception rooms and off-street parking. And the original bells for the servants. Houses that sold before the local agents had time to type up the details – 'Generously proportioned family home, retaining many period features, in the heart of Wimbledon Village with easy access to the City, benefiting from a choice of excellent private schools.' Houses lived in by sophisticated people who could not be served Victoria's party food – toast triangles with smoked-salmon pâté, mini vol-au-vents and Twiglets, cheese footballs, peanuts, or anything encased in flaky pastry.

Victoria caught sight of her sister and brother-in-law hovering in the hallway and sprang towards them, relieved to see their familiar faces in a sea of acquaintances.

'Bottle of red.' Tom pressed a plastic carrier-bag into her hand.

Cooking wine, no doubt. Victoria made a mental note to give it to Consuela tomorrow. But she was grateful that they had come, aware that Tom detested cocktail parties. 'You really didn't need to bring anything,' she said. 'And, before you ask, he's not here yet.'

Tom raised his eyebrows but before he could respond Clara cut across him: 'Don't worry about us. You see to your proper guests.' She spoke with her usual calm assurance. Clara, like Tom, would never have been described as a party animal, far preferring to spend her time researching some obscure point of law in a university library, so Victoria was surprised and touched to see that she had made a special effort with her appearance: she wore a black knitted dress, which was the closest Clara possessed to what other, smarter women would call a cocktail dress. It was not, however, a garment many women would consider wearing to an evening drinks party. Though Clara had donned black court shoes, the opaque black tights she wore with them, not to mention her heavy beaded jewellery and thick glasses, somehow served only to reinforce her dowdiness. Though younger than Victoria by four years, Clara might easily have been mistaken for the older of the two: she had no interest in the touches of make-up that would have accentuated her strong cheek-bones, full lips and soft blue eyes, features which were further hidden by the thick auburn hair that fell heavily across her face and on to her shoulders.

Tom's eyes were already on the miniature club sandwiches emerging from the kitchen. As family, Tom considered himself exempt from any dress code and had complained earlier to Clara that it was a Friday evening when those who really needed to work for a living could scarcely be expected to find time to change. Jeans and denim jacket were his trademark work clothes, an outfit he liked to believe rendered him less official, more approachable, to the poor and dispossessed of the South London housing estate to which he was assigned as the full-time social worker.

In the hallway Victoria made out the Boltons from next door and noted, without surprise, that they were empty-handed. Major Bolton was a stalwart of the Wimbledon branch of the Heritage in Architecture Association and had made a perfect nuisance of himself during the renovations with a stream of helpful suggestions as to period detail. This had been all the more annoying because his own decaying house, stuffed with dowdy furniture and mouldy chintz, was all but held together with linoleum and purple-painted Anaglypta wallpaper. The Boltons had surged ahead and were now creating a bottle-neck at the drawing-room door, having stopped to gawp at the newly painted cornicing. Major Bolton was lecturing no one in particular: 'Good show. Original nineteenth-century colour. Helped them track it down myself. Chap in Wales makes it, natural dyes . . .'

It was all original – or, at least, authentic and sympa-thetically restored in keeping with the period. They had had plenty of time to plan the work, ten years to be precise, the time it had taken them to recover from buying the house in the first place, which had been a nightmare on account of the bridging loan they'd been forced to take out when their Clapham flat stuck on the market. But David had been determined. In the late eighties they had despaired of ever affording a house, so they were damned well going to get one in the crash of the early nineties. The building society had wanted a quick sale, and David would give them one. Six weeks from viewing to moving in, and crossed fingers that the repossessed owners hadn't pushed sardines down the radiators and turned up the heating before their enforced departure. They hadn't. As Victoria subsequently

4

found out from Mrs Bolton they had been a rather nice couple. He was a City trader; she didn't work. Such a shame when he lost his job. But Mrs Bolton had stayed in touch with them and was really quite upset when the wife wrote six months later to say they were getting divorced.

Victoria could only imagine that he had once been paid stonking bonuses: she and David had moved into a scuffed version of a Las Vegas hotel suite, all spotlights and silk-effect wallpaper and marks on the carpet where white leather sofas had stood. The en suite bathroom was floor-to-ceiling black marble, apart from one wall of smoked mirror and the bath itself, which was actually a Jacuzzi. The carpet was white and so deep you needed a special plastic rake thing to comb it out properly. It was all very modern, apart from the kitchen in hand-carved rustic oak. And it had been fun to live in with all sorts of gadgets to play with, like electric curtains and a TV console built into the headboard and sunken blue lights along the garden path.

David had tired of it first. After a couple of years, he had started getting the big cases and big money, and invitations to the houses of judges and QCs. Houses that shared a certain classic English style. He would return home discontented and frustrated and, if the house they had visited was particularly grand, ashamed. He no longer laughed when the doorbell played 'Careless Whisper'. He wanted a house like the others had, with all the vocabulary that went with it. Sofas and pantries and lavatories and cellars and sash windows. Especially the sash windows. Oh, and he wanted a country house, too.

David wanted a country house as only a boy born in a council house could.

Victoria, standing at the drawing-room doorway, estimated that most of her guests must have arrived. Some forty stood around the room and a handful, who were old enough to believe that the best part of a party was to be found in the kitchen, stood in the hallway having been shooed away by Panda. The smokers were braving the chill March evening in the garden. Through the open French windows Victoria could see her youngest sister Annie on the newly laid limestone terrace with her husband Hugo. Annie was smoking what looked like a hand-rolled cigarette and Victoria could only hope that with so many barristers present the contents were legal. Annie and Hugo looked, as ever, blissfully content with their own company, chatting amiably as evening fell.

Victoria's gaze ran across the room, checking that everyone was mixing, concerned that no one had been abandoned. Her guests had formed into predictable clusters. Major Bolton was now holding forth to the neighbours about the dangers of Victorian drain collapse and resulting rat infestation. In the far corner, the barristers had gathered, swapping stories of incompetent solicitors, sleeping judges and the improbable alibis of their clients. In the middle stood the mothers from school. Victoria's son, Alex, attended Wimbledon's most exclusive prep school, exclusive in Victoria's opinion simply indicating expensive, while her daughter, Emily, had recently enrolled in its nursery class. These were the women with whom she swapped school gossip as they stood bunched together by the school gates, all of them waiting to load children, sports kit and musical instruments into estate cars and four-by-fours. Tonight they had swapped the chic casual gear of the school-run – currently silver ski-jackets with Armani jeans – for a blaze of short, slinky designer outfits. Around them, in an outer circle, were their husbands, tired-looking after a week spent from early morning to late at night in the banks and brokers of the City, swapping jokes and laughing too loudly. Moving among them Victoria, in a simple dress of cerise silk, her blonde hair worn up, added a flash of real, if unintended, glamour into a room of little black dresses.

A few brave souls had broken out of their groups and made contact with others. Victoria caught sight of Sir Richard Hibbert, David's head of chambers, backing slowly but determinedly away from her brother-in-law. She moved smoothly across the room as Sir Richard made a run for the garden. 'Tom, there's some people I must introduce you to,' and taking hold of Tom by the arm she steered him towards a cluster of younger men. 'They're barristers in David's set, just started and doing lots of criminal work. I know they'd love to hear your perspective. As someone with real experience of these problems.'

'Well, they do sometimes have a very middle-class standpoint.'

'Exactly.' She pushed him at three smart young men, who broke off from raiding a plate of smoked salmon and cream cheese canapés proffered by a young French waitress in an extremely tight white shirt matched by an extraordinarily short black skirt. Too bad, thought Victoria, someone had to talk to Tom and it was time for them to sing for their supper.

'You must meet Tom Parker,' she said. 'He works on the Southhead estate.'

'That sink estate?' asked one, mildly interested despite the disappearance of more attractive company.

Tom launched into a passionate explanation of how the estate represented so much more than last year's negative headlines, but Victoria had heard it all before and moved away to greet any new arrivals. Then she must check on guests who had wandered outside – and get hold of David. It was seven fifteen and the party was timed to end at eight. At this rate he would barely make the last half-hour. Fortunately she could see no one new to be incorporated into the room, which was now perilously close to being more than comfortably full.

Eleven years ago, when they had bought the house, there had been no drawing room. There had, however, been a lounge. David had instituted the name change shortly afterwards – leaving Victoria to face the derision of her family and pointed remarks about social-climbing – and in the unfortunate situation that Victoria was forced to refer

7

to the room in the company of David and her family she would mutter vaguely about the living room.

The drawing room occupied half of the ground floor, running from front to back to give it that all-important double-aspect. Victoria had overseen the restoration of the room to its full glory: each piece of cornicing, moulding and architrave had been authentically mended, painted and set. She had then created – to Major Bolton's delight – a classic English drawing room, funded with the fees from a particularly gruesome murder that David was prosecuting at the Old Bailey. So it had been a stroke of luck that after three weeks they'd had to abandon the trial and start again after one of the jurors was found to be having an affair with a Murder Squad detective. The three bonus weeks had paid for the gilt mirror over the fireplace, the rugs, table lamps and the bill from the young man who had fitted and painted the white bookshelves on either side of the fireplace. David had got himself in a terrible state about it all – the décor not the murder – and had cross-examined Victoria on every purchase.

But, as she had begun to discover around that time, it was easier to placate him than have another argument.

She had been obliged to scour London's auction rooms – the shops were extortionate – and cart home all manner of mahogany side-tables, silver boxes, ornaments and paint-ings – rarely prints, for David deemed only limited editions acceptable. For the party, Victoria had pushed back the sofas, the two Queen Anne armchairs and the George IV card-table on which were carefully arranged tiny jewelled boxes, delicate china dogs – spaniels, Labradors and setters – and heavy silver photograph frames. Countless pictures of the children were grouped around a central photograph of David and Victoria emerging from the church on their wedding day – this last one depicting David and Victoria gazing into each other's eyes in expressions of mutual adoration.

As she crossed the room, Victoria took in snatches of

conversation: house prices and parking permits, winter uniform lists and homework diaries. All of it lively enough but never passionate, the only interruptions the pouring of champagne and proffering of food. The miniature samosas, which had appeared at the start of the party, were now reappearing for a second round. Victoria began to panic. Soon Panda would be sending out the other B-list canapés: pizza squares, and those awful crab cakes. God, they were edging ever closer to the moment when food stopped altogether.

She *must* call David. Tell him just to get here. People would be leaving soon – some would have dinner reservations and on a Friday night they wouldn't risk losing their tables. And once one left, it would start an exodus until only the bores and the freeloaders were left. David would not even meet his guests, let alone have time to make his precious announcement.

As she crossed the hallway to enter the small study where the telephone was located, Consuela opened the front door. David? Damn it, no. Instead, two young women in severe black suits. Victoria recognised Kitty Standing from David's chamber. Had he invited the lot of them?

'Kitty? How are you? Delighted you could come.'

'Victoria, hi!'

Kitty looked Victoria up and down, smiled insincerely and then brightened at the sight of a tray of champagne. Kitty Standing was hardly London's most talented advocate but what she lacked in brainpower she made up for in ambition and indestructible self-confidence. She turned to the stranger beside her. 'This is Arabella Clevely-Jones. Our most recent addition. She's just been given a tenancy after spending her time as a pupil with us.'

Arabella, tall and blonde, stepped forward and smiled confidently, holding out her hand. 'Everyone calls me Bella. Thank you for inviting me, Mrs Stratford. It's a great honour.'

Before Victoria could reply there was an atrocious howl

from upstairs, which rapidly evolved into a wailing whine. 'My daughter. Please excuse me.'

'Is there anything I can do to help?' Arabella asked, and, not waiting for a reply, followed Victoria upstairs leaving Kitty to grab a glass of champagne and look inquisitively around the hallway.

'I'm sorry about the stairs,' said Victoria, as they went up to the top of the house. They found Emily on the floor, having tumbled out of bed, unhurt but not letting that fact dissuade her from ever more energetic crying.

'Come on, you're fine,' soothed Victoria, heaving her daughter back into bed.

'I'm not. I'm ill,' protested Emily, her features composed in an expression of pained sincerity, her large blue eyes framed by her bobbed hair of the palest blonde.

'Hey, Emily!' exclaimed Arabella. 'What a fantastic bedroom! I wish I'd had one like this when I was your age. How old are you?'

Emily's sobs stopped. 'Four.'

'Four! Wow, a really big girl! Did you choose this animal wallpaper?'

'Yes. And Auntie Annie painted the picture on the wall. It's a zoo.'

Arabella looked impressed at the zoo mural, the beautiful wallpaper and matching swags-and-tails curtains. Victoria knew she spoilt her daughter – the only room that had broken her careful budget – but it had all been OK in the end because of that football manager's drunk and disorderly case. Arabella sat down on Emily's sleigh bed where Victoria was piling up the ten or so toys which had fallen to the ground.

Catching Victoria's distracted look Arabella turned to Emily, 'Listen, maybe you could help me,' she said. 'I've been at work all day and it's been really boring. But there's something that would really cheer me up . . .'

'What?' Emily asked.

'A story. But not just any old story. A story in one of your books that *you* think is great. It has to be funny too.'

She had caught Emily's attention. Emily looked towards her bookshelves and began thinking out loud. Would it be the story about the polar bear, or the mice, or the girl who's really a princess but no one believes her?

'The princess, definitely,' said Arabella firmly.

'Are you sure about this?' murmured Victoria. 'It's not much of a way to spend a party.'

'Quite sure. We'll read a story and then Emily can go to bed and think about which one to read to her mummy tomorrow.'

Victoria felt a rush of gratitude and, fleetingly thinking she herself would have more fun up here, began to back out of the door. 'I'll have some champagne sent up.'

'Only if you can spare someone to do it. I'll be fine . . .'

Victoria sprinted downstairs, arriving breathless in the hall in time to see David striding through the front door. 'Darling! God, I'm sorry! I don't deserve you! Holding the fort. I've behaved abominably!' He kissed her extravagantly on both cheeks. He smelt of expensive aftershave and a hint of whisky. He was one of only a few men Victoria knew who looked better at the end of the day than at the beginning. He did not crumple or crease or spoil in any way: his Savile Row dark suit and white double cuff shirt looked as pressed as they had twelve hours before. And the hint of a shadow on his face only added to his dark good looks. At six foot two, in perfect physical shape with his thick hair swept back from his high forehead, David was not just holding back the years: he was taking them on and beating them.

Consuela moved behind him to take his black barrister's briefcase. He smiled at her: 'Consuela, you look lovely. Thank you *so much* for all your help. I know Victoria couldn't have managed without you.'

Consuela, Victoria's inscrutable Spanish cleaner, rarely smiled. In fact, her habitual expression was one of concentrated anxiety as she moved silently around the house on Mondays and Fridays between nine and eleven. Now, however, she smiled coquettishly at David, inclining her head towards him in a gesture that Victoria could only interpret as an attempt at mild flirtation.

A young waitress inched forward with a tray.

'Champagne? Just what the doctor ordered. Thank you so much.' He took a glass – was it her imagination or did his hand brush the waitress's? – and strode off down the hallway, while Victoria attempted to keep up from some three paces behind him. As he entered the drawing room, everyone within seemed to sense his arrival and Victoria could almost feel some collective greeting of the room as it set eyes upon its long-awaited guest.

David began at once to mingle with his guests, greeting each enthusiastically and managing to recall with accuracy whatever event or preoccupation was foremost in their lives. With the men he compared London and US banking practices. With the women he commiserated about the impossibility of finding a reliable au pair. Sir Richard Hibbert was canvassed as to the best claret to buy that year. And Clara was treated to his views on the absolute necessity of increasing pay for university lecturers. Everyone received in turn his full attention, his rapt approval and approximately three and a half minutes of his time before he sighed that he would *so much* like to talk to them all evening but good manners dictated that he move on to his other guests. It was now nearing eight o'clock but David's arrival had chased all thoughts of departure from his guests' minds.

Victoria felt suddenly weary. Now that he was here she could at least try to relax. He could make the conversation and the introductions for a while. And he was so very good at it because he genuinely loved parties, mixing with an effortless self-confidence to which she felt she could never aspire. Oh, she could do all the right things, careful as she was to remember everyone's name and occupation and even all their children's names for good measure, but she could not quite let go of organising everyone and every-thing and just enjoy herself. And, looking round the crowded room, she had the sudden, rather alarming thought, that she would be much happier when they all went home and she had the house to herself again.

She decided to wander out into the garden in search of Annie and Hugo. At thirty-two, Annie was the youngest of the three sisters. The baby of the family, she had been hopelessly spoilt and indulged, and Victoria and Clara had seethed at the freedoms allowed her that they had been refused. In fact, in every respect their parents had been utterly inconsistent in their haphazard approach to parent-ing. With Victoria they had fussed and worried over every aspect of her development and education. But when Clara was born, four years later, they decided that their attitude to Victoria had made her timid and therefore Clara must be pushed towards greater independence. Clara duly excelled at school and was the only one of the three to go to university, with a scholarship to Oxford. However, by then their parents had decided that she had been pushed too hard and robbed of any childhood fun. In consequence, Annie was allowed to do much as she pleased and it was no surprise when she turned into the wild and reckless teenager that she still at times resembled.

Victoria found Annie and Hugo chatting amiably and inconsequentially. Hugo was monopolising a tray of filo pastries, urging the waitress not to depart quite yet. Annie was inhaling deeply from a cigarette – Victoria was relieved that she could only detect the aroma of tobacco. Annie had contrived, as always, to look effortlessly stylish in a simple dress of white linen, offset by one of her trademark ethnic shawls with an intricate pattern of gold, red and bronze. It was a young look but she could carry it off, still possessed of a gamine figure and a delicate beauty. 'I've just told Hugo that if he eats any more he'll pop,' she said affectionately.

'Nonsense,' said Hugo. 'I'm just big-boned. It's all puppy fat. When I reach forty it'll disappear overnight.'

'You're perfect as you are,' said Annie, and patted his paunch affectionately.

Hugo was very overweight but since his mother scolded him about his weight – and many other topics besides – Annie took the view that nagging him any more would be utterly pointless. She would have to trust that he would lose weight when he felt like it and not before. She offered her cigarette to Victoria, who, checking first that David could not see her, took a quick and surreptitious puff.

'Vicky, you've done a terrific job! It looks beautiful. I hope David appreciates it.'

'Oh, I'm sure he does. It's still not quite finished. Some of the kitchen units need adjusting and the garden's still missing some plants.'

They all turned to look down the small garden. David had been recommended by Sir Richard Hibbert's wife to commission a garden designer whose work she had seen at Chelsea and the result was a Japanese Zen garden, all pale stone, bonsai and white pebbles around a centrepiece stone lantern. It was all terribly trendy but rather incongruous and David was privately worried that it wasn't quite right.

Leaning against a section of bamboo fencing, a stunningly beautiful girl was talking to a young boy. 'Elizabeth is going to get whisked away by a model agency soon,' commented Victoria.

'Not if I can help it,' Annie said, with feeling. 'I don't want her dropping out like I did. I want her to pass some exams. Have something behind her.'

No one could have mistaken Elizabeth for Hugo's daughter: at fourteen, her looks were exotic yet classically beautiful, the product of Annie's youthful affair with a boy from Pakistan who had broken her heart. For a few seconds they forgot the crush of people inside the house and stood absorbing the peace of the garden as they watched Elizabeth and Alex, Victoria's son. Alex, tall for his age with his father's dark colouring, clearly had a painful crush on his cousin. He stood beside her, trying to look taller, bigger and older than his ten years. For the party he had begged to be allowed to wear cream chinos and a blue Oxford shirt in an effort to dress as his father did at the weekend.

Victoria had begun to wonder if it was the very fact that the children hardly saw their father – home after they had gone to bed and working on papers every Sunday – that paradoxically made David so popular with them.

Alex was especially delighted that he had been allowed to stay up while Emily had been sent to bed at six thirty under threat of losing access to the television for a week if she appeared downstairs. David had firm ideas on the place of children and had left instructions that he did not expect to trip over his four-year-old daughter. As they stood silently, listening to the hum and chatter from within, they were joined by Clara.

'Oh, God, witches' coven, I'm off.' Hugo kissed Clara and, with an expression of mock-fear, dived inside to find more food. Victoria and Annie instinctively turned away from the children. Their sister's childlessness was not a taboo subject but neither was it an easy one to discuss amid the buzz of a cocktail party.

'Witch's coven, indeed!' Clara lowered her voice. 'How's the *real* witch, Annie?'

'Don't ask. Hugo's had a dreadful day at the office with her and she's rung three times since he left.'

'Business or personal?'

'Personal. She's now convinced she's got gout.'

'*Gout*!' Victoria and Clara chorused.

'Yes. She's insisting that Hugo takes her to the doctor first thing on Monday morning. But he's got two estimates to do and an installation to supervise.'

'It must be very stressful for him.' Clara sounded concerned.

'But he can't turn his back on her. And he has to work with her.'

Hugo de Longden had the mixed fortune of working in his family's long-established business, designing and building handmade conservatories and summerhouses. The business had been started by his father, Charles, a gentleman builder who combined superlative craftsmanship with effortless charm. The rich and *nouveau riche* of Surrey adored him. His ideas were creative without being outlandish and he had the knack of designing to suit his customers' personalities and tastes rather than his own. De Longden conservatories were a byword for quality and his Surrey customers particularly appreciated the value they added to any house.

Hugo had inherited his father's personality and talent, and after Selchester – an exclusive public school – he had been happy enough to follow him into the business. No one had anticipated that at twenty-five, as his parents' only child, Hugo would have to take over the business following his father's early and unexpected death from a stroke. Her husband's death had come as a terrible blow to Barbara de Longden and the possessiveness that had always characterised her relationship with Hugo grew still more cloying. She insisted that Hugo relinquish his bachelor flat and move in with her, threatening suicide if he refused. Once installed, she proceeded to monitor his movements, his friends and all efforts at a social life. Her favourite tactic was to lurch from one illness to another. Hugo lost count of the times he had to cancel holidays or was called away from dinner parties on account of medical emergencies which seemed miraculously to resolve themselves within a few hours of his return.

She also declared her intention to help him by taking a full role in the administration of the business, so they worked and lived together for five years, until the fateful day four years ago when Hugo had announced his intention to marry Annie. He had, by covert use of a mobile

16

telephone and an elaborate web of misinformation, managed to keep the relationship completely secret from his mother. He knew that marriage to a single parent with a ten-year-old daughter would scandalise his mother, who had in mind that if he really *must* marry then it should be to the virgin princess of a European royal family. Having done everything possible to prevent Hugo marrying Annie, Barbara refused to attend the wedding and afterwards made it her business to disrupt her son's married life to the best of her ability.

As Annie finished her cigarette they heard a rapping in the drawing room, which silenced the room. Victoria jumped guiltily. 'God, he'll be mad if I'm not there.'

'He can wait!' exclaimed Clara, with more than a hint of exasperation, but Victoria had already slipped inside and was squeezing through the packed room to reach David, who was standing by the fireplace. A look of mild irritation passed across his face but was instantly replaced by a fixed, benign smile. 'Darling. Do come over.' Victoria went to stand dutifully at his side. She was pleased to see Arabella slip into the room.

David stepped forward to speak, then paused until the last whispers of conversation had died away and the waitresses had left the room. The room was now perfectly silent. Expectation hung in the air. 'We are honoured that you can be with us tonight. Some of you may have noticed a few changes to the house.'

There was polite laughter.

'In the meantime,' David continued, 'I have been preoccupied with a little court business and Victoria has been spending her time . . . well, let's just say that Victoria has been *spending*.'

David waited for the predominantly male laughter to die down.

'In any event, we are grateful that you can join us tonight and, we trust, for many years in the future. We hope this house is a home not just for us but for our children and in time, if we are so blessed, our grandchildren.'

'God, he's nauseating,' whispered Tom to Clara.

'There is another reason why this house is special. It stands in what I happen to believe is one of the most beautiful streets in the Village.'

This was met by murmurs of agreement from the neighbour contingent, who stubbornly referred to *the Village*, despite it having all the characteristics of a medium-sized town.

'And so it is all the more worrying that the future of our road, and Wimbledon Village as a whole, is under constant threat. From those who have no concept of tradition. From those who would pack our streets with late-night take-aways, raucous nightclubs . . . and worse.'

There was no doubt as to what David meant: the plan put forward last year by the council to build fifty low-cost housing units on the site of a disused school adjoining the Common. He had single-handedly fought the council's plans on behalf of the residents and won in a famous legal victory in the House of Lords.

'The poor and the dispossessed must be provided for, of course. Some of them are, no doubt, deserving of assistance. But there are appropriate places for them. And this is not one of them.'

A chorus of clapping broke out – at which Tom ostentatiously crossed his arms. Clara looked at him anxiously, terrified that he would start heckling.

'But there are new threats and new challenges. I am not a politician by nature but there are times in one's life when one must put duty before personal desire. Most of you will be aware that Sir Reginald Summerston, our marvellous MP, is sadly standing down at the next election. He will be a difficult, if not impossible, act to follow. However, it is vital that a *local* person with *local* knowledge takes on the burden he has nobly shouldered for so long. Today I heard that I have been selected as one of five candidates to be considered as his replacement as MP for Wimbledon Village.'

'Bravo!' cried Major Bolton. The room erupted in applause.

'Who are the other candidates?' a voice from the back of the room called out.

'Two outsiders. Then Charles Lamming, the former defence minister. Oh . . .' David paused for effect and gave a wry smile '. . . and Janet Williamson.'

There were one or two hoots of rather unpleasant laughter. Janet Williamson had hit the headlines last year when she had made a speech at the Conservative Party conference calling for increased maternity pay and a host of other benefits for women. A brash, intelligent northerner, she was exactly the type of unmarried career woman guaranteed not to appeal to the elderly committee whose task it was to choose the Tory candidate in England's safest Conservative constituency. Since, however, it was now deemed unacceptable to have a short list without a woman candidate she fulfilled the role as well as anyone. The inside view was that this was a two-horse race between David and Charles Lamming, a popular minister who had lost his seat at the last election.

The room broke up into groups and David stepped forward to receive the congratulations of his guests.

'He'll be insufferable as an MP,' said Tom to Clara. 'Fucking hypocrite. "Taking on the burden", my arse. He's been scheming for this for ten years. I'm surprised he didn't drop arsenic into old Summerston's drink ages ago.'

Clara gave a wry smile. 'He hasn't got it yet.'

'He will,' said Tom gloomily. 'He may be a bastard but he's a clever bastard. You don't go from a back-street council house to a place like this without brains, hard work and a total willingness to stab everyone else in the back.'

Clara laughed despite herself. 'I hope Victoria knows what she's letting herself in for.'

'It's hardly difficult. He puts his name on the ballot

paper, gets elected, then sits in Parliament until he drops dead. Summerston's done nothing for years and no one's noticed. Most of the voters thought he died years ago.'

But Clara's expression had grown more thoughtful. 'No. I was thinking of the public side. Having to open fêtes, kiss babies, that sort of thing. Plus all those late-night sittings. They'll hardly see each other.'

'Well, that's a bonus, isn't it? Not seeing him? And she won't be opening anything that involves making a speech. Our future prime minister won't miss a chance to grab the limelight.'

'Do you really think . . . ?'

'Yes. Depressing but true. He's good-looking, he'll be great on television and smart enough to scheme his way past the opposition any day.'

On seeing Victoria approach, Tom stopped speaking. She looked vaguely embarrassed. 'I wanted to tell you, I really did, but David made me promise not to say a word,' she said.

'Don't worry,' insisted Clara, adding rather more diffidently, 'Congratulations . . . I suppose this will mean quite a few changes for you both.'

Victoria caught the note of reservation in Clara's voice but was saved from replying by Annie dashing up. 'Wow! Congratulations! How exciting!' In sharp contrast to Clara's, Annie's voice was filled with an innocent enthusiasm. 'Hugo says he'd love to drive round with one of those loudspeakers on election day. He says it's an unfulfilled ambition.'

Despite the laughter that rang out around her, Clara pressed on: 'And you,' she persisted, looking directly at Victoria, 'you're sure about this? You're happy about it?'

'Yes, of course!' Victoria was emphatic. 'And it won't be such a great change, after all. We'll still live here and the children won't have to change schools, and David says he can carry on his work at the bar part-time.'

Clara suspected that Victoria knew full well that this was

not at all what she had meant. She would have liked to say more but realised that this was neither the time nor the place to suggest that life as an MP's wife could only worsen what she increasingly perceived as her sister's near-servitude to her ungrateful husband. Life with Tom undeniably lacked excitement, but neither she nor Tom would have dreamed of making some life-changing decision without hours of careful discussion, whereas Clara had the distinct impression that David would pursue his political ambitions whatever Victoria thought.

'Anyway,' Victoria continued, moving the subject to safer ground, 'he might not even be selected. The first selection meeting is months away, not until June. That's when the five candidates get whittled down to two. Then they go forward for a vote by all the Association members, but that's not until after the summer. David's going to see as many members of the committee as he can. He just needs me to keep the children from under his feet. I'm taking them down to Marlow for the Easter holidays. Are you still coming?'

'Wouldn't miss it for the world,' Clara replied gracefully. 'Only four more weeks of teaching and then it's the university vacation, thank God. And I desperately need to catch up on some reading – something I've found which is quite intriguing, actually. I'll tell you more when I come down. But Tom can only be there for the weekend, unfortunately.'

They both knew this was not quite true. Tom and David were invariably an explosive combination and the two sisters generally contrived to keep them apart. David and Victoria's house at Marlow on the river Thames had been the location of many a stupendous argument between the two men, who clashed over politics, religion and virtually every other subject they ever discussed from sport to literature and cars.

'I'm going to tell the caterers to stop bringing round the food and start clearing away the glasses,' Victoria whispered to Clara. 'That should drop a hint to everyone to push off.' But first she must thank Arabella. Victoria found her talking to Sir Richard Hibbert.

'Thank you very much,' Victoria gushed.

'It was a pleasure . . .'

'She's a great girl, isn't she?' interrupted Sir Richard. 'A brick. Arabella's father and I were at Cambridge. Now he's a Court of Appeal judge and I'm a humble barrister appearing before him next week. Some woman who murdered her husband and is appealing on grounds of PMT, whatever that is . . .'

Victoria and Arabella smiled at each other conspiratorially, and Victoria slipped away to the kitchen, where she found Hugo polishing off a plate of langoustine tails sautéd in garlic and butter. A large blob of butter had fallen on to his tie and Annie was attempting to remove it with kitchen towel. Elizabeth looked on, laughing. 'Hugo, you should only go out in public with a bib.'

'Good idea. I could have one of those plastic ones that catch the food. Save any waste.'

Annie stood back, defeated. 'I think I've made it worse! I give up.'

'Why don't I just take it off?' suggested Hugo. 'Anyway, we ought to push off before I get too comfortable and have to be winched out of your house, Victoria.'

'And we've got to be up early,' added Elizabeth to Victoria. 'I've got an art project to work on. I'm doing a portfolio – Drawing from Nature. Hugo's taking me to Wisley Gardens and we're going to draw some of the magnolias.'

'Actually,' said Hugo, 'it's all a ruse to escape Annie's gardening plans. The alternative is helping with the lawn. I have a nasty feeling that once she's got all the moss out there won't be any lawn left.'

'It's the wet winter,' explained Annie, aware that Victoria's gardening skills just ran to watering her potted summer geraniums, 'but right now I can't imagine that I'm going to be up and about very early tomorrow.'

Victoria never ceased to be impressed by the way in which the lives of Annie, Hugo and Elizabeth intertwined. It seemed to her that this was because of Hugo or, more precisely, his innate unselfishness and generosity of spirit. From the start he had empathised with the painfully shy child with whom he found himself sharing Annie. Unlike Annie's previous boyfriends, he had not attempted to bribe Elizabeth with toys and outings. Instead, he had waited for her to approach him – and when she did they discovered that they shared a love of drawing and design. It was at Hugo's suggestion that Annie had enrolled Elizabeth at her present school, The Maltings, a small progressive establishment that specialised in education in the arts. The fees were beyond Annie's means but Hugo had insisted on paying, albeit without his mother's knowledge.

Around them, Panda had begun ostentatiously to clear up and Victoria, sensing she wasn't needed or particularly wanted in the kitchen, went out to see people off. Consuela was handing out coats and Victoria glimpsed Kitty Standing heading upstairs in search of the bathroom. The downstairs cloakroom must be occupied. She was cross with herself for not speaking to Kitty. David was a powerful figure in chambers and it was his policy to cultivate everyone assiduously.

Mrs Bolton bustled up to her. 'It's been a lovely party. You've worked so hard. I hope David's taking you out somewhere nice to dinner.'

'Oh, yes,' lied Victoria. She had no idea if he had any such plans. 'Probably L'Auberge.' It was her favourite restaurant but they would not have a chance of a table without a reservation made days in advance.

Mrs Bolton kissed her fondly and squeezed her hand. 'You're an asset to that husband of yours. Don't underestimate your own importance!'

Victoria nodded, unsure how to respond. But the Boltons were slightly eccentric, one of a dying breed of residents who had been here for decades and who were now being bought out by the bankers and management consultants who had chequebooks large enough to buy these houses and, just as importantly, to maintain them.

The Boltons left, and after them a steady stream of others. Victoria watched Clara and Tom climb into their battered Morris Minor. Annie, Hugo and Elizabeth were the last to go. Hugo had been obliged to spend ten minutes on his mobile phone placating an irate customer who had telephoned to complain that his mother had been extremely rude to her that afternoon when she had asked for some alterations to the design of her summerhouse. This was not unusual: Barbara de Longden took the view that customers were jolly lucky to have a De Longden building and ought therefore to shut up and be grateful. The call had been awkward and Hugo had then suffered an attack of indigestion, Annie had explained, but after some fresh air in the garden had proclaimed himself as right as rain.

Finally, after Victoria had paid Panda – the cheque actually made out to Pandora Drax-Cairns – and said good night to Consuela, she bolted the front door and gratefully kicked off her black high-heeled party shoes. As she did so she became aware of her aching feet and tired legs, and altogether a feeling of being utterly physically drained. She could hear David settling himself in the drawing room, and she longed for a drink and hopefully some leftover canapés, but before she could finally sit down – she must have spent four hours in those wretched heels – she wanted to check on the children. As she made her way to the foot of the stairs, however, she inadvertently caught sight of her sideways reflection in the hall mirror. She hesitated, then turned to face it. As a teenage girl, and throughout her twenties, her reflection had held no fears for her. Looking back she hoped she had not been vain but she rather feared that she had. In those days, strong blue eyes, high cheekbones, a broad smile had met her gaze and though she disliked her nose – too acquiline – and her resolutely straight hair, back then she had considered the mirror her ally. Like all beautiful girls, she had taken the compliments for granted. And she still received them – how stylishly she dressed, how well she had kept her figure. But they did not lift her as they had before. Now she examined her face in a spirit of detached appraisal. Tentatively, she moved closer to the mirror. The face was still slim, the eyes remained her best feature, the skin glowed, though probably more from make-up than any natural gift. The face that stared back at her was far from old. And yet, for all the clothes, the jewellery, the carefully applied make-up, she felt somehow false. As if the outwards appearance of calm and poise was exactly that – a mere outwards appearance, a mask – and behind it all was someone who felt neither beautiful nor confident. And although she was aware that she had not always felt this way, even beginning to think such thoughts made her feel guilty. It seemed akin to self-pity. She had so much to be grateful for and, really, so little of substance to complain about. She pulled herself back, as lately she had from introspective moments, and forced herself to remember that she was very lucky to have a lovely house, two healthy children, a wonderful family and a husband who worked so hard . . .

'Are you going to be much longer?' David's voice carried impatiently from the drawing room, accompanied by the rustle of a newspaper and the pouring of champagne.

Startled, Victoria stood back. She answered him mechanically. 'Five minutes,' and with as much energy as she could muster climbed the stairs to Alex's and Emily's rooms.

In the semi-darkness, guided by the landing light, she found Emily sleeping, sprawled across her bed, her covers sliding on to the floor and her head pushed up against a large plastic horse complete with mane, bridle and saddle. Emily, coupled with her reluctance to go to bed, was also a wakeful child and so it was with practised care that Victoria gently eased her head on to the pillow, slowly pulled her thumb out of her mouth and covered her up, conscious that the covers would be kicked off in a matter of minutes. She slipped the horse on to the floor, too tired to seek out its plastic stable-block, then crept silently away, careful to leave the door ajar so that the landing light gently illuminated Emily's bedroom throughout the night.

She could not hear any sounds from Alex's room, but she was not fooled. Alex considered it some incontrovertible right – based on being ten years old and the alleged practice of his friends' parents – to ignore bedtime on Friday and Saturday nights. She had detected other signs of a growing independence, most notably his reluctance to allow her to supervise his bedtime since the occasion a few weeks before when his two closest schoolfriends had stayed for a sleep-over and Victoria had made the mistake of overseeing the brushing of teeth and wiping of faces. After their departure the next day Alex had rounded on her and accused her of making him look like a *complete* baby and *totally* embarrassing him in front of his friends.

Tonight, however, Victoria had no desire to enter into complex negotiations over bedtime routines. She opened the door to Alex's bedroom, ignoring the handmade sign: '*Keep Out! Do NOT Enter!!!*' Sellotaped to the outside of the door.

She found him in bed, book in hand, seemingly immersed in his reading. He glanced up and watched as she picked her way across the clutter in his room. It seemed to Victoria that Alex was on a mission to cover all the clear space in there: his walls were decorated with peeling and overlapping football posters, his desk was taken up with neat and rough work thrown together, and on the floor lay last term's school project, a games bag, a French–English dictionary and an empty crisps packet.

'I'm reading,' he announced unnecessarily.

'Very impressive,' Victoria responded. She sat on the edge of the bed, reached deftly under the covers and extracted his Gameboy. They fell into the conversation that was by now so frequent it followed a script.

'You're supposed to be reading—' began Victoria.

'I *am*!' cut in Alex defensively.

'—for half an hour a night,' she continued. 'The Gameboy's for the weekend. You need to keep up with your reading.'

'It is the weekend – nearly,' countered Alex, rolling his eyes theatrically, but his tone was playful.

He was not, thought Victoria, a difficult boy. He wanted to please his parents and his teachers, and craved their praise. Inevitably it was David's praise, rarely bestowed, that he sought above all. She picked up the book Alex had discarded.

'*The Cormorant Castle*,' she read out loud from the cover and turning to the back continued to read out the synopsis, 'When Victorian orphan William Elliott is sent to live with his reclusive uncle in the shadows of the Cormorant Castle, he is plunged into unravelling the centuries-old secret of—'

Before she could continue, Alex interrupted her, 'It's so boring! All he does is wander round the moors and talk to the birds.'

Victoria thought it sounded rather good. She had always enjoyed reading and writing essays and stories but Alex preferred computers and, though he would never admit it, enjoyed maths and science.

'The whole class has to read it and then do this worksheet *and* . . .' he paused for effect '. . . do an essay.'

It seemed clear to Victoria that Alex automatically branded any set book boring and the poor author, whatever the twists and turns of the plot, was dismissed as deadly dull simply on account of being chosen as worthy of study by Alex's class teacher.

Alex lay down and looked up at her. Instinctively, she moved closer to him and smoothed his hair. As they were alone together, he did not flinch away. She swung her legs up and settled down on top of the bed while, wordlessly, Alex shifted so that his head was on her shoulder and she was holding him tight. Sometimes in these moments

Victoria felt a pang of loss, a realisation that his childhood was slipping away and that soon, too soon, Alex would be a teenager and she would find herself pushed away. But for now he occupied that time in childhood when kisses, hugs and play were still welcome, albeit a secret between them.

'Did Dad enjoy the party?'

His tone was uneasy, and detecting the anxiety in his voice Victoria reacted instinctively to reassure him. Alex, it seemed to her, had lately become overly preoccupied with his father's feelings, reactions and responses. 'Of course he did, he loved it!' she lied, having no idea of David's feelings at all. But Alex, she knew, should be thinking about himself, not about his father. She switched the question round, 'Did you like it? You weren't bored?'

'I was a bit,' Alex admitted. 'All people do at these parties is stand around talking on and on and drinking and not doing anything.'

Victoria laughed. 'That's the whole point. To talk, and meet other people—'

'Networking,' cut in Alex. 'That's what Daddy calls it.'

Victoria detested the word but she said nothing. In any case, Alex ran on, 'And I talked to Elizabeth and Clara and Annie.'

Victoria noticed that the 'Auntie' had been dropped from both her sisters' names but decided to let it go. The alternative would entail endless interruptions and corrections to virtually every conversation she held with her children. In any case Alex was rushing on: 'Hugo said that next time we go down to their house we'll go to his workshop and he'll show me how to make a catapult – a real, proper one – and then you can make this stand from bricks and planks of wood, and you put baked-bean tins on it. But they have to be empty ones, so you have to save them up. Can we save some? And then you have a competition to knock them over.'

Only Hugo, Victoria thought, could take a child brought up on computer games and inspire him with enthusiasm for sheds and catapults. But Hugo's natural, unforced zest for life and all its uncomplicated pleasures was irresistible. If previous visits were anything to go by, at the end of the day Hugo would have everyone – children and adults, even David – organised into *ad hoc* teams for all manner of ridiculous games. Last Christmas had culminated in a very drunken game of Twister at past midnight.

At that moment Victoria felt that she would like nothing more than to lie on Alex's bed and chat inconsequentially, holding him while he drifted into sleep. But she was conscious that David was waiting for her downstairs so she detached herself, reached across and turned off the bedside light. She kissed his forehead and tucked the duvet around him. 'Night, night, sleep tight . . .'

'Don't let the bugs bite,' he finished in their familiar refrain.

She left the room, eased the door shut, and, as she did so, heard David mounting the stairs. He met her on the landing, a half-full bottle of Moët in one hand and two champagne glasses in the other. 'I gave up waiting for you,' he said. 'Let's have a drink in the bedroom.'

'I'm starving!' Victoria hissed, but conscious of Alex not yet asleep, she kept her voice to a whisper: 'I need something to eat.'

David was impatient: 'Don't be so bloody boring.'

Since it was obvious that he had no intention of conducting a prolonged conversation in whispers she had little choice but to follow him into the bedroom. It was Victoria's favourite room – one in which David had shown no interest on the basis that no one he wanted to impress would see it. She had been free to indulge her romantic fantasy of toile de Jouy wallpaper, matching curtains and a sleigh bed made up with white linen. But now she took no pleasure in it. She could only hope that Alex would soon be asleep. Standing at the side of the bed, David held the bottle of champagne with more than a hint of unsteadiness and poured two glasses, the fizzy bubbles spilling over and on to the Oriental rug.

'Leave it,' he said, anticipating her reaching for a tissue. He handed her a glass with a theatrical flourish and as he did so she caught the wave of alcohol on his breath. Shocked, she realised he must have had a bottle of champagne during the evening on top of the earlier whiskies, always doubles. And now he had a second bottle in his hand. She had a sense of foreboding, of an incipient row, and the realisation that all her reserves of calm and tact were needed to head it off. These days, it took so little to spark a row – about money, or disciplining the children, or something she had forgotten to do, but all of them at heart about her failure to be the person he wanted. At first it was only when he had been drinking. Then it had started happening when he was stressed or under pressure or some case had gone wrong. Until, these days, it needed nothing in particular to trigger the insults and accusations and criticisms. So now she said nothing. She had lately decided that this was the best approach. Of course, Clara disagreed. Clara said she must stand up to him. But Clara didn't think of the two children sleeping upstairs who would wake to the sounds of their parents' shouting, the ugly, bitter words rising up through the house, and venture from their rooms to be confronted by the sight of their father drunk and their mother crying.

To see that once was enough.

Silently she watched, sipping her drink, as David sprawled on the bed, loosened his tie and took a gulp of champagne. Aware that she was standing self-consciously she moved to sit on the edge of the bed but he reached out and pulled her towards him. She felt him relax, clearly placated. But he did not look at her. Instead, one arm holding her proprietorially around her waist, he gazed up at the ceiling and she heard in his voice a rush of excitement and adrenaline: 'Jesus, that went like a dream! No problems. And the word will have gone out now that I'm standing. I'll leave it a couple of days for the momentum of the campaign to get going and then I'll start canvassing the committee. Silly old buggers, but it's got to be done.'

'Silly old buggers' was David's standard term for the Wimbledon Village Conservative Association committee, with even ruder names applied to Sir Reginald Summerston. He often remarked that Sir Reginald's most lasting contribution to politics would be as a living advertisement for the merits of euthanasia.

'And it won't have done me any harm in chambers either. I think Sir Richard was impressed. You didn't let him near Tom?'

'Of course not,' she assured him.

'Or Annie? Was she smoking a joint?'

'No.' Victoria's voice was emphatic. 'For goodness' sake, everything went perfectly!'

He took a minute to consider this, his expression far away in contemplation of the evening. It was the obvious moment for him to compliment her, to state his appreciation or actually thank her for organising a party that had been nothing short of an unqualified success, but she was to be disappointed. Instead, he put down his glass clumsily and reached over to take hers from her hand, feeling uncertainly to place it on the bedside table.

'And now,' he continued, 'I think we ought to have our own private celebration.'

She should not, she was depressed to realise, be surprised. These days they only ever made love when David was drunk – and in consequence she only enjoyed it when she was, too. And she knew, from the veiled, ironic comments of other women, that she was far from alone in finding that, after years of marriage and the arrival of children, passion had long since died – to be replaced by sex that was as dull as it was infrequent. But right now, she was stone-cold sober and she felt nothing stir in her as his hands moved cursorily over her body, unbuttoning her dress. He began to kiss her in a way that managed to be forceful yet

31

lacking in anything other than lust. Of course she could stop him. Say no and watch him retreat from her. And listen to the bitter accusations: that she was tense and uptight, that she wasn't fun any more, that it was a normal part of marriage and he was hardly being unreasonable. Clever words that would leave her feeling bereft. So she tried to relax and respond as she felt his lips pressed roughly to her neck, his hand lift the hem of her skirt and begin fumbling with the waistband of her tights.

'I hate tights,' he complained. 'You'll have to take them off.'

Hearing the impatience in his voice, she decided that it would be better, or easier, if she did as he wanted. This was just how things were between them now, if not always then most of the time, and maybe she was silly to expect any more. Besides, she reminded herself, sometimes she could will herself to feel something, some emotion, which, though it fell short of passion, could be at least described as enjoyment. So she reached to undress and saw that David did the same, unbuttoning his trousers and letting them slide to the floor. Try as she might she could not avoid the sudden, sharp pang of sadness that overcame her when she recalled how long ago it was since they had undressed each other in the slow, tantalising way of lovers. Instead, he moved back towards her, shifting his weight above her, his breath growing faster as his hand reached to pull down the strap of her bra and grasp her naked breast. She sensed his impatience and understood that all that concerned him was his urgent longing for sex. Wordlessly he took hold of her hair and pulled her head to the pillow. She could feel that the gesture excited him, with its muted undercurrent of aggression. With his other hand he ran his fingers over her stomach and reached between her legs. She felt herself tense up involuntarily.

'God, you're dried up,' he complained.

'I need more time. It's too quick.'

She could sense him reluctantly slowing himself, dutifully

32

exploring her with his fingers, but though his touch was never less than skilful it could not reach her. She felt as far removed as it was possible to be from the sense of reckless abandon that, while she still so desperately craved it, seemed on each occasion to move further and further from her reach. If he could only tell her that he loved her, found her beautiful, still desired her beyond any other woman . . .

'Just relax,' David muttered.

Hearing this she felt a stab of irritation that he could possibly expect her just to relax at his instruction. It seemed to her that the longer he touched her the more tense she was becoming until finally she longed for him to finish. 'I'm fine,' she whispered, and gratefully he read the code between them. Swiftly he eased on top of her and in silence pushed himself inside her until after no more than four or five harsh thrusts he came. She felt his body relax and then, almost apologetically, his lips on her cheek as he murmured lazily.

'Sorry. Too quick.'

And so she lay entwined with her husband, in the most intimate of situations, feeling nothing so much as a sense of relief that soon she could sleep. But after what seemed barely a minute he moved away from her. 'Jesus, I need a coffee.' He did not invite her to join him and she watched impassively as he gathered up his clothes, clumsily fastened his trousers and headed for the door. As she pulled the duvet around her, she could hear his heavy tread on the stairs, then a tap running in the kitchen, then silence.

Try as she might she could no longer suppress the memories of better times. It had not always been like this. In the early days they had been lovers in the truest sense, giving and receiving pleasure with generosity and laughter. David had been skilful and considerate. She had believed then that she had found the perfect husband – he was handsome, charismatic and ambitious. He had worked tirelessly in those early years, making a name for himself at the bar. He was an unknown young barrister with no public-school education or family connection to smooth his path. He had to fight to get every case, let alone win it. But she never doubted that he would succeed. For years they had lived on her secretary's salary, waiting months for David's fees to be paid by careless solicitors, yet Victoria looked back on those days with unalloyed happiness. With no money for going out, and sometimes not even a coin for the electricity meter, they would lie in each other's arms and talk and make love for hours on end.

Of course, there was plenty of money now – and always so many things to spend it on. So how had it come to this? Living a life that seemed so perfect – a life in which they talked but never communicated, had sex but never made love, argued but never reached agreement. Was this, as she asked herself so often, how things were meant to be? Was she foolish to hope for more? After all, they were married, living together as husband and wife, a normal middle-class couple with friends and family of whom few suspected they were anything other than blissfully happy.

In these disturbing moments of truth, she could not deny that they were deceiving everyone. And worst of all, she realised, with a sick jolt, she was deceiving herself.

David was not the man she had married. Oh, he had always been difficult. Edgy and impatient and hot-tempered. But she had loved him in spite of his faults, understood how much it meant to him to succeed, revelled in his victories. Only David took no pleasure from them. With each success he had become more discontented, with each ambition satisfied, more ruthless. He had striven for each precious goal, reached it and discovered too late that, instead of satisfaction, the hunger started all over again. And she was the focus for all the pressure, stress and frustration in his life.

Was it time to divorce him? In theory it would be simple: she could divorce him, the house would be sold, she could go back to work – maybe even get her old job back. The children would get used to it, and she would be free to live on her own without him. Free at thirty-eight, with no qualifications beyond a Pitman's diploma in shorthand and typing – and old enough to remember that freedom's just another word for nothing left to lose. Assuming, of course, that David didn't fight it. In the rows he had always made three things very clear: she could leave if she wanted – but not with the house and not with the children. Although that was bluff – everyone knew that the mother always got custody. Well, nearly always, because on a bad day with a clever barrister and a stupid judge . . .

Her head had begun to spin.

Like every woman she knew why she stayed.

She stayed because she remembered the good times, hoped for better and wasn't ready to give up hope – yet. She stayed because you can love someone who treats you badly, believe in someone who lets you down and see through all the bad to glimpse, just occasionally, the man with whom you had fallen so passionately in love all those years ago.

And she stayed because she wasn't brave enough to leave.

Eventually she fell asleep.

Then she was being shaken awake. She was still in her dress, which was now hideously crumpled, but it was dark outside, save for the harsh light from the streetlamps shining in through the open curtains. David was leaning over her. From the urgency of his touch and the seriousness of his expression she realised immediately that something was terribly wrong. Panic gripped her. 'Where's Alex? Emily?'

'In bed. They're fine.' David spoke with professional calm. 'But there's something else. There's been some rather bad news. And there's no easy way of telling you . . . Clara just phoned. She's at the hospital with Annie.' He paused, giving her time to absorb the information. Then he continued slowly, with a terrible finality in his voice, 'Hugo's dead.'

CHAPTER 2

Annie walked falteringly along the aisle of the parish church of Cobham supported on one side by Clara and on the other by Victoria. In front of her stood Hugo's coffin and as she approached she could smell the sickly sweet scent of the white lilies placed on top of it and in each of the early-spring flower arrangements that graced the Victorian nave. When they reached the front pew, they found that Barbara de Longden had filled it with de Longden family members. None made any effort to move. The three women were forced to wait while those in the second pew squeezed up to allow them to take their places.

Annie had hoped that the picturesque Surrey church would be full, but in the event it was packed, with people standing in every nook and cranny and even in the Norman porch. She felt a lonely pride that all these people had been so touched by Hugo's kindness that they had made journeys from all over the world to be at his funeral. And then she felt a crushing sense of grief that he would never know how deeply he was loved.

She turned round, and saw, directly behind her, David, Tom and Elizabeth, the latter seeming curiously detached, almost as if she was an observer of events towards which she was willing herself to feel no emotion. Beyond them Annie saw a mass of faces, some familiar, others not. She recognised Hugo's old schoolfriends and schoolteachers, his team-mates from the local rugby club where he used to play on freezing Sunday mornings, his customers. His father's customers. And she saw people she would never have expected to come – people whom she would have supposed until then were merely acquaintances – suppliers, rival builders and distant neighbours with whom she had only a nodding acquaintance.

Clara reached across and took her hand. In the five days since Hugo's death Tom and she had been Annie's rock of support. They had been the first to arrive at the hospital and take charge, insisting that she and Elizabeth come to stay with them. They had organised a hundred formalities. They had kept from her a hundred painful details.

Barbara de Longden had attempted to organise the funeral without consulting Annie and Clara had been obliged to visit the vicar secretly. Fortunately he knew Barbara de Longden only too well: four years ago she had tried, unsuccessfully, to persuade him not to marry Annie and Hugo on the grounds that Annie was a woman of immoral character. Clara's intervention with Mr Driscoll had ensured that Hugo's favourite music would be played, his best-loved hymns sung and that a Keats sonnet was included among the readings.

The organist changed pieces. César Franck's 'Panis Angelicus' – Hugo had often listened to it when he came in from work after another draining day. The service was about to begin, and the congregation's subdued conversations died away. There was a rustle as everyone reached for their Order of Service.

Annie gripped the pew in front of her, feeling the waxed wood smooth under her hands. Sunlight filtered through the intricate Pre-Raphaelite stained-glass windows, and Hugo's coffin was cast in the soft sunlight of late spring. She fixed her eyes on the flowers placed on either side of the altar, the white lilacs, tulips and daffodils. And she tried to banish from her mind the absurd but persistent thought she had entertained since she had arrived in the church that suddenly someone would stand up and announce that this was all a ghastly mistake, that there was to be no funeral, and then Hugo would walk in laughing.

There was a stir at the back of the church and Mr Driscoll walked up the aisle. He had been newly appointed when he married them and he had still looked like a schoolboy. Now she felt a twinge of pity for him. How awful to have to conduct such a terrible service in front of so many people.

Annie herself had nearly not come. As they had waited to leave Tom and Clara's house she had collapsed, unable to face the reality of this final confirmation that she would never again see Hugo, hear his voice or speak to him . . . It was Tom who had persuaded her, slowly and gently, that she must be there to say goodbye, to see it not as an ordeal but instead to take comfort from all those who mourned with her. And not to allow Barbara de Longden to have the final word.

The congregation rose to sing 'Abide with Me'. As they reached the second verse Annie could no longer stand. Clara caught her as her legs gave way and she spent the rest of the service sitting, rocked with tears, feeling utterly helpless against the crushing finality of the occasion. She barely heard Mr Driscoll's sermon or the tribute by Hugo's Selchester housemaster. Only David, reading the Keats sonnet she had chosen so carefully, held her attention:

> *When I have fears that I may cease to be*
> *Before my pen has gleaned my teeming brain,*
> *Before highpiled books, in charactery,*
> *Hold like rich garners the full-ripened grain;*
> *When I behold, upon the night's starred face*
> *Huge cloudy symbols of a high romance,*
> *And feel that I may never live to trace*
> *Their shadows, with the magic hand of chance;*
> *And when I feel, fair creature of an hour!*
> *That I shall never look upon thee more,*
> *Never have relish in the faery power*
> *Of reflecting love! – then on the shore*
> *Of the wide world I stand alone, and think*
> *Till love and fame to nothingness do sink.*

As David finished, the congregation was utterly still, moved by the quiet passion and perfect emphasis of his reading.

Finally the prayers were over and the moment Annie had dreaded had arrived. She must follow the coffin to the graveyard where Hugo would be buried. 'You can manage this,' whispered Clara. 'You're not alone. We'll all be there with you.'

'Come on, Mum.' Elizabeth squeezed her arm. She was composed, had been since the night six days ago when Hugo had died in Annie's arms by the side of the road. Annie knew that in time the shock would come but for now Elizabeth was quiet, reserved and practical. As for Annie's mother, holidaying on a remote African game reserve, no one had yet been able to track her down, which – given her uneasy relationship with her younger daughter – had been judged a blessing in disguise by Victoria and Clara. Annie was aware of eyes upon her as she made her way across the lawned churchyard, past the decaying Victorian headstones towards the back of the flint and stone-walled church where smaller, gleaming blocks of white and black marble marked the newer graves.

Victoria and Clara followed close behind. As they approached the grave, Victoria leaned closer to whisper, 'We just need to get Annie through this. Then I think we should take her home as soon as possible.'

'And at all costs avoid Barbara,' added Clara.

Victoria watched Annie as she walked slowly a few paces in front, aware of her sister's physical fragility and her trance-like state of mind in which she appeared utterly removed from those around her.

She felt moved to speak in hushed, despairing tones to Clara: 'I just wish I could *do* something, say something that would help . . .'

But Clara could only throw her an anxious glance. 'I know. But there isn't anything, is there? It's all so cruel and pointless, and there's nothing anyone can do to change it. We can be there but we can't alter anything for her.'

Victoria knew that Clara was right. And she realised at that moment that true, intimate grief was, by its nature, immensely lonely. Victoria felt an awful sadness at Hugo's death, would miss him and always feel love for him, but she knew that Annie's grief was incomparable in its intensity. Watching Annie walk slowly to the graveside she could not be sure that her sister would ever fully recover from the loss of the man who had made her life so perfectly complete.

Barbara de Longden already stood by the open grave. The moment Annie dreaded more than any other had arrived. She had met Hugo's mother on only two occasions but the figure opposite her was unmistakable. Barbara's thin body was clothed in a severe black coat, gloves and broad-brimmed black velvet hat over which was draped a black veil. Her hard face was still discernible, the thin mouth and joyless features set rigidly.

Mr Driscoll began the solemn prayers for interment and each mourner around the graveside threw a handful of soil into the grave. When Annie's turn came, she took from her handbag a small bouquet of dried flowers, tiny snowdrops, anemones and gypsophila. The flowers she had carried on the day of her and Hugo's wedding. She kissed them, then dropped them on to the coffin below.

As she looked up she managed finally to look in the direction of Barbara de Longden. The other woman's eyes could not be seen behind her veil. But at that moment her gloved hands rose and she pulled it back. The expression that greeted Annie was of unadulterated and venomous hatred. Her stare was piercing as she looked deep into Annie's face, holding her gaze, willing her to look away first. Annie dropped her eyes, unable to bear the intensity of the woman's loathing.

Victoria moved to her side and pulled her away, 'Why don't we talk to some of Hugo's friends?'

Annie hesitated. 'I don't know. I'd like to go home.'

'Just for a few minutes,' coaxed Victoria. 'It'll be your

only chance. I don't suppose Hugo's mother is going to invite us back.'

'Victoria's right,' added Clara. 'If you go now, you'll regret it for the rest of your life. The people who've come today represent Hugo's life, every part of it. People you've never met and perhaps never will again. You should meet them and they should meet you. As a tribute to him.'

'And they should meet Elizabeth,' added Victoria.

Annie felt nervous. Even in her grief, she wanted to spare her daughter any encounter with the de Longdens: Barbara had resolutely refused to meet her. Hugo had spared Annie the worst, but she knew that Barbara had referred to Elizabeth's parentage in the most derogatory language. On the two occasions she herself had met her mother-in-law it had been with Hugo over dinner, once before they were married and once afterwards. The intention had been for the two women to get to know each other and to accustom his mother to the idea of his marriage. Both meetings had been an unmitigated disaster. Barbara de Longden had questioned, criticised, patronised and insulted Annie until in the end Hugo had got up and taken Annie home. After the second occasion, when his mother had all but accused her of being a gold-digging harlot, Hugo had vowed that he would never again subject Annie to such treatment and that he would henceforth keep apart his mother and his wife. And so, for nearly five years until today, it had continued.

Clara took Annie's arm and led her first to a group of friends and neighbours. Helen Morgan, Annie's neighbour at Railway Villas, embraced her. 'Don't worry about the house. Everything's fine, the plants are watered and your post is waiting for you. Come back when you're ready.'

Annie nodded. She had not been back to the house since the day of David's birthday party. Clara had collected her clothes and left keys with Helen. Railway Villas was a pair of Victorian cottages, so-called because the old railway line used to pass within a few feet of the end of the garden. It had been abandoned in the 1960s and now the unspoilt

41

houses were two of the most sought-after in the village. Helen, a retired schoolteacher, had never married, declaring that a man would be a distraction from the real love of her life: her garden.

Others approached Annie tentatively. Angus Campbell, the stern but devoted master craftsman who had worked for the de Longdens for over thirty years, spoke to her of how he had known Hugo as a fair businessman, never standing in the way of time off for a new baby or a sick relative. Every one of Hugo's employees came over to her; all had brought their wives, girlfriends or parents to say farewell to the man who had been so much more in their lives than a mere employer. Others whom Annie had never met introduced themselves hesitantly, attempting to offer memories of Hugo. She found these encounters the most difficult to bear, unsure how to reply to them, hearing herself utter words of thanks but little more.

She was relieved to see Sam Swinburne, Hugo's art master at Selchester, approach her, looking every inch the schoolteacher in his sombre suit, with his thinning grey hair neatly parted. Hugo had never lost touch with the teacher who had first discovered then nurtured his artistic talent. They had continued to meet regularly for dinner or trips to galleries and Sam, as a member of the Royal Academy, issued an annual invitation for Hugo and Annie to join him at the preview of the Academy Summer Exhibition. He had been delighted when Hugo had met Annie, thrilled to see in her someone who shared Hugo's outlook and interests so closely, and, naturally enough, he had been an usher at their wedding.

'Have you any idea what you might do next?' asked Sam. He took her hand and regarded her searchingly. 'Please remember that you owe it to yourself to carry on painting.'

'I can't believe I'll ever find the inspiration,' sighed Annie.

'Well, try not to stop completely,' said Sam firmly, 'and

don't feel guilty when you do paint. You'll need something to take your mind off things in the next few months.'

Annie knew that he spoke from experience. His wife had died last year, just a few months after he had retired, and he had found himself alone with neither school nor the retirement plans he had made with her.

Annie answered with what was becoming something of a standard reply: 'I know you're right. I'm just trying to take things one step at a time.'

And Sam evidently appreciating that she did not want to talk, was sensitive enough to bring the conversation to a close: 'Well, do please call me if you ever need someone to talk to.'

People were drifting away, most approaching her nervously to say goodbye, a few braver souls attempting words of comfort and support. Barbara de Longden was organising relatives, and those of whom she approved, into cars to go back to her house for a subdued lunch.

Annie saw, with surprise, that she appeared to be inviting Cal Doyle. He was legendary in the property business. Barely a week went by without some tabloid tale of his deals, drinking and womanising. Born in a Dublin tenement, he had hardly troubled to go to school, and at fourteen he had skipped school, home and Ireland altogether and taken a boat to Liverpool to scrounge a bed with one of his countless aunts. Having started as a builder's labourer, he had worked his way up to become a multi-millionaire thirty years later, specialising in building as many 'executive' homes on Surrey green-belt land as the planners would allow. Cal had certainly been an important customer – many of his Surrey houses featured a De Longden conservatory – but he was hardly the type Barbara de Longden would want as a friend. Annie could only assume that she was making a point by inviting everyone except her daughter-in-law.

The churchyard was almost empty and she could hear the sounds of cars driving away. Hugo's grave was deserted.

Suddenly she wanted very much to be alone with her thoughts and to reflect quietly on the man she had thought of as her best friend. She walked back slowly, under the ancient yew tree and past the brilliant yellow forsythia coming into bloom, stepping carefully around the crowds of trumpet yellow daffodils enclosing clusters of pale pink hyacinth. And still, despite everything that had happened, and was happening, although she was standing at the edge of Hugo's grave, she was still unable to believe that the awful events of the last six days had really occurred.

Images ran through her mind. Hugo driving through the Friday-night traffic. A call on his mobile. The terrible pallor in his face. Hugo collapsing, his hands clasped to his chest. Her own voice screaming into the mobile for an ambulance. The kind doctor who had stopped in his car to try to help. Last, and most awful of all, the knowledge, as she had stood in the street watching the ambulance crew, that Hugo was dead and that no one could bring him back.

As she stood there, lost in rambling memories of his death and their life together, she became aware of a presence at her shoulder. 'If there was any justice in this world, it would have been you.'

Barbara de Longden's voice was unmistakable, and Annie turned. 'Please. I don't want to argue with you.' She tried to move away, but Barbara de Longden gripped her arm, her hold surprisingly tight.

'Argue with me?' She gave a shrill laugh. 'I'm not here to *argue*. I'm here to *tell* you that if my son had never met you he would be alive today. He would have led a decent life, cared for by me, not dragged down into your sordid little world.'

'This is pointless. Neither of us wanted Hugo dead—'

'No. Well, he died while he was with *you*. Which, in my view, means that you are responsible. And I will make it my business to ensure that you never in any way benefit from his death. No, you must be punished.'

'I'm sorry, I don't follow—'

'No, I don't suppose you do. You are as ill-educated as you are common. I have always despised you and I was right to do so, with your silly little paintings and your disreputable ideas. But you'll find out in good time. Justice will be done. Hugo may have been bewitched by you, manipulated by you to pay for your *bastard* child but—'

'That's enough!' Annie was startled by Clara's voice and Barbara de Longden was stunned into silence.

'Stop it!' Clara demanded. 'Stop it right now. No one doubts that you are grieving, that your words are spoken in shock—'

'My words are spoken in righteousness.' Barbara de Longden had rallied.

'But Annie is suffering too, and while you may lack the basic human feeling that would enable you to hold your tongue, I will not stand by and hear you insult my sister.'

'Then I suggest you take her back to where she belongs. To whatever ghastly little bedsit she crawled out of. But don't expect me to forget her. I will have justice for Hugo.'

'Justice?' Clara looked askance. 'Perhaps you should try thinking a little more about *love*.'

'Love?'

'Yes. All that matters here is that Hugo loved Annie, and nothing you can say or do will change that. He loved her simply, freely, unconditionally. And she didn't extract his love through guilt . . . or blackmail.'

'Nothing can compare with a mother's love for her son.'

'Perhaps. But you could never face the fact that Hugo might love someone else. If anyone put Hugo in his grave it was you and the stress of coping with your jealousy.'

Barbara de Longden looked as though she would strike Clara. But Clara stood in front of her with a calm defiance. She had always been the strongest of the three sisters, her brilliant mind coupled with a quiet self-confidence. They stared at each other until finally Barbara de Longden turned away. 'Very well. I'll say no more. You'll find out soon enough. From my solicitor.'

The look in her face was triumphant. Her eyes rested on Annie for a few seconds and then, turning away as silently as she had approached, she walked purposefully towards her car.

'What does she mean?' asked Annie nervously, turning to Clara as she always had in times of trouble. Clara put her arm around her and led her from the grave.

'Forget it, she just wants to worry you. I'm sure it's nothing. What *can* she do? You owned the house with Hugo. He made a will. It's probably something like the wording on the headstone. Perhaps she wants to leave off your name.'

'Actually, it's crossed my mind that's exactly what she'll try to do,' said Annie woefully.

'Then we'll deal with it if it happens. Come on. You've had enough for one day. Let's find Elizabeth.'

Victoria looked anxiously at the kitchen clock. Seven twenty: she had twenty-five minutes to finish breakfast, dress Emily, gather together Alex's school-bags and find three overdue school library books. From upstairs she could hear the sound of David's shower. He avoided breakfast *en famille* and she could not blame him. They were not a family who engaged in sparkling conversation at this time in the morning. Alex, thankfully already in his school uniform, was distractedly eating cereal while immersed in the sports pages of the newspaper and occasionally glancing at a list of spellings he had omitted to revise the night before. Emily, still in her nightdress, fed herself Rice Krispies with agonising slowness.

'Can I have some toast?' Alex mumbled, not troubling to look up.

'Me, too,' said Emily. Whatever Alex did, said or requested she followed suit.

'Is it white bread?' asked Alex.

Victoria sighed. 'No. Brown. It's better for you.'

'I want white,' said Emily.

'There isn't any white. You'll have to have brown,' Victoria snapped, and pushed two slices into the toaster, which stood on the black granite worktop of her hand-painted kitchen, the cream Shaker-style units stylishly offset with aged-brass handles.

'It's OK. I'll have more cereal,' Alex said.

'I'll have more cereal,' echoed Emily, reaching for the Rice Krispies.

'You've already got some!' Victoria exclaimed, turning to retrieve the two slices of warm bread from the toaster. In the meantime, Emily grasped the packet and, shaking it enthusiastically, sent a wave of Rice Krispies into her bowl and cascading on to the table. Victoria shot across the room and wrested the box from her daughter's grasp.

'She's too young to pour her own cereal,' commented Alex, who had recently discovered that referring to his sister in the third person had the delightful effect of annoying her intensely.

'I'm not,' screamed Emily and, anxious to prove the point, lurched again towards the box.

Victoria whisked it away. 'Just eat what you've got there,' she insisted, but Emily had got down from the table and was heading for a counter-attack on Alex in the form of grabbing the newspaper from him. Only the arrival of David in the kitchen proved a distraction.

'Good God,' he exclaimed, regarding the kitchen table, which was now awash with cereal, the two discarded slices of bread, newspapers and spelling sheets. Immaculately dressed in his dark courtroom suit and starched white shirt, he paused, checked that his seat was clean then sat down gingerly.

Victoria spooned coffee into a *cafetière*. Neither she nor David could face breakfast first thing. She preferred to complete the school-run, her least favourite part of the day, and return to an empty house for more coffee, yoghurt and fruit. On school mornings, she regarded breakfast time as little more than a race against the clock, with a quarter to

47

eight the vital deadline. If she left the house then she could beat the traffic, park and drop Alex at five past eight, leaving her ample time to walk with Emily, at a four-year-old's pace, to the school's nursery department, situated beyond the sports field. Leaving even five minutes after the deadline risked immersion in the stop-start misery of Wimbledon's full-scale school-run traffic. The same journey, begun just a few minutes later, would take up to fifteen minutes longer. Moreover, it made it virtually impossible for her to find a parking space and invariably resulted in Emily arriving after eight-thirty registration. Three late arrivals in a month incurred a snooty letter signed by the nursery department head, which reminded parents of the importance of punctuality, the disruption to the class day incurred by late arrivals and ended with a particularly patronising sentence about the poor example set to the children by the failure to observe school rules. She had already had one such letter, and although David had read it, snorted and said that if they wanted punctuality they should damn well provide a car park, she somehow felt ridiculously guilty about it.

'Are you in for dinner tonight?' she asked David.

'Yep. Should be.' He was leafing through the paper in search of yesterday's law reports. 'I'm in Southwark all day.'

'The armed robbery?'

'Mmm. Jury's been out since yesterday morning and I wouldn't be surprised if we get a verdict today. We should wrap up at four. I might be able to head straight back.'

Alex looked up, sensing an opportunity. 'Dad, can we play chess?' He had recently joined the school lunch-time chess club. His progress, however, had been hindered by his inability to practise – Victoria didn't play and David, who did, had managed time for only one game in which he had taken barely five minutes to checkmate his son. Victoria had thought this unnecessarily severe – and said so – which, she now recalled, had provoked an angry exchange centring on the merits or otherwise of letting children win at games.

'Mr Brewster,' Alex continued, 'says that people who want to get in the team need to practise every single day and it's very important to play someone better than you are because that's the only way you get better.'

'I'm better,' Emily chipped in.

Alex ignored her. 'So, can we play?'

David was distracted by the newspaper. 'Sure. No problem.'

But Victoria was gratified to see that he was making an effort of sorts. There had been so many late nights recently – lawyers' dinners and last-minute paperwork for demanding cases – added to which he had been insufferably ill-tempered when he finally did arrive home. After all the work she had put into organising his precious party, he had tested her reserves of tolerance to the breaking point – so much so that she had been moved to point out to him that even she had her limits and that if his parliamentary ambitions were going to have this effect on him then perhaps he ought to abandon the whole idea. He had been surprisingly apologetic. He had promised faithfully to make a real effort to get home early and spend more time with the children. He had also given her his categorical assurance that once his current workload was out of the way, and the MP selection was in the bag, everything would be just like the old days.

She watched as Alex sat back in his chair, pleased to have secured the promise of a game.

'I *can* play,' insisted Emily, never one to let the truth stand in the way of a confident assertion. Victoria sensed the beginnings of a tantrum. In this respect, Emily was her father's daughter: wilful and infuriating but also admirable in her persistence and ambition.

Alex looked at her disdainfully, preparing his retaliation, only to find himself interrupted by Victoria. 'Right, both of you, eat up or we'll be late.'

Alarmingly, it was now half past seven. At least she was ready – one of the few advantages of being woken by Emily at six thirty was the time it gave her to shower, dress and put on her make-up. Today she wore her standard weekday outfit of black jeans and black polo-neck sweater, offset by a simple gold chain and earrings.

David put down the newspaper and glanced at her. 'Doing anything interesting today?' His tone was dutiful.

He had quite clearly forgotten everything she had told him over dinner the night before. 'I'm helping with swimming,' she reminded him. She looked at him for some hint of recognition but his face was blank. 'At the school,' she prompted him. 'Emily's class.'

'Oh, yes.' Signs of recall crossed his face. He had evidently decided to make an effort, if only a polite one. 'But isn't your mother arriving today?'

'No.' Victoria could feel frustration rising inside her. 'She's coming *tomorrow*. She's flying into Heathrow first thing in the morning. Tom and Clara are collecting her.'

A week had passed since Hugo's funeral, and Annie had returned to Railway Villas under the watchful and near-constant supervision of Clara and Tom. As she spoke Victoria felt a twinge of unease that she had not been as available for Annie as she should have. She had managed a couple of visits, for lunch, but since Emily was still only attending morning school, finishing at twelve thirty, she had been obliged to take her, too. And with Emily in tow conversation of any sustained or sensitive nature was near-impossible. And she had been terribly tied down with the PTA newsletter, which she edited – or, rather, produced single-handedly every term, not to mention all her regular appointments. But there was no time to say more to David, who signalled the end of the brief conversation by standing up and tossing the newspaper on to the kitchen table. He kissed the top of Emily's head, veering away from her milky fingers, and patted Alex heartily on the back. 'I'm off.' He kissed Victoria's cheek perfunctorily. 'Have a nice time.'

It was his standard morning farewell and she responded with her equally standard reply: 'Good luck. Hope it goes well in court. Give me a ring if you get a verdict.'

'Will do,' he called back, already striding down the hallway. She heard him seize his briefcase, then the slam of their heavy front door.

With David's departure, she realised that Emily, now merely stirring her spoon through milk and cereal, required swift attention. Victoria grasped her daughter's hand and, with the usual mixture of persuasion and threat, hurried her upstairs to embark on the morning routine of tooth-brushing, hand-washing and dressing, simultaneously shouting suggestions to Alex as to the possible location of the missing school library books. Finally, by the time Alex, with frustrating slowness, had tied his shoelaces, it was five to eight, a full ten minutes past the traffic-avoidance deadline. Yet again Emily would be late for school.

It was four years ago that Victoria had, with a mixture of reluctance and relief, resigned from her job as a legal secretary at Lomax and Sons, Kingston's largest firm of solicitors. Mr Lomax had been devastated, tried desperately to persuade her to stay and declared that he would never find a secretary to replace her. He had grown to rely on her, not just for the office work but for all the other bits and pieces she did for him – soothing difficult clients while he hid in his office, composing tricky letters, even writing his monthly column in the Rotary magazine.

Working had been manageable with just Alex: one child, one flexible childminder and a mother who could be called on in emergencies. With two it had been different, and she had lasted a fortnight after her return from maternity leave. It was not possible, she had found, to be on time for the childminder and the school and work. For example, leaving work five minutes late meant catching a train that left fifteen minutes later – by which time the after-school club had been officially closed for ten minutes – and by the time she had apologised she was a full twenty minutes late for the childminder, who was new and not very flexible and smoked. They would arrive home, Victoria as thoroughly exhausted and miserable as the children, and when David asked her in the second week why she was bothering she hadn't been able to think of a persuasive answer.

Four years on, the reality of full-time motherhood was that she seemed busier than ever. For a start, there was the house. Of course, Consuela was marvellous, and Victoria knew how lucky she was to have her, but so did Consuela's many other employers. Consuela could spare her two mornings and no more.

This, however, was not a Consuela morning, and on her return from the school, where she had been pressganged by Emily's teacher into helping with the annual Easter-egg hunt, she set about the daily task of making the house look halfway tidy. She began in the kitchen, clearing the spills and crumbs of the children's breakfast, before scooting upstairs to make the beds and survey the inevitable scene of devastation in the children's bathroom. There, she neatly refolded the towels trailing on the floor, tidied away Alex's pyjamas and cleaned the sticky blobs of strawberry-flavoured toothpaste off the white porcelain basin and brass lever taps. By the time she had gathered up a pile of David's shirts, loaded the washing machine and whizzed the Hoover over the hall carpet, she was dismayed to realise that an hour had passed and nothing very substantial had been accomplished.

To the sounds of the washing machine churning and the dishwasher humming, she sat down at the kitchen table and began to make a list of all the trivial but essential tasks without which pandemonium resulted: collect David's dry-cleaning, buy a present for Emily's best friend's birthday party, write a cheque for yet another school trip. Her life ran according to carefully compiled and crossed-off lists. She added other items that came to mind: book dentist; call window-cleaner; pay gas bill. And, book facial. She had, after all, reached the age when the claims of various expensive creams and salon treatments invited a more serious interest. In consequence she spent sums of money that, on occasion, provoked David to astounded complaint. But she refused to feel guilty: on the contrary, it seemed to her entirely reasonable that, since she carried out the tasks of domestic life so diligently – tasks which were, in turn, so utterly taken for granted by her family – she should at least enjoy the small compensations of life at home. A manicure every fortnight. A cut and highlights for her hair every six weeks. A St Tropez tan at the beginning of summer. And sometimes, when David had been particularly demanding or neglectful, she went shopping and really gave him something to complain about by spending a large amount of money on some item of clothing. It made her feel better. Much more so than entering into some ghastly row at the end of which nothing would be changed and very probably things would be worse on account of David simmering with resentment for days.

Unable to think of any more jobs, but conscious that she would inevitably have forgotten something, she folded her list and placed it in her handbag. The first warm day of spring had arrived, the muted rays of April sunshine visible through the glass panels of the broad, stained-oak front door. She decided to walk to the Village. Since she never left the house without checking her appearance, she paused to brush her hair in front of the hall mirror and carefully apply her lipstick. It was ten o'clock. If she walked quickly, and took her swimming kit with her, she calculated that she could pop round the shops, go to the bank and, with a bit of luck, still find time for a coffee in Starbucks, and a glance through the new April *Vogue*, before she was obliged to present herself for duty at the nursery-class swimming lesson.

'Are you absolutely sure? You only have to say the word. I can change the flights . . .' Annie's mother spoke with anxious feeling, her voice verging on the despairing as she appealed to her daughter. They sat opposite each other on the pair of homely claret-coloured sofas in the small sitting room of Railway Villas, whose warm buttermilk walls displayed a cluster of well-chosen watercolours. Margaret Elliott had made the offer countless times already, a week seemed such a short stay in the circumstances, but Annie had rebuffed her.

Now Annie was as obstinate as ever: 'No. Really. I'll be fine. I've got Clara and Tom and Victoria and Elizabeth. Helen looks in every day and she's doing the garden as well . . .'

Margaret struggled to think of some persuasive words that would soften her daughter but none came to mind as she gazed at her. Annie looked tired and world-weary, curled up with her bare feet tucked beneath her, dressed carelessly in jeans and a shapeless sweatshirt, her unwashed hair falling untidily about her face. Whereas Margaret, for all her sixty-six years, was suntanned and vibrant, dressed in slim white trousers and a pale pink lambswool polo-neck, her grey hair neatly tied back. They sat in the fading light of the afternoon sipping tea and eating fruit cake, which Helen Morgan had brought round the day before and which, Margaret was pleased to note, was rather dry: she felt somewhat usurped by Helen Morgan. Of course she could see that Helen was a good neighbour – yesterday she had done the first cut on the back lawn – but because Helen was her own age Margaret felt excluded and at a disadvantage. She had missed the funeral and was now being dispatched, or so it felt, after barely a week.

'I'm absolutely fine,' Annie insisted, somewhat too emphatically, leaning forward to replace her plate on the low Indian mahogany coffee table, her cake largely untouched. 'And anyway,' she continued, 'you can't miss Africa.'

Africa was the current stop on Margaret Elliott's nine-month round-the-world trip organised by a company specialising in explorer-holidays for the over-sixty-fives.

She had been attracted by the brochure's promise to offer participants the advantages of independent travel with the companionship of a small group of like-minded individuals. She had found herself with eight others staying in small guesthouses, travelling on ramshackle buses and employing the services of local guides. Like herself, her companions were the type of people who troubled to learn at least a few words of the language, to sample the local food and, above all, to avoid the tourist crowds swarming over the sites as they decanted *en masse* from their air-conditioned coaches.

It was truly the trip of a lifetime. She had found, late in life, that she possessed a desire for adventure and, more to the point, the determination to pursue it. But she had not hesitated for one second to return home when an urgent message from England finally reached the remote South African tented camp where the group was settled for a week's safari – she would have forsaken the entire holiday, except it was clear to her that Annie was wholly resistant to such an idea. She decided to make one last attempt. 'I don't have to cancel the whole trip. I can join them later, in Egypt. Or I can wait and join them somewhere in Europe. It would be terribly easy – I can fly in anywhere, Rome, maybe . . .'

Annie heard her mother's words and concentrated on formulating the sensible, tactful, reasoned replies that she had made to all her mother's entreaties. Because she could not possibly tell the truth: that while, of course, she loved her – and had welcomed her comforting presence for at least the first few days – she now, more than anything, wanted to be left on her own. The truth was that she was tired of talking. And more tired of listening – to all her mother's sincerely meant advice that so singularly failed to comfort her in any way at all. Advice to keep to a routine, eat regularly, go for a walk each day. Advice to confide in friends, remember that she had a family who loved her, pursue her hobbies and interests.

She was sick of rousing herself for walks and trips to

Waitrose and polite efforts at helping her mother with the housework on which she energetically embarked every day. And she had no desire to sit through any more family meals, the conversation stilted and awkward, Clara and Victoria trying too hard not to mention life with their husbands.

She knew her mother meant well – after all, Margaret understood what it was to lose a husband. But that had been three years ago and although her mother had grieved, as they all had, she had somehow managed to live with her grief, carrying on with the small everyday tasks that in time grew into new interests and activities. Her mother had learned to play the piano, joined a theatre club and a countryside conservation group. Her mother, over those years, had accepted the unchangeable fact of her widowhood but refused to give in to loneliness. For her mother, life had gone on.

'I just don't like to leave you like this,' her mother concluded. 'Or Elizabeth, come to that.'

Annie was not about to be drawn into a further discussion about Elizabeth, whose veneer of strength had been shattered by the ordeal of the funeral. Elizabeth would turn to her at one moment, weeping, bereft and seeking comfort, only to push her away and retreat into silence, almost angry in her determination to reject their mutual grief. Elizabeth exhausted and bewildered Annie with the unpredictability and ferocity of her moods – but Elizabeth was her daughter and if Annie could not cope with her then surely no one could?

Annie leaned across the table and took her mother's hands. 'Look, why don't we agree this? You go and join the group in Africa . . .' Her mother, frowning, made to interrupt but Annie pressed on: '. . . and if things don't work out and I find I can't manage I'll ring the travel company and get them to contact you. It's the best way. I've got to manage on my own some time. And I can.

Really. If I need anything, anything at all, I promise I'll be in touch.'

Her mother looked uncertain. 'What if you can't reach me? Some of these places are very remote. I mean, we're camping in the mountains—'

Annie cut in, 'I'm sure they can get through to you somehow. And nothing is going to happen, is it?' She mustered all her strength to say firmly, 'I really will be perfectly all right.'

Looking at her daughter, Margaret saw that she was, if needed, then not wanted. If it had been Victoria, or even Clara, she could have stayed. They had been such easy girls. Annie had been a different matter. Her teenage years had been filled with furious rows and she had stretched her mother's liberal inclinations to the limit with her ethnic clothes, pierced navel and determined quest for tickets to outdoor rock festivals. Now Annie's independence had asserted itself, as it had so many times before. She had always been determined to go her own way, at whatever cost and with whatever consequences. Defeated, Margaret gave a compliant sigh and rose to her feet. 'I'll book a taxi for the morning.'

Annie watched her mother leave the room. Although she sensed her mother's sadness and disappointment, any shadow of guilt she felt was overlaid by a feeling that could only be described as one of relief. Relief that tomorrow she would be alone with her thoughts and feelings. It seemed to her that her mother and, indeed, everyone around her was united in their unquestioning desire to press the future upon her. A future defined in clichés – where time heals and life goes on because that, after all, was what Hugo would have wanted. And although she listened to them all without complaint or argument, she did not believe them. She felt untouchable, as though a wall had been built around her that no one could surmount. Not one of them could reach her because none of them understood the reality. The simple reality was that she had no earthly desire to live in the future. She had lost her dreams, hopes and ambitions. They had existed with Hugo so they had died with him. All that was left was the memories – and it was clear to Annie that the undeniable, unavoidable consequence of Hugo's death was that life, in so far as it continued for her at all, existed only in the past.

'The first draft of examination papers must be submitted, on paper in triplicate and also on computer disk, by May the twenty-sixth for assessment by the Law Examination Standards Subcommittee. The Committee will make amendments in green ink. Amendments must be incorporated . . .'

Clara stopped listening to Kate Dunning's droning voice. Around her the twenty-five lecturers who made up the University of Thames law department fidgeted and gazed out of the window of their cramped meeting room, preoccupied with their plans for the four-week Easter vacation, which began the next day, as Kate continued to set out in mind-numbing detail a host of administrative rules and regulations regarding everything from the font that must be used for examination papers to the correct way to switch on the new overhead projector in the main lecture hall.

Although she was a law lecturer, Kate was so hopeless at teaching that she had diverted herself into the administration of the department as an alternative to being sacked. Now she passed her time hounding her colleagues with paperwork, meetings and e-mails about subjects they were quite well able to understand without her assistance.

Julian Urquhart, their head of department, was openly marking student essays. After fifteen minutes he cut off Kate in mid-flow: 'Marvellous, marvellous.'

'I haven't finished,' Kate protested.

'Marvellous. Now, before we break for the Easter vacation a couple of points.'

Kate sank back in her chair.

'First, congratulations to Clara. Her latest book *Women and Consent to Medical Procedures* was very well reviewed in the *Cambridge Law Journal*. Well done!'

There were murmurs of agreement. She didn't court popularity, but by the end of their three years at the university all the students knew someone whom Clara had helped. She had been known to spend hours sorting out every conceivable problem from unexpected homelessness to rows with parents. And her help went beyond the norm: she was rumoured to lend money, cook meals and even provide a bed for a night.

Clara specialised in medical law. There were only twenty places on the course, which students took in their final year, and they were always fought over by students desperate to be taught by her. She also taught criminal law to first-year students, achieving the rare feat of having as many students at her final lecture as at the first.

This caused Kate no end of irritation. Especially as a one-off lecture Kate had given last year, entitled 'An Overview of the Role of Council Bye-laws' had attracted not a single student. To add insult to injury the student newspaper, *Rag Times*, had just voted her 'Lecturer Most Likely to Send You to Sleep' for the fifth year running.

Julian Urquhart's urbane voice continued: 'Next, Belinda Weaver . . .'

There was a collective groan from all around the table at the mention of the President of the student Law Society.

'Belinda Weaver, the esteemed President, has asked me to remind you about the party to be held after the examinations for the final-year students, on July the twenty-eighth in the refectory. If you could put it in your diaries and make some effort to attend . . .'

There was a rustle of papers as the staff got up to leave, hoping to get some lunch before the staff canteen sold out of sandwiches, but Julian raised his hand: 'Funding.'

There was a sigh around the table.

'You do not need me to tell you that student numbers are

growing but resources are decreasing. We are urgently seeking funding from private sources. Law firms, companies, et cetera. I have to tell you that if we do not secure extra funding then I will be forced to consider staff redundancies.'

'Well, what do you want us to do, Julian? Buy a lottery ticket every week?' The strong Scottish accent of Cameron Hawes rang out around the room. A veteran of the department, Cameron had a brilliant mind and was an expert in the horribly complex area of taxation law. His colleagues stifled giggles.

Julian looked stern. 'I was hoping for rather more constructive solutions, Cameron. If any of you have contacts you could approach . . . although I appreciate that walking into a City law firm wearing jeans and a T-shirt emblazoned with a haggis is unlikely to produce the desired effect.'

Julian fought a hopeless battle to persuade his staff to smarten up. He himself was impeccably turned out in a Jermyn Street pinstripe suit and double-cuff shirt. His male colleagues favoured cords and shabby sports jackets. Cameron wore whatever took his fancy when he woke up. Clara endeavoured to find a clean skirt and blouse each day, but had been known to arrive at work wearing one brown and one black shoe. Kate favoured crimplene slacks and baggy shirts that even someone as immune to fashion as Clara could see were wildly unflattering, especially when combined with her severe short hair and total absence of make-up. Clara felt put to shame by her younger female colleagues who tended to dress in dark suits and smart black court shoes.

'I'm sorry to send you away with depressing news. *Nobis auxilio estote*! '

Cameron snorted, and most of the younger staff looked bemused. 'It means, "Give us a hand,"' Cameron translated haphazardly for their benefit.

Julian continued, 'Well, *bonnes vacances*! If you need me

I'll be at my house in the Dordogne. You have the number there.'

'And if you need me I'll be in Bar Italia in Soho till three every morning,' echoed Cameron, as they got up to leave.

He caught up with Clara in the corridor outside. 'For a moment I thought old Julian was going to mention your other award.'

'Oh? What's that?' said Clara.

'Haven't you seen the student newspaper? You've got the Miss Moneypenny again.'

Clara groaned and Cameron winked at her. 'Yes – "Lecturer Most in Need of a Good Shag". Third year running, isn't it?'

'You know perfectly well it is. Why do they always pick on me?'

Cameron eyed her flirtatiously. Openly gay, he managed to get away with the most outrageous comments in a department that Clara was always grateful had not succumbed to the dull political correctness of the other university faculties. 'It's the glasses, my dear. Men are desperate to cast them off, roll down your blue stockings and uncover the passionate woman beneath the A-line skirt.'

'Really? Perhaps they just don't have another category for me.'

'Well, think yourself lucky. I've won "Lecturer Most Likely to Get Arrested".' Cameron kissed Clara on both cheeks. 'Happy Easter! Don't work too hard.' He left her by the door of her office.

Clara had been at the university for six years and had worked her way up to occupying her own office. She would have hated to share. It was here that she did her research, her writing and her thinking. She tried to work at home, but Tom was always interrupting or wanting lunch or just hanging around trying to help, which she found the most tiresome distraction of all.

She unlocked the door and squeezed inside. Books,

magazines, boxes of court documents, newspaper cuttings and files covered every available shelf and inch of floor space. Students in larger groups were obliged to sit on piles of law reports, their heads wedged between Clara's potted plants. As she inched inside, her telephone rang and she stumbled to her desk just in time to grab the receiver before the switchboard cut her off. 'Clara? It's Victoria. I'm at Marlow.'

'Great. I'm leaving soon. We'll be with you tonight.'

'There's a problem. It's rather embarrassing, actually.' Victoria sounded worried.

'Well, go on. I'm unshockable.'

'I've forgotten my contraceptive pills. They're in my bedside table. I've tried to get an appointment with the GP down here but I'm not on his list and they're all booked up anyway. David's in court all day and coming straight down – I daren't ask him. I was wondering if you could make a detour and get them. You've got a key. I hate to ask but I'm desperate.'

Clara could imagine she was – David was adamant that they would have no more children. She thought quickly. She and Tom lived in Richmond. The last thing she wanted was to have to drive into Wimbledon on a Friday afternoon just as the school-run was choking up every road for miles around, then out again on the A3 hitting all the London traffic. Especially with Annie, who was travelling with them to stay with Victoria and David for the weekend. It was exactly six weeks since Hugo had died . . . Maybe Tom could go. Of course! He was already in town so he could catch the tube. And he had their main set of house keys with Victoria's key on it. 'We're in luck. Tom's in town. He's at a conference in North London. Something about the role of leisure in the inner cities. If you don't mind him going, he can call in on his way back.'

'God, I'm too desperate to be worried about who gets them. I just can't risk it. You know what men are like on holiday. Insatiable.'

Clara could only murmur noncommittally, 'No problem. I'll call him. You haven't changed the alarm code?'

'No, same as ever. Look, I'm really grateful.'

'Don't worry about it. I'll call Tom now.'

After five minutes of complaints, Tom agreed to go. Clara suspected that he was actually quite pleased to have the opportunity to poke around David's office undisturbed.

She gazed at her desk, which was awash with essays, requests for references and the assorted papers that the university churned out by the day. Most worrying of all was the letter from the law editor of the *Sunday Times*, chasing up her overdue article on the Tellium case. She simply must finish it. She planned to do the reading on holiday this week and type it up next weekend after they had left Marlow. Since Hugo's death it had been a struggle to stay on top of her teaching and marking, let alone compose carefully worded legal articles. She and Tom, or one of them at least, had made a daily visit to Railway Villas and at times, after a long working day, she had not been able to suppress the resentment that Victoria popped over only a couple of times a week and David was nowhere to be seen.

She turned her attention to the three boxes that contained her reading – reports of the recent infamous series of court cases in London in which twenty or so women had sued the makers of Tellium. All claimed that they and their babies had suffered serious damage to their health from taking it during labour. But the drug company, Landward Pharmaceuticals, had fought a long, hard and, some believed, dirty battle to defeat them. They had all lost their cases, as had other women who had sued in the US.

The *Sunday Times* wanted a simple explanation of the case, which had received a mountain of publicity as the new Thalidomide scandal. Clara had imagined it would be a simple task. But as she had dug deeper, reading the medical evidence as well as the legal papers, she had become aware that the case was not as straightforward as it had at first appeared. She had become intrigued. The answer, she knew, lay in the US records. In the end she realised that she just had to know more and she spent her own money ordering copies and having them sent by Fed-Ex from the States. The result was a stack of documents on her office floor that she could hardly lift.

She concentrated on gathering together her papers: three boxes of Tellium reading, plus two draft examination papers she had to check and give to Kate. She could just do it in two trips. She slung her bulky handbag over her shoulder, wedged a box under each arm, then manoeuvred open her study door with her elbow. Thank God she had a ground-floor office. As she staggered towards the exit to the staff car park she saw Ben Ford coming towards her. 'You look as if you need a hand.' He seized the boxes. 'God, these weigh a ton. What have you got in here? Kate's body?'

Clara suppressed a laugh. 'Thanks,' she said gratefully. Ben was in his final year, one of her medical-law students. A former City banker, he had given up his well-paid job three years ago and enrolled with the aim of getting a law degree and specialising in medical negligence. He'd also become the heart-throb of his year, with his warm brown eyes and generous smile, his thick dark hair swept back and falling over his collar. Clara tried hard not to have favourites but she had to admit that seminars were much more fun when Ben was present – and that she would miss him when he graduated.

'Any more?'

'Oh, just one.'

'Lead the way, then . . .'

In the end it took the two of them to heave the parcel of US documents into Clara's Morris Minor. 'Reading for the holidays,' she explained.

'Maybe you should try a paperback next time.' Ben was leaning against the boot of the car, his hands resting on the belt of his black jeans and his shirt-sleeves rolled up. He gave her a crooked smile. 'Tellium?'

'Of course, but I'm not writing for lawyers. One of the newspapers wants a piece for its readers.'

'Well, if you need any help getting through it, I'm around all holiday.'

Of course he would be. Clara knew that Ben's mother had died ten years ago during a routine operation for a trapped nerve when Ben was still at school. His father had spent the subsequent seven years trying to prove that the anaesthetist in charge had left the room to make a personal telephone call. The case had taken a terrible toll: unable to take the strain of paying for it and fighting the hospital's lawyers, Ben's father had committed suicide only weeks before the case was due to be heard in court. A week later Ben had left his job and taken it on himself. He had no money for lawyers so he had represented himself in a trial lasting two weeks. He had tracked down the nurses who had been on duty, and the day before the case went to court he had found one who had been present throughout the operation. She had been a reluctant witness but after two hours of Ben's careful questioning she had finally admitted that the anaesthetist had indeed left the room. A few minutes later, when things began to go terribly wrong, the junior doctor had reacted with panic in a situation he was untrained to deal with. Ben's mother's death had been avoidable.

Ben won his case and a large payout, but the law had changed his life in other ways: he never went back to the City, enrolling at the university instead. Although he mixed happily enough with the younger students he had something, Clara wasn't quite sure what, that the others lacked and she often invited him home to share supper with her and Tom. Long after Tom had gone to bed, she and Ben would talk late into the night about law, politics and history.

Now, however, she decided to manage alone: 'I'm sure

you've got heaps of work of your own. Though I could do with a hand. I have to get through all the boxes this week and I'm bound to get distracted.' And then, without knowing why, she found herself telling Ben about Annie and Hugo, and David's party, and all the events of the past few weeks. As the car park emptied they talked about Hugo's life, how Elizabeth would cope with the loss of her stepfather, even about Barbara de Longden.

'Hey, I wish I'd been there to hear you read her the Riot Act! Sounds long overdue.'

'Anyone would have done it,' Clara said modestly.

'No, I don't think so.' Ben's voice was suddenly serious. He looked her in the eye and spoke slowly, choosing his words with care. 'You know, I may be right out of order saying this . . . but I've always had the impression that . . . well, you don't realise how good you really are. How . . . talented. You're a brilliant communicator.'

Clara blushed and tried to sound matter-of-fact. 'I always think of myself as just an academic. Working away in my office while the world goes on around me.'

'Did you ever want the limelight?'

'Once. When I was a child I dreamed of being an actress, but my parents insisted I study something useful so I went into law.'

'I can see you on the stage. You speak so well, with such feeling. You talk about the people in the law cases as if you know them and you're telling us their story. You bring everything to life.'

There was a pause. Clara could not believe she had just told Ben about her childhood ambition. She had told Tom, of course, years ago, but he had just laughed and said it was a damn good thing she had not wasted her life on something so vain and trivial. Ben was still looking at her intently. She dropped her gaze to her watch, and was startled to see that they had been talking for an hour. 'Gosh, I'd better get going,' she said. She was aware that her cheeks were burning and that Ben's eyes were still on her, but she said no more, not wanting the moment to end.

Finally, he spoke: 'Well, remember, if you need any help with those papers, give me a call.'

'I will,' said Clara. 'Thanks.'

And as she drove away she thought that maybe his help might be useful, after all.

Tom hurried along Wimbledon Village high street, his head bowed, studiously ignoring the expensive shops. He was wearing his usual spring–summer conference outfit: a crumpled beige linen suit bought for him by Clara from a mail-order catalogue. For winter conferences he favoured thick corduroys without turn-ups, teamed with a baggy Shetland sweater of faded green. He owned one 'conventional' suit and this he reserved for giving evidence in court cases and other public occasions of sufficient seriousness to warrant donning a shirt and tie. Its last outing had been at Hugo's funeral.

Now his thoughts were full of today's conference. He adored conferences and usually attended three or four a year, although none were residential since the demands of the Southhead estate did not allow him prolonged absences. He always read any papers sent in advance, could be relied upon to ask the first question and mingled enthusiastically with old and new colleagues alike at lunch. At tea breaks he could be found lingering until the end, all the better to stuff his pockets with the free biscuits, which he bore home triumphantly to Clara along with any pens, clipboards, notepads and sachets of sugar that the organisers had been generous enough to dispense.

As he turned into the Ridgway, he was thinking about the need to install a gym on the Southhead. The conference speaker, from New York, had told them enthusiastically of how leisure activities, and sport in particular, could be a force for social change. 'Motivating the Unmotivated' had been the title of her speech and, in her Harlem drawl, she had told of how young and old alike could be persuaded to turn away from the evils of drugs and crime by the provision of a 'leesure culture'.

Tom had been sceptical at the start, not to say bemused by the unfamiliar terminology, but as the day wore on he began to consider the possibilities. A gym and a studio – the gym for the youngsters, the studio for . . . well, the rest of them. He could see the rota for the studio already. Classes for young mothers – and there were plenty of them – for older mothers, for pensioners . . . Yoga, t'ai chi, abs and flabs, stretch and step, funk and Pilates. He was not quite sure how to pronounce the last one but it appeared on all the course hand-outs and he was sure Annie would know. It was so obvious. The next step in his mission to turn round the Southhead.

And it *was* a mission. Tom had all the dedication, energy and self-belief of the Victorian missionary. He had turned his back on the riches of the world and chosen to bury himself in a forgotten place to tend forgotten people. At forty-one he had the energy and enthusiasm of colleagues half his age. When the Southhead estate had been judged by the government, according to a secret Home Office memorandum, to be one of the ten most deprived estates in London, and the memo had been leaked to the newspapers, pressure had mounted on the local council to do something – or, at least, to appear to do something. The director of Social Services had asked Tom, his best social worker, to go into the estate and set up an office there, to be a continual presence, to heal the suspicions between the residents and the police, to reach out to the cynical young and not-so-young.

Tom arrived at the house. He looked up at it, fumbling in his pockets for the keys and mentally calculating how many homeless people it could accommodate if it was converted into a hostel. He guessed ten, plus a resident warden. He pulled out the keys and ran the combination of the alarm through his head: 0503 – 5 March. David's birthday. Trust the arrogant bastard to use his own.

He went to unlock the lower deadlock first and was surprised to find that it was open. Then the Yale, turning half a twist. Perhaps Consuela was there. He went in and felt the lock click silently behind him. He was about to call out to Consuela, worried lest she might think he was a burglar, but then he heard voices.

His first thought was that David was in bed with a girl so he decided immediately to keep quiet. This delicious possibility had long been a topic of conversation and intense speculation between Tom and Clara – Tom arguing that David was too conceited not to be an adulterer while Clara was prepared to give him the benefit of the doubt. However, now there were three voices, and since two were male Tom ruled out the possibility of a threesome in the bedroom: David was not the type to invite competition. Besides, the voices were in the kitchen – one was loud, braying, a man's voice, which accounted for why they hadn't heard him come in. Tom darted into the drawing room, now hearing David's voice. The girl sounded young, but assured. Probably a professional. He strained to listen. They were discussing house prices. Hell, if it wasn't bad enough having to listen to it at every dinner party, you couldn't even eavesdrop without listening to the middle-class preoccupation – no, *obsession* – with how much their houses were worth. He caught the man's voice again.

'Between one and two per cent.'

That didn't sound much. The assured voice continued, 'However, that is for sole agency. We alone would have the right to market the property for a period of eight weeks.'

So they weren't talking about value, they were talking about commission. Next Tom heard David's voice: 'And you're confident you can sell it?'

'The house is in an excellent location and in excellent condition. The style is very good. Did you have the interior designed by a professional?'

'Oh, yes, a London firm.'

Tom took a sharp breath – Victoria had been under orders to design the whole house from top to bottom.

'It shows. We would anticipate good foreign interest. Particularly from Americans. Wimbledon is always popular with our US clients.'

'I'd want to put it on the market in the autumn.'

'We couldn't tempt you to go ahead earlier? We have many buyers waiting . . .'

'Unfortunately not. We have family commitments here over the summer – we're holding a party for my parents' wedding anniversary and they've set their hearts on holding it here. I can't disappoint them . . .'

'I understand. Shall I send you our formal estimate of the value of the house? We can talk again at the end of the summer.'

'Yes, but I'll give you my chambers address and then my secretary can deal with it.'

Tom could hear details being explained and occasionally the girl's voice, but he struggled to make out her words. She must be with the agent, a trainee. He could just hear her talking about the kitchen, something about the doors to the garden: 'They're a wonderful feature . . . so useful in the summer.'

Then David's voice: 'Well, I'll wait to hear from you . . .'

God, they were coming closer. Tom moved swiftly behind the curtains, aware that their precisely pleated folds must now be looking distinctly baggy. They were in the hallway, getting ready to leave.

'Thank you *so much* for your time and expertise,' David was saying. 'It's been most useful.'

'Not at all. Always happy to oblige.'

Then the girl: 'And there will be no trouble selling it . . .'

The door closed but not before four piercing beeps sent the unwelcome signal to Tom that David had set the alarm. Tom, envisaging himself paralysed to the spot all weekend, decided to gamble on there being a time-lag to unset it before the house erupted in deafening peals. He shot out from behind the curtain, bolted down the hallway and slammed the code into the alarm, holding his breath until sure that the silence was to remain unbroken.

'*And there will be no trouble selling it* . . .' Why were they selling? Victoria had said nothing about a move. Suddenly Tom was sure that she knew nothing of David's plan. And why wait until the autumn? Not for some party for David's parents, that was for sure. It was a wonder David could remember their names, let alone their wedding anniversary. He hadn't seen them for years, happy to leave them behind in their Hendon council house – eager, in fact, to put as much distance as possible between himself and his past.

Tom wandered up the stairs and into the master bedroom. Why all this secrecy? Financial problems? Unpaid fees? A secret love child to support? He imagined all sorts of exciting possibilities. Perhaps David was being blackmailed. Or needed to pay someone off.

He looked in Victoria's bedside table and found the pills, slipped them into his pocket and glanced round the room, briefly taking in the fussy wallpaper, the woolly rugs and the heavy cream curtains, which appeared to have some padding in them, he couldn't imagine why. The room as a whole was not his style at all, he decided, preferring something somehow less designed.

He wandered on to the landing and back downstairs. He could not resist going into David's study. The room was faultlessly tidy, the wall-to-ceiling shelves neatly filled with legal books, the leather-topped desk clear except for an arty black-and-white photograph of Alex and Emily – doubtless snapped by some pretentious London photographer. In one corner stood a mock-oak reproduction filing cabinet. Tom tried the door. Locked. So were the desk drawers. Anyway, he had better get going. He patted his pockets to double-check that he had the keys and the pills, then went outside, pondering what to tell Clara when he arrived home.

CHAPTER 3

Annie lay in bed and watched the evening sun glimmer through the half-drawn curtains. She had been awake for an hour or so. She could hear Victoria preparing dinner and Emily playing in the kitchen. From the sound of water gushing through the upstairs pipes she guessed Clara was taking a shower.

She gazed around the room, her eyes barely taking in the cool, flowery blue walls and nautical blue-and-white curtains. David and Victoria had bought the Marlow house three years ago from the proceeds of a huge fraud trial that had kept David in work, and exorbitant fees, for six months. The house, built between the wars in red brick and slate, was neither grand nor luxurious, but David and Victoria had barely noticed it: they had bought it for the gardens – captivated by the expanse of lawn that ran down to the Marlow waterfront – enclosed on either side by huge and ancient weeping willow trees. The interior was 1950s, which explained why David's colleagues only heard about the house, admittedly a great deal, but wouldn't be invited down until it was all done up.

Annie pulled the duvet closer around her and thought about getting up. Her head felt heavy and lethargy engulfed her. The sleeping pills, she supposed, and the tranquillisers and the marijuana. Not that anyone knew about the last two. The tranquillisers had been Hugo's, prescribed for him last year when the stress had got too much. She kept the marijuana carefully hidden from Elizabeth in a locked box under her bed. Packing that afternoon, she had secreted it in her handbag, then bundled whatever clean clothes she could find into a case before rushing out to the car where Tom and Clara were waiting to drive to Marlow. She had paused on her way out to pick up an important-looking letter from the hall table. It had arrived two days ago, franked Belmont & Co, Solicitors. She had not been able to summon the courage to open it.

As they had driven away, she had looked back, miserable at leaving her precious house, so pretty in the April sunshine with the Boston ivy, which covered the pair of cottages, springing into new growth for its annual battle with the blossoming wisteria for space. She loved her house more than ever now. It had been *theirs* and that, at least, could not be taken away. She felt, with relief, that the house still contained Hugo. Or, at least, so many memories of him. The beechwood kitchen they had installed themselves. Hugo's office filled with unfinished designs clipped to his father's old drawing-boards. The oak floors that they had sanded and varnished gleaming in the morning sun. Pictures they had chosen, curtains she had made, school photographs of Hugo at Selchester.

In the still of the house, surrounded by their mutual possessions, she could feel him. She could close her eyes and conjure up his voice and see his face in her mind's eye. She could remember his laughter, the way he had held her, and how it had felt to hold him, too. At these times she inhabited her own private, secret world. And she felt she couldn't leave it. The prospect of admitting, truly admitting to herself, that Hugo was gone and that she was alone was so hopelessly bleak. In her imagination a dismal, joyless future stretched ahead of her, offering nothing more than the challenge of surviving each lonely day, representing not so much a life as an existence. And although everyone kept telling her that in time she would feel differently, she had come to believe, with an increasing degree of certainty, that she would never again feel hope or happiness.

There was a knock at the door and Victoria pushed it open. 'Annie, are you awake?'

Annie thought about feigning sleep, but what was the point? She would have to get up eventually. And she didn't want to seem ungrateful. 'Just woken up.'

'I've brought you a cup of tea. To help you come round.'

Victoria put a mug on the bedside table and sat down. She looked surreptitiously at her sister. Annie had always had an air of fragility, a combination of delicate features and blonde hair, which caused her to look beautiful or terrible depending on her mood. Now she looked absolutely dreadful. Victoria decided to smile brightly and sound determinedly cheerful. This was not solely for Annie's benefit: she was always happy to come to Marlow, would have loved to live there permanently in the small market town by the side of the Thames, if only David would agree to commute. In her weekend outfit of white linen shirt over a pair of jeans she felt more relaxed here than she ever did in Wimbledon. 'Tom's helping me in the kitchen and Clara's getting ready. David's due in about an hour. We'll have dinner in the conservatory. Just the five of us. I'll give the children their tea first.'

'Sounds lovely.'

Annie was trying to sound positive, Victoria realised. 'And you've had a call from Elizabeth,' she went on. 'She's fine. Rehearsals are going great, she said, and tonight they're all going out for a pizza.'

Elizabeth was staying for the weekend with her best friend Celine, so she could take part in intensive rehearsals for the school's end-of-term play, *Romeo and Juliet*. She had won the role of Juliet and, despite Annie's reservations, was determined to go ahead and play the lead. Celine was cast as the Nurse and for the last two months they had spent hours in Elizabeth's bedroom reading and rereading their lines when they were not collapsing into fits of laughter, usually about their drama teacher Mrs Lightfoot and the other members of the cast.

'She said she'd call again tomorrow,' continued Victoria.

Annie frowned and lay back on the pillow, looking up vacantly at the ceiling. 'I just worry about it all. The pressure. And some of the lines. It's not a play about love, you know. It's a play about death . . .' she murmured.

'Come on. You told me how her teacher discussed it all with her. Elizabeth decided to go ahead. You can't make that kind of decision for her. And, besides, I think young people are more . . . resilient than we realise.'

'I can't imagine what it would be like to feel resilient.'

'You will. It's very soon. You can't expect to feel any different.'

Annie turned on to her side and raised herself on one arm to reach for her tea. Victoria was startled to see that she was fully dressed.

Annie caught her look of surprise: 'Sorry. Couldn't be bothered to get undressed.'

'It's OK. Listen, why don't you let me run you a bath? I've got some Chanel bath foam – David brought it back from his case conference in Paris. I'll go and get it, let you luxuriate. Now, let's have some light in here.'

Victoria got up, briskly drew the curtains, and saw Annie wince as the light stung her eyes. Victoria had given her sister the guestroom with the en suite bathroom and a view of the river, hoping that Annie might sit out on the small balcony and watch the life of the river float past. But the French windows had remained resolutely shut. Tom and Clara were in the attic room, sharing a bathroom with Alex and Emily, but Tom wouldn't mind a dose of communal living. She and David had the other first-floor room with the biggest bathroom – there was no question of David sharing. 'I'll go and get that bubble bath. And there's some body lotion, too.'

'Oh, don't worry about it . . .'

But Victoria was already closing the bedroom door, the smile fading from her lips as the catch clicked shut. She felt a heavy, nostalgic sadness that she and Annie seemed to have lost a certain intimacy, and she was aware that this was not entirely the result of Hugo's death. As children, it was Victoria and Annie – the eldest and the youngest – who had formed a natural alliance, leaving Clara the outsider of the three. The pair had shared a happy-go-lucky nature, embracing all that was fun and frivolous in childhood – dressing-up and miming to pop songs, then in time experimenting with make-up and hairstyles. Through it all Clara, quiet, intense and driven, had stood slightly apart, never quite part of the game, until she ceased to join in very much at all and in her teenage years retreated to her bedroom, locked away for hours of study. But as adults or, more precisely, as married women, Victoria had found herself the outsider. It was Annie and Hugo with Clara and Tom who had formed the natural foursome, often meeting up for impromptu suppers and walks in the park and even, over the last couple of years, taking a Whitsun holiday in the Lakes. Although Victoria knew that she only had to say the word and she and David would be politely included, she also realised that it was wiser to say nothing. David had been awkward company on those occasions. He had got on well enough with Annie and Hugo but invariably bickered with Tom, and drew sharp glances of disapproval from Clara for his reactionary views. So now Victoria was the remote one, separated by her marriage and her lifestyle, and with little to talk of except her family and the ambitions of her husband. But she was determined to make this a good weekend, not happy, obviously, in the circumstances but at least harmonious. But, God, it was heavy going.

Victoria stepped into the hallway and bumped into Clara coming downstairs. She mimed to her sister to say nothing, her finger on her lips, edged her into the bedroom and shut the door behind her. Clara's hair was still damp and her appearance was rendered all the more haphazard by her shapeless jeans and an old sweatshirt of Tom's, which she wore oblivious to the large hole under the sleeve. They sat down conspiratorially on the four-poster bed, purchased by

Victoria in an effort to inspire a feeling of romance with its drapes of translucent white muslin.

'I really can't believe how bad she is,' whispered Victoria. 'She seems to be getting worse.'

'I know,' said Clara. 'It's only been a few weeks, of course, but she seems like a . . . like a zombie.'

Victoria hesitated and then murmured, 'Is she smoking . . . cannabis?'

Clara shrugged. 'I don't think so, though I wouldn't be entirely surprised. Maybe it's the sleeping pills – my GP dished them out. The last week with us has been pretty bad and I couldn't have coped without Tom. He's amazing.'

'All that training . . .'

'Oh, he's done all the courses,' said Clara breezily, 'counselling, coping with trauma, teenage angst – you name it, he's got the course hand-out. He's been fantastic with Elizabeth.' Clara's tone grew more serious and, leaning towards Victoria, she lowered her voice: 'Quite honestly – and I know I probably shouldn't judge because I'm not a mother – I think Annie and Elizabeth aren't getting on at all well. The atmosphere when they're both there is awfully strained.'

Victoria nodded. 'Mmm. You'd have thought the whole thing would bring them closer together . . .' It was a clichéd response, she knew, and Clara shot her a look of surprise. 'Well, yes,' she replied, 'but Elizabeth's fourteen and it's hit her very hard. Hugo was a father to her – and now she's having to look after Annie. If it weren't for Elizabeth, I don't think any washing-up would get done in that house . . . It's too much for her. She's got her schoolwork and the play, and she needs some time off to be with her friends.'

'But Annie doesn't see it that way?' asked Victoria, uncomfortably aware that she was trailing far behind Clara and Tom in their analysis of Annie's state of mind.

'Actually, I don't think Annie can think straight at all. Fortunately Tom managed to persuade her to let Elizabeth go to her friend's house for the weekend. He says she should have some fun and not feel guilty about it. Otherwise, he thinks she'll end up getting depressed as well.'

'As well! You mean—'

'I don't know.' Clara sighed. 'I'm not an expert. It seems to me that you can't expect someone who's lost their husband to feel or act any differently. But Tom seems to think there's more to it.'

'Pity Tom's not staying the whole week.' Although Victoria would never admit it, Annie's stay was going to curtail her longed-for week of freedom. She wasn't sure how she was going to keep the children entertained and manage to involve Annie at the same time. The children loved to be active – to ride their bicycles and to go to the leisure-centre swimming pool – but she had the feeling that it would be difficult to prise Annie out of bed. Tom was so good at this sort of thing, so insightful and experienced, whereas she was beginning to feel out of her depth.

But the first challenge was to get through the weekend. Victoria stood up and heaved a suitcase on to the bed, aware that she had a host of jobs to do and that unless she kept her eye on the clock she would run late with dinner. Now distracted by the task of opening the suitcase, she continued, 'Maybe lunch on Sunday will help. I've got the Blessons coming. David's very excited. They're Marlow's oldest family and all the men went to Selchester. He sees it as a real leg up into Marlow society.'

Clara was unable to think of anything suitable to say about a lifestyle so different from her and Tom's – not to mention their own childhood, growing up in a South London suburb. Sunday lunch then had been a tough old piece of brisket, boiled potatoes and carrots. To this day Clara could not face gravy. Their mother's cooking was always dire, but often made worse because she would attempt to cook while at the same time engrossed in her latest historical romance. Latterly Clara had realised that their mother was a far more adventurous, even Bohemian character than any of them had appreciated, and that she had been unsuited to motherhood or the life at home that marriage to their father, the senior accountant in an insurance firm, had imposed on her. But while Clara, dutiful and studious, would always have described her childhood as perfectly happy, she suspected that Victoria and Annie, in their different ways, had reacted against the dullness of it all.

Clara sat lost in her thoughts, only half listening as Victoria chattered on about her lunch menu, which plates to use, the claret David had ordered specially from the Wimbledon wine merchant. She was determinedly unpacking David's clothes from the suitcase that now lay open on the bed, organising and decanting them into an enormous pine chest of drawers.

Clara watched her absently. 'Well, we can't stand by while Annie sleeps her way through it. I'll ask Tom what he thinks we should do,' she said.

Victoria broke off from folding a stack of sweaters. 'Better than asking David. He'll tell her to get a grip and pull herself together.'

'Oh, God. Well, you'd better keep him quiet tonight.'

'At least he'll have Tom to argue with.'

Clara looked unconcerned, 'Oh, Tom can look after himself.'

Her attention had now been caught by the mountain of David's clothes on the bed. Piles of trousers, shorts, polo shirts, T-shirts, boxer shorts and a vast array of socks had mounted up. She rolled on to her front and began nosing through David's clothes, 'Haven't you brought rather a lot? He's only here for the weekend, isn't he?'

'Oh, yes. But if he wants his favourite sweater or his favourite socks and they're not here he goes barmy so now I just bring everything and it saves an argument. I've got another suitpack with his jackets and shirts.'

'Well, if he ever gets tired of them, do pass them on to Tom. He's only brought two tracksuits for the weekend.'

'Tracksuits?' Victoria sounded aghast.

'Yes, it's his latest idea.' Clara shot Victoria an exasperated glance. 'The kids on the estate wear all this sports stuff so he bought them from the market. I haven't had the heart to tell him they only wear designer labels – and they cost ten times what he paid.'

Victoria unzipped a bulging bag and began hanging shirts on wooden hangers inside a wartime utility wardrobe, which the previous owners had left behind. 'You've got to hand it to him, he does try.'

'Oh, yes, he's devoted to the cause of saving the poor, all right. He's on a high at the moment – he's going to launch a campaign to get a gym put into the Southhead estate.'

'Tom? In a gym?' Victoria giggled.

'Yes, he's hardly Mr Universe, is he? I think he sees himself in a managerial role. The gym isn't something fun, you see, it's about motivating the residents, boosting their self-esteem and stopping them smoking.'

'Sounds very serious.'

Clara spoke with a sudden note of irritation in her voice, 'Tom *is* very serious. His opinion on exercising for pleasure is the same as his opinion on everything else, houses, cars, holidays. They're all frivolous extravagances.'

'Come on, he did agree to move house.'

'Yes. After five years of persuasion. And being burgled twice. And having my car stolen. I had to virtually threaten to divorce him unless we left his precious inner-city two-up two-down and moved somewhere decent.'

'Richmond is more than decent.'

'Yes,' cut in Clara bitterly, 'and he still carps about how middle class it is. I really think he'd be much happier if there was rioting in the park and a sit-down anarchist protest in the tearoom. Not to mention a mugging once a week. And God forbid we might spend any money. He absolutely won't hear of putting in a new kitchen. I've got cracks in the floor so big I'll fall down one soon.'

Victoria put the last of several jackets away. 'Well, I

think Tom's a treasure. And he adores you – he'd do anything for you. You know, that's the only thing that really matters . . .'

Clara hesitated, gazing out at the river and the park that lay beyond it. She sounded distracted, 'I know. And I know I'm lucky and that after twelve years you can't expect fireworks. But we seem to be caught in a way of life that's all very . . . mundane. We go shopping, eat dinner and watch television. We don't do anything spontaneous or extravagant. And it's not as if we can't afford it. I suppose it's just that sometimes . . . I suppose I would just like life to be a bit more, well, a bit more *unpredictable* . . .' She trailed off, and for a moment they stood in silence.

Then Victoria gasped. 'Oh, God, I'm supposed to be running Annie's bath! I must dash.' She hurried into the bathroom and Clara heard her rifling through her vast range of cosmetics and beauty products.

'Is there anything I can do to help?' she called.

'Well, actually . . .'

'Don't tell me, Alex needs help with his Latin homework.'

'Unfortunately, yes. It's a holiday project about Pompeii. And you're the only one brainy enough to understand it.' Victoria emerged from the bathroom holding an armful of bottles.

Clara opened the door for her. 'Well, at least you've finished unpacking.'

'No, I've still got David's shoes and sports kit to do.'

At dinner, as yet another awkward silence fell, David got up to pour more wine. Annie's glass was already empty for the third time and Tom was not far behind her. The evening had started badly and, despite David's best efforts at conversation, seemed to be going downhill fast. When Annie had eventually made it downstairs she had been met by Emily going up to bed: the little girl had stopped to ask her for the third time that day when Hugo would be arriving. Meanwhile, when Victoria had suggested that they eat in the conservatory she had overlooked the fact that it was a De Longden, albeit thirty years old. As Annie's eyes watered at the sight of the logo on a discreet brass plate, David had reached for the whisky bottle, hoping to gulp a last drink before dinner, only to find that Tom had just poured the last of it for himself.

Victoria brought out the serving dishes for the main course, helped by Clara. As the silence continued David, in some desperation, turned to Tom and was mildly surprised when Tom spoke to him first. 'Victoria says you've had a terrible day in court.'

'Really? Well, yes.' David appeared taken aback.

'What was the case about?' pursued Tom.

David evidently imagined that Tom was trying to distract Annie from staring blankly out of the window where the odd motor cruiser chugged along before being overtaken by the occasional rowing eight from the riverside club at Marlow Bridge. 'Fraud. Bank employee hacking into the computer and transferring funds to his own account. Not unusual, but the defence are pretty hot and went at it all day.'

'Went at it?'

'Yes.' David spoke without a trace of hesitation. 'Legal argument about evidence. All very technical and rather dull.'

'No. No. I'm sure it's not. I'd be really interested to know.'

Clara, who was bringing a basket of bread to the table, shot Tom a surprised look.

David sighed. 'Very well. There are some records on the man's home computer. The police seized it at the time of his arrest, but the search warrant was wrongly filled out. His defence lawyer is trying to argue that the jury shouldn't be allowed to see the records held on the computer.'

Tom's expression was one of intense concentration. He spoke as if he was mastering the case: 'The computer records show the funds he stole?'

'Yes.'

'And you're arguing that the jury should see the records?'

'Yes. Exactly,' David said, mildly impatient. 'Now, shall I carve this beef? Darling, have you got the black-handled carving knife?'

'No. It's in London,' called Victoria apologetically from the kitchen.

David sighed theatrically. 'It really is the best one. Do try to remember it next time.'

'And this argument about the warrant. Was it very complicated?' Tom went on, reaching for his wineglass, which was nearly empty again.

David looked at him with a mixture of exasperation and curiosity. 'Tom, why on earth are you bothered by all of this?'

'Just trying to broaden my mind,' Tom said airily. 'Do carry on.'

David was hacking at the joint of meat before him when Victoria bustled in with more dishes – artichokes, fennel and roasted onions, each garnished with olive oil, sesame seeds or some exotic sauce.

'Plates, I still haven't got plates!' barked David.

'How did the judge take it all?' wondered Tom.

'Fine,' replied David, testily.

'But you were stuck there all day?'

Victoria returned with a stack of plates, then rushed back to the kitchen. David picked one up and yelped. 'Christ, you could have warned me they were hot!'

'Sorry, sorry.' Victoria hurried in but David was already marching into the kitchen to plunge his hand under cold water.

'Shall I carve?' asked Tom brightly.

'No. I'm coming,' shouted David, and turned on the tap. Water gushed out, splashed on the saucepans stacked in the sink and drenched his sleeve. 'Fuck. Fucking hell! This sink's like a bloody slum!'

Annie jumped and Clara looked highly embarrassed.

Tom sat back happily and, reaching over, poured Annie and himself another glass of wine, thus emptying the second bottle of the night. Victoria was now attempting to dry David – but with a stained tea towel that transferred greasy stock on to his favourite weekend checked shirt. 'Oh, just leave me alone, will you? Bloody hell!' He broke free from his wife's ministrations and strode back, narrowly avoiding Emily who had wandered into the kitchen.

'I need a drink of water,' she announced to Victoria, eyeing the bread and butter pudding that Victoria was preparing to put in the oven. Victoria could see the plan formulating in her daughter's mind: she would hover in the kitchen long enough to inveigle her way to a seat at the table. She decided to head her off – she could see that this dinner was going to require all her powers of tact, and therefore no further distractions. She took down a glass from the kitchen cupboard and began filling it from the tap.

'I want fizzy!' protested Emily.

Victoria regarded her daughter, in a pink and white spotted nightdress, her eyes betraying the telltale red of tiredness following a day of frantic running round the garden, and decided to make a deal. 'All right. You can have fizzy. And a biscuit. But you have to take it to your room. If you're good you can have leftover pudding for breakfast.' She was aware that this was not nutritionally recommended but she had a dinner under way with five hungry adults to feed and, furthermore, she could hear David and Tom bickering about the correct way to carve a joint.

Emily considered the offer. 'OK.' But she had not finished. 'Alex is playing with his Gameboy,' she continued, with an unmistakable note of superiority.

Victoria, while knowing that Emily was trying to score points via the unattractive device of playing the telltale, nevertheless felt a surge of irritation. She had specifically agreed with Alex that he would work on his Pompeii project tonight, the aim being that this would be one holiday when the damned school project didn't get done in a hurried panic the night before the return to school. But she couldn't do anything about it now.

'Well, tell him to put it away and if he doesn't . . .' she slowed her voice, pausing between each word '. . . he'll be in very serious trouble with me.'

Emily beamed. 'I'll tell him.' She grabbed the proffered biscuit from Victoria's hand and rushed off to deliver her message.

Victoria returned to the table and began to pass vegetables, sauces and dressings.

Tom leaned forward. 'So, did you win?'

Victoria could not believe that they were still banging on about that boring case.

David looked blank. 'Did I what?'

'Did you win the argument?'

David looked at Tom directly and spoke very slowly, 'I don't know. The judge will rule on Monday.'

'So you ran out of time?'

'Yes! We ran out of time.'

Tom leaned back and asked, almost as an afterthought, 'When did you finish?'

'Four thirty.'

Before he could ask another question Clara interrupted. 'Annie, let me help you to some vegetables. You've hardly eaten all day,' she said swiftly, shooting Tom a warning glance.

David reached for the wine bottle before starting his meal, only to find it empty.

'You'll need to open another,' suggested Tom, in his most helpful tone.

David got up yet again and marched off to the cellar in search of more red wine.

Meanwhile, Tom set about his food with enthusiasm. He would tell Clara everything in good time but for now he was enjoying the element of investigation. He knew that he appeared to many people as an outdated old liberal, reminiscing about his days as a student protester and still daring to call himself a socialist. But he was not rated as the council's best social worker for nothing. That title was down to his tenacious character. Tom was immensely proud that in the ten years he had previously spent as a children's social worker he had never yet failed to spot a child at risk of abuse. No matter how many times he was turned away by the mother, father or step-parent he kept going back until he saw the child. And when he finally did, Tom could see past the excuses and stories, the tales of falls and accidents, to see the truth in the frightened eyes of the child.

Now he was happy. He had got to the house at four forty. If David had finished at four thirty he wouldn't have had anything like enough time to get there *and* get round the house. To view it properly the estate agents must have arrived at least half an hour earlier. David was in a corner – but the beauty of it was that he didn't know it yet. And Tom thought there was much more still that could be wrung out of his rare advantage over his detested brother-in-law.

David came back, opened the wine and at last sat down to his cooling meal. Tom spoke with his mouth full: 'Wonderful food. You should get started, David.'

David stared at him coldly.

'I guess you don't need these cases running over,' Tom continued.

David looked confused.

'With the election,' Tom explained. 'And you must want to spend some time at the house in London. All that work and expense, you must want to enjoy it now. Have your parents seen it?'

'No. They haven't had time.'

'Oh, that's a pity. We ought to organise something. A family get-together. How are you finding the house?'

David looked at him askance. 'Tom, you amaze me.' He

had taken one mouthful but put down his knife and fork. 'Are you telling me you liked the house?'

'I have to say that's the wrong word. I was *inspired*. No, really. Because when you spoke that night at the party I realised, for the first time, that your house represents something more to you than bricks and mortar. I saw then that it has a . . . soul, a real meaning for you as a family . . .' Tom waved his hand expansively at Victoria and caught Clara's astonished look. 'Yes. A place to live your lives for ever. A base. A home. With your special family traditions and memories cherished over the years. The Christmas tree in the drawing room. The plants growing year by year in the garden. I have to tell you, I was touched. And I don't mind admitting it, you're absolutely right, houses have never meant much to me, but you taught me something that night. What was that phrase you used? "A house for our children and our grandchildren, if we are so blessed." Poetry, David, pure poetry. You taught me the value of establishing a home and tending it, yes tending it, over the years . . . and decades . . . and into posterity.'

David searched Tom's face for signs of the familiar mockery. But Tom's features were set in an expression of utter sincerity. 'That's most . . . generous of you, Tom. Thank you.'

'No, thank *you*, David. In fact, I think I must propose a toast.'

Clara was looking at him as if he had gone stark raving mad.

'To David. The father of the family. An example to us all.' He raised his glass above his head in a sweeping gesture and, while the rest of the table looked on in disbelief, downed half its contents then helped himself to more.

There was a pause before Clara rallied. 'Alex is doing so well. We went through the Latin and he grasped it all with no problem at all.'

'That's what his teachers say,' sighed Victoria. 'He can do it but he just doesn't try.'

'Couldn't you inspire him, David?' asked Tom. 'But on second thoughts I suppose they didn't do Latin at Hendon Secondary Modern. Isn't that where they had the drug bust last year, all those sixth formers caught with Ecstasy?'

David ignored this. 'Alex just needs to pull his finger out. He's got two years until the Selchester Scholarship exam and it's damned competitive.'

'I'm surprised,' said Tom. 'I wouldn't have thought many parents would want a school like Selchester these days. Cold showers and dormitories, all that public-school stuff.'

David replied with irritation: 'Tom, intelligent parents will always want the best for their children. Selchester has been around for four hundred years. The cream of the country has always sent their children there. They must be getting it right, in my book.'

Victoria remained silent. She was dreading the day when Alex would be sent away to school – it was the cause of at least half the rows, but David was adamant that he must go. She looked across at Annie, who had barely touched her meal. 'Come on, Annie, try a bit. Is there anything you'd rather have?'

'Actually, I think I'm going to have a lie-down. Please excuse me.' She rose unsteadily to her feet.

'I'll come with you,' said Clara, happy to have an excuse to get away and attempt to work out what on earth Tom was up to.

With their departure David, Tom and Victoria lapsed into an uneasy silence. There followed a desultory conversation and Victoria tried desperately to think of some subject on which David and Tom could agree. But somehow they always came back to the same old political debates.

When Clara came back Victoria gratefully and swiftly served the pudding and listened to her sister talk about the Tellium case, while at the other end of the table Tom and

David's voices rose in passionate argument. After two hours Victoria had had enough. She got up to load the dishwasher, make coffee and finally plead a headache, which allowed her to go to bed, followed soon after by Clara. Only David and Tom's drunken state persuaded them to follow their wives to bed rather than argue, as they often did, into the early hours of the morning with neither taking the slightest bit of notice of the other's point of view.

As soon as Tom came to bed, Clara tackled him. 'I want to know what this is all about. Now.'

Tom laughed. 'All the best mysteries unfold slowly. I'm going to brush my teeth.' And with that he disappeared on to the landing and into the children's bathroom. Clara lay fuming in bed. But Tom on his return seemed to take an age to get undressed, carefully folding his shiny new tracksuit, and fiddling with his trainers, his watch and his wallet. Clara watched him dispassionately, noticing all the more these days how thin his arms and legs seemed compared to his increasingly bulging stomach. As a student Tom had been lean. Now, as he approached middle age, he just seemed wizened.

'For God's sake, Tom!'

'All right, all right.'

'It's to do with this afternoon, isn't it?'

Tom got into bed. 'Yes.' And detail by detail he told her about David's plan to sell the house, the lies about his parents and the girl's parting shot. ' "And there will be no trouble selling it . . ." she said,' he concluded.

Clara was stunned. 'Maybe he's just getting it valued. People do that, don't they, get an estate agent round to find out what it's worth just for the fun of knowing?'

'So why all the secrecy? Why get the valuation sent to his chambers? Listen, I was there and I'm telling you I *know*, I absolutely know, that he was serious.'

'And this girl was confident it would sell? When she said – what was it – "It will be easy to sell . . ."'

Tom said nothing. He was lying on his back staring at the ceiling. 'No, she didn't say that.'

'But you just said—'

'I mean, she didn't say it like that. Jesus.' Tom paused, saying nothing.

Clara shook him. 'What? What is it?'

Tom rolled on to his side, propped himself up on one elbow and looked at her, his face suddenly serious. 'I assumed she was an estate agent, that David was there with two of them, the man who was in charge and the girl who was younger and therefore his assistant or trainee or something. But she wasn't with the agent. She was with David. It's all because of the way she said it. I wasn't listening because I'd made a wrong assumption. She didn't say it would sell easily. She asked a question. She said, "And there will be no trouble selling it?"'

Clara looked at him uneasily, 'Tom, are you sure? It's just a tone of voice and you were eavesdropping.'

'Clara, I'm as sure as I've ever been about anything.'

And as she looked at him, Clara believed him. For a while they lay pondering the situation.

'What are you going to do?' she asked eventually.

'I think it's what *you* are going to do. She's your sister.'

'I don't want to get involved,' said Clara, definitely. 'It's their business, their marriage.'

'And what are you going to do when he finally decides to tell her? When the house is sold under Victoria's nose? How are you going to look her in the eyes knowing that you knew and you did nothing to warn her?'

'You don't know that's going to happen.'

'No, I don't. But she ought at least to be warned that something's going on.'

'But—'

'But nothing. You *are* involved. Because of what you know. It's like someone who suspects a child is being ill-treated. Once they have that suspicion they can't forget what they know. They have to act. Surely you have a responsibility to her. And what about the kids? What if he *is* planning to bugger off? Christ, Alex's life is going to be miserable enough at that awful school without his father playing around on the side.'

Clara said nothing.

Tom went on, 'You have to speak to her. The sooner the better.'

Clara sighed. 'OK, OK. I'll do it in the morning. I don't know how I'm going to put it.'

'Don't worry about that. Just tell her what happened. What she chooses to do after that is her business. But you can't say nothing.'

Clara felt miserable. Dealing with the students' problems was easy compared to this – Victoria's marriage had always mystified her. Clara could see that David was a powerful, domineering figure and that some women might find that attractive – not that he appealed to her. But what disturbed her was not so much his personality as his effect on Victoria. Over the years of their marriage, as he had grown more successful and confident – and also, Clara had detected, more selfish – so she had observed Victoria cast ever deeper into his shadow in which, year by year, she appeared diminished and almost, at times, subservient. Admittedly, she could see that it would take a strong woman to challenge David. But at other times she was infuriated by her sister's passivity, her refusal to confront her situation and to fight for a more equal relationship. And in her more judgemental moments Clara wondered if it was all a type of bargain in which Victoria had traded intimacy and companionship for other rewards, the houses, and the clothes and the store cards, rewards which were in fact entirely material.

Tom moved closer to her and she was jolted from her thoughts as he began to rub her shoulders. 'Don't worry, love. Just talk to her in the morning, get it over with.'

Clara frowned, still unwilling to be drawn into interfering in the minutiae of her sister's marriage. 'What if she doesn't believe me?'

'Then that's her decision. But she has to know the facts.' Tom's hand moved across her breasts, which he began kneading with increasing urgency. His voice was slurred after too much red wine. He never had been able to hold his drink. 'Anyway, I don't want to talk about her,' he murmured. 'Sooner or later she's going to have to stand up to him.'

'But—'

'Ssh. Come on. Forget it . . .'

Now his hands were moving over her body, but never lingering long enough to bring her any pleasure. Tom had been a radical postgraduate student when they had met in Clara's first year at university. He had secured with ease his first degree in economics, but while his contemporaries had left for jobs in the City, he had studied for a master's in social work. Looking back, she saw that she had fallen in love with his mind, not his body – and if she had assumed that the years would improve Tom's lovemaking then she had long since realised her mistake. But although she still loved him dearly – and, anxious to please, he would always do as she asked, she wished that he could just get it right without being reminded. He began fumbling amateurishly between her legs, covering her face with wet kisses and cooing into her ear, 'Does Mrs Tiggywinkle want Peter Rabbit?'

Clara, as usual, could think of no reply to this. She tried to bring some erotic thoughts to mind that might move her body to respond to Tom's ever more insistent manoeuvrings. A picture of Ben Ford came involuntarily to mind: his tall, slim frame, the long thick hair, the rise of his arm muscles as he heaved the boxes into her car.

'Would Mrs Tiggywinkle like Peter Rabbit to water her garden?'

'Oh . . . yes,' mumbled Clara, trying hard to put some

enthusiasm into her voice. It wasn't that Tom was selfish or rough or lazy. He was just inept. He disappeared beneath the covers and she felt the roughness of his tongue imitating a monotonous movement of licking an ice lolly. But in the silence she could try to recall Ben's voice and when she caught it in her mind she felt a thrill of secret pleasure.

As Tom rose from the depths of the bed after barely a minute and lunged on top of her she struggled to keep Ben's voice in her mind, aware of her own disloyalty but desperately needing the tantalising image of Ben to stay with her.

Tom let out a series of grunts as he pushed himself inside her, and as she felt his paunchy stomach settle on hers, she imagined in its place Ben's hard, youthful body. And when, after a few seconds, Tom came, Clara lay back, glad that it was over for at least another week – and wondered when she would next see Ben Ford.

As the Marlow church clock struck half past midnight, Victoria and David were lying in bed.

'He's just a fucking do-gooder!' David fumed. 'He says he's got his principles. That doesn't stop him drinking my wine and eating my food but criticising everything I do to pay for it.' David mimicked Tom's speech, '"Oh yes, Victoria, I could just manage some more cheese . . ."'

'Please, darling, he's only in the room above us. He might hear,' Victoria whispered desperately.

'Good. He might get the hint and fuck off to worship at Karl Marx's grave or whatever else he does in his free time. Assuming that heap of a car could get to the end of the road. Well, if he tries it again tomorrow I'm not holding back. I'll tell him where he can stick his principles.'

'Please, please, darling, can we just keep the peace for one day?' Victoria begged. 'For Annie's sake. He's going on Sunday morning.'

'Yeah, pity he's not taking his frumpy wife with him. God, Clara's not a bad-looking woman so why doesn't she make an effort? I'm surprised those students of hers don't have a whip-round for her, get her a new pair of glasses instead of those jam-jars she wears. And her hair! She looks like that sheepdog your mother had. Does she actually own a hairbrush?'

'I think her mind is on higher things.'

'Well, she certainly doesn't waste any thought on her appearance. Christ, with the two of them it's the Ugly Bug Ball here.'

'Tom's not all bad.'

'Yes, he is. He's opinionated and outdated and small-minded. God knows, those people on that estate must be desperate if they go to him for advice.'

Victoria experienced a wave of panic. She had to keep everything harmonious for one more day. On the spur of the moment she thought of something to win David round: 'Look, I wasn't going to mention this but—'

'What?'

'Well, I didn't want you to be cross . . . but I forgot my contraceptive pills.' She hurried on, before David had a chance to erupt, 'It's all right. I've got them now.'

'And you've taken one?'

'Of course.'

'You haven't missed any?'

'*No*, I told you, it's fine. I was in a rush packing and Emily was playing up and somehow I forgot them. I know I'm disorganised and silly but it's all OK because I phoned Clara.'

'Clara! I can't believe she needs the pill. I bet Tom can't even get it up.'

'I phoned Clara and, as luck would have it, Tom was in town. He went to the house for me and brought them over with him.'

'How?'

'Darling, they have a spare key in case the alarm goes off or something and we're away. Anyway, it was really nice of him because he had to leave his conference early and he missed the question-and-answer session at the end, which Clara says is his favourite part. So, you see, he does do *some* good things and try to help.'

'And – and when did he go?'

'I don't know exactly. This afternoon. He didn't say.'

'*When?*'

'Does it matter?' Victoria turned to look at him and decided to think carefully. 'I know! It must have been about a quarter to five. He told me he saw the mobile library parked on the corner when he came out of the house and that's when it comes, every Friday. I take the children. I remember Tom mentioning it because he said that no one in our road needed a library, we were all rich enough to pay for our own books, and it should be sent somewhere that it was really appreciated and not wasted on housewives reading recipe books.' Victoria gabbled on, terrified that David would be furious: 'So you see he's not all bad. It was terribly out of his way and he didn't complain at all. Actually, he told me it had been a pleasure to go to the house.'

David lay back on his pillow. Then he turned to Victoria and, to her amazement, kissed her gently on the forehead. 'I suppose all's well that ends well. But you must try harder to remember everything. Lots of London families have week-end houses in the country and the wives manage perfectly well.'

'I know.'

'Never mind. Get some sleep.'

And as Victoria dozed gratefully beside him, David lay awake staring at the walls and thinking carefully about the events of the day.

Next door Annie was lighting a joint. As she began smoking she started to feel more relaxed. It would help her sleep. Her eye caught her handbag. She had avoided picking it up as if the letter it contained would somehow jump out at her and unfold itself so that she could no longer ignore the information it contained. Now it did not seem so intimidating. She inhaled deeply, the windows open to air the room. David, with his parliamentary ambitions, would go mad if he found out she was smoking dope. She reached over for her bag and sat on the bed. She knew that Belmont & Co had been the de Longden family solicitors for decades. It must be a formality. But her hands were shaking when she opened the letter, and when she read it she was filled with disbelief. She was asked to make an appointment, at her earliest convenience, to discuss the future of Railway Villas. There were no more details. No clues.

She could not possibly go. She would ask Clara to telephone them, try to find out what it was all about and make some excuse on her behalf. Whatever it was, it would have to wait.

When Tom eventually came down to breakfast he found the kitchen filled with the remnants of Alex and Emily's breakfast and David finishing a plate of bacon and eggs. At the sight of him, David put down his knife and fork, 'You'll have to excuse me,' he said. 'Papers to go through.'

'Oh, your fraud case,' said Tom affably. 'It really is taking up all your time, isn't it?'

'Absolutely,' said David. He smiled back. 'Such a pity I've got to work on it all day.' And with that he picked up all the newspapers and strode off to his study, slamming the door behind him.

Victoria was preparing a tray for Annie when Clara wandered in. 'Children not around?'

'No. Alex has gone to a tennis lesson and Emily's watching a video.'

Tom was ploughing through a basket of croissants. Clara absent-mindedly helped herself to cereal and sat down. She was relieved that Tom was there, secretly hoping to avoid any conversation with Victoria about his trip to the house.

'Victoria, you must show Clara the garden after breakfast,' said Tom enthusiastically. 'She's desperate to see it.'

Clara looked at him darkly but he was not to be put off: 'If you like I'll watch Emily. Give you two girls some time on your own.'

Victoria, who was placing a rack of toast on Annie's tray, sounded enthusiastic: 'I'm not going to turn down an offer like that. I'll just take this up to Annie. Then I'll show you the plot where we're hoping to put a tennis court – if we get planning permission.'

'I can't imagine that'll be a problem round here. Aren't tennis courts compulsory for these houses?' muttered Tom, as Victoria went out.

'Shut up,' hissed Clara. 'Will you stop being so obnoxious!'

'I don't think I'm the one being obnoxious in this house – as you need to point out to your cosseted sister,' Tom retaliated, 'when you're alone together.'

Clara sighed, and they spent the rest of breakfast in silence. But when Victoria returned, Tom all but pushed them out of the conservatory doors and into the garden, closing the doors behind them.

Victoria looked bemused. 'Is Tom all right? He seems very odd this weekend, if you don't mind me saying. Strangely . . . cheerful.'

'Oh, I think it's just this conference. It's inspired him.'

'You ought to send him on them more often.'

They walked down to the waterfront and the ducks swam over, hoping for bread which, thanks to the park visitors on the opposite side of the river, they had come to expect in huge quantities.

Victoria was enthusing about their plans for the house: 'The tennis court's going to be round the other side. So you can't see it from the river. We're going to shield it with trees so it all blends in. I'd prefer a swimming pool but David says pools are terribly common . . . The Blessons have a tennis court so it's obviously the smart thing to have.'

'Victoria.' Clara had decided to get this over with. She

felt slightly sick. She was the family intellectual, but Victoria was no fool and she was anticipating some searching questions.

Victoria had adopted a knowing expression. 'Yes, I can guess what you're thinking. The expense. But it's some special new surface so we'll be able to use it all year round and have tennis parties.' She was ambling back up the garden, occasionally bending down to pull out a weed or poke about in search of greenfly.

Clara had little choice but to follow her. 'Victoria, it's not that. I need to talk to you.'

'Is it Tom? Is there a problem?'

'No, it's not Tom. It's . . . David, actually.'

'David?'

Victoria was tugging at a dandelion. Clara spoke slowly, hoping to get her full attention. 'Yes. David. And the house. Selling it.'

'Selling this house?'

'No,' Clara continued, 'not this house. Your Wimbledon house.'

Victoria stood up and brushed traces of soil from her hands. 'Clara, we're not selling it.'

'Well, that's just it. Tom thinks you are.' Clara wished they could just stand still and get this uncomfortable conversation out of the way.

But Victoria had wandered over to examine a border planted with roses. She looked unconcerned but spoke deliberately: 'Go on.'

'Yesterday, when Tom went for the pills he overheard David with some estate agent. David was discussing selling the house.'

'You mean Tom eavesdropped on David talking to an estate agent?'

'Well, yes, but not deliberately. He didn't go to spy on anyone,' insisted Clara.

Victoria was continuing to inspect her roses, and

although Clara could not see her expression, she caught the note of questioning suspicion in Victoria's reply: 'No?'

'No. He just overheard,' repeated Clara.

'I know,' said Victoria.

Clara could not hide her surprise. 'You know?'

'Yes, David told me all about it this morning.'

'Oh.'

Victoria turned to face her. Her expression was defiant and her features set hard. Clara was aware of her sister looking older than her thirty-eight years. 'Yes. And what Detective Tom heard was David getting a valuation of the house. Not to sell but because he wanted to take out extra life insurance to cover the mortgage. So he can look after me and the children if anything happens to him.'

'But he didn't tell you earlier?'

'No, because he didn't want to worry me about the size of the mortgage. He arranged it without me knowing to protect me.'

Victoria's cheeks were flushed and she turned her gaze from Clara to the river, folding her arms as if to protect herself from any more allegations.

Clara thought quickly. 'But he told you this morning. Why now?'

Victoria was losing patience. 'Probably because he worked out that Tom had been to the house and was about to come up with some ridiculous story about him selling it behind my back.' Victoria's voice rose. 'Which, from where I'm standing, looks exactly like what's happening. I'm just surprised that you're going along with it.'

'I'm afraid there's more. There was a girl—'

'From the agency. That's not illegal, you know. Or suspicious.'

'You see, Tom got the distinct impression that David . . . well, David was *with* her.'

'Clara, I'm surprised at you.'

'I'm sorry, but I have to tell you. You – we – need to face the facts.'

Victoria stared at Clara, turning to confront her, '*Face the facts?* Well, let's do that. David is not selling the house. He is not with some girl. He has told me everything.' Her voice was shrill. 'And, no, I'm not a naïve wife. I don't expect perfection after fifteen years. If something goes on at a conference or some trial miles away then I wouldn't be totally surprised. But I've never had any real evidence to think that it does and if – if it does, then it's a one-night stand and that's all. David wouldn't do anything to upset our lives. Mine, the children, his. He's got too much to lose. Money, respectability, a seat in Parliament. He may not be a saint but he's certainly not stupid, and he's the last one to throw it all away for a bit on the side.'

Clara struggled for words. 'But can you be so certain?'

Victoria interrupted her: 'Clara, what is your problem?'

Clara's mouth was dry. 'Look, I'm only trying to warn . . . to let you know.'

'Warn me? So I can do what exactly?'

There was a pause and the reply they both knew so well remained unspoken until Clara adopted her most persuasive tone: 'Look, you've said before that you're not happy. That things between you and David have . . . changed. You don't have to put up with it – we're not living in Victorian times. You can get a divorce and start again.'

Victoria wondered why it was that whenever Clara tried to be supportive she always sounded so patronising. She tried to keep her voice even: 'I know we're not living in Victorian times. Just as I know that I can get a divorce. And has it ever – just once – occurred to you that if it was *all* so very simple then that's exactly what I would do? You know as well as I do that the divorce itself is simple. It's sorting out arrangements for the children and the money that always causes the problems—'

Clara cut in: 'Money? You can't stay because of the money! Victoria, that is just such a – such a – cynical and false and dishonest way to lead your life.'

'Christ, you really think you know it all, don't you?'

Victoria exploded. 'Wise, sensible Clara. Or do I mean prissy and judgemental? Maybe money doesn't matter on Planet Clara, but I have two children and I have to care for them and house them and bring them up. And David, in case you haven't noticed, isn't the sort of man to let me leave with the money. How would I survive?'

Clara, fighting to stay calm, attempted to reason with her: 'You'd get your share of the house. And he'd have to pay maintenance—'

But her argument was cut short by Victoria's dismissive interruption: 'Yes – like all the other fathers being chased by desperate mothers who can't pay the bills. He's a barrister, he's self-employed – with the right accountant he'll get away with the legal minimum. And the children – they love their father, you know, whatever you think of him. How can I uproot them, make them change school, not be there when they come home because I'm out working – always assuming he doesn't sue for custody?'

'That's very unlikely,' insisted Clara.

'Unlikely,' echoed Victoria contemptuously. '*Unlikely*. I have to be certain. I have to balance my life with that of the children – and before you interrupt me and tell me I can't sacrifice my life for them, let me tell you that at the very least I would have to be damned certain that leaving is going to be an improvement.'

Clara was exasperated. 'Then you'll never go. You'll always accept his word that things will get better after the next case or the next promotion or the next bloody social-climbing manoeuvre he's got planned. And the longer you leave it the harder it will be to leave all this behind. You'll end up like – what's that phrase? Yes, a bird in a gilded cage.'

Victoria gave a hollow laugh. 'I think it's time for honesty on both sides here. Yes, I spend David's money. Why shouldn't I? I helped him make it, went without for long enough, and now I'm going to enjoy it. It's not a crime, you know. I get in the car and drive to the hairdresser's – I don't murder anyone when I get there. Just because Tom wants to live in a wigwam in Richmond Park doesn't mean everyone else has to squeeze in with him. I think you should look at yourself before you start criticising everyone else so freely.'

Clara was stunned into silence as Victoria ran on, 'Because I'm not the only one being dishonest around here. Why don't you take a look at your own marriage before you start wading into other people's? David may be a bastard but I'm not the one moaning about how bored I am. Or how I want some excitement in my life. Believe me, I've got more than enough drama to keep me going. And I've got a reason to stay. What's yours?'

'That's nonsense,' snapped Clara, but she was rattled, colour rising to her cheeks.

'Is it? I think you're getting bitter. And envious. I'm sorry, but it's true. You see what I have, all this,' Victoria gestured at the house, 'and you envy it. You said yourself that Tom wouldn't spend any money. Well, David does, on me and the children, and it makes you jealous.'

Clara felt a rush of indignation. 'That is simply not true. I'm just trying to let you know the facts. And the fact is that David only came out with this – this explanation about the house, which is what this conversation is about, let's remember, once he knew you would find out from Tom.'

But Victoria was oblivious to her words. She carried on, the words tumbling out as if she had rehearsed them: 'David was trying to protect me, to provide for me. I can't help it if Tom can't do that for you. Perhaps you should have married someone rather more successful in life.'

Clara paused for a second, then slapped her sister hard across the face. She could not remember ever having felt so incensed. Victoria was reeling across the lawn and Clara was flushed with rage. 'Well, being provided for is something you're really rather good at. So much so that you've turned into a spoilt, selfish cow.' Clara's voice carried across the water causing walkers on the other side of the river-bank to stop to listen. 'I came here to help, but now I'm more than happy to leave you to it. Look at yourself – you can barely be bothered to have Annie here for the week. You think every problem can be solved by throwing money at it. You're prepared to sacrifice Alex's happiness and send him to that awful school just to suit your social-climbing husband.'

At the mention of her son, Victoria flinched. Clara had hit the mark but she did not pause. 'It's true,' Clara continued. 'I don't have a bathroom full of perfume and a wardrobe full of designer clothes, but I do have a life. One that consists of more important things than giving orders to my overworked cleaner. And as for this house, I've had quite enough of it so I will be leaving with Tom. Right now. Annie can stay if she wants, but if she needs some sympathy over the next week she'd be much better off coming with us. I imagine your idea of support is leaving her with a pile of glossy magazines while you go shopping. I'm going to pack.'

'Clara, wait . . .'

Clara turned on her heel and marched up the lawn. She threw open the conservatory doors and strode into the kitchen. Tom was still at the breakfast table. 'Come on! We're leaving,' she said.

'What?'

'Now,' Clara barked. 'As a result of your advice to have a quiet word with my sister.'

Tom rose to his feet wordlessly and followed Clara upstairs. Long years of social work with volatile clients had taught him when it was safer to say nothing. Clara ordered him to explain the situation to Annie while she threw their clean and dirty clothes alike into a suitcase before heaving it downstairs. Tom emerged with Annie and followed in Clara's wake.

'Clara, I'm coming too,' Annie said, sounding unusually resolved, as they walked downstairs.

'Good, you can come home with us.'

'Actually, I'm going back to Railway Villas.'

Before Clara had a chance to respond, the door of David's study opened and he stepped out. 'Leaving already?' he asked pleasantly.

'You're a lying, conniving bastard,' spat Clara.

Tom looked at his wife with astonishment. Clara continued bitterly, 'But, as one lawyer to another, I can't prove it.'

'And as one lawyer to another, and I'm a rather better one than you are, you never will,' said David coolly. 'So why don't you take your little suitcase, get in your little car and go back to your little house?'

'Fuck you,' said Clara, and bundled Annie out of the door and into the car.

'Come back in if your car won't start,' called David after them. 'I have the number of an excellent garage.'

Clara and Tom prayed as they never had before that the Morris Minor would start and mercifully it did.

As they chugged out of the gravel drive and into the distance, Victoria watched them from the side of the garden. She waited until the car was out of sight before turning and walking back to the kitchen where she began silently to prepare for tomorrow's lunch with the Blessons.

CHAPTER 4

The offices of Belmont & Co had occupied a double-fronted Victorian building at the top of Cobham high street for over fifty years. The old-established family firm was a byword for solid respectability and Michael Belmont, who had taken over the firm when his father retired, looked every inch the provincial solicitor in his sober suit, with his receding hair swept back and his belt visibly straining round an expanding waistline. As well as running the firm, he was chairman of the Cobham Rotary Club, honorary president of Cobham Cricket Club and a churchwarden at Cobham parish church. He was also the de Longdens' family solicitor.

As he ushered Clara and Annie into his office, Annie was glad that she had come. Clara had cajoled her into making an appointment, arguing that whatever trivial matter it concerned was best sorted out and quickly forgotten. Michael's office was an oasis of calm, the deep-red carpet showing off the mahogany furniture set against walls displaying his framed certificates and diplomas. He directed them to two velvet-backed upright chairs and settled himself behind his leather-topped desk, empty apart from a sheaf of papers and a photograph of his wife, Beth, pictured smiling alongside their two fresh-faced daughters.

He cleared his throat. 'Annie, I want to say before we begin how terribly sorry I am about all this. Dreadful business. We were both at the funeral.'

'Yes. I wanted to say how beautiful the flowers were. I

know Beth organised it all. I've been meaning to write to her . . .'

Michael waved his hand. 'Think no more about it. All in good time. Now . . .'

There was a knock at the door and Michael's secretary, Marilyn, came in with a pot of coffee and a plate of biscuits. As she poured the coffee into white porcelain cups, Michael offered the plate to them, which they both refused. Realising that neither was in any mood to eat he put the plate by his side and involuntarily picked up a digestive biscuit.

Once Marilyn had left the room, Clara spoke up: 'Is this about Hugo's will?'

Michael sighed. 'Well, yes, in a way, but the situation is slightly more complicated than one might wish.'

'Complicated?' asked Clara, an expression of surprise crossing her face.

'Let me explain. In his will Hugo left everything to Annie. He also left a small bequest to Elizabeth with,' he checked his papers, 'his painting materials and art books.'

Annie looked pleased. It was typical of Hugo to be so thoughtful.

'Unfortunately, however, Hugo's will cannot be seen in isolation from the loan.'

'Loan?' interjected Clara. 'What *loan*?'

Annie stirred. 'I never mentioned it to you. It was just a formality . . .'

'Would that it were,' interjected Michael, his heavy-set face betraying an uncharacteristic flash of anxiety. 'Let me elaborate. Two years ago Hugo took out a loan from Northland Bank. He needed capital to modernise the business, move to bigger premises. He bought a new computer system to keep track of customers' orders and send them mailshots, that type of thing. Frankly, the investment was long overdue. De Longden Conservatories was being run from a card-index filing system and Hugo knew it couldn't go on like that. The bank was happy to lend the money. But, well, Barbara de Longden was firmly opposed to the idea. She felt things should go on as they were. And I imagine that she found the idea of a computer system . . . shall we say unappealing?'

'Because she wouldn't be able to operate it,' cut in Clara.

'I couldn't confirm that,' said Michael tactfully. 'Whatever the reasons, Hugo could not secure his mother's co-operation so he went to the bank independently. Naturally they required security for the loan, and since his mother refused to allow the business to be used as security, he was obliged to offer them Railway Villas instead.'

'Did you know about this?' Clara asked Annie urgently, turning to face her sister.

Annie avoided her eye. 'Yes, I did. We owned the house jointly, so when Hugo took out the loan I had to sign the papers for the bank saying I agreed to the house being used as security. I remember, I had to visit a solicitor in Weybridge who explained it all to me and I signed the papers there.'

Clara's eyes met Michael's. He said resignedly, 'I know. I think you'll find that Annie did give proper consent.'

'But I still don't see the problem,' Annie said. 'The house is only security. As long as the payments are kept up that's all that matters. The house is irrelevant. And there have never been any problems about making the payments. The order book is full. Even without Hugo they can get a manager in and carry on.'

'Yes, they could,' agreed Michael. 'But Barbara de Longden has made it clear to me that that is not her intention.' He paused, looking from Clara and back to Annie. 'I'm very sorry. What I have to tell you is going to come as a shock. You see, Barbara de Longden has agreed to sell the business. She's quite within her rights. It's a private company and, after her husband's death, she alone inherited it. Hugo was technically an employee . . . one might say regrettably in the circumstances.' At that point Michael Belmont broke off, as if to remind himself that he was, after all, Barbara de Longden's solicitor and was not there to represent Annie. He cleared his throat and resumed his steady explanation: 'Mrs de Longden has made it crystal clear to me that she will not meet the payments to the bank. The loan was in Hugo's name *personally*, so she's quite within her rights to ignore it.'

'Surely she has a moral responsibility!' exclaimed Clara. 'All the money has gone into the business – which she's selling. She should give some of the proceeds to Annie to pay off the loan.'

Michael looked uncomfortable. 'Many people would agree with you. But the fact is, moral responsibility or not, she has no legal responsibility for it. The payments are due to the bank from Hugo's estate and if they are not met then the bank is well within its rights to repossess Railway Villas.'

A stunned silence fell over Clara and Annie. Annie tried to take a sip of coffee but her hand was shaking so violently she was obliged to put the cup down. 'Would they do that?' she asked, in a whisper.

Michael paused uneasily. 'Please understand that I'm speaking off the record here. The bank's district manager is vice-chairman of the Rotary here and I took the opportunity last week to have a quiet word with him about it. It seems he has very little discretion – these things are all run from departments in London, these days, I'm afraid – so if the payments aren't made . . .'

'Annie will lose her home,' concluded Clara. 'Can you pay it?' she asked Annie.

Annie gave a hollow laugh. 'Clara! Paying off that loan was taking half the profits of the business. And I've still got the mortgage, school fees and all the bills.'

Clara thought desperately. 'What about life insurance? Did Hugo take out insurance?'

'He tried,' said Annie, 'but he failed the medical.'

'Unfortunately, the loan is a substantial liability,' Michael added. 'In fact, according to my calculations, it represents three-quarters of the value of Railway Villas. By the time the loan and the mortgage are paid off, Annie should just about have enough left for a deposit on a small flat.'

'This is unbelievable!' protested Clara. 'How can Barbara de Longden have arranged all this so quickly? How has she found a buyer?'

'The buyer is Cal Doyle.'

Annie gasped. 'So that's why he came to the funeral. I couldn't work out why he was there. He was always making Hugo offers for the business, but Hugo always refused. He said Cal Doyle was a playboy who just wanted to buy the De Longden name. Then he'd get rid of all the staff and have everything made in plastic in a factory in the Far East.'

Clara's face betrayed her outrage, and colour flooded her cheeks. 'This is obscene! It's not even two months since Hugo died. Barbara's behaving appallingly.'

'Well, I can't comment on that,' murmured Michael. 'However, it seems that, admittedly in some haste, Mrs de Longden has reached an agreement with Doyle. Again, she's within her rights – the business is hers. Ownership would have passed to Hugo on her death. Of course, no one imagined things would turn out as they have . . .'

Annie was determined to be brave. Michael Belmont was trying so hard to be sympathetic but she knew he was the last man in the world to be able to cope with some tearful woman collapsing in front of him. She swallowed hard. 'What do you think I should do?'

Michael leaned forward. 'Annie. Strictly speaking, I cannot advise you because I represent Barbara de Longden and I can see that there is some . . . conflict of interest between you. But let us suppose that you were to ask me my advice informally, as a friend rather than as a solicitor . . .'

'I'm asking you as a friend,' said Annie firmly.

'Sell the house as soon as possible. It's springtime, the

weather's fine and the estate agents are full of people looking for character houses like Railway Villas. The May bank holidays are approaching and plenty of people are viewing. I know it's hard. It's very soon after . . . But if you let the bank repossess it will end in a forced sale by them and you won't get as much money. Plus you'll be landed with their costs and possibly credit blacklisted if it goes to court. This way you get the most money – and I think you'll need every penny. It's the most dignified way.'

'Is there no way out?' asked Clara.

Michael raised both hands from the table. 'I've racked my brains. Truly I have. And, please, go to any other lawyer you like and see what they suggest. But my honest opinion is no. Sometimes in life it's a question of limiting the damage, and I think this is one of those times. And there's one other thing, Annie. If you do decide to sell . . .'

'Yes?'

'Take this piece of friendly advice. Don't mention to anyone that you're a widow. People have a nasty habit of lowering their offer if they think you're alone and vulnerable.'

A widow. The word hit Annie. And, try as she might to retain her composure, she found herself dissolving into hopeless tears in Michael Belmont's office.

Victoria's week was not going as she had planned. Lunch with the Blessons had been a nightmare. William Blesson was a droning bore, his sole topics of conversation were his schooldays at Selchester and his days in the Army. His wife was a crushing snob and their children, twelve-year-old twins, were obnoxious brats who had sneered at the house, priced Alex's toys and ignored Emily. To top it all, after lunch David had disappeared to the end of the garden with William Blesson, and two bottles of their best wine, where he had sat seemingly captivated by a never-ending stream of Army anecdotes.

She was exhausted from all the cooking and now the

children were driving her mad. She had imagined an idyllic two weeks – she had planned a boat trip to Windsor, a picnic by the river-bank and an Easter-egg hunt in the garden. But they'd done all that and there were still two days left of the holidays. So now Alex was following her round the house telling her how bored he was: all his schoolfriends were at home in Wimbledon, there was no one to play with and all the things his father had promised they would do together – swimming, a bike ride and a trip to the cinema – had turned out to be just that. Promises. Victoria had stepped in to take David's place – but it wasn't the same. Emily was happily copying Alex's pester-power tactics and Victoria was reduced to sitting the pair of them in front of videos and stuffing their mouths with leftover Easter eggs.

And she felt depressed. The row with Clara had wounded her more than she cared to admit and she was doubly hurt that Annie had decided to leave too. Then David had disappeared: he had returned to London on Sunday evening to begin his charm offensive on the Wimbledon Village Conservative Association committee before the first selection meeting. Before his departure, he had left her a list: Victoria was to do a draft of his speech, sort out his favourite chalk-stripe suit and choose something suitable to wear for herself. He thought navy blue, not-too-high heels and definitely not trousers. Rumour had it that Charles Lamming had lost a safe Hampshire seat on account of his wife's choice of a chic Armani trouser suit, which the Tory ladies had found too sophisticated for their tastes. Charles Lamming, David had decided, was his main rival and as such he was strongly promoting Janet Williamson to make it to the final two with him. He was confident that in a head-to-head he could leave her standing.

For the fifth time that day Victoria took up pen and paper. She sat at the dining-table in the sun-filled conservatory, praying that the children would allow her an uninterrupted hour. It had all been so much easier when

David was starting out. If his caseload had got too heavy, he had handed over the papers of some of his cases to her. She would read the thick stack of statements and legal argument, summarise them for him, then prepare his opening speech, questions to the witnesses and closing remarks. She had enjoyed it, sitting beside him in bed on a Sunday morning, working on some case of theft, assault or fraud. And she was good at it. Though David never gave her credit, it was Victoria's clever turn of phrase that often stuck in the jury's mind. Or her careful reading that spotted the flaw in the defendant's alibi.

Of course, she was just a legal secretary, and when she had got pregnant with Alex she gave up the part-time law degree that Clara had spent years persuading her to take up. David encouraged her to drop out, telling her that one lawyer in the family was more than enough and that by supporting him she was working as a lawyer in a kind of way. She had supported him in every way. Those had been the years when, burdened by the mortgage on their new Wimbledon house and with all the expenses of a new baby, he had been only too grateful for her salary, which had kept them afloat. Now he had fees rolling in and juniors to do his groundwork for him. Kitty, maybe. She put the thought out of her mind.

But as she opened her writing-pad and picked up her pen, she could not still the disquiet provoked by Clara's words, the uncomfortable feeling engendered by accusations that had held too much truth to be discounted. She sat, quite still, looking out on to the calm river but unconscious of the boats, walkers and children playing on the bank beyond. Was it possible that what she had always viewed as her pragmatic approach to life, her refusal to be drawn into introspection and self-analysis, was actually the shallow response of someone who had neither the inclination nor the honesty to face the truth? Was she, in fact, so blinded by the trappings of middle-class wealth – the private school, the country house, the designer clothes – that she could not see the fault lines that lay, hidden but ever-present, below the comfortable surface? It was a disconcerting thought. But even as she allowed herself to consider it, her thoughts were overtaken by the intrusion of more powerful feelings. Feelings of fear, at the prospect of change, maybe even of being alone, of having failed at a marriage in which she had invested so much. So much time and so much love.

And she did still love David, which was why she could never believe that he was hatching some plan to sell the house. It seemed impossible that, after all this time and all they had been through together, their mutual love could simply cease to exist. However trying his behaviour, she refused to believe it. And because she still loved him, and this was what Clara had forgotten, she could not deny him his dreams. His unquenchable ambition was so much a part of him, it so defined him, that to have refused him his chance of Parliament would have seemed so very cruel. It would have made her the selfish, demanding one, and that was not a role she had ever contemplated – it would have felt far too dangerous, uncertain and fearsome. It was all much easier, and safer, to stay in the background – which was why, whatever Clara's barbed comments, she didn't hold any concerns about becoming an MP's wife.

Victoria pulled herself back to the speech. She was running ahead of herself. She forced herself to concentrate on the task and the blank sheet of paper that lay in front of her, and that, far from being daunting, was actually rather exciting. She felt a rush of creativity at the challenge it presented. The key to this speech, she realised, was to put herself in the shoes of the committee members. She thought for a while. Of course, they weren't really interested in politics – all the candidates said the same things anyway – they were interested in the personalities. She would tell them about David and the family. After a few seconds she began to write: 'I stand before you today with my wife at my side, my family in my heart and my country in my thoughts . . .'

This was going to be easy, after all.

Jan Marsh lit a cigarette, causing Tom to search desperately through his desk drawers for an ashtray. Strictly speaking, he shouldn't have one at all on account of the council's no-smoking policy in all its premises.

'It's brewing up again.' Jan flicked ash expertly into the white plastic cup Tom had rooted out of his bottom drawer. 'It's the summer coming. Always makes the gangs worse.'

Tom could think of nothing to say. His extensive training did not extend to altering the seasons. Instead he asked her what was happening with her plan for a community bank and how she was getting on with Sean's new probation officer. At least Jan tried: still young – only thirty – but not yet totally worn down by her fifteen-year-old son, she was one of the handful of residents who always came to Tom's meetings and even believed that things on the Southhead could change.

Sean and Ali were late, as Tom had known they would be. Neither could risk arriving on time only to sit waiting for the other. As the unofficial leaders of their two groupings, maintaining face was all-important. Tom shied away from calling them gangs, whites on one side and Asians on the other, but no one else on the estate or in the press bothered to pretend they were anything else. Sean and Ali had been born in the same hospital, truanted from the same school, and now caused their mothers to despair of their obsessions with sport, cars and girls. The difference in race provided them with reason enough to hate each other. And each had twenty or so young teenagers behind him to follow his lead.

Tom did his best to look welcoming when the two boys eventually sauntered in, neither acknowledging the other as they sat down on either side of Jan. Sean nodded at his mother. 'All right, Mum? What's this all about, Tom? He been causing trouble again?' He jerked his head in Ali's direction.

Before Tom could reply Ali retaliated, 'It's not us who's been shoplifting in Patel's. Steaming through, nicking everything you can lay your thieving hands on . . .'

And they were off. Accusation and counter-accusation about real and imagined insults and wrongs. After five minutes Tom held up his hands. 'Actually I'm not interested.'

Jan looked up from lighting her third cigarette.

'But that's what you're here for!' protested Sean.

'Not today,' said Tom. 'Today I want to talk to you about a gym for the estate.' And looking at the two boys, he knew that, for the first time ever, he'd got their attention.

Annie had not expected this reaction. She had steeled herself to tell Elizabeth and had expected her to respond with despair or anger. However, Elizabeth was lying on her bed, still in the hated school uniform, considering the situation with a calm maturity beyond her years.

'So, we can't pay the loan unless we sell this house,' Elizabeth repeated, 'but if we do sell the house we can pay off the loan and live somewhere else.'

Annie was caught off guard by her daughter's ability to make it all seem so simple. Elizabeth's composure threw into sharp relief her own confusion and doubt – which found expression in the anxious thoughts that now intruded on her every waking moment.

'Where will we move to?' Elizabeth asked.

'It depends how much we get for the house. We'll probably have to leave this area.' She decided there was no point in hiding the truth: it would emerge soon enough. 'And I'm sorry, it won't be a house, it will have to be a flat.' Annie caught Elizabeth's involuntary glance around her room, which was cluttered with a teenage girl's life – schoolbooks and clothes, posters and make-up. The room was dominated by an old oak chest of drawers, the top littered with magazines, scented candles and cheap jewellery scattered around a lava lamp. Every drawer was open, clothes spilling out on to the room's striped cotton rug. 'But you'll still have your own room,' Annie reassured her, 'and you'll be able to get a bus to see your friends.'

Elizabeth considered this. 'So, when are we going to move? Will it be before the play?' She sounded momentarily alarmed.

'No! Definitely not. Not for a while. We have to sell the house first, and find another place to live.' As she spoke the words, Annie felt her mood falter. She could barely consider the practical implications herself, let alone explain them with a calm reassurance.

Elizabeth frowned. 'But I still don't get this problem with the business. I mean, does it have to be so bad? Can't you talk to Hugo's mum about it? Maybe we could pay it off in small bits. I mean, you could try.'

Annie knew that it was only her daughter's naïveté talking, the response of a fourteen-year-old who still believed that the world was destined to be kind to her, and she made an effort to appear to take the suggestion seriously. 'Well, in a way we have tried. Clara and I both spoke to her solicitor. But no, I don't think there's any alternative.' She did not mention that Barbara had already defaulted on the two loan repayments due since Hugo's death and that only Clara's intervention with the bank – and the covert assistance of Michael Belmont – had bought them time to sell the house.

Elizabeth rolled her eyes. 'Well, I suppose we'll have to tidy up before people come round.'

And Annie knew that she should offer some light-hearted aside that would lift the moment and look to the future, but no words came. Instead, she slumped into her chair, retreating into silence, concentrating all her efforts on stopping her tears.

Elizabeth sat up and leaned forward. 'Mum, it'll be all

right.' Her voice was reassuring and optimistic. 'We'll find somewhere – it could be really nice! You're always saying how much work the garden is here. And we don't need lots of money – we can paint it ourselves. Tom can help, and Clara. And I can get a Saturday job.'

Listening to her daughter, Annie felt a hopeless guilt at her own weakness. Try as she might, she could not pull herself from this interminable despair in which every task – from getting up in the morning to climbing the stairs at night – had become the most enormous effort. Even the contemplation of moving house, no, being *forced* to move house, seemed an impossible burden.

Whereas Elizabeth, although she grieved, by turns tearful and resentful at the loss she had suffered, was still at heart the same person she had been before. Despite all that had happened in the three months since Hugo's death, she was essentially unchanged, still moody and sulky and unpredictable, one moment ranting about the unfairness of some mark she had received at school only, the next minute, to answer the telephone to one of her coterie of friends and stand laughing helplessly, her anger instantly forgotten.

And Annie, in that second, looking at her daughter's face – filled with optimism in the midst of this dreadful news – suddenly understood the difference between them, the reason why Elizabeth could still love life. The difference was that Elizabeth possessed the quality of acceptance. Acceptance that Hugo was dead and that nothing could change that unalterable fact. Elizabeth grieved for the past and not for the future – a future that still enticed her with all its promise of dreams and adventures, of ambitions to be fulfilled and love to be discovered.

Elizabeth, in short, could live without Hugo.

Clara held out for three days before she gave in and looked for Ben Ford. Not that she was actually looking for him: she needed to check some detail or other in the library. At last she was making progress with her research. Her teaching had dwindled to the odd revision lecture and tutorial and in the four weeks since the Easter weekend her diligence had yielded more intriguing discoveries.

The law section of the university's 1960s concrete and glass library was packed with students revising for their summer examinations. Files, books and bags tumbled over the scuffed library desks while the harassed librarian tried to re-shelve the books left scattered around by anxious students. There was a winding queue for the photocopier and Clara felt the familiar irritation that students, these days, seemed far keener on photocopying articles than reading them. She wandered up and down the shelves of law reports, casually looking out for him. But she could see no sign of him. He must be working at home, she thought. An astute move: for most students, working in the library usually meant ten minutes of study before they were lured away by their friends for an hour-long coffee break in the refectory.

She encountered Anthony Chang thumbing through the latest edition of the Weekly Law Reports. He looked harassed but smiled ironically when he saw Clara. 'Research for my latest article,' he explained. 'I'm trying to get it finished before I'm made redundant.'

'It won't come to that,' Clara reassured him. 'Julian does it every year – the "savage cuts are looming" speech. Then he heads off to the Dordogne, works his way through a case of Beaujolais and forgets all about it.'

'I hope you're right,' said Anthony gloomily. 'I'm getting married next year, and if there are redundancies it'll be last in first out. In other words, me.'

Before Clara had a chance to reply he let out a sigh. 'Don't look now but it's that awful student.'

They both tried to seem engrossed in reading but out of the corner of her eye Clara could see Belinda Weaver's barrel-like body bearing down on them. There was no hope of escape. She noticed that Belinda had dyed her hair, presumably with an inexpertly applied home-colouring kit, because her brown bob had taken on a distinctly crimson tinge, which was as unflattering as the flared jeans from which her thick ankles protruded.

Belinda thrust invitations in the shape of a champagne flute into Clara and Anthony's hands and whispered loudly, 'Post-exam party, for students and lecturers. I know it's not until July but I like to get organised. There is a charge, but that includes a glass of sparkling wine.'

Clara smiled weakly. 'Wonderful. I'll definitely be there.'

Anthony stayed silent despite Belinda's enquiring gaze. She continued, unfazed, 'It'll be great. Unfortunately the rest of the committee aren't really pulling their weight but I don't mind doing it all. Anyhow, it's a break from revision. Can you let me have the ticket money by the end of the week? And we're asking the lecturers to bring a plate of food.'

'How hospitable,' said Anthony drily.

'Yes. My idea.'

As a lawyer, Belinda would win her cases by wearing down the opposition, Clara decided. Perhaps she should be advised to go into commercial law. Or probate. Certainly something that involved as little contact as possible with the living.

Belinda turned her attention to Anthony. 'Any last-minute revision tips? What I should revise?'

Anthony appeared to think for a moment. 'Yes.'

Belinda's face lit up in expectation of an unexpected advantage over the other students. 'Revise everything. Absolutely everything. Then revise it again,' and with that he walked off to the newspaper rack, leaving Belinda open-mouthed and staring after him.

Clara decided that she would look conspicuous if she hung around the library any longer. She went back to her office and finished the first draft of the Tellium article. She had made the connection she suspected. The US cases had been the key. But now she paused over the final sentence. Should she say it? Of course, there was no proof. The paper might not even publish it. And it could get her into trouble. There was no point calling Tom. He would publish the wildest accusations on principle with no heed to the consequences. She stared at her closing sentence. Should she write her suspicions or, at least, hint at them? If only Ben were here. Her thoughts were interrupted by the telephone.

'Clara, it's Ben.'

Clara felt a surge of elation. She concentrated on keeping her voice and conversation professional. 'Hello, Ben. How's the revision?'

'Deadly dull. Except for your stuff, of course. How's Tellium? I looked in the paper this Sunday but your article wasn't there.'

'Late, I'm afraid, family commitments, but it's finished now. Well, almost. There's something I can't quite decide. A hunch . . .'

'Sounds intriguing. Can I play Watson to your Holmes?'

Clara laughed. 'I can't take you away from your exams.'

'Yes, you can. Even law students are allowed to eat. Why don't you pop round for a bite of lunch? You can't expect me to work without eating.'

'Well . . .'

'I'm in the cottages backing on to Richmond Park, off the Hill. See you in fifteen minutes.' And with that he put down the phone.

Clara knew exactly where he lived. It was all in his file. The same file that was currently sitting on her desk for no better reason than the enrolment photograph it contained of him, stapled to the inside cover . . .

She went downstairs to the cramped ladies' lavatory and peered at herself appraisingly in the small mirror. She brushed her hair and took off her glasses. She had only a lipstick in her bag, one that when she had tried it at home seemed rather orange in hue, but she had carried on using it anyway, careless of its effect. At least she was wearing a dress, sky-blue linen, and she'd shaved her legs, which mercifully had begun to tan in the May sunshine as she had sat in the back garden ploughing through the Tellium reading.

She turned away, suddenly feeling foolish. Ben was only being friendly. He could have his pick of any of the girls on his course. The first blush of warm weather had seen them appear in her seminars dressed in tight jeans and cropped tops looking even slimmer and younger than usual. She guessed that the other boys would have no chance against Ben. Ben who was charming and worldly-wise and handsome and rich. With his own car and a house. Of course girls yearned for him when the alternative was to be smuggled into a university hall of residence to spend the night on a single bed with an inexperienced eighteen-year-old.

She replaced her lipstick, smoothed her dress and headed for her car. Ben's cottage was one of a late-Edwardian row of six, originally built for the workers of Richmond Park but long since sold off to wealthy young couples yearning for period features. Ben's was number two. She took in the neatly tended front garden, then rapped on the door with the brass knocker. She was hungry but guessed this would be a bread-and-cheese affair. When Ben opened the door she was startled to see him holding a colander of fennel.

'Hi! Come in.'

It had only been a week since she had last seen him – in her office for a medical-law revision tutorial – but each time she encountered him she was struck anew by how extraordinarily attractive he was. She followed him into the hallway and through to the kitchen.

'I'm a bit behind, I'm afraid,' he said apologetically. 'Problems with the pasta.' He gestured to a gleaming machine alongside which stood a bowl of freshly prepared tagliatelle. 'I think I put too much water in the dough and it was threatening to turn into . . . gloop is probably the only word for it. I'll pour you a glass of wine and just finish off.'

'Fine . . .' Clara was lost for words. She gazed round

what had to be a handmade kitchen, which opened into a dining-area for six. The marble-topped table was set for two with bone-handled cutlery, crystal glasses and white napkins.

Ben caught her glance. 'I hope you approve. Most people keep the kitchen small and knock through to make a big living room, but I figured that since I was going to be on my own . . . this way I can cook but not disappear from sight. I've kept the front room separate but it's pretty small.'

'I think it's a perfect idea. Did you think of adding a conservatory?'

'One day. But I like the garden as it is.'

The walled garden was tiny and cobbled. Clara could imagine Ben and his friends sitting outside on warm summer evenings and talking into the early hours. As she had done with her student friends all those years ago . . .

Ben poured her a glass of Sauvignon and began sautéing the fennel, chopping herbs and mixing salads. A small armchair stood in the corner and Clara sank into it, sipping her wine and struggling to relax. She was aware that she had crossed a line in coming. Admittedly it was a modern-day blurred and ill-defined line. In her day she had regarded her lecturers with awe, addressing them respectfully as 'Professor' or 'Doctor'. Nowadays everyone was on first-name terms: students spoke to her with jokey informality, and lecturers often invited the more articulate to drinks or dinner parties. Just as she had with Ben. But now they were alone, in Ben's house, and neither Tom nor anyone else had any idea that she was here. She felt uncharacteristically nervous, almost at a disadvantage, and the absurd idea came to her that at any moment Kate would burst through the door and order that she be arrested by the university authorities for fancying a student in contravention of university regulations.

'Kate hauled us all into a meeting yesterday,' said Ben casually.

Clara jumped, spilling wine over the floor. He gave her a

puzzled glance. 'Jesus, I thought she only had that effect on students.' He reached for a tea towel, came over and began to mop up the wine.

'Oh, no, she terrifies the staff as well.'

'She wanted to tell us about the exam timetable. How we'd be beheaded if we turned up late or didn't write our names in triplicate on every sheet of answers.' He looked up at her from where he was hunched on the floor. 'Are you all right? You seem a bit . . . edgy.'

'Oh, no . . . it's just been a difficult time.'

'Since your sister's husband's funeral? Hugo, wasn't it?'

'Yes. And the Easter vacation was a nightmare – an awful family weekend with my other sister that ended in a row and we left early. I came back to the university to try to get some serious research done.'

'Sounds fascinating. You do have an eventful life.'

'Only when my husband gets involved.'

As soon as she had said it, Clara regretted mentioning Tom. Ben got on well with him, although at times Clara suspected that he hid boredom well. Right at this moment, though, she didn't want to think about Tom. It was as if he inhabited a separate world, and here, with Ben in his house, she had moved into a totally different one.

The pasta was boiling and Ben was bringing salad to the table. 'Please, do sit down.' He pulled out a chair. 'I'll get you some more wine.'

Clara watched him carefully, aware of the movement of his limbs beneath his button-down shirt and canvas jeans before finally giving in and allowing herself to wonder, just for a second, what he would look like undressed.

He sat down next to her at the dining-table. 'That dress is great, it really suits you.'

Could he read her mind? Clara stuttered, 'Oh, gosh, thank you. I'm hopeless with clothes. This was actually my sister's – that's Victoria, the oldest one. She gave it to me when it got too big for her.'

'Then she must be far too thin. The colour's perfect.'

'Usually I just wear black.'

'Yes, I'd noticed. The Lady in Black. That's how I thought of you before I found out who you were.'

'Well, I'm sure that's better than most of the names lecturers get called.'

'Better than Miss Moneypenny?' said Ben, looking her straight in the eye.

Clara blushed furiously. 'I've learned to live with that one.'

Fortunately Ben changed the subject and began asking her about the weekend. They talked about David, politics and houses, Ben adding casual anecdotes about everything from tennis courts to the latest gossip among the students. When they had finished the pasta, he opened a second bottle of wine and brought a *tarte Tatin* to the table.

'Where did you learn to cook like this?' exclaimed Clara.

'I bought it,' he admitted. 'I know my limitations and pastry's one of them. But I did pick up a bit from my mother. She was French. When I finished school I went to France for a year to stay with my grandmother and she took it upon herself to teach me.'

'Grandmotherly cooking?'

'Not really. She was sophisticated, very chic. She ran a beauty salon in Deauville. Off the Place Morny. She used to shop every morning in the market, then go and beautify the local ladies. Lots of them are Parisians – they have holiday houses on the coast there. It's only a couple of hours' drive from Paris.'

'Sounds wonderful.' Clara smiled bravely, conscious of her own heavy auburn hair which, thick and shoulder-length, she had worn in the same style for years.

'Oh, it is,' he assured her. 'The beach is beautiful and all the designers have shops there.' He smiled disarmingly. 'I even got roped in to helping out at the salon, washing hair and clearing up. Listening to conversations about clothes, make-up and massage.'

'Massage?' Clara rubbed her neck involuntarily.

Ben eyed her. 'Too much time bent over your books. Which reminds me, what's the mystery about Tellium?'

'Well, you know the drug was for stopping women going into premature labour? The women who had taken Tellium in pregnancy lost their case because they couldn't prove that Tellium had caused the problems with their babies. As I had begun to suspect, when I went through the papers I found that there is a second drug that's mentioned, Vartren. It's given for high blood pressure. Well, all the women took that as well, but in the early stages of pregnancy, so no one connected the two. I think they might be linked.' She could see that he was interested. It was one of the many things she liked about him, his enthusiasm and the tenacious way he approached the law.

His expression was thoughtful. 'There's an interaction between the drugs?'

'I think there might be. Landward Pharmaceuticals makes both of them. It was the US cases that showed me. All the women in the US took it as well.'

'Why didn't their lawyers pick it up?'

Clara was thrilled that he had asked exactly the right question. Tom would have gone off on some rant about the evils of multinational corporations, but she and Ben thought exactly the same way. She took up the point eagerly. 'Probably because they were only looking at their own client's cases. I guess I'm the first person to read all the case notes and see the pattern.'

'Are you going to print your suspicions?'

She looked troubled. 'Well, I can't prove it. I need a form of words that isn't libellous.'

Ben sat back, thinking. 'Yes, it's difficult.' He poured more wine. They thought for a while.

Then Ben spoke up: 'Would something like this work? "The case has perhaps not ended with this last court hearing. Lawyers for the women are now exploring a possible connection between Tellium and the use of Vartren"?'

'But I don't know if they *are* exploring a link,' protested Clara.

He leaned forward, smiling at her with excitement. 'It doesn't matter! If they are, no one can force the lawyers to admit it. It's privileged confidential information between lawyer and client. And if they're not, your article might persuade them to look at it anyway.'

How could she have missed such a simple tactic? 'Ben, that's brilliant! And the paper won't be at any risk of libel. They're just reporting what the lawyers are doing.'

He gave a self-deprecating shrug. 'Well, I'm just a student. You're the expert. If you think it would work . . .' He raised his glass. 'To you, Clara, and your crusading journalism.'

Clara felt blissfully happy, flattered, exhilarated and relaxed all at the same time. She smiled at Ben and he grinned back. 'I'll make us some coffee. Why don't you go into the sitting room? It's more comfortable there.'

Clara rose to her feet. She felt pleasantly hazy and carefree. Tom and she never had times like this. Even at the weekends Tom was always dashing over to sort out some crisis at the Southhead, preparing interminable memos for his department boss or reading the stacks of magazines and newspapers he had delivered every week. The kitchen was piled high with Sunday newspapers and copies of *Social Work Weekly*, which Tom refused to throw away until he had pored over every page. Perhaps she should get a shed in the garden for them.

Ben's front room was as restful as her own house was chaotic. If it had been designed to evoke Paris in the 1950s it had worked. Two large, framed black-and-white photographs of Paris hung on opposite walls. One showed the Eiffel Tower rising from the morning mist, and in the other children played on a barge as it made its way up the Seine. An old battered two-seater sofa in soft cream leather occupied the window bay. To each side stood a pair of Art-Deco table lamps, their blue-glass stems glinting in the sunlight. Shelves of books lined either side of the small stone fireplace and Clara felt a thrill of pleasure on seeing her own textbook *Medical Ethics for Law Students* among other law books and novels. Ben came in with mugs of coffee and a box of marzipan *calissons* tucked under his arm. She sat down on the sofa and was guiltily pleased when he ignored the matching leather armchair and sat beside her.

'I'm so pleased you came,' he said, then paused. 'To be honest I was afraid you might not. With me being just a student.'

'No! Kate might think like that but I don't. You're not a different species.'

'Oh, I don't know. Belinda might be! But being older than the others can be tricky. The first term was awful. I felt like an OAP, among all those faces straight from school. They knew how to write essays and summarise books, and I'd forgotten everything.'

'But you've caught up. I know you'll do well in the exams.'

'That's not why I wanted you to come. Rather the opposite. I know you'd never show me any favouritism—'

'That's hardly a problem. The papers are anonymous, anyhow.'

'I asked you because . . . well, because I admire you so much. Because you represent what being a lawyer should be about. Not money, glory or fighting the other side for the hell of it. It should be about people, and that's what you've taught us. How the law really affects people's lives. I just wanted to tell you that.'

The longer Ben spilled out his praise for her, the further Clara's spirits sank. Of course he would see her like that – as a professional, an example to him, which was exactly what she was supposed to be. What had she expected? A declaration of love? She had stupidly fantasised about something she knew she could not have. She was his teacher, after all, quite apart from the inconvenient fact that she was married to Tom. But . . . now that it was obvious that this was a forbidden attraction shared by her alone she was engulfed by an awful disappointment.

She must pull herself together. 'Ben, that's very kind of you. We don't often get much praise. Students pass their exams and move on. It's rare to get any feedback, let alone any compliments.'

'So I haven't made a total fool of myself?'

Clara paused. It appeared that she was the only one in danger of doing that. 'No, of course you haven't.'

'Because, if you take away the teacher–student thing what is there between us? A couple of years.'

'Hardly. Actually, I'm thirty-four.'

'Hey, I'm twenty-seven. So it's seven years. My lucky number. How old's Tom, if you don't mind me asking?'

Clara had to think for a moment. 'Forty-one. Seven years older than me. We met at university.'

'Oh,' said Ben smoothly. 'Was he your lecturer?'

Before they knew it they were both laughing and trying not to spill their coffee.

'No, he was not! He was a postgrad at my college. He tried to recruit me for some sit-in he was organising against cuts in housing benefit. Or maybe the housing-benefit demonstration was the year after. Perhaps it was apartheid. Anyway, I told him it was a waste of time and he set out to convert me. I should have been warned . . .'

'But you've been together a long time. Are you going to have children?' He looked aghast. 'God, sorry, forget I ever said that. It's none of my business.'

At that moment Clara felt that she could tell Ben almost anything. She rested her head against the back of the sofa, the warm sun streaming across her face. 'Maybe. It just hasn't happened. I don't think there's a medical problem, it's just that . . .' She decided to change the end of the sentence: 'It's just that my husband and I only make love twice a month' was hardly the sort of declaration she could make to a final-year student. '. . . Life is so busy,' she concluded lamely.

'You should make more time for yourself. Do something to relax. It would help your neck problem.'

'How did you know about that?' said Clara, surprised.

Ben gave her a furtive smile. 'Don't you remember when you were a student? All the times you mimicked your lecturers' voices and mannerisms? Did you think you were immune?'

Clara looked at him spellbound. 'Oh, God, what do I do?'

'Well, I don't think I've ever been to one of your lectures when you haven't been rubbing your neck by the end. Mostly on the left.' Ben showed her. 'Like you're all knotted up.'

Clara was mortified. 'What else do I do? I wasn't even aware I did *that*.'

'I really couldn't tell you. All I'm prepared to say at this point is that your catch-phrase is "Experiment by reading the case, not just photocopying it." I think you've probably said that at every lecture I've ever attended.'

Clara covered her face. 'I don't want to hear any more. It's too embarrassing.'

'OK, OK, I'll stop. But only if you let me have a go at your neck.' Without waiting for a reply he reached over and took the coffee mug out of Clara's hands. 'Sit on the floor,' he said. And she did. Without hesitating or objecting or even speaking. Instead, for the first time in many, many years, she acted out of pure instinct. She sank down into the soft carpet.

And at that moment she knew it was the beginning. The point at which she had crossed from actions that still conceivably had an innocent explanation to others that she could never admit to Tom.

As Ben's hands caressed her neck she knew without the least doubt that she wanted more. As his fingers stroked her shoulders she hoped they would stray still further. She no longer cared about the state of her make-up or her unfashionable underwear or the bodies of the young girls with which Ben might compare hers. So when she felt his lips on her neck she did not resist. She let him kiss her hair and cheeks, and push her down on to the floor where he held her and kissed her mouth. The years of talking between them were over. When Ben stood up, it was in silence that he took her hand and led her upstairs.

Their roles were now reversed. He was the teacher and she the pupil. He slowly undressed her and as her clothing fell to the floor he was enthralled, or kind enough, to make no comment until she lay naked on his bed. 'Clara, you're so beautiful . . .'

She made to protest but Ben placed a finger on her lips. 'Yes, you're beautiful. You just need someone to tell you so. Over and over again until you believe it.'

He drew the curtains, then lit candles, and warmed richly scented oil with which he traced the outline of her breasts and, with tantalising slowness, explored her body. As he kissed her breasts, his fingers stroked the soft inside of her thighs until, when she thought she could bear the anticipation no longer, his touch was no longer gentle as his fingers thrust inside her and she clung to him as the shock of forgotten pleasure overcame her.

And when all the undressing was done and there was no trace of shyness left between them, only then did he make love to her with a passion she had up to that moment believed was for ever to be denied her. Clara lost track of time and then of herself. Everything that had previously defined her now seemed irrelevant in the private world they had created. Nothing could be as important as being here with Ben. So that after they had made love, and he had held her and kissed her, it was she who moved to sit astride him drawing him into her to satisfy her again.

She understood now why people had affairs, why they risked their jobs, marriage and children's happiness. It was a drug, to feel passion after so long without it. She was intoxicated and she knew that she had to return for more, knew that this could never be without risks but prepared to gamble again and again. They lay together through the afternoon and he held her in his arms. When the spell ended, as it had to, it was Ben who broke it. 'Will Tom be worried?'

Clara gave a bitter laugh. 'No. It's . . .' she reached for her watch '. . . six thirty.' She was astounded: the afternoon had passed so quickly. 'He'll be on his way home. He'll assume I'm in the library. I usually am.' She felt a lurch of panic – not about Tom but because Ben had mentioned his name. Was this his way of hinting she should leave? Or that she should not come back at all? Perhaps this was the way things were with young men nowadays. Superficial encounters that only silly, deluded older women invested with great significance.

'Because,' said Ben, frowning, 'if he was to find out it might be more difficult for you to come back.'

Clara felt a surge of relief. 'Tom won't find out. He won't notice a thing.'

Ben smiled at her and stroked her face. 'Tomorrow, then?'

'Yes, tomorow.'

Clara had hoped to get home first and have a shower – if she was cast as an adulteress, she might as well play the role properly – but Tom was already in, hunched over the pine kitchen table scribbling on an A4 lined pad. Clara concentrated on sounding ordinary, neither too attentive nor too preoccupied. She settled on a tone of casual interest. 'What are you doing?'

Tom did not look up. 'Thinking of who I can write to about the gym. Money for it. Local businesses, the usual bigwigs. I don't hold out much hope of the council. We'll need donations, not that the rich and famous will be interested in Southhead – not fashionable enough for them.

It's easy if it's money for premature babies or cuddly animals.'

'But Sean and co. don't come into either category?'

'Nope.'

Clara wandered over to the sink and poured herself a glass of water. She felt hung-over. Her eye caught the chipped tiles around the sink and the fact that the vinyl wallpaper, with a 1970s design of yellow tulips on a brown background, was peeling off the walls. The only new item in the kitchen was her globetrotting mother's latest post-card, from Istanbul, telling her that she had arrived at a *cultural crossroads*. God, even her mother led a more exciting life than she did. She felt like Cinderella after the ball. 'Tom! We're going to have to do something about this kitchen. Look at the floor! These cork tiles, there isn't a single one that isn't cracked to pieces. And the cooker, it's a museum piece. We could have proper fitted units and a dishwasher, with everything built in.' She waved despairingly at their free-standing cooker – the upper grill section was held on in one corner by a piece of green garden wire and half of the oven door handle had long since fallen away.

'It's a perfectly good kitchen,' said Tom absently. 'This table's got years left in it.'

'Tom! We bought it when we got married. Twelve years ago. Cheap pine with two matching benches. People have chairs nowadays.'

'I'm sure it'll come back into fashion. I could sand it down, paint it for you.'

Clara despaired. Only Tom's efforts at DIY could make their battered old table look worse than it already was. 'I'm going to get some quotes,' she declared.

Tom looked up. 'Well, don't be persuaded into ordering anything. We'll have to discuss it. I'll want to be in on it.'

That was precisely what Clara was afraid of. Afraid of Tom's niggling questions and objections. And plain tired of his attitudes. Now, as she looked at him bent over the table,

dressed in some ridiculous jogging suit with the single word
'Streetwise' emblazoned across the front, the sight of him
irritated her. She didn't feel the least bit guilty. She'd left
the place and the man she wanted to be with to come back
to this dump. It *was* a dump. Even the estate agent they had
bought it from last year said it needed 'updating', which
Clara took to mean ripping out the interior and starting
again. She felt sick of the house, but most of all she was sick
of Tom.

'I'm going to have a shower,' she snapped.

'OK.' Tom was still compiling his list. 'You'll need to hit
the mixer tap – it's sticking on the bath setting again. I've
put the mallet up there.'

But Clara had already slammed the door behind her and
was half-way up the stairs.

Lucretia Stanley and Victoria sat in the dining room of
David's London club. In the background old men in
worsted suits shuffled about, and waiters kept an eye on the
few women present to check that they did not encroach
into forbidden rooms. As far as Lucretia could make out
women were banned from nearly all of them, except the
main dining room and the ladies' lavatory, located half a
mile away in the basement. In front of them stood two
glasses of champagne and the day's dinner menu printed on
the club's thick embossed paper.

They were the only women dining alone. The other
tables were filled with solitary old gents or groups of
businessmen cracking jokes and attempting to impress the
boss. Occasionally they threw furtive glances at the two
glamorous women sitting by the window, which in turn
overlooked St James's Park. Most would have judged
Victoria better-looking but Lucretia far sexier, dressed as
she was in a sleek grey cashmere dress that clung to her
body in a most distracting fashion.

Lucretia guessed that Victoria would lunch with her
women friends but seldom go out to dinner with them. She

was hardly a friend in any case. They had spent years bumping into each other at cocktail parties, enjoying companionable if brief conversations, but this was their first meal alone. In short, Lucretia knew that if Victoria had altered her schedule to accommodate Lucretia's daytime business commitments it could only be because she wanted something.

The young waiter came to take their order. Lucretia ordered a salad to begin with and a salad to follow. One of the many responsibilities of running a clothes shop was the necessity to look good in the cashmere clothes she sold. Not just sweaters but dresses and skirts and huge piles of pashminas. The pashmina craze had all but funded her move to a mews house in Wimbledon and she hoped it would continue long enough to pay for her redecorating plans.

'I'll take the asparagus to begin,' said Victoria, 'and then the roast chicken.'

'I suppose running up and down those stairs all day keeps you slim,' remarked Lucretia, as the waiter took their menus.

'Oh, that and the gym. I'm not as good as David. He always goes five times a week, but I try to make it twice. Do you go?'

'Actually, I loathe gyms. I see quite enough bodies every day, handing them clothes in the changing rooms.'

'Then folding them up afterwards.'

'That's the least of my worries. Lipstick's the real problem. Some people just throw things on and ruin them in the process.'

They moved on to talk politely about Lucretia's shop, Victoria's house and the current June heatwave. Lucretia found Victoria dull and would have preferred to be at home, curled up in front of the television with her Siamese cat on her lap. It was not her sort of place, she decided, looking round at the flock of white-coated waiters. She supposed it was David's choice. The chairs were *faux*-Louis XIV, the carpet deep scarlet and the tired red and gold curtains that framed the window in enormous drapes of dusty velvet and brocade completed the *ancien régime* effect. She preferred something more modern, but here it was all fuss and flourish as white-gloved waiters removed silver domes from every dish and flambéed at least half the desserts on the menu. But Victoria had phoned twice, offered her a choice of umpteen dates and it had been difficult to refuse.

Besides, it was now mildly entertaining to see how long it would take Victoria to get on to the subject of the Wimbledon Village Conservative Association of which Lucretia was a committee member. The first selection meeting was only a couple of weeks away. In the event it took until the arrival of their main courses.

'Of course, you'll be at the first selection meeting. There are twelve of you, aren't there?' said Victoria casually.

Really! Victoria knew full well there were twelve. Her husband had been attentively courting all of them for years. The man probably knew their birthdays, blood groups and postcodes by heart. Like the professional woman she was, Lucretia Stanley came straight to the point. 'I think this is what you need to know. Yes, there are twelve committee members, but half of them are deaf or senile and probably both. I flatter myself that I'm in the other half, but at forty-five that may be optimistic.'

Victoria seemed to relax a little, though more because they had got to the point of the evening than her own self-deprecating comments. Actually, Lucretia knew she looked bloody good for forty-five: she was slim, tanned and only her hairdresser would ever know that her blonde hair was dyed from its true mouse-brown. She picked at a piece of cress before continuing – salads here did not appear to have advanced beyond lettuce, cucumber and salad cream.

'As far as the selection of the candidate is concerned, there are three people who really count. The others will follow their lead. Viscount Clement is the most important. He's chairing the meeting. He's old-fashioned but he'll make sure it's a fair contest.' She could not resist adding, 'I'm sure that's what David wants more than anything. Fair play?'

'Oh, yes.' Victoria had adopted an expression of sincerity. 'But don't let me interrupt you.'

In other words Lucretia should keep up the flow of information. Very well. 'Then there's Major Bolton. He's not the old fool he seems. Don't underestimate him. The old ladies on the committee worship him so he's got quite a bit of influence. Finally there's Hilda Rudge. She's dangerous. She doesn't like anyone very much, especially not career women. Oh, it's fine if they're teachers or nurses but she thinks all the other jobs should be left to men. And she's an old battleaxe. Make sure David stays on the right side of her.'

Victoria looked thoughtful. She seemed to be calculating how far she could push her luck. 'Do you have any ideas about the candidates?'

'Not much. Seems to be the usual spread. A local person, that's David. A woman, that's Janet Williamson. A young chap. An old chap who's given heaps of money to the Party. And the ex-MP, Charles Lamming. I don't really know any more than that.'

'No. Please. I don't want to pressurise you . . .' Victoria looked uncomfortable, obviously fearing that she had asked too much.

Lucretia felt suddenly sorry for her. It was evident that this dinner hadn't been her idea. 'It's OK,' she said kindly. 'It must be tough doing all the groundwork. And you're not doing anything wrong. I'm sure all the candidates try to find out about the committee, it's only natural.'

Victoria spoke haltingly: 'I really appreciate you coming tonight. And, actually, it's an unexpected pleasure. I hardly ever go out in the evening.'

'Why on earth not?'

'Homework. Baths. And David always seems to need food or drinks or his clothes putting out.'

'The joys of married life. I can't comment on that. Given that the husband I love isn't married to me.'

At last Victoria laughed. 'That's a neat way of putting it. But it must be hard for you.'

The ice had been broken, and for the next two hours they allowed themselves wine, dessert and chocolates while Lucretia told Victoria about her secret life as the mistress of a prominent City banker. A man who had promised faithfully to leave his wife for the last six years, but somehow a crisis had always intervened to prevent him packing his bags. Lucretia had watched and waited while he dealt with his son's exams, his daughter's wedding and the long drawn-out final illness and ultimate death of Freddo, his wife's pet Labrador. And if she had long ago realised that he would probably never leave, she had settled for what snatched time she could have as an alternative to none at all.

When they left the restaurant at eleven, Victoria had resolved to see Lucretia again. She was funny, interesting and wise. Her life seemed exciting and lonely in equal measure. She was different from all the other women with whom Victoria mixed, most of whom talked exclusively about their hugely talented children and their dull, neglectful husbands. She was vivacious, inspiring and *brave*. Victoria had been delighted when Lucretia had promised to book a table at Bluebird in the King's Road, for an indulgent evening out. Most of all it had been fun – and that was a commodity in pretty short supply.

CHAPTER 5

Annie was in Cobham Care, the town's only charity shop, leaving piles of clothing and books, and arranging for items of furniture to be collected. She didn't want to get rid of any of it but wherever she ended up moving to would be small and she couldn't afford to keep it in store. And she might as well use the Volvo while she still had it. It was a company car – which accounted for why it was going back next week: De Longden's no longer made the payments to the car finance company. Beth Belmont looked on sympathetically, tactfully storing away the bags of Hugo's clothes to be sorted later and most definitely not to be displayed in the window.

'I've kept a few bits,' said Annie, 'the suit he wore on our wedding day and his old rugby jersey but . . . there just isn't any room.'

'You mustn't worry about it,' said Beth. 'Hugo wouldn't want you making yourself miserable about anything. He wanted you to be happy. It was obvious.'

Before Annie could reply she heard a commotion in the street outside, shouting and swearing. At the back of the shop she turned to look out of the window where she could just see two men apparently engaged in a heated argument on the pavement. She had no desire to investigate: there was enough trauma in her own life without other people's problems.

By the time she left the shop the argument was still in full swing. With horror she recognised Cal Doyle and Angus Campbell, Hugo's old foreman. Angus saw her, but Cal

Doyle was oblivious to her presence. She heard his voice, with its Irish accent, ring out: 'Just get one thing straight. I've bought a business, not a museum. Yes, there are going to be changes—'

'Shall we discuss this later? In private?' muttered Angus, looking uncomfortably at Annie.

But Cal Doyle had still not seen her. He continued, in full voice, 'And anyone who doesn't like it can have their P45 ready this afternoon. If you've got a problem with the business being sold, take it up with Barbara de Longden. She's the one who sold you out, not me.'

Angus did not reply. Instead he looked at Cal Doyle and gestured in Annie's direction. 'Mr Doyle, this is Annie de Longden, Mr de Longden's widow.'

She had never come face to face with Cal Doyle before. He towered over her, six foot two at least, with the reddish, tanned complexion of a man who had once been an outdoor labourer and who still had a builder's muscular physique.

Doyle was suddenly silent. He moved over to Annie. 'I'm sorry. I didn't see you. I meant no disrespect.'

Annie could think of nothing to say. She ought to berate him, scream at him for robbing her of her home, but no words came. She knew that later she would be furious with herself for not speaking up in the calm, assured way that Clara would have done.

Cal Doyle seemed to want to break the silence. 'I see you've got a for-sale board on your house. Are you moving away?'

She could not meet his gaze. 'Yes. Somewhere . . . different.'

There was an awkward pause. He shifted slightly. 'Ah, well. Probably for the best. Make a new start and all that. You're still a young woman. Move on.'

Annie could take no more of his platitudes. She felt the world spin around her. Barbara de Longden had set out to ruin her and Cal Doyle was her accomplice. True, it was business to him – and she couldn't imagine that he would have any interest in their family feuding, even if he knew about it. But if he was not the author of her misfortune, he was certainly its main beneficiary. And if what she had heard about him was true, he would ruin the business, destroy everything that Hugo and his father had created. Now he was pretending to sympathise with her situation. She felt as if her life was being erased before her eyes in the space of barely three months.

She had put the house on the market after the meeting with Michael Belmont through a new firm of estate agents with a reputation for being enthusiastic and hungry for sales. In the first weekend there had been eight viewings. The agents were supposed to conduct these but three of their staff had gone down with food poisoning and Annie had been obliged to do the viewings herself. She had trailed round with a succession of well-heeled young couples, some pulling grizzling children behind them, enduring their scarcely concealed appraisal of her and the house. Talking about the work that she and Hugo had done had been unbearable and by the time the final couple had arrived on Sunday evening she was half-cut on vodka and tonic.

Two offers had come in on Monday, both well below the asking price. Tom and Clara had smelt a rat and the following evening came round, accompanied by the rather queasy-looking young estate agent, posing as purchasers. Then, on their drive back to his office, the agent had suggested that the house could be picked up for a bargain price in return for a quick sale. Clara had torn a strip off him, threatening to sue him within an inch of his professional life if he did not fulfil his legal responsibilities to get the best price. So the Stimpsons had upped their offer – on condition that Annie agreed to a quick sale – and contracts were due to be exchanged any day. Annie had not even begun looking for herself.

As she stumbled towards her car, Angus Campbell stepped forward and took her arm, holding her as she fumbled for her keys. She heaved herself in and Angus closed the door. As the engine started and she moved off, she could just hear his voice through the open window: 'I think you're the one who made a pretty good job of moving her on, Mr Doyle.'

'How could you? How *could* you?' shouted David. 'It's my favourite tie. I always always wear it with this suit.' He stormed round the bedroom followed by Victoria, who was in turn pursued by Jean-Pierre, her hairdresser, Simon, his friend, and Emily. It was nine o'clock with an hour to go before they were due at the Wimbledon Village Conservative Association offices.

'Calm down. It's at the cleaner's. Consuela can go and get it.'

David held his head in his hands. 'But it should be here! Two hours to go to the most important meeting in my life, my entire life up to now, and I have no tie!'

'There are lots in here,' suggested Simon, happily fingering the dozens of silk ties in David's wardrobe.

'Leave them alone,' bellowed David. 'In fact, get out, all of you!'

Victoria, Jean-Pierre and Simon formed a procession out of the bedroom and took refuge in the guest bedroom, tailed by Emily.

'I don't know how I'm supposed to work in conditions like this,' exclaimed Jean-Pierre, in his thick French accent. 'It's hardly a Mayfair salon.'

'I'm sorry. He's tense.'

'We can see that, sweetie,' sighed Simon. 'Highly strung, is he?'

'You could say that,' muttered Victoria, hearing David bark orders at Consuela, who had been cajoled into coming in on a Saturday morning with the promise of double pay. David's voice rose from the depths of the house, followed by the sound of the front door slamming and Consuela's footsteps scurrying in the direction of the cleaner's.

'Well, if he's like this over his tie, I hope he doesn't end up with his pinkie on the nuclear button,' mused Simon, scouring a tray of nail varnish for a colour that Jean-Pierre had decreed must be pink but not too pink, with the merest hint of red.

Emily, bewitched by the sight of so many brightly coloured small glass bottles, began to finger them inquisitively.

'Purple!' she exclaimed.

'Emily,' said Jean-Pierre, 'you sit quietly like a fairy on a mushroom and if you are good Simon will paint your nails.'

Emily sank, mute, to the floor. Alex was nowhere to be seen and Victoria presumed optimistically that he was working on his current school project, 'The Rainforest'.

Jean-Pierre started to blow-dry her hair. He had come as a special favour to her: he was not supposed to come at all. The chic Wimbledon salon where he was senior stylist absolutely forbade staff to see clients on the side but, like all their other rules, Jean-Pierre ignored it. He could not support his lifestyle on his salary, so the bundles of cash he made from new mothers with crying babies, desperate mothers with wandering toddlers, doddery old ladies and anyone else who couldn't make it to the salon came in very useful. And Victoria, with David under her feet, had sounded desperate on the telephone. It was such an important meeting, her husband wanted her to look just right and Jean-Pierre was the only person who could get some body into her hair. And he had felt sorry for her: she was one of his favourite clients, always on time, easy to talk to and a good tipper.

Jean-Pierre had arrived with Simon, his current friend, a landscape gardener with ambitions to become an actor who had trained as a make-up artist in one of many previous lives. On her last visit to Longchamp Hair and Beauty Jean-Pierre had looked appraisingly at Victoria's reflection in the mirror and declared her tired. She must have make-up that lifted and brightened her but not so much that she ended up looking like a 14th *arrondissement* lady of the night. He had gone on to countermand David's instruction that she should wear navy blue: with her blonde colouring she would look washed-out. Taupe was perfect, and they had spent a happy lunch-hour in Swatches – Wimbledon's *in* boutique of the moment – arguing over hemlines and cleavage before settling on a mid-knee suit with gilt buttons. 'Other-wise you will look like a tax inspector.' Jean-Pierre had grimaced. 'The gilt is for a little glamour.' Now he began to lift and dry her hair.

'Today, we will do a chignon. This, I think, is right . . .'

'But—' began Victoria, thinking it rather over the top.

'Yes. I am right. Do not argue with Jean-Pierre. I am the best in Wimbledon, if not London, not that that is saying much. Like being a chef here. There is little competition. This will be perfect.'

Victoria was too exhausted to argue. David had come in at ten o'clock last night and taken yet another look at his speech. Fortunately he liked the final version, but he had then spent four hours practising it, as he had been doing for weeks, in front of the drawing-room mirror, insisting that she stay up to watch him, then ask him interview questions until three in the morning. She could not help but be impressed by his perfectionism – but if she never heard a word of that speech again it would be too soon.

Simon was painting her nails. She supposed that he was the junior partner in the relationship. Jean-Pierre, in black leather trousers and an immaculate white T shirt, kept up a steady stream of comment and criticism, but Simon seemed happy enough. Jean-Pierre had firm opinions on hair, make-up, clothes, gardens and interior designs. Other subjects held no interest for him. Doubtless he had chosen Simon's designer jeans and found just the right blue shirt to go with them.

Jean-Pierre looked around the guest bedroom. 'This room you have not done bad. But you must change these curtains. Flowers is not right here. I think stripes.'

Victoria looked at him with irritation, but she knew why the Wimbledon ladies put up with his tactless comments about them and their houses. He was always, infuriatingly, right. He had perfect style, with a sense of perspective and fit that enabled him to analyse a person or a room and see how best to display beauties and hide faults. And he meant well.

'Now you do the top coat,' he barked at Simon.

'Oh, he's a one, isn't he?' exclaimed Simon, but he reached for the bottle of clear varnish.

Victoria wished she could stay in the bedroom all day, listening to their banter and gossip. Next they were off to lunch, then dinner and afterwards a club or two. And tomorrow a day trip to Paris. How wonderful to be free of children, husband and responsibility. Travel was not an ingredient that David thought necessary in their lives, refusing to undertake any prolonged car journey, flight or ferry crossing with the children. Marlow was far more practical. But, then, maybe she had become unadventurous, too.

Jean-Pierre declared himself finished and sprayed her hair and vast swathes of the surrounding air with lacquer. Simon hovered in the background.

'The Master has finished,' declared Jean-Pierre. 'Now the disciple may begin.'

'Begin what?' exclaimed Victoria.

Jean-Pierre gave her an exasperated stare and spoke as if to an idiot: 'Your make-up. You do not think you are able to do it?'

Victoria knew when she was defeated and said nothing as Jean-Pierre settled himself down on a chaise longue and got ready to complain at Simon. 'Do not touch her hair with foundation!' he ordered, as Simon unpacked make-up and brushes.

He put down a bottle of moisturiser. 'If you don't shut up I'm leaving.'

Jean-Pierre sat back sulkily. 'Very well. If you cannot accept advice from the best . . .'

Simon ignored him and set to work. As Victoria closed her eyes he began to apply moisturiser and then foundation. He chose creams and browns for her eyes and began softly stroking on mascara. 'Hold very still,' he whispered, as he applied eyeliner before touching and retouching his handiwork. It seemed to take an age – she would have done it in five minutes between interruptions from the children. But Simon was not to be rushed.

Finally, he declared himself finished. Victoria did not dare look in the mirror. Jean-Pierre's opinion counted for more than her own. She turned to him.

Jean-Pierre paused. 'Yes. This is not bad. Actually, it is quite good.'

Simon let out a sigh of relief. 'Praise be! The thumbs up. The Emperor has spared me to live another day.'

Victoria turned to look at her reflection. It was her face, but a remembered face from five, ten years ago. She looked younger and brighter. Her eyes were somehow bigger and her mouth fuller. She smiled at Simon. 'You're a genius. Thank you.'

Jean-Pierre harrumphed. 'Well, the *genius* and I must go. You must get dressed. I have left you the right tights. Do not even think about choosing a different pair.'

David's voice rang out, calling for socks. Simon fussed around painting Emily's nails and packing his bag and Alex came in wanting to watch television. Once she had paid Jean-Pierre, settled a happy Emily with Consuela and negotiated with Alex a maximum time-limit for computer games, she and David hurried out of the house with ten minutes to spare.

The Association occupied surprisingly shabby offices on the ground floor of a Wimbletown town house a few minutes from their own. David walked silently beside her fingering his tie, which Consuela had successfully retrieved. She guessed he was more nervous than he cared to admit.

This was the last but one hurdle to his life's ambition. To be a Member of Parliament, and thereafter who knew? She felt a sudden stab of sympathy for him. She could support him in the background but he had to go out into the limelight and withstand the pressure of delivering the perfect speech and answering all manner of questions. As they reached the front door of the Association's offices he slowed down and turned to her, his brow creased in concentration. 'OK. There's just one thing I want to say.'

'I'm listening,' she said keenly.

'Just don't fuck this up.'

And ignoring the pang of hurt which crossed Victoria's face, David indicated, without another word, that she should take his arm, and they advanced into the Tory meeting room.

Victoria, still stunned by David's blunt rudeness and attempting to attribute his last remark to his nerves, masked her feelings with rigid self-composure. She saw at once that the other candidates and their wives were already there, sipping the usual ghastly coffee and making nervous conversation with the twelve committee members. David swung into action, greeting each of the committee in the manner of one who has rediscovered a long-lost lover. As a tactic for disarming the other candidates it was highly successful. Albert Weekes, the West Country businessman and one of the Party's most generous donors, found his conversation about milk quotas with Major Bolton interrupted by David enquiring as to the progress of Mrs Bolton's recovery from a recent hernia operation. Charles Lamming's exchange with Lucretia Stanley was similarly sabotaged by David's interest in her battle with the council to have the business rates on her shop reduced.

Victoria noticed Janet Williamson standing alone. And the young man talking to the Association chairman, Viscount Clement, must be Adam Burdett, a former speech-writer to the Prime Minister. David was worried about him, but surely he was too young at twenty-six to be a serious contender?

After ten minutes Viscount Clement called the meeting to order. Victoria had been surprised to learn from Lucretia that he was only in his late forties, but the humiliation of his wife running off with his racehorse trainer – not to mention mounting half his jockeys beforehand – had left him dependent on his housekeeper, who put out ageing tweed suits for all formal occasions, regardless of the weather. Today he was in some green outfit and was efficiently lecturing the candidates, who must wait in the back office to be called in one by one. Spouses could attend the meeting, but only the committee could ask questions after the candidate had delivered a ten-minute speech.

The committee took their places, clearly relishing the rare opportunity to exercise some real political power. For the rest of the time they delivered leaflets, filled in canvass returns and held endless fund-raising raffles. Today, in their dusty committee room with its peeling campaign posters, they had the chance to select the candidate for the country's safest seat and, more interesting still, to grill those who wanted to represent it. An air of anticipation filled the airless room. Lots had been drawn as to who went first and, as luck would have it, it was Janet Williamson. To Victoria, it seemed portentous. Together with all her other disadvantages, Janet Williamson had the thankless task of warming up the room.

She stepped up confidently and took her place behind the small desk that doubled as the tombola stand at the Association's summer fête. Her dark grey suit was well cut to hide her bulky figure, and although she had clearly made an effort with her make-up it seemed to consist mainly of thick swathes of bright blue eye-shadow. But she had done her homework. She spoke with ease about the issues within the constituency and she tried to address what were her obvious shortcomings: 'I know how important it is for residents to see more policemen on the beat. Where I come from, in Newcastle, we know a bit about crime, though I guess fewer residents here are actively engaged in it . . .'

They liked that. It made them feel superior. There were a lot more politically incorrect jokes, some stories from her years spent campaigning for the Conservative Party and finally a line about her spinster state: 'I know that many of you might prefer a male MP. Well, I'm prepared to do many things for this party but a sex-change operation seems a bit drastic. But if it's traditional male qualities you are looking for, like a determination to fight for my constituency to the bitter end, then I can offer you that as a woman. And I don't suppose any of us would tell Margaret Thatcher that she lacked balls.'

It was a risky line but she carried it off. Victoria found herself clapping loudly, before she remembered that Janet Williamson was the competition and stopped her palms meeting. But it was hard not to like her and a damned pity that this committee would never be adventurous enough to select her.

There followed some difficult questions though. Hilda Rudge, the retired headmistress of an obscure girls' boarding school in Northumberland, asked Miss Williamsom why she worked as the director of the Council for Divorced Mothers in a tone that suggested women should be either mothers or divorced but not both. Victoria had the distinct impression that most of the committee were scarcely bothering to listen to Janet's answer, which was peppered with statistics about poverty among single-parent families.

Then Viscount Clement asked if she had plans to start a family as a single parent herself, given that she was so supportive of them. And as if that was not enough, Major Bolton bowled her an utterly incomprehensible question about which Army assault rifle she favoured for issue to British soldiers. Janet Williamson looked relieved to sit down.

Who would be next? Young Adam Burdett. The political speech-writer. Cool, confident and utterly shallow. His speech was filled with well-honed soundbites. Building for the future. Inspiration in education. Encouragement for enterprise. But little sound or practical advice about how all these laudable goals were to be achieved. Hilda Rudge went for the kill: 'Do you think you should come back in twenty years' time when you've learned a little more about life?'

He never recovered. Albert Weekes fared scarcely any better. A prosperous businessman, who had donated a fortune to the Party, he clearly laboured under the misapprehension that the committee would be impressed by money. As he reeled off details of his business deals and successes, half the committee glazed over with boredom while the other half regarded him with unconcealed distaste. Rich was acceptable, their faces said, but never *nouveau riche*.

David was next. Victoria felt her stomach turn over. So many years of waiting, planning and preparing but all of it might come to nothing in the next twenty minutes. David's face, however, betrayed no sign of nerves. If anything, he appeared to be among friends. He went over to the desk but chose to stand in front of it. He was close to the committee and he spoke to the twelve members in the friendly but authoritative tone he had used over the years to hundreds of Crown Court juries. He was not there to lecture them, his voice seemed to be saying, but to mirror their own thoughts and views – and if occasionally they were uncertain as to what those views were exactly, then he was happy to give them some gentle guidance: 'I stand before you today with my wife by my side, my family in my heart and my country in my thoughts . . .'

At this point he paused and appeared to look for Victoria in the audience. When he found her, he greeted her with a smile of quiet love and tenderest devotion. This had been practised with increasing irritation for half an hour the night before. The committee loved it. It was political drama crossed with soap opera. There were to be no dull statistics, no tedious explanations of policy. David spoke of his hopes and dreams for his family: 'I believe that parents, not governments, know what's best for children. Doubtless there are some social workers who would like to close down every boarding school in the country and set up hippie communes in their places. Fortunately, as Conservatives, we believe in decency, which is why Victoria and I have chosen Selchester for our son Alex.'

A loud 'Hear hear' was heard from Hilda Rudge. David said nothing about Emily's education but Victoria had judged, when writing his speech, that half of the committee probably didn't believe in educating girls. David sailed on. A brief reference to strong defence, a passionate plea for capital punishment and, most of all, endless references to the importance of family life. Victoria thought it was all very simplistic, and she had written it, but she knew how to please an audience. And they were pleased. No one could be bothered to ask a tricky question. Indeed, they hardly seemed concerned to ask him anything at all. David navigated the inevitable enquiry on Europe, then sailed through a point on discipline in schools – much more needed – before rounding off with his response to asylum seekers: far fewer wanted. He came and sat next to Victoria, took her hand and kissed her cheek, whispering into her ear and smiling endearingly, as if to greet her with yet another protestation of love. 'That should keep the old buggers happy. The only danger now is Charles Lamming.'

David was right. Charles Lamming was neither a young upstart, a buffoon, nor a woman. His wife sat demurely in the corner, dressed for the occasion in a navy blue suit cut on the knee. She gazed at her husband with the Tory wife's required expression of rapt attention. As Charles Lamming began his speech, Victoria could feel David tense beside her. This was his nightmare scenario: the selection of Charles Lamming with Janet Williamson chosen to go through to the final two as a token woman.

He spoke casually of his time in the cabinet. He played

on his time in the Army and as defence minister: 'The Secretary of State for Defence is always at an advantage when he's been a serving soldier. Active service is a privilege and not, as some young people seem to believe, the name of a pop group . . .'

He followed this up with a couple of inside anecdotes about the Queen. Viscount Clement looked impressed and Lucretia Stanley appeared to fancy him. He was tall, distinguished and rich. In other words, the perfect candidate. Victoria felt as though she was watching a disaster unfold before her but was powerless to prevent it. With a feeling of sick dread she wondered how she would cope with David if he were not selected. She began thinking of what she could say, other constituencies that David could try for, but all the while she knew that inevitably she would take the blame. David would be unable to accept any explanation for his failure other than her own devastating incompetence.

The applause when Charles Lamming finished speaking seemed agonisingly prolonged. Then the questions began. He appeared to have woken up the entire committee. Maybe the mention of the Queen had jolted them into life. An elderly dowager asked him if he felt the Queen should abdicate. No, he personally knew that she was doing a wonderful job. Another old lady asked him what he thought of bringing back hanging. Yes, he was an unequivocal supporter of capital punishment. The applause got louder as the questions got easier. Victoria could see that David's expression of polite interest was growing increasingly fixed.

After what seemed an age Viscount Clement asked if there were any more questions. There were none and Charles Lamming made to sit down. 'Just one moment,' said Viscount Clement, 'I have a question. Something that has come to my attention this week.'

If there was a note of warning in his voice it went

unnoticed by Charles Lamming. He looked utterly unconcerned and went so far as to give Viscount Clement his
most debonair smile. Viscount Clement responded with a
grim expression. He was consulting papers in front of him.
'Am I correct in saying that you were an officer in the
Hobshire Regiment from 1977 to 1982?'

'Quite so.' Charles Lamming's voice was urbane. 'I
served in Northern Ireland and all over the world. I joined
at twenty-one, trained at Sandhurst and held a commission
for five years—'

Viscount Clement cut him off: 'Indeed. Though it is not
the start of your career that is at issue.' Something in the
tone of his voice caused those present to still themselves. He
continued to speak very deliberately: 'It is not your time in
Northern Ireland, or anywhere else overseas for that
matter, which concerns us today. But rather one particular
day. The eighteenth of February 1982. At your regiment's
headquarters. There was a lunch in the officers' mess. A
lunch at which you were present.'

The faintest signs of anxiety betrayed themselves in
Charles Lamming's expression. 'I don't recall . . .'

Viscount Clement's face hardened. 'Then let me refresh
your memory. One of your brother officers was celebrating
his engagement to be married. A good deal of alcohol was
consumed, as may be expected at an event of that sort, wine
and then spirits. The lunch continued for some two or three
hours. The officer concerned was one William Blesson.'

Victoria stole a glance at David, but his expression was
one of benign interest: he was regarding Charles Lamming
and Viscount Clement as one would lambs frolicking in a
meadow.

'After this lunch you left to attend to your duties. That
afternoon there was rifle practice on the firing range for
young recruits. The practice was organised by your NCO,
Roy Lane, a sergeant of many years' service and several
commendations for bravery. But you, as his senior officer,
were in charge.'

If Charles Lamming could at least attempt to hide his feelings, his wife could not: Victoria saw that she wore an expression of stricken dismay.

'When you arrived at the range, the practice was under way. Sergeant Lane was adjusting the targets. You said in your statement to the subsequent court martial that you had not been aware of his presence, that you believed dummy ammunition was in use. Unfortunately Sergeant Lane *was* present and the ammunition that day was *live*. The demonstration shot you took at the target missed and hit him in the head. He died in hospital six days later after a decision was taken to turn off his life-support machine.'

Charles Lamming interjected – Victoria had to admire his cool: 'I welcome the opportunity to set the record straight on this. Those events were tragic, serious, and thoroughly investigated. There was indeed a court martial – at which I was cleared of any wrongdoing.' He looked at Major Bolton. 'I am sure that those who have served in the Army would agree that accidents can happen in the most well-ordered circumstances.'

A murmur of sympathy went round the room.

Charles Lamming continued, 'Moreover, I am sure that you will appreciate that my career, indeed every aspect of my life, was thoroughly investigated by the security services before I was given clearance to serve as Secretary of State for Defence.'

It was a good point and Victoria expected it to end there, but Viscount Clement continued. 'I fear, however, that these events and your interpretation of them may yet come to be re-examined. And we cannot risk that re-examination causing harm to the Party. I have received papers from lawyers acting for Sergeant Lane's family, or rather his son. Mrs Lane accepted compensation at the time of her husband's death and agreed not to take any further legal action. Her son, Brent, is not bound by that undertaking. He is now nineteen, having been just a baby at the time of his father's death. Four months old, to be precise.'

A faint gasp of sympathy for the young Brent Lane echoed round the room.

'Brent Lane will be bringing civil proceedings for the wrongful killing of his father. He is seeking damages for the loss of his father and wants a criminal case to be opened to see if there is a case for a murder charge to be brought.'

At the mention of *murder* shocked gasps rang out and everyone began chattering to their neighbours. Charles Lamming attempted to speak above the mêlée: 'This is unfounded nonsense! I was cleared, and I am shocked that this tittle-tattle should be aired here to discredit me.'

'Quiet!' commanded Viscount Clement. The room fell into silence and Charles Lamming stood before him, a schoolboy before his headmaster. Viscount Clement sounded seriously riled: 'I assure you that after twenty years of public service I do not deal in *tittle-tattle*. The full outline of Lane's case has been supplied to me by his lawyer, a Miss . . .' Viscount Clement peered at the papers in front of him '. . . a Miss Kitty Standing. She believes this is in the public interest, and I for one agree with her. The case alleges a cover-up by the officers at the lunch that day to protect their brother officer. They are all to be interviewed under oath.'

He looked up at Charles Lamming. 'This appears to me to be a matter of the utmost seriousness, and potentially highly damaging to both you and the party you seek to represent. Is that not the case?'

Charles Lamming appeared to be struggling for words. Beads of sweat had broken out on his forehead and he was regarding the room with an expression of despair. The committee, in turn, were looking at him with expressions ranging from shock to outright distrust. Viscount Clement, whom he had succeeded in mortally offending, was staring at him with distaste. Seeing that Charles Lamming was at a loss for words he spoke up: 'It seems to me that you have two choices. To explain this entire sorry story to us now, or quietly, and with dignity, to withdraw your candidature.'

His tone left Charles Lamming and the entire room in no doubt as to which course of action he preferred. And Victoria could guess that the committee would unanimously share his opinion. They would tolerate an extramarital affair, just about put up with financial irregularity, but the shooting by his own officer of a sergeant decorated for bravery was beyond the pale.

Viscount Clement continued, 'I suggest that we take a short break for you to consider your position, Mr Lamming. Then the committee will make its decision.'

'How did you do it? And how are you going to get away with it?'

Victoria and David were settled on a sofa in the bar of the Cannizaro Hotel sipping champagne and celebrating David's selection – with Janet Williamson – as one of the two candidates to go forward to a meeting of all the members of the Wimbledon Village Conservative Association in September. The committee had retired and emerged in less than half an hour with their decision.

'Darling, there's nothing to get away with. I'm not involved.'

Victoria looked at him with disbelief and admiration in equal measure. In the glory of success he had suggested drinks and lunch at the nearest hotel. It was like old times. He had even thanked her for the speech.

He grinned at her. 'It's quite simple. Let us suppose that a young, idealistic lawyer, someone like Kitty Standing, goes to a party.'

'Idealistic? Kitty?'

'Well, she is for the purposes of this story. She goes to a drinks party or a dinner party. Anywhere, in fact. The drinks flow and one of the officers who was present at that fateful lunch starts talking about how there was a cover-up. That much, by the way, was true. Charles Lamming was blind drunk but they all swore he was stone-cold sober. Kitty hears the story. Her heart is filled with indignation. A terrible injustice has been perpetrated. She cannot sleep for thinking about it . . .'

Victoria gave a cynical laugh and started picking at the bowls of nuts in front of them.

'In fact,' continued David, getting into his stride, 'she is tormented. She resolves to track down Roy Lane's family. When she arrives, only Brent is at home. Nineteen years old, unemployed with no qualifications, he's watching daytime TV. He's happy to have company and she tells him the whole story – how his family has been the victim of a terrible injustice. He believes her. He believes her when she tells him that all the failures and problems in his life result from the loss of his father. And he especially believes that he is entitled to compensation. So he agrees to start a case. Kitty will organise legal aid for him. He can sit back, do nothing, and wait for his cheque.'

Victoria interrupted, 'But what about the officers?'

'Surprisingly easy. They're older now, they've long since left the Army and most of them have it on their conscience. They also loathe Charles Lamming. As the saying goes, there's nothing worse than your friend's success. Interestingly, only one refused to co-operate. William Blesson. He doesn't believe in breaking ranks. But he did tell the whole story to a friendly barrister one day over a bottle of wine by the Marlow riverside.'

Victoria sat back. It was all falling into place. But there were still questions. 'But how did you persuade Kitty?'

'Easy. She's ambitious. When a powerful member of chambers tells her to do something she does it.'

'And she won't say the whole case came from you?'

'Not if she values her career. Believe me, she won't talk.'

'And why didn't you tell me?'

David looked at her as if she was an imbecile. 'Because I wanted you to look surprised when it all came out.'

'Surprised? I was astonished. But wasn't it just the most incredible bit of luck to find this out from William Blesson?'

David shrugged. 'Not really. I'd tried lots of other avenues. But Lamming's financial affairs are squeaky clean. And there's no sign of a mistress. But there had to be something – there always is. You just have to open the right door and the skeleton comes tumbling out. I knew Lamming and Blesson were in the same regiment so I invited the Blessons to lunch . . .'

Their club sandwiches and a bottle of wine arrived. Victoria looked at David and saw the relief and happiness on his face. Whatever she thought about his tactics for winning, she was delighted for him. 'We're a team, aren't we? My speech-writing and your strategy. We can do anything!'

David did not reply, tucking into his sandwich instead. Seeing her face fall, he turned and squeezed her knee. 'Victoria, you've been *wonderful*. And I've been ghastly to live with. I want to make it up to you. Right now. I'm going to go out after lunch and buy you a very special present to say thank you.'

If Victoria would have preferred an hour or two alone together without the children, she was wise enough not to say so. David was making an effort at last. Maybe his becoming an MP might mark a turning-point, a fresh start, a new chapter in their lives. She decided to be positive. 'If you're sure—'

'I'm certain,' David cut in. 'It's the least I can do.' He put down his glass and took her hand. Leaning towards her, he lowered his voice, fixing her with his eyes so that the rest of the room faded away and she was only conscious of his gaze. 'Victoria, don't falter now. Please, bear with me . . . help me . . . stay by my side. It's so close. I'm almost there – and you know, you absolutely know, that I can't do it without you.'

In his shabby office on the other side of London Tom read the letter, then reread it. He could not believe it. He was used to fighting and arguing his case in front of one committee after another before being refused outright or offered half of what he had requested. But this gave him everything. Errol Knight, Britain's middleweight boxing champion, was going to pay for the gym: he wanted to put something back into the estate where he had grown up. Or more precisely, thought Tom, the estate he had fought his way out of.

Errol would pay for everything Tom had requested. Not that Tom had even dared to hope that he would reply. But here it was: money for a gym, a studio and a café. It would be in part a boxing gym but the Social Services committee would have to put up with that. They had virtually laughed at Tom's request for funding, pointing out that they were already overspent on their budget with months to run until the end of the financial year.

Errol would like to open the finished gym, and he kind of hoped it might be named after him. Tom could see no problem with that. At that moment Tom would have renamed the entire estate after him. He sat back in his second-hand chair in his dilapidated office. The kids would be ecstatic. And if boxing was something of which he did not wholeheartedly approve, he was not about to impose his middle-class values on them.

The priority now was to find a builder and start ordering the equipment. But first he must tell Clara. He picked up the telephone to call home. The phone rang and rang, but there was no reply. He was sure she'd said she was staying at home to tackle the ironing. She must have dashed out to the library. Never mind, he'd tell her tonight. There were more important things to get done first. Clara might criticise him for coming to the office on a Saturday but she would have to admit that this letter had made the trip well worth it.

Later that evening Annie was also trying to telephone Clara. Victoria had just called to say that she and David would not be able to make that evening's performance of

Romeo and Juliet after all. David had gone shopping only to receive a desperate call on his mobile from a senior judge whose wife had been caught drink-driving after a liquid lunch. Unfortunately she had called the arresting policeman a common little man and was now languishing in a cell in Beaconsfield police station. David was driving down to do an urgent bail application. It was one of those situations in which he couldn't say no.

Annie had understood, but now she had two spare tickets and there was no reply from Tom and Clara. She supposed that she could not expect things to be any different. Clara and Tom had their own lives to lead, popping over once in the week and again at the weekend. And as for Victoria, she appeared to be immersed in David's political adventures and Annie hadn't seen her for a week. Besides, it was obvious that Victoria and Clara were avoiding each other, each telephoning and casually asking whether the other would be present before committing themselves to visit. Whatever had been said at Marlow, it had clearly created a rift between them that neither seemed willing to heal and Annie, seeing her two sisters estranged, felt ever more depressed as her family fractured around her.

She couldn't wait any longer. The Stimpsons were due any minute. They had offered the asking price, Annie had accepted, and now they wanted to come round and measure up. She could hardly refuse. The house was a mess but they would have to put up with it. She looked around the cluttered kitchen in which she had once taken such a pride. Now pots, pans and plates were piled in the sink and the antique kitchen table was strewn with newspapers, an overflowing ashtray balanced on top.

These days, the house had to manage without her. Elizabeth got up, made her own breakfast and caught the bus to school. Annie usually surfaced at around midday. If she was feeling energetic she would tackle the washing-up. If not, she went back to bed. She dealt with her financial situation by not opening any envelope that was brown or official-looking. She would have to sort something out, though – her debit card had been refused at the supermarket yesterday and she had had to put the week's shopping on her credit card. She couldn't ask Victoria and David – they were still paying off their builders – and Clara and Tom had done so much already.

The bell rang and she heaved herself up to let in the Stimpsons. She was wearing an Indian print skirt and an old blue shirt of Hugo's. She had heaps of Indian and African clothes which, when ironed and carefully matched with a scarf or belt, looked stunning on her slight frame. Now she didn't iron them and the effect was more shabby than chic. But what did it matter?

Mrs Stimpson was standing outside with a clipboard and pen. As Annie opened the door, she pushed her tortoiseshell designer sunglasses into a mass of blonde hair, then looked Annie up and down. In her mid-forties, Mrs Stimpson favoured zebra-print leggings, a crisp white shirt and a complexion that was heavily reliant on twice-weekly use of her sunbed. Her husband hovered anxiously behind her, dressed in expensive American jeans and sweatshirt.

'We won't get in the way,' Mrs Stimpson said efficiently. 'Please, just wander around.'

'We know the way.'

They came into the hall and looked appraisingly at the walls, which Annie had only last year painted picture-gallery red.

'Shall we call you when we've finished?'

Her cue to push off. That was fine by Annie. 'I'll be in the garden.'

She left them unpacking an enormous tape measure and sheets of A4 paper on which Mrs Stimpson had typed lists of what was presumably to be measured, changed, discarded and improved.

Annie wandered into the garden, sat on the lawn. There was no sign of Helen Morgan. She lit a cigarette. But she had reckoned without Mrs Stimpson's voice carrying through the open windows: 'It's all very *alternative*, you see, sweetie. And that's fine for some people. Arty people, I suppose. But we want something more classically taste-ful . . .'

Mr Stimpson's fainter voice could be heard, 'What do I do with these papers?'

'Here. Each sheet represents one room. Then there are six headings. Number one, measurements. That's where you write down the measurements. Two is floors – that's tiles, floorboards or carpet, which do we have? Three is walls – meaning, wallpaper or paint? Four is structural changes. Five is where to put our furniture and any new pieces that will be needed. Finally there's number six, lifestyle.'

'Lifestyle?' Mr Stimpson sounded confused.

'Yes, you know, is such and such a room a *formal* room, for entertaining, or somewhere we would use for someone *informal* . . . like your parents.'

'I see.'

From the snatches of conversation Annie learned that fitted wardrobes in cherry-wood veneer were to be installed in the main bedroom. Elizabeth's room was to become Mrs Stimpson's office, with a new range of built-in furniture. The floorboards were to remain downstairs but white carpet was to be laid upstairs – so Mr Stimpson would need always to remember to take his shoes off when he came in and leave them in the new shoe-rack to be purchased and placed in the hall. Hugo's office was to become a formal dining room and wallpapered in broad cream and navy blue stripes, with curtains in identical fabric. As for the kitchen, the solid beech was coming out and new white lacquered units with gold fittings installed. This, it appeared, was more modern and would give an impression of space, particularly with shiny white tiles on the floor instead of the existing dull quarry tiles. By taking out the old larder there would also be room for a dining-table in the kitchen, presumably for use by Mr Stimpson's parents.

But the first job was to repaint the gloomy red hall, replacing it with a shade of pale pink, over which Mrs Stimpson herself would stencil a multicoloured motif of creeping ivy.

So it would all change, Annie thought. A life together obliterated by a few weeks of building work.

In the end, the Stimpsons stayed for an hour and a half. No sooner had they driven off in their black open-top Porsche than Sam Swinburne drove up in his battered Land Rover. She was trapped. A few seconds later she would simply have ignored the doorbell. Although she knew she should be grateful for his kindness in visiting and calling so regularly, all she felt was irritation that she was about to be forced into more conversation. She struggled to raise a smile as Sam emerged, in faded tan corduroys and a checked open-necked shirt, with a bunch of mixed carnations and a stack of art books. If only he had telephoned before setting out she could have put him off.

'Annie. Hello!' Sam greeted her with warm ebullience. 'I've brought those books I promised you. Lovely day for a drive over. I think a flaming June is upon us! And these as well . . .' He handed her the flowers and Annie made every effort to receive them appreciatively.

'Thank you. Sam—'

'It's a pleasure! Let me just put these down on your hall table.'

She stood aside wearily as Sam bustled in. 'Sam, I'm just on my way out . . . Elizabeth's school play.'

'Oh, super! Send her the best of luck from me. Break a leg and all that. Now, very quickly, let me just show you a couple of these books.'

Annie resigned herself to standing politely at Sam's side, pretending to peer intelligently at the reproduced photographs of Victorian paintings while half listening to Sam's earnest, schoolmasterly commentary: 'You see, Annie, I thought these would be useful reading for the exhibition I was telling you about – "Art in an Age of Empire". I gather they've assembled the most superb Victorian collection. Did I mention it's at the Tate – not that Modern one, of course – and the landscapes are particularly special.'

Annie recalled dimly that Sam had invited her to a preview in a week's time and, although she had not actually accepted the invitation, he had clearly assumed that she was coming.

'You see,' he continued, 'although one naturally thinks of Hunt as an exponent of sacred themes, his landscape work is very important and, of course, the religious element of his work can be seen in those paintings as well.' He pointed at a photograph in which Annie struggled to see the significance of a flock of sheep grazing on a cliff-top.

He was now leafing enthusiastically through a particularly large volume, seemingly unable to bypass any photograph without proffering an explanation. 'Boddington! Apparently this is the largest collection of his work ever assembled under one roof. Most exciting. You can see here how he's captured the sunlight in these trees . . .' He pointed at yet another photograph. 'Naturally, one can't appreciate the skill just from a photograph but I think it gives a useful impression nonetheless . . .' He continued, turning pages, and Annie struggled to maintain even the illusion of paying attention. She really did feel terribly tired and hazy. She needed a strong coffee at the very least, but if she offered Sam a drink he'd be there for hours. He was in full flow, however, and impossible to interrupt.

'Now, just one last thing to show you,' he said, for the umpteenth time, 'a rather intriguing Inchbold.'

There was a knock on the door. Annie didn't know whether to feel exasperated or relieved. She opened it to find Helen Morgan on the step. 'I brought these round. Broad beans.' She held out a colander and caught sight of Sam. 'Hello! How are you?'

Sam broke away. 'I was just showing Annie something rather interesting. Do have a look.'

Annie knew that she could not let this develop. The two

of them would be unstoppable. When Hugo had been alive they had quite often made up a foursome over tea in the garden . . . Abruptly she stopped the recollection forming too clearly in her mind. She decided to be blunt and if she appeared rude – too bad. 'Actually, Sam's just leaving. He popped round to drop off some books. I've got to go out to Elizabeth's school play.'

Helen gave her a wry look. 'Not a problem. You must get ready. Could I have the colander back when you've finished with it?' And Annie could have hugged her when she added, 'I was just about to make some lemonade. Would you like to join me, Sam?'

'Gosh, well, I don't want to intrude . . .'

'You wouldn't be at all,' said Helen. Annie felt a surge of gratitude and relief as she observed Sam carefully closing the uppermost book before arranging the half-dozen volumes into a neat stack.

'Do have a glance through,' concluded Sam, wandering without urgency towards the front door, which Annie was now holding open, 'and I'll telephone to organise meeting up at the Tate. Oh, and give some thought to our painting trip. I always find it a most inspiring setting.' He turned to Helen, his expression enthusiastic. 'Devon in August. It'll be the third year I've put together a little party and, if I say so myself, the work that emerges is really very good.'

Annie nodded earnestly, while making a mental note to come up with excuses for both of Sam's suggested trips, until the protracted goodbyes were over and she gratefully closed the front door. She knew that Sam was being kind and that he had nothing but her best interests at heart. But it all felt somehow overwhelming – the prospect of travel even to London appeared beyond her and any idea that she would venture on holiday was simply an impossibility. She was faintly aware that she never now left Railway Villas unless it was absolutely necessary to do so but at the same time she saw no particular reason to do otherwise. At least she felt safe at home, indoors with the curtains usually drawn, more often than not leaving the telephone and the door unanswered.

By the time Annie had downed a strong coffee, washed her face, and discovered something vaguely smart to wear – blue linen trousers and a white T-shirt, which would just have to do – it was past seven o'clock and she arrived at the school after the play had already started. She edged in at the back of the hall, which was crammed with parents, grandparents and teachers, plus a few unfamiliar faces. Talent scouts. The school had a growing reputation for grooming the stars of the future, a reputation enhanced when last year's head girl had gone on to play a single mother in *Stretton Surgery*, the country's most popular soap opera.

Elizabeth was not on stage. When she appeared at the end of Act I, Annie's stomach tightened; she felt as if she was watching a stranger. Elizabeth was no longer the quiet girl with the downcast eyes who had sat on Annie's bed and cried with frustration at her inability to learn her lines. She was an Italian girl in Verona and the lines were mere lines no more. They were Juliet's expression of her thoughts and feelings.

> 'My only love sprung from my only hate,
> Too early seen, unknown, and known too late,
> Prodigious birth of love it is to me,
> That I must love a loathed enemy.'

Annie repeated the lines inwardly. She knew them all, the cues and the exits. But she could not speak them as Elizabeth did. There was a magic ingredient and Annie knew the audience provided it. An audience that to Annie appeared as a vast, terrifying mass but whom Elizabeth simply accepted: they were no threat to her because she could hear their laughter and feel their approval. The scenes with Celine as the Nurse were a riot.

When the play broke for the interval there was a surge of prolonged applause. Sandra Hollis, chair of the parent–

teacher association, rose from the front row: 'The PTA will now serve wine and canapés in the dining hall.'

Annie had last encountered Sandra Hollis two weeks ago when she had arrived at Railway Villas unannounced, supposedly to offer her sincere condolences but actually to advise Annie that Elizabeth should be withdrawn from the play for her own good. It was not fair on Elizabeth to place her under such pressure so soon and, moreover, account must be taken of all the hard work by the other youngsters, not to mention the PTA who had painted the scenery and made the costumes, and who deserved the play to be a success. After all, with talent scouts in attendance, the children's careers were perhaps at stake! And if her own daughter, Jessica-Anne, could help in any way by taking over the role then she would just have to put in the hours necessary to learn the lines. Annie had thanked her but told her firmly that the situation had already been discussed with the headmaster so Jessica-Anne could stay as Lady Capulet and need make no further efforts on Elizabeth's behalf. Sandra had left ten minutes later.

Now Sandra was attempting to supervise the mothers serving drinks, seek out her own daughter to give her a word of advice about voice projection, and engage Pete Mallinson from the Theatre Life Agency in exclusive conversation. Annie took a drink and drifted towards the edge of the room. She hoped she looked inconspicuous enough to avoid being drawn into conversation. There was no sign of Elizabeth. As an excuse to turn her back to the room, she began to survey a display of sixth-form collage work, which had been expertly displayed on the bare brick wall.

'Escaping the crowds?'

Annie realised that the question had been addressed to her. She half turned to see Martin Hollis standing by her side, his balding head tilted at her with an expression of concerned interest.

'Annie, Elizabeth is a natural. You must be very proud.'

Before giving her a chance to reply he carried on, 'Look, I haven't seen you since . . . since Hugo, and I wanted to say that if there is anything, anything at all you need, then you only have to call.'

'Thanks. I'll let Sandra know if something comes up,' said Annie, while not imagining any event that would induce her to call on Sandra Hollis.

'Hey. Let me give you my mobile number. Best way to get hold of me.'

He fished a card out of his blazer pocket. Martin Hollis, short and stocky with the sort of pale, fleshy face that never tans, ran a successful computer-supply business, which provided his wife with the income, if not the social status, she required. The latter she sought to acquire through membership of Cobham's most exclusive gym, weekly golf lessons and the dedicated pursuit of power within the PTA. Though universally derided, her energy had secured her success in gaining the chairmanship two years ago and she showed no sign of loosening her grip on power. The PTA was dull and time-consuming but it put her in an excellent position to further Jessica-Anne's career. Jessica-Anne had already appeared in a television advertisement for fabric-conditioner, holding a towel to her face in ecstasy, and was in the final two for a role as the love-child of the local policeman in *Gilbert Street*, a new daytime soap opera set in Manchester.

Martin Hollis slipped his business card into Annie's hand. 'Anything at all. Shelves need putting up, washing machine leaking, I'm your man.'

'Thanks again.'

He beamed at her. 'It's a pleasure, always happy to oblige. And, of course, I'll have some time on my hands, with Sandra away.'—

Of course, she would be. The Maltings were taking their production of *Romeo and Juliet* to the School Drama Festival, to be held that year in Oxford. The cast were praying for good weather, hoping to re-create the hot, fevered atmosphere of Verona in the Oriel College quad where they were to put on the play in the open air. They were to give five evening performances, the last in front of the judges. Sandra was accompanying them – ostensibly as their self-styled wardrobe mistress, but really to bully the poor judges into giving Jessica-Anne the festival prize for Best Actress.

When the audience returned for the second half, Annie felt more relaxed. Elizabeth was not only in command of her own lines but when Romeo, a sixth former presumably chosen for his good looks rather than his wooden delivery, forgot his, Elizabeth swung effortlessly into her own speech. Only Annie, and a frowning Mrs Lightfoot standing as prompter by the side of the stage, detected that anything was amiss.

Where had Elizabeth's confidence come from? Certainly not her mother. And if it was from her father it could not be as a result of knowing him. Annie's relationship with Salim had been romantic, illicit and short-lived. Annie had been an eighteen-year-old fashion student, scouring the Brick Lane shop Salim's father owned for cheap and exotic fabrics. That day Salim had been there alone. How odd to think that such an unusual occurrence had led to such far-reaching consequences. He was never usually left in charge but his father had needed to go to the bank and his brothers were at school. Otherwise he would never have spoken to her.

Salim's parents had arrived in the East End twenty years earlier from Pakistan and had worked every day from then to build up their textile factory. Salim, the adored elder son, was destined to take over the business and marry a cousin from Karachi. Both events had been settled for years. But Annie had paid no heed to this when they had made love in her digs. She was in love with the tall Pakistani boy with thick black hair and deep brown eyes. He had laughed at her white skin, had pushed her reddish blonde hair up to his and intertwined the colours. But he had concealed nothing from her, had made her no promises. And she could still see the expression on his face when she had told him she was pregnant.

But she did not want to dwell on that. Elizabeth had been born and a few months later Salim was married to the girl he had known of since childhood yet who was a stranger to him. She recalled the snatched telephone calls at her parents' house, her father hovering obtrusively in the background, when Salim had begged to visit his daughter. But Annie had refused. Her mother, whose liberal inclinations had not extended to reacting with joy at the idea of her daughter's teenage pregnancy, had filled Annie with stories about feckless absent fathers, children crying because their birthday had been forgotten or the longed-for weekend visit had been cancelled at the last moment.

Annie wanted none of that for Elizabeth. He could send money but no more. And each month since then whatever amount Salim could hide from his family had arrived in her bank account. It was their only contact. He would have had trouble tracking her down, even if he had wanted to. After three months living with her parents, Annie had had quite enough of her mother's helpful advice and moved to the first of so many rented flats. She had worked whenever she could, waitressing, then in a launderette, as a receptionist, and a spell as a live-in housekeeper. She was hopeless at the last job and had been sacked with a week's notice. Her parents had helped out, of course, and somehow Annie had started her curtain-making business. Elizabeth had grown up doing her homework on a kitchen table covered with yards of fabric – chintz to be made into swags and tails for conservative customers, rich eastern material to be elegantly draped for the more adventurous. Once, when there had been no money for a TV licence, the only sounds in the flat for months had been Annie's Singer sewing machine and the transistor radio.

How had Elizabeth survived? Annie's boyfriends had come and gone. They had moved every couple of years, slowly working their way up to the flat in Raynes Park, where Annie had started making curtains for the rich women of Surrey who had neither the skill to make their own nor the inclination to buy ready-made. Women who wanted au pairs, gardeners and conservatories. She thought fleetingly of the day when Hugo had arrived to quote for a summerhouse at a Weybridge mansion and caught Annie as she fell off her stepladder while fixing a too-high pelmet. Much later, he had promised her that he would always be there to catch her if she fell.

There was no one to catch her now. But Elizabeth had survived. As she watched her on the stage, Annie knew that the scenery might fall down or the stage collapse, but Elizabeth would always remain standing. All the upheavals of her childhood had moulded and strengthened her to withstand whatever life threw at her. In fact, thought Annie, gazing at Elizabeth feigning death in the burial vault of the Capulets, she could perfectly well survive without her mother.

CHAPTER 6

Clara and Ben had had their last lunch together. At least, for the next two weeks. For Clara, it was undeniable that she was committing adultery with one of her final-year students, but she drew the line at doing so during his final examinations. Ben's started today, but she had needed a last goodbye so she had stolen out for a couple of hours on Sunday morning, excusing herself to Tom with a story about late alterations to an examination paper. He had barely looked up from the brochures for sports equipment that battled for space on their sagging double bed with the umpteen Sunday papers he insisted on purchasing each weekend. He had become something of an overnight expert on step machines and treadmills and all manner of weight-lifting equipment.

So she had gone with ease to Ben. She had drunk wine with him in his bed, lying naked on the covers to escape the June heat that lingered in the cottage. In the last few weeks they had fallen into a routine. Ben would get up early and work from eight o'clock. Clara would arrive at one. She no longer allowed him to cook: his time should be spent studying, not shopping, cooking and clearing up. Now she had brought wine, cheese and bread from the bakery in Richmond. They ate quickly, aware of the time passing, before rushing upstairs. Ben had taken to calling this his revision break. He would remind her laughingly that only a few weeks ago she had lectured her students on the importance of working methodically and taking regular time off to allow themselves to absorb the seemingly endless facts they were required to memorise.

In the short time they had been together Clara had felt herself transformed. She no longer hid her body from him. How could she when he had spread her out and touched every inch of it in so many different ways? And told her she was beautiful, desirable and perfect so many times. Their lovemaking had changed: no longer tentative and exploratory, they had become wilder and more desperate at every meeting. Ben took her with all the force in his body and she found herself crying out to him to be still harder with her. Afterwards they would lie breathless and laughing, and she returned home each time with ever-greater resentment that she could not stay. Her only comfort was that Ben would be returning to his books, working from late in the afternoon to late at night. She agonised that he would fail his exams and blame her. So despite his efforts at persuasion she had enforced their separation. And to comfort them both, she had agreed to go to Deauville with him in August.

That was going to be tricky. A snatched couple of hours during the day while Tom was at work was one thing. Disappearing for the weekend was another. But Ben's descriptions of Deauville had enthralled her and, more than that, she wanted to be with him for the day and the night. To *sleep* with him, in his arms, knowing that she could wake the next day with him beside her. Leaving was becoming the hardest part.

At least he could call her. Two weeks ago she had gone out and bought a mobile phone. Tom had been scandalised. She left it switched off most of the time, checking the messages whenever she could. She was still surprised at the number Ben left – never less than two or three a day and often more, inconsequential chat, what was she doing, where was she going, he missed her. Occasionally, just occasionally, she was faintly disturbed by the impression that she was Ben's whole world whereas she . . . was married. Retrieving the messages could be difficult to manage surreptitiously, especially when Tom had asked her why her law school colleagues were leaving them on a Sunday evening.

Before Ben, when she had read about married people who had affairs, she had supposed that lying to one's partner would be the worst part. But it had proved to be easy. Of course, Tom was hardly a challenge. She had bought new clothes, highlighted her hair, lost six pounds and he had made not a single comment. And as for guilt, it was Ben who inspired guilt in her. Guilt that she was monopolising his time, guilt that he would fail his exams and lose his place to train as a solicitor. Above all, guilt when she had slept with Tom. Fortunately, it had only happened once but to refuse might have alerted him to something amiss. She had imagined Ben, and conjured up a picture of a French hotel room in August.

But Deauville was still a long way off. Until then she would distract herself with work. As she unlocked her office door she saw her answering machine bleeping furiously. Last-minute desperate queries from students, no doubt. She would call them back and resist telling them that if they didn't understand the subject now it was too late to do anything about it. She settled herself at her desk and let the contents of her postbox fall from her arms. The usual requests for references plus advertisements for conferences and new textbooks. Belinda Weaver wanted an urgent reference for a job in a Birmingham solicitor's firm specialising in matrimonial cases. That was going to require some careful wording – divorces in the Midlands were going to get a whole lot messier with Belinda involved.

As she pressed the replay button, the mechanical voice told her dispassionately that she had twelve messages and the tape was full. But before she had a chance to listen to any of them, the telephone rang. 'Clara Parker? *The* Clara Parker?'

The woman's voice was unfamiliar and vaguely awe-struck.

'Yes, I'm Clara Parker. Have we—'

'No. You don't know me. And I want to apologise for calling. I know you must be very busy and important, and people like you with their names in the papers probably get called up all the time but I just had to say something about your article.'

So that was it. Between making love to Ben, falling out with her family and attempting to avoid Tom she had completed the Tellium article for the *Sunday Times*. It had appeared yesterday in the Review section, prominently placed on the third page, accompanied by a photograph of a sleeping baby cradled in its mother's arms with the caption 'Is any baby safe from the devastating side-effects of drugs?' Clara had thought it distinctly over the top. That was not the point of her sober, carefully argued article. But the subeditor had clearly been determined to liven it up and her final paragraph had appeared in italics: "*The case has perhaps not ended with this last court hearing. Lawyers for the women are now exploring a possible connection between Tellium and the use of Vartren.*" The very words Ben had suggested three weeks ago. But what did this woman want?

Clara spoke professionally: 'I see. Thank you. It's very kind of you to call.'

'But don't you see? You've started something here. For TAG. When we've met at the meetings, lots of us had talked about Vartren but no one had ever made the connection. You're the first. This could change everything.'

What meetings? What group? But there was no time to consider this. The woman was rushing on: 'So, you see, I was so excited when I read that an expert like you was taking an interest. And you're a lawyer. I read in the paper that you had written a textbook, so you must know all about it. I could ask you.'

'Ask me what?'

There was an audible sigh. 'About TAG. The Tellium Action Group. How we continue the fight.'

There was a pause. Clearly the woman was expecting Clara to give her some guidance, but Clara was an academic, not a protest leader. For once she wished Tom was around to give her a few tips on direct action. He would have her occupying the Landward Pharmaceuticals building in no time.

'I'd love to help you, I really would. But although my area of specialisation is medical law, I'm a teacher not a practitioner.'

The woman's voice was confused. 'What do you mean?'

'I'm an academic. I analyse cases. I teach the law. I don't go into court and argue cases myself. You need a solicitor for that.'

This provoked an agitated response. 'I know about solicitors. I've spent the last five years talking to them. But how are we supposed to pay them? They don't work for free, you know. After we lost the last case they took all our legal aid away. A few of the solicitors are carrying on, but they're working for nothing and they can't give us much time.'

'I'm very sorry, but I really don't see what I can do to help.'

There was a pause. The woman's voice lost its edge. 'I'm sorry. I don't want to get annoyed with you, it's not your fault. But it's been such a long fight, exhausting, and when we lost last year . . .' Her voice broke. She was struggling to speak through tears. 'You see, we really thought we would win. We *know* it's Tellium. But they had the best lawyers. They picked holes in everything. And they had a team, one barrister and all the others below him. We had so many different solicitors involved and it was a nightmare trying to sort out our information. I know we made mistakes, got a few facts wrong, and Landward got hold of every little slip-up and made us look stupid.' She broke off, trying to control her sobs. 'But how could we get it perfect? My son

– he's six – he's brain-damaged and I'm trying to look after him and do this case and, of course, my husband couldn't take any more, he walked out last year . . .'

Clara was lost for words. She had no idea how to help this nameless woman. And she had even less inclination to walk right into a legal minefield, which appeared to have exploded all around. She decided to play for time. 'Look, I'm very sorry to hear your story. Let me take your name and telephone number and I'll have a think and see if there's anything I can do. But I have to be honest. If the courts have ruled on this it probably is the end of the road.'

The woman's voice was suddenly uplifted. 'Thank you! You've no idea . . . I'm Laura Turner, TAG secretary.'

Clara wrote down her number. After prolonged thank-yous and goodbyes she finally got her off the line. Then she played back the messages. Each was from a Tellium parent, mostly women but also the occasional father. Some told of their despair, of children unable to talk or walk and unlikely ever to do so. Others simply thanked her for writing the article. They were all clearly despondent and felt forgotten. Knowing the legal position, Clara judged that they were probably realistic to feel that way. Twelve voices of people whose lives had been ruined, thirteen if she counted Laura Turner, rang out in the silence of her office.

She sat back and surveyed the cosy disarray of her office. Beneath the apparent chaos there was an underlying order and predictability. The summer vacation followed by the autumn term and its fixed timetable of classes and meetings. Then the Christmas holidays, February mocks, Easter, then summer examinations. There was no uncertainty in her life. It was all so simple, so straightforward – Victoria had got that right. Teaching provided her with a safe sanctuary in which to sit and analyse the disastrous events of other people's lives. And Ben was wrong: she did not care about people or changing their lives. Yes, she might counsel students and inspire one or two to greater efforts. But really she was an observer of events, hidden away behind the protective walls of the university. Whatever idealism she had once possessed had long since been forgotten. She could not even sympathise with Tom's crusades. She was certainly not the person to galvanise a demoralised set of parents to recover from defeat and fight yet another exhausting legal battle. The most she could do was ask around her colleagues for any ideas before calling Laura Turner in a couple of days.

Annie held the estate agent's particulars of 18 Albert Road in her hand and looked up at the decaying Victorian building with dismay. The midday sun beat down and she still felt nauseous from the half-bottle of supermarket vodka she had consumed the night before.

'As we say in the details, the property requires some work but, of course, that is reflected in the price.'

Of course. The estate agents had presumably sent their most junior employee to show their most derelict property. Jason was about nineteen, perspiring in a trendy suit and running his hands through his spiky gelled hair. He pulled a set of keys from his pocket. They wandered up the uneven concrete drive avoiding the huge dandelions and thistles growing up through the enormous cracks. Annie guessed that 18 Albert Road had once been a fine Victorian house, but nothing of faded grandeur remained in a building that had long since been cheaply converted into four flats. She looked up at the brown peeling paint on the window-frames. Greying net curtains hung at most of them, and here and there a lopsided roller-blind. Loose wires from television aerials trailed down the front of the house and looking up to the roof she could see that the clay chimneys were collapsing. Jason led her past the front door, with its cracked panes and bundles of free newspapers and pizza menus sticking out of the letter-box.

'The basement flat has its own private entrance,' he said, attempting to sound enthusiastic. Annie felt almost sorry for him, but she was beyond thinking of anything suitable to say. They walked round to the back of the house, passing the remains of a rusty moped, which had presumably been taken apart by its owner, then abandoned in despair.

The basement door was located at the bottom of a flight of five steps.

'Mind yourself. It's a bit slippery,' advised Jason.

Annie clung to the side of the wall, attempting not to slide on the slimy moss and grime that coated the dank steps beneath her shoes. Jason inserted the key in the flimsy lock and tried to open it without success. He tried again, then took out the key to check its tag. 'Yep. Eighteen Albert. Basement.'

'Here, let me try,' suggested Annie.

The key just about slid into the rusty lock. She turned it but the door remained shut. Finally she gave it a hard shove with her shoulder whereupon it sprang open, sending her stumbling into a tiny hallway awash with post and flyers. Jason stopped to gather up the papers. 'As you can see, we haven't had many viewings recently.'

When Annie looked through to the living room she could think of a hundred reasons why. The smell of damp and decay was suffocating. Despite the heat outside, the flat was cold in a way that could only mean the chill had entered the walls after many months without heating. What little light might penetrate it was blocked by the filthy windows. As she walked into the living room she saw that the flat had not even been cleared out. In one corner stood a collapsed armchair in faded and torn maroon Dralon, surrounded by heaps of old TV listings magazines and telephone directories. A heavy old-fashioned telephone with a dial hung off the wall and next to it a teak-veneer shelf unit teetered precariously. The dark brown carpet was stained and bunched in thick folds.

Anxious not to linger, Jason led her briskly through to the kitchen. Annie by now knew what to expect. She glanced at the warped Formica units, the filthy electric cooker coated with rivers of congealed cooling oil and the rusty, stinking fridge. 'Who lived here?' she asked.

'An elderly lady. She's in a home now. Her son's selling it for her.'

Annie felt a spurt of hatred for any son who could allow his mother to live like this.

Clearly Jason felt embarrassed. 'He did say that she didn't like anything to be touched.'

He took her through to a tiny bedroom, which at least was empty but for a pair of thin green and brown flowered curtains hanging from a cheap pine curtain rail. 'This is the biggest bedroom . . .' moving briskly on he led her into a second room '. . . this is the second.'

Annie guessed that you could just about get a single bed into it.

'And the bathroom's down here.'

She followed Jason along a short, dark passageway. Annie could have predicted the limescale-coated green plastic bath and basin, and lino that was peeling away from the walls. She avoided looking at the lavatory. She turned and wandered back through the flat, followed by Jason.

'As I say, the price does reflect the work that needs doing. Most of it's cosmetic.'

'Surely it needs a damp course, not to mention—'

'I couldn't say. You'd need to get a survey. We can suggest a surveyor. Do you need a mortgage? We have an in-house financial adviser who can advise on mortgages, life assurance . . .'

Annie had stopped listening. The stark reality was that this was all she could afford. She had looked at every available Surrey property in her price range, which hadn't taken long. There was only a handful within reasonable distance of the school, and Albert Road was one of them. Its one redeeming feature was that the bus for Elizabeth's journey to school stopped almost outside the front door.

At least the money from the sale of Railway Villas would provide a good deposit, but she would still need a mortgage. Victoria had said that she and David would guarantee it. Though nothing had been said, Annie knew that it was her responsibility to make the payments and she would have to get a job, but even so there was no certainty that she could manage the school fees too. A letter from The Maltings had arrived last week, reminding parents that the autumn-term fees were due by 1 September at the latest.

It was this flat or homelessness. The Stimpsons were completing their purchase and moving in next month. She couldn't wait a day longer. Whatever she felt about Albert Road it was vacant and the awful son was willing to exchange contracts as soon as possible. He wanted the money. And she needed a place to live.

Nancy Masters tapped her short, French-manicured nails against her low marble coffee table, indicating to her Hungarian au pair where she should set down the coffee tray. 'Thaaanks,' she drawled, and the girl hovered nervously before Nancy waved her away.

'Ute's very willing,' said Nancy, in a voice that left little doubt that this was the only characteristic to recommend her. Victoria noticed that Ute was also fat, frumpy and badly dressed in sagging jeans and what appeared to be one of Hayden Masters' old shirts. Victoria knew the score. Nancy was not about to introduce some nubile French or Spanish girl into her home to tempt her husband away from his purpose in life – providing for his wife. Ute may be unsightly but then that was really rather the point of her.

Nancy had arrived in England six months ago, and had invited Victoria to a coffee morning with Philly Bingham, a fellow mother at the school where Nancy had recently enrolled her son, Connor. All three women had sons in the same class. Alex and Philly's son, Rufus, were old friends, but Connor was becoming popular with his classmates on account of the hundreds of electronic toys and state-of-the-art computer games that filled his enormous bedroom. Also, he had a home cinema in the basement with all the latest films. And Nancy Masters served fabulous teas with real chips and American burgers followed by tubs of expensive ice-cream.

Philly Bingham was attempting to stare discreetly around the room, taking in the sound system, the television and the acres of mahogany furniture. Philly, thought Victoria, would probably describe herself as an old-fashioned Englishwoman from an old-established English family. Philly's own drawing room consisted of good but shabby furniture, a few faded rugs and a Labrador. On no account would Philly allow into her house a television the size of the one Nancy possessed. But, then, Philly couldn't afford one. She and her husband had inherited their house from Algy's father, and although Algy had a prestigious job valuing paintings for London's smartest auctioneers his salary barely kept them in pasta.

There followed a stilted attempt at conversation.

'So, Nancy, how are you settling into London?' asked Victoria politely.

'*Weeell*, I'm finding my feet. I've located the American library, signed on with an American doctor. Of course, the US school was full so we had to put Connor into the local one.'

Nancy was really getting into the English way of life, then.

'And Hayden?'

'*Weeell*, he's kinda busy at work. They've been doing a big takeover. The cab comes for him at six.'

Philly sounded bright. 'Oh, that's not too bad. I know these banks can demand the most ghastly hours. So he has the evening with you?'

Nancy looked nonplussed. 'I mean the cab comes at six in the *morning*. To go to Canary Wharf. He's up at five. He gets home most nights at around eight.'

'Gosh.' Philly was aghast. 'How does he keep going?'

'Oh, he's pretty health conscious. I watch his diet and I

don't let him drink alcohol in the week. And we go jogging at the weekend, that kinda thing.'

Wow, thought Victoria, life was a bundle of fun for Hayden Masters.

'But I still have some things to sort out,' continued Nancy.

Philly seized deftly on the opportunity to make some suggestions. 'Maybe we can give you some pointers. Algy and I have been here for ten years so we know virtually everyone.'

Nancy seemed doubtful. 'I'm kinda hoping to find a decent hairdresser. I find the salons here a little . . . dull.' Her eyes took in Philly's chubby face and her lank brown hair, pushed back for the occasion with a velvet Alice band. 'You see, I need *volume* in my hair, but I cannot find anyone here who can really backcomb.'

Victoria thought that Nancy's hair was immaculate already, platinum blonde with the ends curled neatly outwards. But she knew just the man to take her on. 'Jean-Pierre. He's excellent. I'll write down his number for you.'

'Is he American?'

'French.'

Nancy looked disappointed, but evidently decided to change the subject. 'Let me pass you some biscuits.' She got up, revealing a pair of beige Tod's loafers with those knobbly bits on the heel that Victoria never quite under-stood the point of. For driving, maybe? Philly took two biscuits, Victoria one and Nancy left the plate untouched. At least there would be plenty left for Ute to snack on.

'And how is Ute doing?' enquired Victoria.

Nancy sighed. 'I suppose I can't complain. We had such a wonderful Mexican lady in Dallas. All legal, of course. We paid for her to be naturalised. Hayden can't take any chances with employing *aliens*.'

Philly choked on her biscuit.

Victoria translated: 'Aliens are illegal immigrants. It's the American term.'

Nancy pushed on regardless: 'But it's so hard to get domestics here. Ute is my third au pair already.'

Philly and Victoria exchanged a glance. Consuela had been with Victoria for nearly five years.

Nancy brushed a non-existent crumb from her spotless white polo shirt. 'She's fine with cleaning and shopping, but she struggles a little with Connor's homework. And I really cannot trust her with the ironing. I'm having to have all that sent out.'

'Perhaps she has difficulties with the language,' said Philly, trying to be helpful.

'I can't help that! She has to take responsibility for her own learning.'

'Quite.' Victoria could see that this was going in a decidedly dodgy direction: Philly was looking at Nancy with undisguised distaste. Victoria often found this type of occasion fraught with difficulty. If you put together a group of bored women, added a dose of social snobbery and mixed in a strong element of competition, the result could be a tense couple of hours. Philly, realising that she had neither Nancy's looks nor her money, evidently decided to move the conversation on to her own ground.

'Talking of homework,' Philly said, 'Rufus has just started advanced maths with Mr Knightly. So's Alex, hasn't he?'

Victoria murmured. She saw the way this was going.

Philly turned to Nancy. 'Is Connor doing advanced maths?'

'I really couldn't say. Ute deals with all that.'

Touché. Philly turned back to Victoria. 'Perhaps it's only the *top-stream* boys who are doing it. Those they think will get scholarships. I'm sure Connor will catch up soon,' she added patronisingly. 'They do move them between streams, you know.'

'Scholarships,' repeated Nancy. 'Do you need a scholarship? I kinda thought everyone in this neighbourhood could pay for education.'

'A scholarship is not about money,' Philly said testily. 'It's about, well, recognition for the boys who are top of the class. When they move on to their senior schools, at thirteen, the boys who have come top in the entrance examinations are awarded a scholarship to that school. It's a wonderful privilege. It's something they can be proud of for the rest of their lives.'

Nancy Masters looked as though she didn't give two hoots about scholarships now or at any other time. 'Do you mean those boarding schools?'

'Yes,' said Philly proudly. 'Rufus is down for Selchester.'

'So he's going to live there? All the time?'

'No, not during the holidays. And we're allowed to see him at weekends. We can go down every third Sunday and take him out for lunch.'

'You're allowed . . . ?'

'Yes. It's all much more relaxed than when my husband went. Algy was there for weeks before he saw his parents. And of course, there are wonderful social events. The July garden party. And the summer concert.'

'It sounds great . . . for you,' said Nancy drily.

'Oh, it is. It's a super way to meet people and network. The boys meet people who'll be useful to them for the rest of their lives. A Selchester education is a passport to the world,' Philly concluded happily.

'Yeah. You're right there. Your English class thing, I guess. Hayden's been dealing with some Selchester old boy in his takeover. The British bank he works for has just been taken over by a US bank.'

'There you are, you see,' cut in Philly. 'Selchester boys are at the top everywhere. Banks, auctioneers, the BBC, politics . . .'

'Not this guy. They just sacked him. Put in a thirty-two-year-old from Harvard.'

Philly was lost for words.

Victoria decided that she had listened to more than enough about schools. She was not opposed to the idea of boarding: her reservations were centred on Selchester, a school so committed to its austere traditions that it refused to publish a prospectus. Future Selchester parents received a poorly photocopied two-page document detailing the school calendar and suppliers of uniform. It was a far cry from the glossy brochures that Victoria had received from other schools anxious to appeal to a new generation of parents who had not themselves boarded. Victoria had spent hours poring over text that would assuage the fears of the most anxious mother given its emphasis on family values, pastoral care and a visiting policy so liberal that parents appeared to spend every weekend at the school. Looking at the photographs of the facilities on offer, each school offering as standard an Olympic-sized swimming pool, a theatre and a state-of-the-art science block, she had almost felt disappointed that she herself would not be moving into one of the cosy study-bedrooms pictured.

She decided to change the subject to something they could all agree on: politics. Neither Nancy nor Philly were on the selection committee but they both knew people in Wimbledon – Philly in particular, thanks to her children's clothes sales. Unprepared by her education to earn a living, Philly had taken to holding monthly sales of children's clothes in her home. She designed them with the help of drawings from stacks of Victorian ladies' magazines supplied by Algy and then had them made up, allegedly by grannies in the West Country but, Victoria suspected, more likely by newly arrived immigrants in a sweatshop in the East End. Philly specialised in smocked dresses for girls and corduroy knickerbockers for boys. She also churned out hand-knitted Arran sweaters, blue-and-white-striped Breton T-shirts, and had just started a line in made-to-measure wild-silk bridesmaids' dresses. Neither Emily nor Alex would be seen dead in any of Philly's garments so Victoria was reduced to buying the odd item and giving it to Consuela for one of her many nieces or nephews. At least it kept her on the right side of Philly.

Now Victoria adopted a tone of high seriousness: 'David's busy preparing for the final selection meeting in September. I know he'd be interested in any views you have as to what is *especially* important in the constituency.'

Philly leaped in, obviously keen to cultivate the wife of the next MP: 'I'm sure David knows all there is to know. Please tell him if there's anything we can do, anything at all for the election, to let us know.'

'That's very kind. I'll pass it on.' Victoria smiled, thinking that in the absence of any real competition from the other parties there would hardly be an election campaign in Wimbledon at all. The real battle was in September for the seat. David was secretly hoping that the Conservatives would lose the next election. Then there would be a clearout of the old guard and more room for youngsters like himself. Thinking of this, Victoria continued, 'I'm sure I won't see much of David when there is an election. He'll be working heart and soul to get the government back.'

'Is there going to be an election soon?' asked Nancy.

'Probably not until next year. The government has only been in office for three years. They could even wait another two before they go to the polls.'

'Well,' concluded Nancy, 'put us down for the campaign fund. We'll give all we have to keep those darned Communists out.'

After a further hour of chat, interrupted only by Ute serving more coffee, Victoria made her excuses and left.

Had these things always been so boring? She had once enjoyed a chance to gossip and keep up with all the news from school. And she had held plenty of coffee mornings herself – they were so useful for entertaining divorced mothers. It was much easier to invite singles to coffee than to a dinner party, where you had to find some presentable man to pair them off with and make sure none of the husbands were getting too friendly.

She lived only a few doors away from Nancy but

Consuela would be Hoovering so she took a roundabout way back, enjoying the sun and the buzz of the taxis whizzing past. Lucretia Stanley and Janet Williamson crossed her mind. Were they only invited to coffee or lunch, never to dinner? She felt a momentary pang of sympathy for Janet Williamson. Fat, worthy, sensible Janet, who would spend the summer swotting up for the September selection – only to realise when the day came that she had never been in with a chance.

It was a warm June evening, clear and fresh after a light shower, but even the late sun could not lift the atmosphere of oppressive neglect that lay over the Southhead estate. Clara locked the car, tested the door-handle, then mentally castigated herself for displaying so little trust. She walked the few yards to the doors of the community centre in search of Tom, his guest speaker and whatever handful of residents he had cajoled into attending his meeting to launch the idea of the gym. Each of the double doors to the hall displayed a poster in garish red: 'Have Your Say – The Gym: Use it or Lose It.' Catchy wording – the part about having your say was just right. But how much interest could Tom stir up in a place that was either to be endured or escaped?

It was with surprise that Clara entered the hall, its walls painted a faded municipal green and every window covered by wire mesh grilles, to find that it was nearly full. Perhaps fifty residents, she guessed, most standing and the majority smoking in defiance of the prominent no-smoking signs nailed to all four walls. She looked for Tom and spotted him standing next to a man who, from his previous description to her, had to be Brendan McCarthy, the famed trainer to Errol Knight and a host of other British boxers before him, and the man Tom was relying on to propel the gym to success. Brendan – short, barrel-chested, red-faced – was surrounded by a cluster of teenage youths and was holding forth to his uncharacteristically respectful audience.

Before Clara could approach Tom, he moved away and set off for the back of the hall where he began deftly setting out extra rows of chairs. She recognised Tom's thinking: always set out fewer chairs than you think you need or the meeting will start with rows of empty seats – guaranteed to deflate the atmosphere. Then he looked up, saw her and waved. She pushed her way past the groups of people and excited children, past a noticeboard covered with plans and schedules and a picture of a thermometer showing how much money had been raised to date, its red line reaching the top.

'Quite a turnout,' she said, aware that she was not quite able to keep the note of surprise from her voice. But Tom did not appear to notice. 'Brendan's the draw. People have seen him on television. And Jan's covered the estate with posters.'

'Jan?'

'Over there.' Tom gestured to a tanned woman in a red sundress, her bleached blonde hair piled high on her head. She was placing a sheaf of papers on each seat, 'I'll introduce you.' But before he had a chance to do so he was waylaid by a shaven-headed youth in a football shirt who had no hesitation in butting in on their conversation.

'Tom, someone says that Errol's going to turn up.'

Clara knew that Errol was not going to turn up, Tom having earlier informed her that he was on holiday in St Lucia. Realising from the youth's urgent tone that Tom was likely to remain occupied for some time in tactfully explaining this, Clara turned away and found a seat. The air in the hall was uncomfortably close, and she felt conspicuous in her navy linen skirt and jacket, a new acquisition, and her strappy sandals. Her nails were painted a dark pink, lending her hands and feet an unfamiliar elegance. She felt like a visitor from another world, all too identifiable as someone educated and prosperous, whose presence could almost be interpreted as patronising. Which it wasn't, of course. Tom had so much wanted her to come and she would have done so even if Ben had not been in the midst of his exams. But still she felt uneasy and out of place.

Tom, though, was perfectly at home. She observed him laughing and chatting, asking people to take their seats, marshalling Brendan into position behind a fold-up plastic-topped table, issuing assurances that everyone would have time to ask questions and speak to Brendan afterwards. And he did it all with a light touch, she had forgotten that, a touch he had become adept at using over the years to mask his underlying seriousness of purpose. She leafed through the stapled papers in her hand, the agenda for the evening's meeting, drawings of the proposed gym, a questionnaire – 'What do YOU want from the Gym?' – draft exercise-class timetables, ideas for a crèche and workshops on everything from debt to parenting, even plans for an extension to house offices that could be used for legal advice and counselling. Tom was nothing if not ambitious, visionary even, and as she read on she was jolted back into recent flashes of conversation at home when Tom had mentioned most of this, except she hadn't been listening. But it was the same for most wives, surely? Half listening, feigning interest in their husbands' work, but past that stage in a relationship when one wanted, needed even, to know and share every part of the life of the person one loved.

She had not been listening then or now. But when the room fell quiet she looked up and saw that Brendan had risen to speak. Tom was now seated at his side, looking relaxed and sitting back with the air of a man who is watching a success of his own making unfold before his eyes. Brendan's voice rang out: 'Right. I'm Brendan McCarthy. I used to be a boxer but I'm a bit past that now so I train them.'

He didn't look 'past it' at all to Clara. His enormous

head was joined to colossal shoulders with no sign of a neck. It was difficult to judge his age, probably late fifties, but Clara would have backed him against any of the youngsters in the room.

'I grew up on an estate like this in Liverpool.'

That explained his accent, which Clara had been struggling to place – a weird mixture of Irish, Liverpudlian and Cockney.

'But I got out of there. Out, up, and I never went back. And, looking round this room, I see faces who want that too. To get out, find a better life, go places in the world. Not all of you, though. Some are happy to stay here. Maybe you've got kids and you can't leave. But others- . . . well, that's where boxing comes in.'

Clara recognised that air of uncompromising self-confidence, which, more than any attempt at false empathy – or, worse still, sympathy – would appeal to this audience. She caught Tom's eye – how long had he been looking in her direction? – and smiled. Bringing in Brendan had been a stroke of genius to give the project the credibility it needed, which Tom was astute enough to know that he alone could never provide. She had forgotten how good Tom was at his job. Brendan was in full flow now, scathing of other sports, particularly football, and uncompromising about the efforts that would be required from those wishing to participate. Now there was total silence in the room. He picked up a glass of water in his huge hand and took a gulp. 'But only a few make it. They're the ones with the gift. They're strong and fast and hungry for it. But they've got something else, too. And I'll tell you what that is . . .'

They wanted to know. Clara could feel it.

'Discipline. A disciplined body. And a disciplined mind. And that starts with training. Running, circuits, weights, then more running. And more bloody running when I'm not there, training for the next session. And you go on a diet. Lose the fat, build muscle, eat decent food – not the crap most of you live on. If you smoke, you give up. If you drink, you give up. Well, most of the time. I never managed to keep to that one.'

Brendan's audience allowed themselves a nervous laugh. Clara watched as the boy next to her discreetly dropped his cigarette on the floor and ground it out with his trainer. More of the same followed. It was clear that Brendan was going to be in charge and anyone who couldn't accept that had one option, which was to leave. The air now was thick and Clara could feel her make-up turning moist, and probably smudged. Stupid, really, to wear foundation on an evening like this but she had got into the habit of applying make-up every morning lest she should unexpectedly encounter Ben and look anything less than her best. In consequence she felt unkempt and less than confident without it.

And still Tom hadn't noticed. She didn't know whether to feel resentful or, more pragmatically, grateful that his indifference enabled her to conduct this double life without challenge or consequence. Because there were no consequences. Her life was compartmentalised, her time with Ben existing in its separate, secret world, its only intrusion at home when she allowed her thoughts to wander to him and had to pull herself up short, suddenly conscious that her smile betrayed her. She had supposed that this was how philandering men ran their lives, each segment of work, home and mistress contained in a box in the mind, each to be opened when the others were closed. And now it was easy to see the attractions of such an approach, the freedom it gave her to live for the day, to enjoy the moment, secure in the knowledge that what Tom did not know could not hurt him. And as long as the boxes stayed closed, as long as Tom did not suspect, there was no reason to think beyond each exciting day to the future. Actually, there was no incentive to do so when the present was so beguiling and the alternatives, to give up Ben or leave Tom, to enter into irrevocable and agonising decisions, were so painful to contemplate.

Applause broke out. Brendan sat down, but before Tom had a chance to rise to his feet four or five teenage boys had surged forward to Brendan. Shaken from her thoughts she joined in the clapping, not that she had been listening to Brendan's final words, and heard Tom calling for a five-minute break before they opened the meeting to questions. She did not imagine such a break had been scheduled: Tom was going with the flow. The blonde woman in the red dress, she had forgotten her name, was giving him an enthusiastic thumbs-up from her seat in the front row, and all around people were talking loudly, the atmosphere one of excited anticipation. Five minutes. Tom was at Brendan's side, the room was abuzz, plenty of people were going out for fresh air. She picked up her handbag and slipped out with them. To call Ben. Just for five minutes. Just to hear how today's exam had gone. Just to hear his voice.

Annie put down the telephone. Sam had reluctantly accepted her excuse for missing the preview of his Victorian paintings exhibition – the sudden, fictitious onset of gastric flu – but had pestered her again about his tedious Devon painting trip. *Yes*, it was a terrible shame she couldn't make the exhibition and, *yes*, she had loved the books, which lay unopened on the hall table, and, *no*, she hadn't made a decision about the holiday.

She ignored the doorbell. Helen Morgan, she guessed with more vegetables or flowers: Helen brought something every day in a thinly disguised attempt to keep an eye on her. She heard footsteps retreating and the click of Helen's gate.

Too bad. She must start packing. The move was just weeks away. Contracts had been exchanged on 18 Albert Road so all that remained was to pack up Railway Villas. She had managed to collect a few cardboard boxes. There was no money for removers so Tom was hiring a van and they were doing it themselves. Tom had been brilliant – more help, it had to be said, than either Clara or Victoria. It appeared that they were still not speaking but Annie had the uncharacteristically resentful thought that they could have come separately . . .

She supposed this was the way things were going to be from now on. Helen Morgan had lent her a book on bereavement, *Life after Death*, which had warned curtly of how friends and family tended to fall away in the weeks and months after the funeral. The book went on to recommend a sensible diet, regular exercise and a new hobby to fill the time – none of which Annie had taken up.

Before she could start she heard the sound of a car in the driveway, then the ring of the doorbell. This had happened several times. The first time, about a week ago, she had made the mistake – at midday in her dressing-gown – of answering the door to a blaze of sunshine and the sight of Cal Doyle in a dark navy business suit.

He had shot her a quizzical glance. 'Bad time?'

She had been wrong-footed. 'I . . . overslept,' she had mumbled, running a hand through her unkempt hair, conscious that she must look dreadful but not really caring.

At least he'd got straight to the point. 'Do you know anything about the accounts programme on the De Long-den computer?' He paused. 'I'm sorry . . . I know you probably don't want to be reminded, but it's pretty desperate. Unless I can figure it out, I can't do this month's payroll. I've been stuck in the office all morning and I'm not getting anywhere.'

Annie wondered what on earth this had to do with her – and he seemed to read her confused expression perfectly. 'You're my last hope,' he continued. 'Barbara de Longden says she doesn't know and it's up to me now.'

Annie could imagine the tone in which this had been said and, however much she tried, she couldn't quite stop a hint of sympathy arising for Cal Doyle's predicament – not to mention that of the poor employees who wouldn't be paid on time, if at all. 'I don't know,' she began. 'I never used it myself.' She struggled to think clearly and then remembered. 'There are instruction manuals for some of the programmes. Hugo kept them in his study.'

'Anything at all that might help. I'd be very grateful.'

And Annie could see that he would be. She was aware that a harder woman would have given him short shrift – but what purpose would that have served? She wasn't one to hold a grudge and, besides, she had no reason to dislike him personally. She had gone off into the study, leaving him in the hallway, and returned with a stack of computer manuals. 'I've no idea if they're any good,' she said dispiritedly.

'I'm sure they will be.' His voice was surprisingly kind. He glanced through the sitting room door at the cardboard boxes waiting to be filled. 'If you need any help lifting heavy things, just give me a shout and I'll send a couple of lads over.'

Annie raised a polite smile. 'Thanks. I will.' But she did not mean it.

And he seemed to know that, but did not press the point. Instead he had regarded her for a few seconds before uttering a brief but warm goodbye and making for his car.

In the days that had followed the doorbell had been rung three or four times, preceded by the sound of a car on the gravel drive, but on each occasion she had been in bed and eventually the car had driven away.

Now, a week later, the bell rang yet again. Whoever it was pressed their finger long and hard so that it sounded insistently through the house. Bloody hell! More in anger than curiosity she stormed out of the kitchen and threw open the door.

Martin Hollis stood on the step, his red Jaguar parked behind him. He was perspiring slightly in his usual navy blue blazer and grey slacks. He smiled at her and spoke in his unmistakable nasal tone, 'Hi! Hope I haven't called at a bad time.' And, without waiting to be asked in, he stepped past her. 'Thought I'd pop round. Heard on the grapevine that you were moving soon.'

'Yes, in a week, so there's lots to do.'

'Good time to have a break, then.' There was a pause. 'Kitchen this way?'

Annie was resigned. 'Yes, I'll put the kettle on.'

Martin Hollis beetled off down the hallway, glancing around nosily before he settled himself at the kitchen table. 'Nice place you've got here. Get a good price?'

Annie ignored this.

'Shame about the move. Going far?'

Annie had no desire to have her impoverished circumstances relayed to Sandra and then around the school. 'No. Just up the road.'

'Great! We wouldn't want to lose you. Sandra was only saying last week you must come over to Sunday lunch.'

Annie knew somehow that this was one invitation that would never materialise. She lacked any of the commodities that attracted Sandra – money, connections or fame, to be precise.

'Now, is there anything at all I can do?'

'I don't think so. It's all packing.'

'What about the new pad? Need any shelves? Electrics?'

'Oh, it's all fitted out.'

'Still, you might think of something. I'd welcome the chance, actually. Sandra has her little man to do all those things and a chap likes to feel useful.'

'How is Sandra?'

'Not too good, actually. Bit of a crisis last night. The Oriel College front quad may be all hoity-toity but you can't get away from the fact that it's in the open air. Poured down on them last night; had to abandon it in the end.'

'So Elizabeth said.'

'But she's still in Oxford?'

'Yes. She phoned.'

Annie handed Martin a mug of tea and sat down.

'Any sugar?'

'I'll have a look.' She heaved herself up and started rooting about in the near-empty cupboards. Martin was chatting happily about his latest business idea – installing computer-controlled sound systems in Surrey houses. 'You have a keypad in every room and a central console. You can play a different CD at a different volume in every room.' Annie resisted asking why anyone would want to do this. 'The new houses have them, but not the old ones. I think there's a lot of potential.'

He droned on about computer chips, boards and sensors. Annie wondered how long he planned to stay. 'Have you got appointments round here?' she asked.

'No. Whole day's free. Advantage of being your own boss. Not that being top dog doesn't have its responsibilities, but I like to think I can juggle the balls quite nicely. You see, business is not just about seeing opportunities, it's about getting out there and grasping them. With both hands.' He seized his mug to illustrate the point. 'Take the domestic market. It's all about lifestyle now. Furnishings are old hat. People want a house that suits the way they live. That's where I come in. Music in every room, that sort of thing. You should get it installed in your new place. I could do it at cost price.'

'Thanks. I'll let you know.'

'Do. I want to help. It can't be easy. How's Elizabeth bearing up?'

'Difficult to say. I think the play has distracted her.'

'Good. It's certainly distracted Sandra. Not altogether unwelcome, I have to say. She's a bundle of energy. And since Jessica-Anne dried up – I expect you heard, their first performance in Oxford – she's been desperate. They've been going over the lines every day . . .'

Annie could imagine. More followed about Jessica-Anne and the further bad news that she had lost the part in *Gilbert Street*. Martin downed the last of his tea. Good, she could get rid of him. 'Lovely cuppa – any chance of another? I'll just pop up to the little boys' room.'

Martin Hollis took himself upstairs, leaving Annie with no option but to boil the kettle again. He seemed to be gone an inordinately long time – no doubt taking the opportunity to have a surreptitious poke around upstairs. On his return, he settled himself even more comfortably than before and launched into a tedious account of Sandra's own childhood acting ambitions. Annie decided to say nothing, hoping that her failure to take part in the conversation – or was it a monologue? – would encourage him to push off. But, if anything, he appeared to be warming to his subject: 'But, as I was saying, Sandra isn't going to give up. Oh, no. She's decided to give Jessica-Anne a new look. She's going to get her hair highlighted, made blonder. All these teenage parts want blondes.'

'I'm sure Sandra knows what she's doing.' There was a pause. Annie saw that Martin was staring at her.

He lowered his voice. 'Let me hazard a guess. I don't think *you* dye your hair, do you?'

Annie's hand went involuntarily to it. 'Well . . .'

'No! I knew it. You're a natural blonde. With a little bit of red. You can't fake that.'

'Thank you.' Annie realised as soon as the words had left her mouth that she had said the wrong thing: Martin Hollis looked pleased with himself.

'You see, Annie, whatever happens in life you can't change your nature. A man is a man. And a woman is . . . a woman. It's very simple. I like to think I understand you ladies.'

Annie kept silent.

'And ladies, much as they might try to deny it, have certain . . . needs.'

It clicked. OK, she knew she just needed to keep calm but her stomach tightened and panic surged through her. She got up. 'Well, I'd love to sit and talk. But I must get on.'

It was her second mistake. Martin got up too. He came over to where she stood by the kitchen sink, pretending to wash up. She sensed him too close behind her, and then the touch of his hand on her hair. 'You have beautiful hair. You are a beautiful woman. I want to make you happy. And I know I can . . .'

She froze. 'No!'

'*Yes*, sweetheart. Let it happen. Don't fight it. I saw it at the play, the way we talked. I want you and – though you can't admit it to yourself yet – you want me.'

Annie spoke with all the firmness she could muster. But her hands were shaking. She managed to put down the glass she was rinsing on the drainer, 'No, I don't. I want to be alone.'

His hand was on her shoulder. 'You can't be alone. You need a man ... in your bed.' With his other hand he reached for her waist and then her hip.

She still had her back to him, terrified to turn round, 'Please. Please stop it. I don't want this.'

'Come on, relax, let it happen. You must need it. All women do. You're not some feminist. You were married, you're used to getting it—'

When she felt his lips on her neck she knew she had to fight. 'Get off me! I don't want you. I never have.' She must face him. Swinging round with as much force as she could manage she squared up to him. 'And I never will. I want you to go. Now.'

'Hey. There's no need to be like that.' But he had backed away. 'Come on. I can be good for you.'

'I don't think so. I really do want you to go.'

She shrank from him and, seeing her weakness, he moved across. She felt a sickening shock as he groped for her breasts. 'I'm not going ...'

Annie knew she was way out of her depth. She'd read about this type of thing. What did women do? His hands were clutching her all over now and he was pushing his mouth against her lips. She felt the weight of his body pressing against hers.

'Stop it!'

But he did not stop. He was reaching for the front of her shirt, his fingers searching to touch her body beneath it. She struggled for breath. There was nothing she could hit him with, no strength in her body to wrench him away. She was running out of time. 'I'll call the police!'

He laughed. 'No, you won't. You know me – you let me in.'

He had his hands inside her shirt now, running his fingers under the straps of her bra. 'I'm not going to stop.'

And then, struggling and wrestling with him, she found her voice: '*If you don't go I'll tell Sandra.*'

The effect of those few gasped words was immediate: he let go of her and wiped his mouth on the sleeve of his blazer. 'You wouldn't.'

'Yes, I would. I will tell her that you came round here and tried to force me to go to bed with you.'

He was appraising her now. His voice was sullen, yet aggressive too. 'I just followed your signals, *sweetheart*. You led me on, love. You encouraged me.'

'You know that's a lie! Will you just bloody well go?'

He was summoning his dignity, straightening his tie and smoothing his lapels. 'Well, all I can say is you'll regret it. You won't get any other offers.'

'I don't want any other *offers*.'

'Just as well. You're hardly a great package.'

'Especially not from a creep like you.'

That stung him. He walked out of the kitchen door and into the hallway. 'There's a word for women like you.' He had reached the front door, was searching in his pocket for his car keys. 'You play your little games.' He opened the door and paused, then spat the words towards her: 'You lead men on. Well, I'm telling you, you're a *bitch*. A *frigid bitch*. I should have known.'

And with that he slammed the door behind him. Annie stood paralysed in the kitchen. Then she ran to the front door and bolted it. She slumped against it, straining to hear his car. When the engine started the most powerful feeling of relief flooded through her. She could hear the car screeching out of the driveway. He was gone.

She stood still for a minute, frightened that he might come back. And then she sank to the floor. Yes, she was crying again, but so differently from all the hundreds of times since Hugo's death. She missed him so badly. And the world without him was unbearable. Wherever he was, whatever place he had gone to, she had to be there with him. It was a relief to know, without any doubt, that this was the end. There would be no more struggle, no more attempts to survive. She was at last giving herself up to the inevitable.

As she got up she felt lighter and happier than she had since before Hugo's death. Everything had fallen into place. She did not have to continue. She would be free of the misery and worry, and the deep, deep depression that engulfed her every waking moment and with which she could struggle no longer. Free of Albert Road and Martin Hollis and the pile of unpaid bills. Free of Barbara de Longden and the awful Stimpsons. She walked deliberately into the kitchen and then she washed up. She stacked the plates and the mugs and wiped the kitchen table, pushing the chairs in and picking up stray crumbs from the floor. She folded the newspapers and put them in the pile for recycling. She reread her mother's last postcard from India. Next she filled a jug of water and went round watering the house plants, refilling it until each was done. And when the washing machine was running and the sitting room had been tidied, she went into Hugo's office and took two sheets of writing paper from his desk.

The first she addressed to Clara and Tom. She made sure that it covered everything. She would like to be buried with Hugo. They should take whatever they wanted from the house – the rest could be sold and the money kept for Elizabeth. There would be enough money from the sale of Railway Villas, if carefully managed, to pay for her education. Please would they thank Victoria and David for everything, especially David's reading at the funeral. She had forgotten to do this. She was sorry to burden them with the responsibility of Elizabeth. But they would do a far better job than she would and, really, that was the most important thing. She loved them very much.

The next letter she wrote to Elizabeth. It took an hour to find the words but in the end there was nothing more to say:

My Dear Elizabeth.
Do not ask any questions.
You only need to know that I love you very much.
With my everlasting love. Mx

Elizabeth was away until next week but she called every night at ten o'clock. When she got no reply she would call Tom. He would come round and know what to do. She took one last look round Hugo's office, holding his photograph in her hands, the pictures, the drawings, all the silly bits and pieces of a life – his school rugby medal and the wonky clay pot he had made when he was seven. His pencils were standing in the gaudy mug they had bought from that tacky tourist shop in Biarritz. His old tweed jacket still hung over his office chair: when she pressed it to her face she could still detect the faint smell of him. Then she picked up the letters, enveloped and addressed them, then propped them on the hall table where they would be easily found. All she needed now from downstairs was the vodka bottle from the kitchen, so she fetched it, taking the opportunity to close all the windows at the same time.

The pills were on her bedside table. She sat on the edge of the bed and counted them, first the tranquillisers, then the sleeping pills. She considered getting up and going to wash her face and brush her teeth. But now she was keen to avoid any more delays. She supposed that people would imagine one might hesitate at this point. Ring the Samaritans. Draw back from the brink. They were wrong. She took the pills singly at first and then in handfuls. One didn't hesitate, you see, because this was something one wanted more than anything else in the world. When she had finished the tranquillisers she started quickly on the sleeping pills, terrified that she would fall asleep before she had taken enough. And when she had finished she lay back on the bed, pulled the soft duvet around her and closed her eyes.

CHAPTER 7

Cal Doyle was storming into Annie's bedroom with a crowbar. And Helen Morgan was hovering behind him. He grabbed the empty bottles on her bedside table. 'What have you taken? Tell me. Now.' Annie felt someone shaking her and pushing her eyelids open, staring into her pupils like a madman.

'Nothing . . .' Her throat was so dry she could hardly speak. She felt as though a blow to the head had knocked her out and most of all she just wanted this man to leave her alone.

'OK. Have it your way.' Cal turned to Helen. 'Call an ambulance. Don't take any bullshit. Tell them it's an emergency. An overdose.' Helen hurried out of the room and Cal began to shake Annie again. 'Get up! Come on, get up!'

Annie felt as if the room was spinning around her and, although she was becoming aware that this was not a dream, she felt an irresistible urge to sleep. Why was this shouting man wrenching the covers off her? Now she was cold! She tried to pull them back, but somehow her arm wouldn't move properly. She closed her eyes again. She was just so tired and she really, really wanted to go back to sleep. Maybe he would just go away . . .

'Right, girl, you're coming with me.' He put one arm under her back and the other under her legs, scooped her up and out of bed. She tried struggling but at the best of times she was no match for an Irish builder. And this was hardly the best of times.

She didn't try to speak. The room was wheeling round too quickly even to think. She had no idea where she was or what was happening. But she was moving. No, she was being moved. They were heading to the bedroom door.

'Where's the bathroom?' He sounded impatient. What was the hurry?

She didn't reply.

'Jesus . . .'

He found it across the landing. Holding her, he kicked open the door. 'Annie, listen to me. You're going to throw up.'

'No . . .' she slurred. She was not. And he couldn't make her.

The next thing she was aware of was Cal Doyle bending her over the lavatory and shoving his fingers down her throat. 'Fuck off,' she wanted to say but she had started to gag. She was falling over but he was holding her and ranting on and on. She couldn't catch it all but he was telling her to bring it up. *Bring it up. Bring it up.* And his fingers were pressing deep inside her throat. She felt a gut-wrenching wave of nausea from the depths of her body. There was nothing she could do to stop herself. Held in his arms, she vomited pills and vodka, and the remains of a bar of chocolate. She thought each time was the last. But every time she felt it was over, her stomach somersaulted and she was sick again. In between, Cal Doyle flushed the lavatory. He smelt of expensive aftershave and dusty building sites.

How long were they there? She would never know. At least until a paramedic team arrived – and did something that felt worse than her burst appendix, almost worse than childbirth. They laid her on the bathroom floor, put a rubber tube down her throat and pumped out her stomach.

Later that night Railway Villas was full. Clara and Tom and David and Victoria. Helen Morgan. Sam Swinburne. Cal Doyle. And Annie was upstairs in bed, having discharged herself from hospital an hour earlier. There had been a short conference among the doctors about whether to have her sectioned and compulsorily detained but faced with two lawyers, one of whom seemed to know an awful lot about medical law, and an officious social worker, who was pretty hot on patient rights, they had relented and allowed her home on condition she was not left alone.

There was little chance of that. The kitchen was crowded. Victoria was cooking pasta, Helen was making a salad and Cal was opening a bottle of wine. But there was tension in the air. Clara broke it, glaring at Cal. 'I hope you don't think you're some bloody guardian angel.'

Cal raised an eyebrow. 'No. I do this sort of thing every day.'

'Personally,' said Helen, who was drizzling olive oil over a tomato salad, 'I don't know what would have happened without Mr Doyle. Most heroic.'

Clara was livid, glaring at him over the top of her glasses. 'Let me tell you where we would be without him. Annie would still have a home and none of this would have happened.'

Cal said nothing. He took a packet of cigarettes out of his pocket, lit one and offered them round. Victoria gladly accepted. David looked at her askance. 'Darling, you really shouldn't—'

'Oh, shut up! If you hadn't been so obsessed with your precious meeting I might have come down more often.' She lit up with shaking hands. 'I feel so guilty! She's my little sister and I abandoned her—' She began to cry, but carried on making pesto from Annie's basil plant and a lump of Parmesan brought back from Sam's earlier shopping trip into Cobham.

Tom stepped in: 'Look. We can all argue about why this happened. I don't think it's fair to blame Cal. May I call you Cal? Thanks. This is all a result of unfortunate circumstances. But we have to look forward. Consider the positive. There are challenges to be met here—'

'But the reality,' cut in Clara, 'is that she has to move

next month. She's signed a contract with the Stimpsons and they don't strike me as the understanding type.'

'Not to mention telling Elizabeth,' added David, who had made no move to go to his wife's side. He poured himself a glass of wine, while Tom stood with his arm round Victoria. There was a pause. Sam Swinburne was sketching Cal Doyle's profile on the back of the envelope that had contained Annie's note to Clara and Tom.

Annie was lucky to be alive. Helen Morgan had seen and heard Martin Hollis leave, skidding recklessly in his haste to get away. She had waited. She knew Annie was in but she'd rung before and got no reply. But she was worried. She had gone out into the garden and seen that everything was shut up – which was odd, considering how hot it was. So she had pottered and worried and eventually decided to go round again with a marrow. But Cal Doyle *had* been heroic. She'd seen him turn up three or four times that week but Annie had never answered the door. So when he had driven in she'd been curious about him. They'd talked for a few minutes and she'd told him about Annie not answering earlier, how there had been some sort of row in the kitchen – not that she liked to eavesdrop – and how this cross-looking man had stormed out. She had reluctantly repeated the words she'd heard the man shout at Annie. Mr Doyle didn't seem too shocked. Instead, he'd peered through the letter-box. That was when he had seen the letters on the hall table. The next thing she knew he had run to his expensive car, dashed back with that crowbar and, in quite remarkable haste, broken down the front door then charged upstairs. She had asked if he was insured for the door and he had been really rather curt at that point. But no matter, he was awfully decisive and the rest, as they say, was history. Admittedly not the nicest type of history. She had kept well away from that bathroom but even from downstairs the noises were gruesome. Thank goodness Sam had turned up with those new watercolour paints and they'd waited together for the ambulance.

The telephone rang.

'Elizabeth,' said Clara and Victoria simultaneously.

David stood up. 'I'll do it.'

'Remember what we agreed,' called Victoria after him. 'We're telling her nothing. Annie wants her to carry on with the play.'

'Hi. Elizabeth!' They all strained to hear him. He sounded utterly relaxed. 'How's the play? Great! Go for it. I have a vision of you collecting Best Actress!' He chatted inconsequentially. Then, 'Your mother? She's just popped out . . . Hmm – with Victoria. Girls' thing. They've gone to look at curtain fabric . . . Yes, it *is* late, isn't it? I think a friend of Victoria's imports fabric and sells it from home. They've gone round to her house . . . Philly from my birthday party? Do you know, I think you're *right*. They did mention her name. That's right, she lives in the Village . . . What am I doing here? Good question. Helping Annie with a bit of the legal work for the move. Well, anything I can.'

There was a pause while David listened to Elizabeth, seemingly for ages. At last he spoke again: 'Look, I hear what you say. She has been a bit down about it all. And you're right, the move is a big wrench. But take some advice from an oldie like me. I think she's rallying . . . Yes! She's been much more positive today. We're all having a great time. Tom and Clara are here . . . No, it's all fine. It's a ball. I'll get her to call you tomorrow.'

The kitchen was stunned into silence. It wasn't the lies, they were a necessary means to an end, it was how brilliant David was at constructing a giant pack of them. He strolled back to the kitchen and took a sip of wine.

Tom was grudging. 'I suppose you have to be a lawyer to lie like that.'

'It helps,' said David. 'But what would you have said? "Good luck with the play. By the way, your mother's just tried to top herself "?'

Sam got up and went upstairs to check on Annie.

'We have to draw up an action plan,' Tom said. 'I suggest Annie comes home with us and stays until she's feeling better. Then she can go to this appointment with the hospital psychiatrist on Tuesday.'

David snorted. 'I don't see how analysing her dreams or reliving her childhood is going to help her move house.'

'No, you wouldn't,' retorted Tom. 'It's not like that at all. He'll treat the depression and probably start her on some cognitive therapy.'

'Cognitive bollocks, more like.'

Victoria spoke up: 'Actually, I think she should come to Marlow. I'm going down there next week for the school holidays. I can drive her up for the appointment. And we can just relax or wander round the town.'

Clara wanted to object. She had still not spoken properly to Victoria, and things had been tense at the hospital. Clara and Tom had got there first, alerted by Helen's message on their answering machine. Then Victoria had arrived and an hour later David had turned up, straight from Beaconsfield, complaining that he had been called away from a tricky magistrates' hearing. Sitting in the hospital corridor, Clara had talked briefly to Victoria, both of them too shocked to be coherent, before lapsing into the silent state of waiting relatives. Now she sat at the kitchen table knowing that she should argue for Annie to stay with her and Tom. But at the back of her mind was the fact that Ben finished his last exam on Monday. She was desperate to see him, but she could hardly do that if Annie was there. She realised Tom was talking to her: 'Surely it would be better for her to be with us, nearer to the hospital . . .'

She avoided his eye. 'Well, yes . . . but Victoria has more room. And Alex and Emily might be a distraction.'

Tom looked surprised, but Annie was her sister so he couldn't argue.

Clara changed the subject. 'So, Mr Doyle, you still haven't told us exactly what you *were* doing here this afternoon.'

If her tone was accusatory, Cal ignored it. He exhaled slowly. 'Problems with the computer. I wondered if she knew anything about it.'

Clara glowered at him. 'You wanted *her* to go to the De Longden office and help *you* with the computer?'

'Yeah. Well, I can't ask Barbara de Longden. She's swanned off on a cruise. And before she went she made it clear that she didn't intend to have any more dealings with me.'

'She always was a snob,' said Victoria, laying the table. Then she realised what she had said. 'Oh, I'm sorry. I didn't mean that you . . . I didn't mean to imply . . .'

'Darling, if you must come out with these tactless comments, do stop wittering on afterwards,' snapped David.

But Cal was cool. 'Forget it. I know what Babs thinks of me.'

Victoria giggled. 'So what will you do about the computer?' she asked, dishing up pasta and making sure to give Cal twice as much as anyone else. Helen was bringing the salad to the table and Tom was slicing some bread.

'Oh, some bloke's been recommended to me. A local. Martin Hollis.'

'Never heard of him, I'm afraid,' said Tom. He really rather liked Cal. And he couldn't see why Clara was being so hostile to him. Tom never worried very much about arguments over money and surely the important thing was that Cal had saved Annie's life? 'Actually, Cal, you might be able to give me some advice. About a gym . . .'

Clara raised her eyes heavenwards. But Tom started droning on and then Cal was on to it, too: 'Hey, I know Brendan. Watched him box a couple of times when I still lived in Liverpool. Mind you, I was just a youngster and he was coming to the end of his career then. But he fucking scared me.' He looked up quickly at Helen. 'Sorry, I wasn't thinking.'

'Oh, don't worry about it. I've heard all sorts of language

from the children in my time. I was a schoolteacher,' she explained.

'Were you just watching him?' asked Victoria.

'Well, I got in the ring a couple of times with him. Only sparring. I was working on the sites then, I didn't have time to do it seriously.'

'And what type of work was it?' enquired Helen.

'Did it all. Brickie. Chippie. Labouring. Bit of pipe-work . . .'

Helen looked more confused than before.

'But then I got the van and a couple of lads and started doing my own jobs. Tarmacking driveways, then extensions, pools – you name it, we built it. Never looked back. Of course, it was the eighties that made us. Council contracts. Even built a crematorium up in Leeds.'

They could think of nothing to say to this last achievement. Clara stepped in. 'And now you cover the Surrey countryside with executive homes.'

'Only because people want to buy them. Not everyone's like your husband – most people can't wait to get out of the cities.'

Privately Victoria shared Clara's opinion that Cal Doyle's houses were a blight on the landscape. Huge detached mock-Georgian, with pairs of *faux*-Greek columns framing the front door and triple garage blocks located to the side. Six bedrooms on average – except that they were called suites on account of the bathroom that went with each.

Cal was no fool, though, and he had caught Clara's tone. He continued, 'You see, the people who criticise my houses the most are usually the ones who can't afford them. Stuck-up Surrey types who call them vulgar and over the top. But,' he waved his fork in the air, 'most of my houses I sell off plan.'

Helen looked confused again.

'You buy the house based on a drawing, before it's built,'

he explained. 'I can't build enough to meet the demand. Talking of houses, where's Annie moving to?'

'Not a house,' said Clara sourly. 'A flat. A very small basement flat. It's all she can afford.'

'I see.' He was as cool as ever. 'Where is it?'

'Albert Road,' said Sam, 'but I've only seen the outside. We drove over last week. Unfortunately, the man selling it wouldn't give her keys until she pays him the money. She asked him if she could go in and clean it up a bit but he wasn't having any of it.'

'Albert Road? What number?' asked Cal.

Sam thought. 'Eighteen. Do you know it?'

'*Know it?* I bloody converted it! God, that must be fifteen years ago. When I first came down south.'

'Oh.' Sam looked surprised. 'I got the impression it had been done a long time ago.'

'Well, cash flow was a bit of a problem then. Not one of my luxury jobs. A quick in-and-out with a few plasterboard walls.'

'Pity you didn't make a better job of it. For Annie's sake.' Clara helped herself to more salad. She had left most of her pasta as part of her drive to lose another six pounds before she saw Ben again.

There was yet another awkward pause. David was looking thoughtful. 'So, Cal, I guess you're pretty interested in politics. Keeping the right type of government in power.'

Victoria couldn't help catching Clara's eye, and they exchanged a wry smile. David had spotted a potential donor. And before they knew it, he, Tom and Cal were arguing furiously about taxation policy. Victoria chatted to Sam and discovered that he lived just up the road from Marlow, in Maidenhead where he had settled to be close to Selchester. He still went into the school to take a sixth-form art class every week and, realising that he was anxious for company, she found herself inviting him to Marlow whenever he was free. She looked across at Clara, who seemed to be in another world.

When they had finished dinner Tom, Cal and David were arguing furiously about live animal exports. Helen cleared the table and offered to wash up while Sam quietly picked up his sketchpad. There was little option but for Clara and Victoria to wander into the garden. It was dark now, past ten, but the scents of the garden had been accentuated by the soft rain that had fallen a couple of hours earlier. The perfume of the night stocks planted at either side of the cobbled pathway filled the air, mingling with honeysuckle and roses. They walked together on to the lawn and down to the end of the garden in an uncomfortable silence.

'I can't believe it's come to this,' began Victoria. 'If only I had spent more time, listened more carefully . . .' She was crying. 'I should have *been* here. Or had Annie come to live with us . . .'

And Clara, walking beside her, realised that she could have spoken every one of Victoria's words herself. In the near-tragedy that had passed so close to them, their own rift now appeared to her as little more than an irrelevance. She linked her arm in Victoria's and they walked slowly around the lawn. 'I know,' she said, 'and, believe me, I feel just the same. I've been very . . . distracted. But we can't change the past. Tom's right – Annie needs professional support, and whatever we've got wrong in the past we've got a chance now to put it right.'

Victoria pulled out a tissue. 'Do you think we should tell Mummy? Get her to come back?

Clara looked resolute. 'No. Or, rather, Tom thinks not.' She was uncomfortably aware of how much she depended on Tom's advice and guidance right now. 'He thinks that Annie should make up her own mind.'

Victoria sniffed. 'Tom's so good in these situations.' She paused, 'Listen—'

'It doesn't matter,' Clara interrupted.

'No, it does,' insisted Victoria. 'I should never, ever have said those things about Tom. He's a fantastic person and you're so lucky to have him. The things I said weren't true.

211

I just wanted to hurt you. I know you and Tom were doing the right thing, trying to protect me, and I know how David must appear to you. But he's not all bad, you know.'

As she said this she was aware of how hollow it sounded. So she started talking about the last selection meeting and how it had brought them closer together. She left out the part about William Blesson and Charles Lamming's unfortunate officers' lunch. She knew Clara would not approve of David's tactics. And she couldn't very well mention that she and David had made love the night before – admittedly not with much passion but after a couple of bottles of wine between them better than on recent occasions, and even at his laziest David could be bloody good in bed.

And Clara listened, but only distractedly. She felt she was receiving an apology she did not deserve. She recalled her own accusations on that April day by the Marlow riverfront – that Victoria could not be bothered to have Annie, that Victoria was too distracted by her own selfish concerns to care for her sister . . .

In the cool evening air her secret life weighed heavily upon her, and Clara felt a desperate need to confide in someone. Having an affair, she had discovered, was intimate but also lonely. She wanted to talk about Ben and release her feelings of doubt and worry about the future. What would happen when he left the university this summer? Would he want to continue? Could she carry on like this indefinitely?

But could she confide in her sister? Victoria might tell David and who knew what might happen late one evening between him and Tom, after some drunken, acrimonious family dinner?

In any event the moment passed. As they stood leaning over the fence, trying to make out the vegetables in Helen's immaculate garden, Cal wandered out to them. He took out a cigarette and passed it to Victoria. 'Hey, your husband's not looking. Have a fag.' He held a light for her in his cupped hands. 'Tom's with Annie,' he continued.

'I've just been looking at some of Sam's drawings. He's pretty good.'

'Oh, he is,' gushed Victoria. 'He's exhibited at the Royal Academy. The boys at Selchester worship him.'

Cal appeared to grasp neither reference. 'His wife died,' he was saying.'

'Yes. Terrible. Nearly two years ago now. Which is one of the reasons he's so good for Annie. He understands.' Victoria led them back up the lawn to the teak table and four chairs that stood on the cobbled patio. They sat down, Cal stretching out his bulky legs.

'Are you married, Cal?' asked Victoria.

'No.'

There was an uncomfortable silence. His tone did not invite further questions. Instead, he asked, 'What about your family? Is there anyone else apart from you two who can help? What about Elizabeth's father? Shouldn't he be told?'

'You know about him?' exclaimed Clara.

'Barbara de Longden said something.'

'Plenty, I imagine. Well, the problem is,' continued Clara, 'we don't know where he is. Annie and Elizabeth never see him. He just sends money.'

'So he's not a total bastard, then.'

'Actually not at all.' Clara's voice softened. 'When Annie got pregnant his parents sent him away. To Pakistan. By the time he got back Annie had had Elizabeth, and Mother had persuaded her to drop him.'

'And your mother. Is she coming?'

Clara glanced at Victoria and decided to evade the question. 'Well, we don't know where she is either. I mean, we know she's somewhere in Asia . . .'

Cal raised an eyebrow in what was becoming a customary gesture.

'. . . because her last postcard was from India,' continued Clara. 'But she may be in Thailand now. Or possibly Indonesia. We just have to wait for her to call.'

'And your father?'

'He died three years ago. This trip is Mother's mid-life crisis. We don't actually know when she's planning to come back.'

Cal appeared to be reflecting on a family that was in part suicidal, in part unreachable and all seemingly intent on arguing about every conceivable subject under the sun.

Helen brought out a tray of coffee. David had gone to read the paper in the sitting room, she told them, and Tom was cleaning the loo. They discussed arrangements. Victoria would bring forward her trip to Marlow and take Annie down on Saturday, in two days' time. In the meantime, Helen would stay at the cottage. She was sure Sam would hang on, too, and Clara and Tom would come down each evening.

Cal said nothing. Victoria, observing him discreetly, thought he was attractive in a rough sort of way. Not her type – his thick dark hair needed a good cut and his clothes were too crumpled for her taste: she preferred a man to look well-groomed. There was something charismatic about him, though. He was powerful but he didn't throw his weight around. Most of the time he just sat and observed them all. All things considered, he didn't seem a bad type. Quite human, really, considering everything she had read about him in the papers. And in truth, whatever Clara said, it was Barbara de Longden who had cheated Annie. How could he be expected to know that the sale of De Longden Conservatories was in large part a devious plan to make Annie homeless? Looking at him smoking in the night air, Victoria could only imagine that he was planning to put as much distance between himself and their mad family as soon as possible.

Clara held a plastic beaker of cheap, warm red wine. In her experience of student post-exam parties the red wine was marginally better than the white, which was always too sweet, and the beer was to be avoided at all costs. The refectory was full. Groups of students, high on the feeling of relief that their examinations were over – and the exotic combinations of drinks they had been throwing back since lunch-time – swarmed around their sober lecturers.

Or, rather, ex-lecturers. Clara always noticed a subtle change in students once their exams were over – nothing radical, just an air of confidence that came from knowing that they no longer needed you. Of course, the most dramatic changes had taken place already. They had arrived three years earlier, desperately nervous, hopelessly ignorant and in a state of perpetual worry. Slowly they had learned to read as a lawyer, write as a lawyer and speak as a lawyer. And now they were ready to leave, realising that they had learned all they could from the lecturers, who had once seemed so dazzlingly brilliant – but now appeared hopelessly dull.

Belinda Weaver had not been celebrating: as she was explaining to Cameron Hawes, she had her responsibilities to consider. 'You see, I can't just go off and enjoy myself. There was this room to set up, decorations to put up, and then I had to wait for the wine and glasses to be delivered. They were supposed to come between two and three but didn't turn up until nearly four and, of course, I had to sit here all that time, which would have been all right if the committee had been here to relieve me but they all disappeared to enjoy themselves.'

Clara noted without surprise that Belinda was dressed in a smart navy suit while Cameron was in the current student gear of khaki combat trousers and ripped olive-green T-shirt.

He turned to Clara. 'So, Moneypenny, how's the Tellium campaign?'

Clara looked at him with mock-seriousness. 'What campaign?'

'The article you wrote for the *Sunday Times*,' added Belinda helpfully. 'Actually, I read it and referred to it in my exam answer.'

Cameron looked irritated. 'I was assuming Clara could remember writing her own article. No, I meant the calls coming into the office.' He glanced at Belinda. 'Don't you have someone to supervise? I don't know how the building's still managing to stand without you.'

He took hold of Clara's shoulder and steered her towards the row of refectory tables, now covered in paper table-cloths, where two groups of students had formed around the wine and beer at one end and the food at the other. Clara had intended to bring something wholesome, like a quiche, if only to help them soak up the booze, but she had been so behind with her work that she had just grabbed a couple of bags of peanuts from the kitchen cupboard.

Cameron reached over, picked up a bowl of crisps and carried it off amid protests from the students. 'You haven't graduated yet, you know,' he called to them over his shoulder. 'Not till after the exam meeting. Until then you are still in my power. Be grateful for what crumbs fall from my table.'

There was laughter. And Clara recognised Ben's voice. She knew he was standing behind the tables, helping to pour wine, but she had purposely not looked in his direction since she had spotted him when she arrived. She could not risk the slightest gesture, let alone comment, that might reveal their relationship to the prying eyes and gossiping tongues of the hundred or so final-year students. Not to mention the staff, who were even worse.

Now, involuntarily, she looked up. He was no longer laughing, just smiling at the girl who stood to the side of him: Francine Lewis. Clara hadn't taught her since criminal law in the first year. But she saw her around often enough – cigarette in one hand and mobile phone in the other, or climbing in and out of her Golf GTi. Daddy, apparently, was a wealthy City type. Now Francine was staring up at Ben, her brown eyes fixed on his, and her *mane* – that, unfortunately, was the best word – of glossy auburn hair falling over her shoulders. Clara took in her clinging strappy top, her bare midriff, and the diamond that nestled in her belly button. Finally, as Anthony Chang moved away from the food to get another glass of wine, there was no one between them to obscure Clara's view and she saw, with something like shock, that Francine Lewis was wearing skin-tight hot pants. Had those come back? Denim, with little sequins decorating the pockets, and cut so high that you could actually see the crease of the girl's bottom. And below them her slim, tanned, waxed, oiled, faultless legs.

'Are you looking for a pair?'

'What?' Clara swung back to Cameron.

'Are you looking for a pair of hot pants? You seem quite attracted by them. Unless the sight of Francine Lewis has prompted you to come out. In which case be my guest. The more the merrier.'

Clara rallied. 'No. I think you should reign as the only queen on that front.' Good, that had got him laughing. And distracted. She moved quickly on to Tellium. 'The article was fine. It's the telephone calls I've had ever since that have been the problem.'

'I wanted to tip you off about that. Kate's on the warpath. She was holding forth in the staff-room last Friday – you weren't in?'

'Family crisis.'

'Yes . . .' He hesitated, then continued, 'Anyhow, probably just as well. You see, once your answering machine gets full, the callers start ringing the law school office.'

'So then the secretaries take a message?'

'Simple, isn't it? They don't mind and the callers are happy. So, no problem. Wrong! Remember Kate's involved. She was arguing that it constituted a misappropriation of law school resources.'

'Oh, really!' Clara was genuinely annoyed. 'Hasn't she got anything better to do than stir up problems that don't exist?'

'No. And here she comes now.'

Kate was approaching with Julian Urquhart. Clara guessed that he was seeking safety in numbers. She knew that the best way to tackle Kate was to take the initiative so she launched in: 'Kate, I hear you've been complaining about Tellium calls to the office—'

But before Kate had a chance to respond, Julian stepped in. 'Marvellous, marvellous. Read your article, Clara. We need more like that. Campaigns, profile, *scandal*.'

'Have you gone mad, Julian?' queried Cameron.

'My dear boy, it's all about publicity, these days. Getting your department's name in the papers. That way, they're less likely to cut your funding. I was reading an article on it the other day, "The Culture of Celebrity in Post-millennium Academia". I'll lend it to you.'

'Thanks, I'll clear my diary,' said Cameron.

But Julian had not heard. He addressed Clara, 'So carry on, my dear! And anything the department can do to help, let me know. In fact, see me next week in my office. Tell me how the campaign's going.' And with that he slipped off to pour his wine into a plastic Swiss cheese plant.

Cameron turned to Clara. 'Well, it looks like you've got yourself a campaign.'

Clara sighed. 'I'm not sure I want one. And I think I may need help with some of the stuff on legal procedure.'

'Happy to oblige. As ever.' Cameron winked. 'Let's have lunch next week.' Then he turned to Kate with an ingratiating smile. 'What a result! Perhaps you could be Clara's research assistant, Kate. Do you good to study some law. You might even end up teaching it.'

'Cameron, good administration is as vital to the department as—'

But at that moment Kate's voice was drowned by Belinda bellowing for quiet. 'I'd just like to say a few words . . .'

Clara looked across at Ben, who was staring straight at her. She held his gaze for a moment, then slowly left the room in the direction of her office. She could only hope he would take the hint and follow.

He did. A few minutes later they were together again after two weeks apart. Ben knocked gently at the door and pushed it open, smiling softly at her in a way that chased any thoughts of Francine Lewis from her mind. He spoke with new-found authority. 'I've missed you. Come here.'

Pausing only to lock her door, Clara fell into his arms. They kissed and clutched each other with insatiable urgency. Whatever vague plan Clara had had of slipping back to Ben's cottage was chased from her mind. Ben swept the papers from her desk and pushed her back, leaned over her and unbuttoned her blouse to kiss the soft flesh beneath the black silk. Only then, after she had begged him seemingly a hundred times, did he push himself into her with reckless passion. She buried her face in his neck and clasped his shoulders, crying out in pleasure and relief at touching him again.

'Ssh . . .'

'I don't care. I can't help it.' She was heedless of caution. At that moment only Ben mattered.

So when, at the height of their lovemaking, there was a knock at the door, it was Ben who gently covered her mouth with his hand and stilled himself until, after an agonising delay, footsteps could be heard retreating. And then he came, and kissed her, and – when she had thought all passion was spent – slowly made love to her again.

Dr Gove's consulting room, in the mental-health unit of St Edward's Hospital, contained three low grey-upholstered chairs and one table on which was placed, somewhat ominously, a box of tissues. A large no-smoking sign dominated the far wall and the others were dotted with soothing pastoral landscapes. Sam would have approved. It was not actually called the mental-health unit. Annie's appointment card, for an assessment interview with Dr Gove, Consultant Psychiatrist, directed her to Hamilton House – presumably to avoid embarrassment when asking for directions on the large South London teaching-hospital campus.

Now she sat facing Dr Gove as he ran through a series of what he had described as standard questions, occasionally referring back to the notes from her emergency hospital admission. They covered her medical and family history, sketched in the bare dates and details of Hugo's death and her own suicide attempt in a way that seemed curiously matter-of-fact.

Dr Gove made a note and looked up at Annie, who was in a pair of jeans and a pale blue striped shirt borrowed from Victoria. His voice was low and measured. 'So, you're now thirty-two. And you have a daughter, Elizabeth, who's fourteen, currently on a school trip, due back in a couple of days,' he summarised.

'Yes,' she agreed.

'And you discharged yourself from hospital four days ago?' he asked casually.

She shifted awkwardly in her chair. 'Yes.'

'Against medical advice?'

Annie faltered, but he raised a wry smile and added, 'It's all right. I'd probably have done the same myself – I've seen the food there.'

Annie couldn't help but smile back. He really was terribly . . . normal, not at all threatening or intimidating, and he didn't appear to be trying to catch her out. She guessed that he was around forty, dressed in the kind of crumpled old suit that suggested he had little interest in clothes. He had the air of an academic, although the engraved silver wedding ring he wore hinted at an alternative outlook. She guessed that he read the *Guardian* and, for good measure, rode a bike to work.

He looked through some notes attached to the clipboard. 'The A and E registrar referred you to me as a priority appointment.' This did not seem to require an answer and he went on smoothly. 'You've been staying with your sister – Victoria, isn't it? – since then?'

It seemed a perfectly straightforward enquiry. 'Yes. She drove me here today. She's waiting downstairs.'

He looked up. 'Do you get on with her?'

It was a simple enough question, and ordinarily she would have said yes, of course she did. But there was something about Dr Gove that distracted her from the polite or obvious answer. As if in this room, in the quiet stillness, the simplest questions demanded a more searching and honest response.

'Yes,' she said hesitantly. 'I mean, Victoria's an easy person to get on with. She doesn't have ups and downs . . . whatever's going on in her life . . . Her husband's quite difficult,' she added. 'Somehow it doesn't seem to affect her, she just gets on with it . . .' Annie tailed off.

There was a pause. Dr Gove appeared to be thinking, twisting his pen between his fingers. 'Not someone you could confide in, then,' he concluded.

And Annie could only nod. And she knew then that Dr Gove instinctively understood that there had been no one in her family or among her friends to whom she had been able to reveal the true extent of the despair that had crept over her until she could struggle no more and had surrendered, broken and defeated.

Her voice emerged as if of its own accord, at times faltering, but at last speaking what she knew was the honest truth. 'I couldn't confide in her or anyone else. Sometimes I spoke to Tom – my brother-in-law. But I couldn't ever *really* say what I felt.' She stopped, knowing that at last, in this room, she could take the time to compose her words and that Dr Gove would not interrupt or make suggestions or tell her what to think. There was silence between them, and then she continued, 'I had to put on this brave face. That's what everyone wanted. They were always giving me advice or telling me it would get better. But it was as if they were speaking a different language from me. I knew I shouldn't be feeling this way but I couldn't help it. Everything I did was so exhausting. I remember one morning starting to change the bed, then trying to put a clean duvet cover on – only I felt so tired and I couldn't get it to fit properly . . . I just gave up and left it off and I still haven't put a clean one on.'

She looked up at him, wondering what on earth he thought of her, but he just nodded and didn't look remotely shocked or disapproving. And, seeing that, she went on, 'I had to try to hide the feelings and pretend that everything was all right. And sometimes, when I did let myself think about what had happened, I felt it was all so unfair. I mean, you're not supposed to feel that, are you? You're supposed to feel sad and – and mournful.' She looked at him for confirmation of her words.

Instead he said quietly, 'Are you saying you felt angry?'

'Yes. Yes, I did.' She was stunned by the force of her own voice. 'I still am. Angry that someone like Hugo who was such a good person, so kind and loving, so *young*, for God's sake, should die. He was only thirty-four,' she said bitterly, 'and awful, horrible people go on living until they're really old. And we were so happy together – we didn't do anything to hurt anyone – and one day it all got taken away. Why did it happen to us? Sometimes – I know this sounds awful, but sometimes I look at couples in the street and I think, Why did it have to happen to us and not to them?' Her voice cracked. 'Do you think that's a terrible thing to say?'

'I think it's a very natural reaction.' Dr Gove's voice was kind. 'I would be surprised if you didn't feel angry. But I also think you suppressed your anger . . .'

Annie dropped her head into her hands. 'I had to. Sometimes I even felt jealous of my own sisters. And I couldn't talk to my mother – she's so positive and no-nonsense. Until, in the end, I couldn't face anyone at all and I just hid myself away. It was such an effort pretending to be someone I wasn't, putting on this act. I couldn't do it any longer.'

There was a pause. At last he spoke. 'Annie, that sounds like a very lonely place to be.'

His words hit her with the force of their understanding and perceptiveness. And there was nothing more to say while she cried, and he let her, saying nothing, until when she could cry no more he spoke with a calmness that was more comforting than all the advice she had received in the past months. 'Annie, you're still in the early stages of recovering from a bereavement. And you're also suffering from serious reactive depression brought on by the death of your husband. And, I imagine, there are other things that have happened in your life, in the past, so that Hugo's death – devastating in itself – brought them to the surface to affect the way you feel now. But your depression can be treated . . .'

Annie raised her eyes. 'I don't see how.'

He nodded. 'No, you won't. That's the nature of depression. A kind of darkness, if you like, in which there appears to be no light or hope of change.'

Despite herself, Annie looked up.

He caught her gaze and held it. 'What I would suggest is a course of antidepressants . . .'

Annie went to object but he carried on speaking.

'. . . Just as a short-term measure to correct the chemical imbalance in the brain, raise the serotonin levels and allow you to participate in a course of therapy – if that's what you want. It's certainly what I would recommend. You could come back and see me on a weekly basis, initially for a three-month period, and we can review things at the end of that time.'

He paused. 'Annie, I've no doubt you intended to kill yourself. This wasn't a cry for help. But you're here now and if I didn't believe that you could be helped I wouldn't make false promises.' He caught the confusion on her face and gave a half-smile. 'You don't have to believe anything. I'd be concerned if you weren't sceptical. All I'm suggesting is that you need to be open-minded about the possibility of feeling different.' His voice slowed. 'Depression is an illness. It's not a character defect or a sign of weakness or a moral failing. You're not a bad person. You're not a bad mother. But you are sick.'

Annie looked at him. He had told her how she felt – weak, hopeless and ashamed of causing so much trouble. And especially ashamed that people would think she had tried to abandon her daughter – but, God, it hadn't been for want of loving her. In fact, it had almost been because she *did* love her, because somehow she had believed that Elizabeth would be better off without her.

But something in his words had struck her – *the possibility of feeling different* – and though he was a stranger to her she felt herself drawn to trust him. To want to believe what he said instead of disregarding it – as she had so much well-meaning advice.

He looked hard at her. 'Would you be prepared to make a commitment to a course of treatment? To give it a go?' he asked.

And in the room she heard herself speak, quiet but with a steady resolve: 'Yes. Yes, I would.'

Clara looked at her watch. She should have left ten minutes earlier – she had a sheet of first-year examination marks to collect and check from the law school office – but the temptation to linger, to prolong her departure proved, as ever, too strong. Especially on a day like this, in the warmth of Ben's garden, filled with the scent of honeysuckle, and the lure of a lazy August afternoon stretching ahead. And now that his exams had finished, and he had so much time on his hands, Ben seemed even more reluctant to see her leave. He reached across to pour her more coffee but she shook her head. 'I really have to go,' she said softly. 'Julian will be asking questions.'

Ben leaned towards her. 'Just tell him you're counselling some poor student. A third-year, suffering terribly with post-exam stress disorder.'

Clara smiled. But she was thinking of how her life had become divided: her normal life in one category and her life with Ben in the other. Two worlds that she must, at all costs, maintain separate from each other. But it was not a simple division. Now, as she sat with Ben, she felt herself torn between the desire to stay and the necessity to go. A necessity that was not, however, altogether unpleasant. For outside the walls of Ben's cottage lay the life in which she existed in so many roles beyond that of lover: as a wife and sister, tutor and colleague, each with their duties but also their rewards.

Ben got up. 'Before you go, I've got something to show you.'

She suppressed a twinge of anxiety. She really was late. But Ben had disappeared into the kitchen and she could hear the rustle of papers. He returned with a large white envelope. 'Hotel brochure,' he announced. 'It's all booked, of course, but I thought I'd get a copy so you can see where we're going.'

He pulled it out of the envelope and placed it before her, resting his arm on her shoulders while he flipped over the pages. 'This is the pool . . . and the gym. Here's a photograph of the beach with the boardwalk – we can go rollerblading, if you like.'

It looked beautiful – elegant and tranquil. The perfect escape for two lovers. Two lovers, Clara thought wistfully, who must escape to be together.

His voice was enthusiastic: 'And if you want we can drive to Bayeux to see the tapestry.'

His voice faded in her mind. She did not know why but, looking at the beautiful pictures, she felt uneasy. Which was ridiculous because she wanted so much to be with Ben, alone without deadlines, truly free to be together. But now that this longed-for holiday was no longer a dream, now that the dates were set and the bookings made, she was filled with a sensation of . . . fear. She struggled to make sense of it. The time for fear had surely been months ago – in that first kiss, when she could have stopped this, but all she had felt was passion and excitement. It was so much more serious now. And it was the questions that made her afraid. The questions that recurred in her mind, that could not be ignored for ever.

How long could they carry on like this? How long before she made a mistake, forgot her careful story, allowed the wrong name to slip from her lips? How much longer, in fact, could she continue to be a wife to Tom and a lover to Ben?

Annie lay on one of Victoria's expensively upholstered sun-loungers at the foot of the Marlow garden, listening to the lap of the river against the bank and sipping a glass of home-made lemonade. Sam Swinburne was sitting a few feet away, sketching the trees that stood across the river in Higginson Park. She could hear the sounds of lunch being prepared in the kitchen and, upstairs, Alex playing some convoluted war-game in which it was Emily's role to get shot and lie down dead. David had not yet arrived with Elizabeth. He was collecting her later that morning from Oxford where the cast had stayed for a few days after their triumph in *Romeo and Juliet*: they had won the prize for Best Production and Elizabeth the prize for best actress. Since any event was an excuse for Victoria to go shopping, she had dragged Annie into Marlow that morning to find a present for Elizabeth. When they couldn't decide between a portable CD player and a pair of Versace sunglasses, Victoria solved the problem by purchasing both. Then they had stopped for morning coffee at Burger's tearoom on the corner and Annie had surprised herself by eating two toasted teacakes and a chocolate slice.

Sam was mixing colours for the clear blue early-August sky. 'I always find sky tricky.' He sighed. 'Tend to make it a bit bright.'

'Try adding a touch of grey,' suggested Annie. 'I know it sounds odd but it can help . . .'

They talked inconsequentially while Sam experimented with different shades of blue and grey, and back to blue again. She was beginning to enjoy his company. He didn't ask any intrusive questions and – apart from nagging her about the Devon painting trip – didn't make any demands. She felt bad that she had been so irritated by him. He was kind and easy-going and they shared so many interests, from painting to reading and, of course, gardening. And since the Volvo had gone back, it had been jolly useful to run errands with him in his car.

'How long do you plan to stay here?' Sam asked absently, dabbing at a cloud.

'Victoria says as long as I like. But the Stimpsons are moving in this Saturday so we're going to take everything over to Albert Road, clean it up and see if I want to stay or come back.'

'Hmm. Good not to make any rush decisions. See how you feel when you get there.'

Annie was surprised by how sanguine she felt about it all. Maybe it was the antidepressants, or her session with Dr Gove. The events of the week before seemed to have receded – not in such a way that she had forgotten them but in the sense that she felt herself looking back with more detachment than she would have thought possible in such a short time. She could not have described how she felt now. Calm, perhaps.

The silence was broken by Victoria coming down the garden with another jug of lemonade. 'David's just phoned on his mobile. He'll be here any minute. And Tom rang earlier.'

They all laughed. Tom called at least three times a day, having put himself firmly in charge of the operation to nurse Annie back to health. He had given Victoria precise instructions from some old conference hand-outs he had saved on 'Suicide Among the Young'. He had warned her that one attempt was often followed by another and therefore that she must supervise Annie at all times and shield her from any bad news. So Victoria had not attempted to contact their mother – last heard of in Egypt 'immersed in the wonders of Pharaonic culture'. And Victoria did not mention the calls Tom was fielding from the Stimpsons, who wanted to know what time they could arrive on Saturday and if the house would have been professionally cleaned. Or the school-fees reminder that had arrived at the house, which Victoria had paid. Or a strange visit from a nervous-looking man in a red Jaguar, who had accosted Tom while he was watering the garden and asked if he was Annie's new boyfriend.

Most difficult of all, no one had yet felt able to broach the subject of Cal Doyle. Annie knew that she should write to him. Seeing him was unthinkable. One of the many advantages of staying in Marlow was that she could walk down the high street free of the danger of bumping into him. She could not imagine even being able to look him in the eye, let alone speak to him. But what could she write? What words could overcome the tangled feelings of shame and embarrassment at all the trouble she had caused, which were overlaid by an uncomfortable sense of indebtedness? It was difficult to know how to feel towards someone who had, albeit unwittingly, played a small part in driving her to despair only to intervene in the most dramatic circumstances to save her from herself.

They listened to the crunch of David's car pulling into the gravel driveway.

'You wait here,' said Sam tactfully, getting up from his easel. 'This needs to dry anyway. Victoria, can I give you a hand in the kitchen?'

As Sam and Victoria sauntered up the lawn to the house, Elizabeth appeared. Annie stayed where she was, determined to appear as normal as possible. It had been decided, in consultation with Tom, that Elizabeth need not be told anything, at least not until the move was out of the way and things had calmed down. Annie had her story well prepared, having gone over it a hundred times in her head. But as she watched Elizabeth walk towards her she saw immediately that something was wrong. 'Hey, why the worried face?' Annie smiled. 'I thought you'd still be basking in glory. Congratulations, love.'

Elizabeth leaned down to embrace her mother but there was a palpable stiffness in her cursory kiss and they broke apart too quickly. Annie decided to ignore it. 'Have a seat. I want to hear all about it.'

'It was nothing. Just an announcement by the judges and a bit of clapping, and I got this plastic trophy thing.'

'Well, where is it?'

'In my bag. I'll show you later.'

Elizabeth did not sit down. She went over to Sam's picture. Even in jeans and an old white shirt, the sleeves rolled up to show her dark brown arms, she looked beautiful.

'Were there any talent scouts there? Did you get approached?' Annie asked. Perhaps Elizabeth, knowing Annie's views on child models, was anxious about breaking the news of some modelling offer.

'No.' Then a pause. 'Did Sam do this?'

'Yes, it's very good, isn't it? The way he's caught the water . . .'

Elizabeth's tone was accusatory. 'I thought you liked him.'

'I do like him. He's a very kind man.'

'But not your type?'

Annie was bewildered. 'What do you mean?'

'I mean, you didn't let him stand in your way?'

'Stand in my way?'

'Mum! Do you have to repeat everything I say? It's really annoying.'

'Sorry. I just don't follow.'

'No. Neither do I.' Elizabeth was looking at her now and the hurt and accusations in her eyes were unmistakable. 'I mean, how could you? I know you miss Hugo but I just don't get it. *How could you?*'

This was the conversation Annie had hoped not to have. But there was no escape. She could hardly just get up and walk away. 'Look, Elizabeth, you have to understand how I felt. I was lonely, everything was just getting too much. At the time it seemed the right thing to do. But I can see now that it wasn't. And, most of all, you must realise that I don't intend it ever to happen again.'

Now Elizabeth spoke with withering scorn: 'So it was just a one-night stand, was it?' She rushed on, 'I suppose you're going to say it didn't mean anything. Have you any idea how humiliating this has been for me? It totally spoilt Oxford. They were all talking about it. Everyone knows.'

Annie was perplexed. 'One-night stand?'

'Yes. And with Martin Hollis. I mean, he's such a slime-ball!' Elizabeth was looking at her in disgust.

'What were they saying?'

'Mum, if you don't know I don't know who does. What do you want me to do? Spell it out?'

'Yes, I do. All of it.'

Elizabeth stood sullenly but Annie had decided to take control of the situation. 'Elizabeth, sit down and tell me everything that happened.'

Her daughter reluctantly obeyed but demonstrated her unwillingness by only perching on the edge of Sam's seat. She sighed deeply as if about to launch into an extremely tedious account, 'Martin Hollis came down one evening last week. We were all in the Oriel College bar. Sandra wasn't there. She was going through Jessica-Anne's lines. So . . . he came charging in, glared at me and asked for Sandra. I'd just won Best Actress so I thought it was going to be some family pow-wow about that. Anyway, we didn't see him again, thank God, and in the morning I went down to breakfast. And Jessica-Anne was sitting with Celine. Celine was looking really odd. But I sat down and then Jessica-Anne made some really bitchy comments about how I shouldn't have left you alone. Because . . .' Elizabeth stopped and looked out to the river.

'Go on,' prompted Annie.

'I don't want to say it.'

'Go on,' said Annie. 'It's fine. It really is. I've got a fair idea.'

Elizabeth sniffed. 'Because you were like a . . . bitch on heat.' And then her sullenness and aggression disappeared, and she was crying softly. 'Jessica-Anne said that you'd got her dad round to look at the washing machine. And you'd tried to persuade him to go to bed with you. And when he wouldn't you got really nasty and said you'd tell his wife.'

Annie passed her a tissue. 'Carry on.'

'I mean, I know it's been difficult and everything but I didn't think you would. And Martin Hollis is so horrible. He's always trying to come into the changing room and Sandra has to keep him out. That's why she does the wardrobe, I'm sure. Well, she does Jessica-Anne's costume – mine hasn't been cleaned for weeks. It really stinks.'

Annie laughed. Elizabeth looked up. 'How can you *laugh*, Mum?'

'Because it isn't true. Well, some of it is. Martin Hollis did come round. But I didn't make a pass at him. It was the other way round. And I threw him out. I promise you, nothing happened.'

Elizabeth looked up, wanting to believe her but evidently unsure. So Annie went on, slowly, 'Elizabeth. I swear on Hugo's memory, nothing happened. Martin Hollis is just a frightened, pathetic little man who was terrified I'd tell Sandra that he'd come on to me. So he got in first with his story. Besides,' Annie said, 'there's nothing wrong with the washing machine, is there?'

Elizabeth considered all of this. 'No ... but if nothing happened, what was all that stuff you said before – about being lonely? And *it seeming the right thing to do*. And it not happening again?'

Then, looking at her daughter, Annie decided that the time had come for honesty between them.

In the kitchen, Victoria was feeding Emily and Alex sandwiches and making David an omelette. They had not yet reached the halfway point of the school summer holidays, which appeared to her to start earlier and finish later every year. Already the children were driving her mad.

'Juice, Mummy,' called Emily.

'Can I have some?' said Alex.

'Can you hurry up, darling? I've got to be in Beaconsfield in an hour.'

Reaching for the orange juice from the refrigerator, Victoria resisted pointing out that a sandwich would have been quicker. Instead she said, 'This case is taking up a lot of your time, isn't it? It's only a drink-drive – isn't that something for someone more junior to take on?'

'It would be except the wife was three times over the limit. And since the husband's a judge it's going to hit the papers big time when those vultures get hold of it. Unfortunately, he's sent drunk drivers to prison before, usually with some pompous homily about learning the error of their ways. We've managed to hush it up so far but it'll come out at the trial. They want the best.' David spoke without a trace of irony.

Victoria finished pouring juice. 'I hope they're paying you well.

'Any ice-cream, Mum?' chimed Alex.

'Any chocolate?' said Emily.

'Will you wait, Emily?' David snapped, then turned to Victoria. 'Don't worry,' he said sourly, 'you won't starve. Anyway, the Dubai cheque is due in any day.'

In the last year David had developed a lucrative line in defending expatriates caught with drink or drugs – usually both – overseas. In truth, he didn't do much – he relied on local lawyers to prepare the papers and go into court – but he was a reassuringly expensive presence. In particular, he was good at holding the hand of an anxious mother, whispering a stream of soothing platitudes, while in the background the harassed father telephoned countless banks to raise a second mortgage on their suburban semi to pay the legal fees. He had done a drug bust in Dubai involving a twenty-three-year-old nurse, and a couple of cases of drug smuggling in southern Spain.

Victoria dished out ice-cream and passed David his omelette, which he ate standing up. He continued, 'Talking of which, I'm going to Paris next week. Drug bust in

Marseille. Some nineteen-year-old public schoolboy's got himself in a tangle with the mob there. When the police raided their warehouse, he was holding two kilos of pure cocaine.'

'So why isn't the case heard there?' asked Victoria.

David fixed her with an irritated glare. 'I'm sorry, darling. Next time I'll get the French prosecutors to organise things the way you think best. They've decided it's sufficiently serious to be dealt with in Paris.'

Alex had caught his father's tone and looked up. Victoria decided to end the conversation. 'When will you be going?'

'Monday. I should be back Thursday, Friday if it drags on. Can you pack a case? I'll fly Sunday evening.'

'Fine.' She heard the brittle edge to her voice but David did not appear to notice it or, if he did, ignored it. He put down his plate and picked up his keys and papers. 'Oh, and I'll need some casual gear. I think that'll go down better with the officials there – an English pinstripe suit might put their Froggie backs up.'

'I'm sure you're right,' Victoria said, without conviction but anxious to head off any further bickering.

'OK, I'm off.' He kissed Emily, patted Alex on the back and strode off into the hall. 'Oh, and, darling, could you make a start on the speech?'

'But the selection meeting is weeks away!'

'Yes, but Janet Williamson has been sighted – in our road, can you believe it? Having tea with Mrs Bolton, two silly old bags together. I want to be prepared.'

Victoria followed him into the hall He kissed her briefly and grabbed his bulging briefcase. 'See you later.'

He didn't specify when. Victoria watched as the front door slammed behind him – and calm descended on the house.

CHAPTER 8

Tom was feeling frazzled. He prided himself on being good under pressure, but the August heat was unbearable and he was running hither and thither at everyone's beck and call. There was the van to organise for Annie's move, not to mention all the other arrangements he was helping put in place, and that awful Stimpson woman had somehow got hold of his office telephone number and was calling him three times a day with an interminable number of enquiries she appeared to be reading off a list. Meanwhile Clara was hardly at home, pleading piles of exam papers still to mark and her meeting with that Tellium woman to organise. He approved of all that, of course, but it couldn't have come at a worse time.

Without Jan to help him with the filing – she came into the office most mornings now – he feared he would disappear altogether under a pile of internal memos, council policy documents and boxing gloves.

Now Brendan was screaming at the thirty or so teenagers who stood around in the baking-hot community hall. They included Sean and Ali, the unofficial leaders of the estate's two factions, both keen to lay claim to the new gym. This was their second session. During the first, Tom had watched from his office as a trail of puffing youths followed Brendan jogging briskly round the estate. For the second session in the improvised gym, Brendan was yelling at them to jump higher and stretch further as they progressed in ever-slower circles around the hall, interspersing his instructions with a steady flow of colourful insults.

Brendan stood next to two huge red punch-bags, which had been suspended from the ceiling, a pile of old boxing gloves to his side. When they were all breathless he called, 'OK. Take a breather. Don't waste your energy talking.'

There was little chance of that. Sean looked as though he was going to expire on the spot and Zareb had slumped to the floor. Only Ali looked capable of walking.

'Right. We're gonna start punching.'

A few managed an interested glance in his direction, but the rest were bending over in a desperate effort to breathe, not caring if their neighbour was brown or white.

'OK. You.' Brendan pointed at Vince. 'Come over here.'

The boy staggered to his feet. Brendan took his hands and reached down for a pair of gloves. 'Now, the secret is not to punch the bag.'

Vince looked blanker than normal.

'The secret,' Brendan continued, 'is to punch *through* the bag. Otherwise you stop the punch on impact. And if you do that you lose the force. So imagine you're punching to the other side of the bag. Here, like this.' With his bare fist, he slammed into the bag sending it spinning before catching it and steadying it expertly. 'Now. You try.'

Vince squared up to the bag. Tom watched with growing interest. He could begin to see the attraction in all this. Vince took his arm right back and punched with all his might. The bag hardly moved. A snigger ran round the hall as Vince swayed and narrowly avoided falling over.

'Try again. Punch through.'

The second punch set the bag swaying. Vince looked pleased with himself.

'Ah, well, not bad for a beginner,' observed Brendan.

Tom knew that Vince was hardly a beginner: he had served six months in a young offenders' institution for grievous bodily harm against his mother's boyfriend.

Now Brendan had them all lining up for a try. 'Hey, Tom, can you hold the other bag?'

Tom got up reluctantly and gripped the other punch-bag,

praying that at least everyone would get their aim correct. Sean was good and so was Ali. But Zareb was the best, virtually sending Tom sprawling to the floor. As he walked away, he spoke in a low aside to Sean: 'Tom nearly went flat on his back. Bit like your mum, eh? Isn't that how she used to earn her living? Flat on her back?'

Sean stepped towards him, but before he had a chance to defend Jan's doubtful honour Brendan's voice rang out: 'Right. Circuits.'

Zareb and Sean circled each other dangerously. But Brendan had come over. 'And that includes you two nancy-boys.'

They turned to glare at him, but they took off their gloves and the moment passed. Tom gave a sigh of relief and meandered towards the double doors, keen to get back to the safety of his office before he was called upon again to act as an unwilling human target.

The Saturday of the move had arrived and the contents of Annie's house had been carefully loaded into the white van Tom had hired. As Annie and he drove away from Railway Villas, Clara and Helen stood at the front door waving them off. Helen was holding a watering-can. It had been decided that the Stimpsons wouldn't know a hosta from a dandelion, and since Annie couldn't bear the thought of the garden dying, Helen was going to give it a last watering before they arrived. There was a hose-pipe ban so it would take an age, but Helen had told Annie in her most schoolmistressy tone that if Mrs Stimpson didn't know about gardens when she arrived then she would very quickly learn. Mrs Stimpson, thought Annie, was going to meet her match in her seemingly innocuous neighbour. In the meantime, Clara was going to dust and Hoover the house, and hand over the keys.

Tom put on the scratchy radio. As they drove through the tree-lined lanes of Cobham, Annie reflected that he was just the company she needed. He knew when not to talk. In any case, she had discussed the move with Dr Gove at their second appointment. It had lasted another two hours, but he had intimated that they would soon have to reduce this to one on account of limited NHS resources. No matter: by the end of the session she had slowly begun to see the move not as something to be dreaded but as just another of life's changes. Because what was life if not a series of changes? It would take time but she would turn 18 Albert Road into a home – once she had found a job, or maybe started curtain-making again. Ironically enough, Mrs Stimpson had asked Tom if he knew of anyone, and while Annie did not relish seeing the changes to Railway Villas, Mrs Stimpson's money was as good as anyone's – and she appeared to have plenty of it.

Twenty minutes later they arrived at Albert Road. Tom eased the van inexpertly into the drive, crunching the gears and narrowly avoiding another that was parked there. 'Well, that's good, isn't it?' he said cheerily. 'Neighbours doing building work. Come on, then.'

He jumped out and Annie followed him, hearing banging and drilling emanating from the house. Her heart sank: Railway Villas had been so quiet and this house was plainly filled with young couples who got builders round on a Saturday then spent Sunday doing noisy DIY. But she was moving in and that was that.

'Shouldn't we take some boxes with us, Tom?'

'No, no, no! First rule of project management: assess the task before you begin.'

He was halfway up the drive now. She smoothed down her navy shorts and dark red T-shirt. She had even ironed them, after finishing a huge pile of Elizabeth's washing yesterday. She would not retreat back to the sanctuary of Victoria's house: she had resolved to stay at Albert Road, whatever state it was in, leaving Elizabeth in Marlow where, it had to be admitted, she was getting increasingly – and vocally – bored, despite her resident worshipful audience of Alex and Emily.

They went around to the back of the house. Annie noticed the old maroon Dralon chair and the teak shelf unit dumped next to the rusty moped. Typical. The horrid son's idea of clearing the flat. Then she looked down the dank steps to her new home. There was no front door. Before she had time to consider why burglars would bother to steal a heap of tat, Tom called her.

She went gingerly down the steps in her blue plimsolls. A cloud of dust greeted her. And in the middle of it, holding a sledgehammer, she made out the unmistakable figure of Cal Doyle. 'Hey, there! Tom, Annie, we've been expecting you.'

We? Annie made out a cluster of men labouring in the kitchen. 'Where's the door?' she asked.

'Took it off,' said Cal. 'Don't worry, I've done it before,' he added, winking at her.

Annie felt a wave of embarrassment wash over her.

'Cal's just making a few . . . improvements for you,' explained Tom breezily. 'Getting the place a bit more comfortable.'

'Comfortable?' repeated Annie, staring aghast at the piles of dust, bricks and tools that lay all around the floor of the tiny flat.

'I'll show you,' said Cal Doyle. He put down the enormous sledgehammer and strode into the kitchen. Annie had little choice but to follow. 'This is Dave. He does the electrics. And this is Little Dave – Dave's son. He's helping out with the heavy work. And this is Joe. Best brickie this side of the Irish Sea.'

Dave, Little Dave and Joe looked at her and chorused hello.

'Now, we're just taking the kitchen out,' Cal continued.

'You're taking it out?'

'Yep. So we can get the new one in.'

'But . . . there isn't a new one.'

'Ah, well, that's where we've had a bit of luck. Some fussy woman who's just moved into one of my new houses – at The Chapters – doesn't like the kitchen we put in. Says it's too *cream*. Well, I don't get it – cream's cream to me. Anyway, she wants it out so she can put some German job in. All stainless steel – can't see it'll suit myself. We've gone for the period look there. But it's not my place to argue. Not with the ladies, anyway. She wanted it out – so we ripped it out. She even tipped me a tenner for my trouble.'

Annie started to speak but Cal was in full flight now: 'So, the kitchen will go in this corner. Not that you'll get it all in – the kitchens at The Chapters are the size of rugby pitches, the Americans like them big, you see – but we'll take the best units and fit them. And you'll have more room in the conservatory through the French windows.

'But there aren't any French—'

'There will be soon. Once we've finished knocking through.' As if on cue, Little Dave began smashing his way through the back door, sending bricks tumbling to the floor. 'Best leave him to it. Now, in the bedroom . . .' Cal had disappeared down the hallway.

Annie stared in disbelief at Tom. 'Did you know about all this?'

'Yes.' Tom was looking insufferably pleased with himself. He took Annie's arm and propelled her into the bedroom, where Cal was waving at the walls.

'Now, this room's a wee bit small, but there's no answer to that.' He banged on the far wall. 'This wall could be rotten, dangerous. Might fall down at any minute on some kiddie.'

The wall looked perfectly sound to Annie but there was no chance to interrupt.

'So we'll have to take it down to be on the safe side. And when Joe rebuilds it, the wall will be a bit further out. About four feet.'

'*Four feet!* Don't you need planning permission for that?' exclaimed Annie.

Cal paused. 'Well, if you want to get technical about it, but no one's ever noticed when I've done it before. Don't worry,' he finished heartily, 'I'll deal with any busybodies.'

Annie had no doubt that he would. But before she had a chance to ask any more questions he had charged off to the bathroom. 'Now, we'll just put a white unit in here. Simple but classy.'

'Did it fall off the back of a lorry?' enquired Annie.

'No, the back of a boat. It's Italian. I've got a mate down the docks sells me anything that's got a bit chipped.'

Tom laughed. 'Tell Annie about the conservatory.'

'Ah, yes. Not a De Longden, I'm afraid, but I figured you wouldn't mind that. It's UPVC. Now, I know some people get all la-di-da about plastic but it means there's no maintenance. And you don't want to be wasting your time painting it every year. The conservatory's going to lead off the kitchen so you can use it for entertaining.'

'But . . .' stammered Annie, wondering how she was going to pay for all this.

'Don't worry. You don't need planning permission for a conservatory,' Cal assured her.

By now all efforts at further conversation were drowned by the cacophony of crashing and drilling from the kitchen, which was also sending clouds of dust into the living room.

'Let's go outside.'

They stood in the bright sunlight. Cal lit a cigarette and offered Annie one. She would have liked to refuse but she needed one.

'Good girl. You don't want to be breathing in all that dust.'

Annie was struggling to collect her thoughts, let alone call to mind any suitable words. Cal passed her a cigarette and cupped a lighter for her in his dusty hands.

'When can I move in?' was all she could think to ask. 'I mean, all my stuff's in the van. Shall we come back this afternoon?'

Cal looked askance. 'Oh, no. You don't want to be doing that. You see, the damp course is going in this afternoon and the chemicals from that will give you an awful bad headache.'

'It's all taken care of,' interrupted Tom. 'Cal's said you can stay at his house.' A look of horror must have passed across her face because Tom added quickly, 'Well, not exactly *his* house. His show house in The Chapters. There are six of them. Cal took me round, and very nice it is, I must say. He's just had an offer for the show house but the people aren't moving in for a couple of months. They're coming from California. So, you see, you and Elizabeth can stay there.'

'No,' said Annie firmly. 'We can't. It's – it's out of the question.'

Cal shrugged. 'The house is standing empty. It's no trouble to me.' Sensing that Annie had more to say he moved away tactfully to inspect a portion of the basement wall.

Annie turned to Tom. 'I can't possibly stay in his house!' she hissed. 'I can go back to Marlow. We'll be perfectly all right there.' She glanced round to check that Cal was out of earshot. 'Anyway, why is he doing all this . . . for me? And why is he doing it himself? I thought he had armies of people to do everything.'

'He has,' said Tom, without irony. 'I think he's just getting them started.' He paused. 'It's a long story. I'll tell you later. But I think there are two ways of looking at it. The first is that he feels pretty bad about the whole thing. He told me he had no idea about the loan or Barbara's motives or that you had been forced into selling Railway Villas. He thinks it's a bad business – made worse because you've ended up here,' Tom gestured to the unappealing exterior of Albert Road, 'which he also had a hand in. He told me it was one of the first conversions he did, years ago, when money was tight, and it was obvious he cut all the corners he could.'

Tom coughed as another wave of dust drifted from the basement. 'The second interpretation is that if any of this got out it would seriously compromise his image. People buy his big Surrey houses because Cal's worked hard in the last few years to make a good name for himself for quality work. People know that if they buy one of his houses they won't have cracks appearing in the walls six months later or half the garden disappearing because their house was built on some old rubbish dump. He's protecting his reputation.'

'He's always in the papers,' observed Annie thoughtfully.

'It's all a front for publicity. Keeping his name in the public eye – and his houses. Which is all the more reason why he doesn't want any of this to get out. "Millionaire Builder's Dodgy Dealings" isn't the sort of headline he's after. It only takes one disgruntled employee to go to the tabloids. But this way, sorting you out with the flat and giving you somewhere to stay in the meantime, he can distance himself from Barbara's shenanigans. It's his business reputation we're talking about, and this is a small price to pay for it.' Tom adopted his most persuasive tone: 'But don't think about him, think about *you* – and Elizabeth. Accepting Cal's offer would mean you'll be close to Albert Road – and Elizabeth would be near her friends.'

Annie nodded. She couldn't help but see the advantage in that. She thought of Elizabeth, complaining about how boring Marlow was – how there was nothing to do, no one to talk to and how all her friends back home were having the most fantastic, interesting, brilliant summer without her . . .

'And you would be near to us,' Tom continued, 'and the hospital for your appointments.'

Annie felt herself weaken. Staying in Marlow was easy – and Victoria had put so much effort into keeping her and Elizabeth entertained – but at the end of the day she was still a guest in someone else's house. It would be nice to have a bath without worrying that she was taking all the hot water, or cook a meal for herself – and, much though she loved them, it would be nice to have some peace and quiet away from the incessant bickering of Alex and Emily.

Cal wandered over. He seemed to read the indecision on

her face. 'No need to make a decision about the house right now. Let me know if you want it. The offer's open.' Before she could reply he had stubbed out his cigarette and was saying, 'Now, I need to be getting on. Can't stand around chatting all day. And I haven't eaten.' He pulled out a wad of grubby notes. 'Could you just be an angel and pop down the greasy spoon for us? It's on the corner. Eight bacon butties and four teas. Two sugars. Oh, and any Mars bars if they've got them.' With that he disappeared down the steps again.

Annie looked at Tom with amazement and exasperation in equal measure. 'Tom, I just don't know about all of this. And I'd like to know *exactly* what's been going on.'

'Fine,' said Tom, in his most professionally reassuring tone. 'Let's walk down to the café. Wouldn't mind a bacon sandwich myself.'

And as they stood watching fatty bacon being slapped between thick slices of white bread, Tom continued his explanation. 'You see, as I was explaining before, it's all about project management. We did that at the leisure conference I went to. It was called "Planning for Change", very good speaker, some sort of management consultant—'

'Yes, all right,' said Annie. 'I get the picture.'

'So, you see, project management is all about bringing together resources. Identifying what you have at your disposal, then organising them according to your needs.'

'Tom, how am I going to pay for all this?'

'You don't have to.'

'Cal Doyle works for free?'

'Not normally, I grant you, but this isn't "normally".'

God, would Tom never get to the point? 'I still don't see how all this has happened. I mean, how did he find out about all of this – Barbara and everything?' Annie sounded exasperated.

'Oh, Cal and I got talking after dinner at your place.'

'My place?'

'Yes, after your . . . *suicide attempt*.' Tom prided himself, Annie knew, on not shying away from the uncomfortable truth. 'And I explained about Hugo's death and Barbara de Longden. But he didn't know about the loan. He suspected, of course – Angus Campbell had filled him in on quite a bit of the story after that row they had in the high street. That's all OK now, by the way. Angus is staying on to run the business for Cal.'

'Good,' said Annie impatiently.

'Rather neat, isn't it? But, if you'll let me get to the point. As I said, I think Cal feels rather bad about it all and this is his way of putting it right. Not that he's a pushover. He's not going to give you the money. But then, strictly speaking, he doesn't owe it to you. That's Babs's responsibility.'

'Babs?'

'That's what Cal calls Barbara de Longden. We've all got into the habit now.'

'*All*? Well, who else does he know, for goodness' sake?'

Tom thought for a moment, 'Me. Clara. Victoria and David, of course – David's keen to get to know him better. Helen, who thinks he's a real gentleman. And Sam, of course.'

Annie slumped against the counter.

'Yes,' continued Tom, 'we all got to know him over dinner, when you were asleep upstairs. Then it turned out that he knew Brendan so I invited him down for the first training session. He was damned useful, put up the punch-bags – which was a stroke of luck because the council works department had said they couldn't do it for three weeks. Then we went for a drink. That's when we fitted the pieces together about Martin Hollis – your mystery caller in the red Jag.'

Annie wasn't listening. Cal Doyle, whom she had hoped fervently never to see again, now appeared to know her entire familly and be intimately involved in the running of their lives. At least he couldn't meet her mother: no one knew where she was.

'He's amazing. Much more than just a builder. He knows everyone, he's got contacts all over the place. And he's still pretty handy with his fists. Did a few demo punches with Brendan.'

'But . . . has he said anything about me?'

'No. He made a few polite enquiries, you know the sort of thing, but that's all.'

By now they had almost reached Albert Road. Annie stopped. 'Tom, I can't face him. Even if I did accept his offer of the house . . . You have no idea how embarrassing this whole thing is. It's not that I'm not grateful . . . but I was *sick* over him,' she wailed.

'Well, isn't that all the more reason to speak to him? Show him you're quite normal underneath.' Tom grinned at her. 'Even quite likeable. Look, you don't have to come in but it seems to me that you're the one with the problem about all this, not him. Judging from a few of the stories he's told me, he's seen a lot worse than you throwing up. And he's doing the flat. You can't avoid him for ever.'

Annie knew Tom was right – that she should accept Cal's offer and just feel glad that something was going well at last. But it was always easier to dole out sensible advice then to follow it. She had never found it easy to ask for help, preferring to struggle on alone . . . but look where her stubborn pride had led her. The more she thought about it, the more self-defeating it seemed not to accept Cal's offer. She knew exactly what Elizabeth would say: Elizabeth would go mad if she found out that Annie had turned down the chance to live in a Cal Doyle house just round the corner from all her friends. And they could hardly stay at Victoria's for ever: judging by the work Cal was doing it looked as if several more weeks as house guests would stretch ahead of them. As for Cal, she knew instinctively that he was not the sort of person to make her feel beholden to him, that he would do what he had offered, no more and no less, and when it was all finished he would move on to his next deal or project with no backward glances.

When Tom stopped and looked round at her, she took the bulging bag of sandwiches and chocolate from his outstretched hand. 'I'll wait in the van,' he said.

She set off round the path and down the steps, hearing the noise long before she entered the living room. When she did, Cal was swinging the sledgehammer at the wall, which shuddered, then crumpled, thin chips of plaster flying through the air. When he saw her he put it down.

She had to say something now. Get it out of the way. But faced with him, and the memories of the last time they had been alone together, it was difficult to sound coherent. 'Your sandwiches,' she stuttered, 'and the change.' She put down the notes on what remained of the mantelpiece and turned to face him. Her voice echoed round the small, bare room. 'Look, about the house . . . The Chapters . . . About your offer . . . If it wouldn't be causing you any trouble . . .'

He was absently picking slivers of plaster off what remained of the wall but his voice, cutting in, was decisive: 'Good. I'll get the keys to Tom. You can take it from there.'

'Thanks. Look . . . I just want to say . . .'

He looked at her. 'Annie, there's nothing to say. Nothing at all. There're only two questions I need to ask you.'

He had caught her by surprise, the half-formed speech in her mind left unsaid. They stood alone in the room, faint sounds of drilling emanating from the back of the flat.

'Two questions,' she repeated. 'All right. Go ahead.'

He spoke deliberately but with an underlying seriousness in his voice that she had not detected before. 'The first, most important question, is are you OK?' He was looking at her directly now, his dark brown eyes holding her gaze.

'Yes. Thank you. I'm going to be fine.'

There was the slightest pause. The awkwardness between them seemed to have passed. But she wondered what was to follow.

'Well, that's all right, then. The second question is, what

colour tiles do you want in the kitchen? I'll leave some samples here. Pop back in the week and let me know.' He smiled at her and picked up the paper bag. 'Now, if you'll excuse me, builders' break.' And with nothing more to say, he turned his back on her and ambled into the kitchen.

Clara sat in the modest lounge of Laura Turner's three-bedroom detached home, which was situated in the middle of a sprawling estate of identical houses. She looked around the lounge, which was spotlessly clean and all but filled by a floral three-piece suite. From the stripes on the pink carpet, Clara could see that she had been Hoovering before her guest's arrival. Ornaments – coloured glass animals and miniature porcelain baskets of flowers – were neatly spaced around photographs of a young boy. On the window-sill stood a collection of china thimbles, and behind them pristine net curtains masked the neatly tended patch of lawn. Laura bustled in with a tray. She had clearly brought out her best china, white with a pale blue swirling pattern of roses and ribbons. A paper doily covered a plate of Rich Tea biscuits. She pulled out a nest of occasional tables, put out coasters and poured the tea. Laura Turner, like her house, was small and neat. 'I hope you didn't have any trouble finding us. People get lost on this estate. And there's no one to ask for directions – they're all out at work during the day.'

A lonely place to live, thought Clara. She refused a biscuit. She had lost a stone now, since she had started sleeping with Ben, and she wanted to lose still more.

'Jamie's asleep,' Laura went on.

Clara was surprised. It was three o'clock in the afternoon.

'He often sleeps after lunch.' Laura settled herself in an armchair. 'It tires him. That's when I get on with the housework. And he doesn't sleep well at night – usually wakes up between three and five and I can't get him back to sleep.'

'So what's his routine?' asked Clara.

'Oh, it varies. He's usually awake at six. Then I get him up, give him his breakfast – that takes till about eight – and get him dressed. Then we look at his books or watch a video. The time flies and then it's lunch. Sometimes my mother comes over, but it depends on the buses. She doesn't drive.'

'I see. And school?'

'Well, we're trying, but I've only been offered one and that's residential. It's too far to drive every day. I think he's too young to go off yet – he's only six. Of course, I could move. I have thought about that.'

Clara was seeking to make sense of Laura's situation. She remembered Tom saying that clients often assumed you knew far more about their circumstances than you did. How could she find out more without appearing to pry? 'And do you get any help? With Jamie.'

'I have a carer twice a week. It used to be five times but that got cut down when he was five. Which is silly because I need more help now. The carer's supposed to come in and help me bathe him – but he needs a bath every day. He gets so messy when he's eating. Of course he doesn't feed himself, but even so it goes everywhere. He gets frustrated, it's not his fault. And quite often he needs, well, you know, a wash during the day. Down below.'

'I see,' said Clara, struggling to take it all in. 'Do you ever get a break? A holiday?'

'There's the respite care centre. They're very good and the staff love him. But they can only offer us one week a year – they're a charity.' She laughed hollowly. 'Last year we went to Dorset. That's when my husband told me he was leaving.'

What could Clara say? Jamie was unable to walk, feed himself or use the toilet. He couldn't read, maybe he couldn't speak – and he was six. How could this woman cope with a child who would never grow up? Clara got irritated with Emily after a few hours – how much worse was it to live with that every day and know that the situation would never improve? But then, might it improve in some small way?

Laura was continuing: 'You see, the worst thing is the lifting. I'm only five foot two. It was easier with my husband around . . .'

'Does he visit?'

'About once a month. He's got a girlfriend now. He gives me money, but I daresay that'll drop off once she has the baby.' Curiously, her voice softened. 'I don't blame him. He always found it harder than me. I have a mother's love, I suppose. He did try. But he put so much faith in the legal case – he got really involved because he was so angry about what happened to Jamie. When it all went wrong it was the final straw. Of course we shouldn't have . . . but we'd thought about how we could spend the money. All for Jamie, of course. We would have got a bungalow so he could be on the ground floor and we could get the wheelchair everywhere. You can't get it through the doors here.'

'But for now you have to stay put?'

'It's easier. My mother can get here. She's offered to move in but I don't think I could take that.'

'I know the feeling,' said Clara. 'Mothers tend to take over, don't they?'

'I knew you'd understand. I figure we're happier on our own.'

'But . . . well, I want to be very cautious. I can't promise you anything.'

Laura's face told Clara that she was beyond disappointment.

'But I have asked around. And you could start a new legal case against Tellium, a different one, based on the interaction between Tellium and Vartren. And you might want to think about approaching it differently, with one solicitor representing everyone. It's called a class action. It saves costs and makes the paperwork easier.'

Laura thought for a while. 'I don't know. TAG is pretty disorganised at the moment.'

Clara felt a rush of enthusiasm. 'Well, how about holding a meeting to relaunch the group? Then you could discuss the way forward. And I could recommend a solicitor – we were at Oxford together and he's very good.'

'Oxford?' Laura seemed electrified. 'And he'd take it on?'

'I've spoken to him and he's interested. If you give me a date when you could organise a meeting, I'll liaise with him.'

'That's what we've always lacked, someone to co-ordinate everything.'

Clara knew that Laura was edging her towards this unwanted role. She had only come reluctantly knowing that she had to have something to report to Julian when she saw him later that week. But before she had a chance to speak, a muffled sound came from upstairs.

'Jamie,' said Laura. 'Come and meet him.'

There was no way out. Childless and never maternal, Clara reluctantly followed Laura up the stairs.

'Mind the stairlift. It's at the top. Just ease your way round it. I don't know how I'd manage without it – the council gave me a grant.'

Laura led the way towards the increasingly urgent sound of crying. There were gurgles, too, and sounds that might have been words but somehow weren't quite clear enough. Clara knew then that Jamie could not talk. She wanted more than anything to avoid this meeting. She had no idea what to say to him and even less what to do. Tom would have known exactly how to handle it. But Tom wasn't here and she had no choice.

When she walked into Jamie's bedroom, where the balloon-patterned curtains were closed against the afternoon sun, she hesitatingly looked down at a small, handsome boy, his dark blond hair falling over his face. The room was like any other child's, with heaps of cuddly toys and a mobile hanging from the light-fitting – but this child was not like any other. She could see, as she looked closer, that he wasn't ... *normal*. God, what an awful word to come to mind. She felt guilty and ashamed. She forced a smile at him, feeling fake and insincere, and he looked at her with a kind of puzzled blankness, seeing her but unable to comprehend who she was. That was it, the blankness, the outwards sign that this brain-damaged boy would never communicate fully with the outside world. But he did communicate with Laura – those sounds, which were so nearly words, and which Laura understood perfectly: 'That's right. We've got a visitor. A lady . . .'

She was unhinging the rails that were fitted to either side of the bed. 'To stop Jamie falling out,' she explained. Then she reached for a pair of clean shorts and a spotless white T-shirt that lay ready on the chest of drawers. She began manipulating Jamie into the clothes, while he lay motionless on his back. 'You have to be organised, you see, when you're on your own. You can't leave him while you rush off and find something in case he hurts himself.'

She spoke softly to Jamie: 'Come on, love, let's get you downstairs. Have a drink. Then we can sit in the garden. Look at your books.' She turned to Clara. 'Could you bring that book on the bedside table there?'

Clara picked it up. The cover said it was suitable for children of between eighteen months and three. She opened it. The story seemed to be about a train's journey through a town, and all the people and animals it collected on the way. There were pull-up flaps and you could lift them up to see inside the carriages. Tom's words from all those weeks ago came back to her: 'You are involved . . . because of what you know.' Clara watched Laura pull her son to a sitting position and then, incredibly, pick him up and carry him to the stairlift. At that moment, she knew she had to help her.

Annie lay in the sunken bath and pushed the lever of the hot tap to send hot water gushing into it. From Tom's florid description of The Chapters during their drive over from Albert Road she had expected gold taps and had been half disappointed to see that these were chrome. But on closer inspection they turned out to be German chrome, with elegant operating-theatre-style levers that sent softened water cascading out of the elegant arched nozzle. Cal Doyle clearly built to suit sophisticated tastes – and enormous budgets. After three days she had still not worked out how anyone would use all the rooms in this house. Seven bedrooms, seven bathrooms, two downstairs cloakrooms. Did these people spend an inordinate amount of time reading on the loo? Then there were the third-floor games room, the gym and the staff flat above the three garages – where the entire contents of Railway Villas was more than comfortably stored. Not to mention the kitchen, the dining room, the conservatory, the pair of ground-floor offices and the family room – the latter big enough to house three generations. Oh, and the sauna.

She could just hear muffled music from Elizabeth's CD player in her bedroom. Elizabeth adored the house and more than once had voiced the hope that the work at Albert Road would take an extremely long time indeed so that they could remain in luxury at The Chapters for as long as possible. She had not met Cal. True to his word, he had left them to it. But there had been plenty of other visitors: Clara and Tom, of course, Victoria – though not David, who was working – Sam and Helen. All had been unable to resist asking for a guided tour.

Annie had chosen a small bedroom on the garden side of the house with comparatively simple white décor. All the bathrooms were done in different styles but she liked this one best for its simple white marble tiles and shelves. One of the others had an entirely mirrored wall and that was more exposure to her reflection than Annie welcomed. Predictably, Elizabeth had bagged the master bedroom and its opulent bathroom.

Annie pressed one of the three chrome buttons to the side

of the bath and sent hundreds of little bubbles welling around her. The other two, she had discovered, sent up hard or soft jets of water to provide an underwater massage. The show house had been more than furnished: not a detail had been missed, up to the expensive L'Occitane bath oil she had decanted guiltily, using only a few drops, and the lush white towels that lay over the heated towel rail.

All in all it was like staying in a luxurious hotel, a pleasant interlude but impossible to think of living like this all the time. For a start, how did one manage to keep it all clean, or work out how to use half of the appliances? Tom and Clara had come over on the first night with takeaway pizza and a bottle of wine, which they had consumed at the eight-seater table in the vast limed-oak kitchen. Tom had been like a schoolboy, deafening them with the integral sound system as he worked his way through the show house's collection of CDs, mainly popular classical hits but at the bottom of the pile he'd dug out some Van Morrison. They hadn't figured out the dishwasher, which appeared to rely on some complicated electronic coding, so they had washed up – until Tom had sent a teaspoon spinning into the waste disposal unit. There had been an agonising moment when its quiet Swiss hum was jolted into an ominous banging but Clara found the master switch, cut the power off and fished out the mangled spoon with a pair of barbecue tongs. They had found the barbecue built into a side wall alongside a brick-cobbled terrace, which looked out over a landscaped garden obviously designed, unlike the house, to be low-maintenance.

Tom had declared that you needed an induction course before moving in – otherwise you had no hope of mastering the ice-maker, maintaining the water-softener or even switching on the zillion-programme washing machine. All in all, he had concluded, the house was perfect for a lady rocket-scientist with a very large family and a passion for holding parties.

Annie had discussed houses with Dr Gove at this week's session. It had again lasted two hours but he had said they would reduce to one when he came back from holiday. The room had been hot and he had sat in his shirtsleeves, his tie loosened. She had wondered where he would go and whether he had children. It wasn't that she was interested in him – he was too academic to excite such feelings, and his appearance was rather drab – but it seemed unfair that he knew so much about her and she was allowed to know nothing about him. But, then, they weren't there to discuss Dr Gove's travel plans.

'So, you moved house this week?' he asked.

'Yes – well, almost. It turns out there's some building work to be done. Tom organised it. I'm staying somewhere else until the work's finished.'

Anyone else would have asked about the building work. But by now she was getting used to the nature of Dr Gove's questions so the next was not a surprise: 'And how did that feel, Tom organising the work for you?'

She allowed herself time to think. 'To begin with I was uncomfortable,' she said eventually. 'Guilty, really. As though I should be doing it myself. And it's all a bit complicated because the builder who's doing the work is Cal Doyle, the man who found me . . .'

Dr Gove did not look in the least surprised. He never did. She had come to the conclusion that he was utterly unshockable – one of the reasons why he was so easy to talk to. That and the fact that he never interrupted.

'He's lent me a house until the work's done.'

'He's lent you a house?' repeated Dr Gove, drily.

Annie laughed. 'Yes. I know. It sounds rather grand, doesn't it? But he's a builder – well, a property developer, really – and it's a show house that's standing empty. It's just business to him – Tom thinks he doesn't want any bad publicity. And eventually I thought, Why not? Why struggle on my own when someone's offering to help me?'

Dr Gove nodded. 'I get the impression that accepting

help has always been a problem for you. That you associate independence with strength. Whereas accepting help arouses feelings of guilt, perhaps weakness. But it strikes me that there are a great many people who love you and want to help you. Even this Cal Doyle – whatever his motivation – is offering assistance that is clearly very useful. I wonder how it would *feel* just to sit back and take that help?'

Her voice slowed. 'I don't know. All I know is that I'm tired of struggling. Tired of pretending to be someone I'm not.' She looked up. 'I want to move forward.'

And that was the cue for Dr Gove to suggest gently that perhaps they should set some targets. Nothing too demanding, he had explained, just some things for her to do before their next session. What did she think would be possible? She had suggested two things: first, to accept Sam's invitation to join his painting trip, and second, to approach Cobham's two interior-design shops to see if they needed a curtain-maker. Dr Gove had suggested a third: choosing the tiles for Albert Road.

When she left the hospital, she had gone straight home to telephone Sam, then made appointments to go into Cobham Interiors and A Place Like Home later that week. All that remained was to go to Albert Road and look at Cal Doyle's sample tiles.

Julian Urquhart had popped out of his office to explain to Clara that he was running a little behind schedule; would she mind waiting in the law-school entrance lobby for him? He would be about twenty minutes. She settled down on one of the sagging vinyl chairs. The law school was deserted. All the students were away for the holidays and most of the staff had disappeared too. She had finished her exam marking, seen Ben every afternoon and prepared an impressive account of events on the Tellium front for her meeting with Julian. She had been surprised to find that she felt genuinely excited about it. James Agnew, who had been one of her most brilliant Oxford contemporaries, had said he was interested in the case, and Laura Turner was currently setting up a meeting with what remained of her committee. Clara had also found time to write another article, this time for the *Medical Law Journal*, which would be a more detailed, scholarly reworking of her piece for the *Sunday Times*. And she'd done a first draft of Belinda's reference, which was proving as difficult to word as she had feared.

Cameron Hawes emerged from the staff-room clutching a pile of exam scripts and a cup of coffee. 'I'll need it just to stay awake. First-year contract law. God knows what a hash they've made of this. Apparently half of them left the exams in floods of tears.' He settled himself next to Clara. 'Have you finished your little bundles, Clara?'

'All done. Wrapped and dispatched to the external examiner for a second marking.'

'A paragon in our midst. How long can it be until you're canonised – St Clara of the Library?' He put down his coffee. 'Waiting for anything special? Or just soaking up the scenery?' He waved at the glass-fronted cabinet displaying examination regulations and the student noticeboard now plastered with advertisements for secondhand textbooks.

'Julian. He wants an update on Tellium.'

'*Marvellous*,' impersonated Cameron.

'But he's running late, should be with us in about ten minutes.'

'Good . . . You see, there's something I've been meaning to mention to you.'

'Sounds mysterious.'

Cameron put down his bundle of exam scripts and moved closer to her. 'Hmm. Well, you'll have to tell me that. You see, I think you ought to know about a – a rumour that's doing the rounds.'

'Another!'

'Afraid so. But this one's about you.'

Of course, she guessed immediately. But that simply couldn't be possible.

Cameron hesitated. 'Ben Ford.' He looked at her closely. 'Some of the students seem to have got it into their heads that you know him really rather well.'

She faltered and recovered. 'Cameron, obviously I know him. I interviewed him for his place here. And I've taught him every year – he's just done my medical-law course. And he's been round to dinner – with Tom – but so have plenty of the others.'

Cameron was now regarding her with an unmistakably questioning look in his eye. 'You've never been round to his place?'

'Cameron! What sort of a question is that?'

'Clara, we've known each other a long time and you've often stood up for me. I'm trying to help.'

Unsure of what to say she played for time. 'What exactly have they been saying? And how do you know all this?'

'I know because I keep my ear to the ground. And my eyes open. Miss Moneypenny seems to have transformed herself into a Bond girl lately ... But more particularly because I hung around after the post-exam party. Your disappearance – and Ben fleeing the scene five minutes later – didn't go unnoticed. The students were clucking like a bunch of hens.'

'That means nothing.'

'True. But I gather that's not the real problem. It's your car that presents the difficulty. It's been seen outside Ben's cottage.'

'Who by?'

'Francine Lewis. In one of those awkward little coincidences that life throws up, it turns out that her brother lives in number six, four doors down from Ben. And your car is pretty conspicuous.'

Bloody Tom! Why couldn't she drive a Ford Fiesta like every other woman lecturer? But no, Tom had to save the planet – and the Morris Minor – from extinction. 'Oh,

God.' She sat back. She had never really believed that anything like this could happen. She had been so careful, so discreet. She had thought of everything, or so she had told herself. They had a life together that was totally private – *secret* – from the outside world. Only yesterday they had been planning their trip to Deauville, where they would emerge from behind closed doors and walk hand in hand for the first time ever.

Cameron leaned towards her. 'Look, keep your head. It's only a rumour. No one can prove anything as long as you refuse to discuss it. I've done a lot of work like this—'

'In *taxation*?'

'No. I don't broadcast it but I do an advice surgery for gay men in London, every Thursday night. We hire a room above a gay pub in Earl's Court. We get a lot of this type of thing from our clients – rumours at work, nasty innuendos about their sexuality. People getting hauled in to see the boss and quizzed about whether they've got HIV. And in that situation you've got two choices. Either to be honest and open about your situation and fight any reaction it provokes, or to say nothing. No one has the right to pry into your private life so long as it doesn't affect your work.'

'But, Cameron, this is more complicated. There are university policies about not having relationships with students.'

'Clara, they can write all the policies they want but it won't stop people falling in love or even just having a shag. The problem is if it affects the professional relationship between the lecturer and the student. Or if the lecturer is using their position of authority to extract sexual favours. But Ben's hardly some starstruck eighteen-year-old. And, forgive me for saying it, I don't see you as a *femme fatale* leading him on. Policies are there to protect vulnerable students – but they can't alter human nature.'

Cameron took a swig of coffee and checked that the lobby was still deserted, 'More importantly, I know you wouldn't have given him any favourable treatment in the exam.'

'If anything I marked him down. I recognised his handwriting.'

'Fine. And there's a second mark anyway. If they don't tally there can be a third. I assume you didn't show him the exam paper in advance?'

Clara gave a faint laugh. 'No. Rest assured.'

'My friendly advice to you, then, is to say nothing. Don't answer any questions or be drawn on any aspect of it. With a bit of luck it'll all die down now that they've left for the vacation.'

'Cameron, I really—'

He got up, picked up his coffee and his papers. 'Don't mention it. And one good thing will come out of this – you won't get the Miss Moneypenny Award next year.' He meandered off to his offce.

Before she had a second to collect her thoughts, Julian's door opened. 'Clara, so sorry. Rather tricky telephone call. Some student who wants to get out of Roman law.'

Clara followed him into his immaculately tidy office. All the students wanted to get out of Roman law, but Julian taught it and therefore it was a compulsory second-year subject, long after it had been dropped by nearly every other law school in the country.

'I did explain,' Julian continued, 'that Roman law is the most excellent training for the young legal mind.' He bustled about his office, gesturing Clara to a chair and sealing himself in a leather captain's chair that he had purchased – like most of the contents of his office – from his own funds, declaring the university-issue furniture ghastly. Clara had discovered years ago, from Cameron naturally, that Julian had been left a sizeable inheritance by his father, which enabled him to work as a lecturer but live to a standard considerably above that of his colleagues.

She was thinking furiously. Cameron might advise her to say nothing but, faced with Julian in person, that was easier said than done. She was well aware that beneath the bumbling exterior lay a sharp legal mind and years of experience in cross-examining recalcitrant students on their various misdemeanours.

'Clara, a couple of points. How's Tellium going?'

A couple of points. Why two? Clara made a determined effort to sound her most professional. 'Very well. I'm organising their action committee and hopefully James Agnew will take on the case . . .'

'Sound chap. He'll do an excellent job.'

'I think so. And I'm preparing another article so that should generate some interest among the legal community.'

'Marvellous! This is just what we need. Putting the law into action. "Making it relevant", I believe, is the current phrase. And you're keeping on top of everything else?'

'What? Oh, yes. Marking, references, all under control.'

'Good. You certainly sound in top form. By the way, I'm off to the Dordogne next week so I'll be out of action for a couple of weeks. But you have the number there if you need me. I'm actually hoping to get a piece on the Emperor Augustus finished. Very interesting chap. Now,' Julian looked worried, his brow creasing, 'one other thing. Nothing to worry about, I'm sure.'

Clara would have given anything to be anywhere else. She prayed for the telephone to ring or for some frantic student to bang on the door, but all was silent. She repeated Cameron's mantra over and over in her mind: say nothing.

'The point is – and I'd appreciate your comments on this – something came to light at the last heads-of-department meeting. I'm sure it won't affect you but . . .'

Clara braced herself. Her palms were damp and she felt faint with dread.

'Landward Pharmaceuticals have just offered the biology department a sizeable donation. Only last week. Of course, there may be no connection, but they have something of a reputation for underhand tactics.'

'Oh . . . fine.'

Julian looked up in surprise. 'I thought you'd be furious about it.'

'Well, I am – It's blood-boiling, dreadful. But I suppose one has to expect this sort of thing from Landward.'

'Quite. But what I wanted to assure you of was my absolute support. They can give all the money they want to the university, but while I'm head, this department will act with total correctness. We can't just cave in to every multinational corporation that wants to give us money in return for hushing up the unpalatable truth.'

At that moment, Clara could not have cared less if Landward Pharmaceuticals had purchased the entire university and turned it into a theme park.

'You see,' continued Julian, 'this is about our reputation. A reputation takes years to build up and it can be destroyed with one foolish error of judgement. One must not only act correctly, one must be *seen* to act correctly. And if you drop out of the Tellium case then doubtless the wrong conclusion will be drawn.'

'Doubtless.'

'Well, I'm glad to have cleared that up. Clara, you are my safest pair of hands on the staff.' He sighed. 'If only everyone was so level-headed. Some of the younger members of staff require an inordinate amount of supervision.'

'Oh?'

'Mentioning no names, but take the post-exam party . . .'

Clara had hoped he wouldn't.

'I couldn't help noticing some of the younger ones indulging in over-familiar conversation with the students. Those students may be leaving but, still, one must maintain certain standards.'

'Absolutely.'

'Still, such are the burdens of office. Mustn't complain.' Julian got up. 'I gather that the weather in the Dordogne is absolutely super now so I shall return invigorated for the trials of the autumn term. Not to mention the exam meeting . . .'

The exam meeting could last all day, lecturers making decisions that might affect the students for the rest of their lives. The law school awarded three types of degree: firsts for the brightest, seconds for the majority, and thirds for those who preferred parties or sport to study.

'Yes, last week of August, isn't it? It's in the diary,' said Clara.

'Marvellous.' Julian held open the door of his office for her. 'Are you going away?'

'Me? Oh, maybe a few days. Nothing planned.'

'Hmm. Try to get a break. Mind and body, all that sort of thing.' And with that Julian closed the door, leaving Clara standing, drained and shell-shocked, in the still-deserted law-school hallway.

On the other side of South London, Tom had been summoned by Jan to her flat. She was lying on her red-velour settee, the inevitable cigarette in one hand and a bottle of calamine lotion in the other. 'I'd have come down to the office, Tommo, but I can't walk with this sunburn. Can't move. Here, can you do my feet? I can't bend down there.' She pushed the bottle at Tom. 'The cotton wool's on the floor.'

Tom got up reluctantly and dabbed the tops of Jan's reddened feet with the pink liquid. This was not the strict definition of hands-on social work.

'Ooh, that's better.'

'You ought to be more careful,' said Tom, starting on the other foot.

'I know, but you don't realise till it's too late. Of course, I've got very delicate skin, always have had – did I tell you I was entered for that Pears soap competition when I was a little girl?'

'Yes, I think you mentioned it.' Tom was screwing the top back onto the bottle and looking for somewhere to dispose of the cotton wool.

'Give it here,' said Jan, taking it from him and dropping

it onto her teak-effect coffee table, where it jostled for space among a pile of TV listings and *Real Life* magazines. In fact, there was barely an inch of clear space in the room. Between Jan's huge three-seater settee, two black leather-effect armchairs, an outsize TV and a murky-looking fish tank there was barely any space left for the octagonal coffee table.

'Anyhow, you're here now. You see, I've told you before, it's brewing up – you mark my words. And what I want to know is, what are you doing about it?'

'Jan, I can't work miracles.'

'Never said you could.'

'I don't think things are *that* bad. The gym's up and running, the building work's starting in September.'

'Yes, but it's August now. It's the heat. And there's trouble already. That Ali, he's leading it, hanging around those stairs causing trouble.'

Tom had heard it all before, countless times. And the worst thing was that Jan wasn't as prejudiced as some of them. It was just that she could think nothing bad of Sean – who, Tom suspected, was trading dope and worse on the estate. So was Zareb, and if there was any fighting it was going to be over that. 'Even if there is trouble,' Tom said, 'it's going to be between the kids. I don't see the estate going up in flames.'

'You weren't around to see it the first time,' said Jan.

'So what do you suggest?' Tom already knew what her answer would be.

'Get the police to arrest the lot of them, lock them up – before it's too late, Tom.'

Tom felt suddenly weary. He was making progress here, he knew it, but for every step forward there was another back. No, that was defeatist. There were new challenges. He got up. 'Look, I hear what you say. And I *will* speak to the police – about *everything* that's going on here. I can't take sides.'

Jan was mollified. 'Well, I'm glad you've listened to what

I had to say. Excuse me if I don't get up. You know your way out.'

Tom had reached the lounge door.

'Oh, and Tom . . .'

'Yes?'

'Why don't you make us both a nice cuppa before you go?'

Tom was home early – Clara had expected him to stay for Brendan's training session. It was unfortunate that he would find her in the bath but not disastrous. She heard him call out, then climb the stairs.

'Brendan cancel?'

'Brendan? No. Just felt like getting out of the office . . .' Tom perched on the downturned lavatory seat, reached out and absently stroked Clara's soapy knee.

She decided to get this over with. After her meeting with Julian, she had gone straight round to Ben – checking first that no black Golf was lurking in the vicinity but parking several streets away. He had calmed her down, taken her to bed, then shown her his photograph album of Deauville. At first she had suggested cancelling the weekend, but Ben had just laughed and asked if she really thought Francine Lewis was going to turn up in Normandy. Ibiza, maybe, but not some French coastal town. And after he had kissed her and held her and made love to her a second time, in a way that was now comfortingly familiar but never predictable, she had been reassured. But she couldn't delay breaking the news of her departure to Tom any longer.

Tom was his usual attentive self. 'How was work?'

'Oh, all quiet. Did some more on Tellium. Talking of which, Landward Pharmaceuticals have only gone and given the university a whopping donation.'

Tom looked askance: 'Bloody disgusting. I hope it hasn't put Julian off. Did you speak to him?'

'Yes.' Clara paused. 'Good and bad news, actually.'

'Tell me the worst.'

'The best is that he says not to worry about Tellium, that I should just carry on with the campaign.'

'Sounds remarkably right-on for Julian.'

'Well, hold your praise. There's more. You know I told you he was worried about funding in the department? Well, he wants a reorganisation to try to make some economies. And he needs to hold a meeting to plan it all.'

'But you're safe?'

'I think so – I've been there a long time. That's not the point. Tom, you know these big companies, when they want to discuss something, how they all go away to some hotel and do team-building and brainstorming?'

'And Julian wants the whole department to go to the Ritz?'

'Not quite. But he does want us to go down to the Dordogne, just before the exam meeting. All the senior staff, so we can get away from the university and talk creatively about the department – what direction we should take, what our goals should be, that sort of thing. And by going to the Dordogne he can keep it low-key, stop the rest of the staff panicking . . .'

Tom looked surprisingly despondent. He picked up the bottle of her new French bath oil, a present from Ben, and fiddled with the cap. Without much hope he asked, 'Are partners invited too?'

'Afraid not. I did ask, but Julian said it's only for a weekend and his house doesn't really run to putting up everyone . . .'

'So, who's going?'

'Oh, the usual crowd.'

She kept it vague. Tom never went to the university, these days, and there was no reason why he should. And this way, if he did accidentally encounter anyone from the department, she could say they hadn't been invited so knew nothing about it. God, it was getting complicated, though.

Tom put down the bottle and stared morosely at the floor. 'I see. It's very short notice. Can't you get out of it?'

Clara wanted this conversation to end. 'I don't see how I can . . . The way the funding cuts are biting at the moment, we all have to take the situation pretty seriously.'

She reached across to Tom and squeezed his arm. 'Hey, it's only a couple of nights. I leave on the Friday and I'll be back Sunday. You'll hardly notice I've gone.'

'I will, you know. I'll phone you every night.'

She had known that was going to be a problem. Tom sighed and got up. 'I'll pour us a drink. Then we can discuss your travel plans.'

'Oh, that's OK. I'll get a lift from someone. Or a cheap flight. But I'm not sure about the phone. This place is Julian's retreat. His sanctuary from the outside world, he calls it. I've an idea he hasn't got a phone at all.'

Seeing Tom's face fall she added quickly, 'But you can call me on the mobile.'

Tom looked scarcely more cheerful. He rose heavily to his feet and made for the door. Listening to him retreat downstairs she settled back uneasily into her cooling bath. And felt the first twinges of guilt pricking her conscience.

CHAPTER 9

Victoria emerged from Temple tube station with relief. The heat in the underground carriages was stifling and she had stood wedged between a City businessman with dreadful body odour and a group of chattering foreign-language students. She had hoped that by waiting and travelling mid-morning the train would have emptied but she had found it packed to the doors. The air outside was scarcely cooler but at least it was fresh – or as fresh as London air in August can be. Fortunately, she was only up for the day and she would catch the evening train back to Marlow where Elizabeth was minding Emily and Alex. David was due back from Paris in a couple of days and she wanted to have made some progress on his speech.

She walked briskly to his office, feeling the thin fabric of her summer dress sticking uncomfortably to her back. It was her own fault. She should have got a copy of his CV before she had gone to Marlow so that when she tackled the section on his career – which was really about his suitability to be an MP – she had all the facts in front of her. And the facts had to be absolutely, indisputably and irrefutably correct. The committee would not want a repeat of the Charles Lamming fiasco. David wanted to appear as the candidate of utmost propriety.

She had resolved to go to his office, print off his CV from his computer and at the same time pick up the Dubai cheque that David's clerk had phoned to tell her had arrived in chambers earlier that week. She needed to bank it because the kitchen man had phoned twice requesting payment. The cheque would more than cover it, of course, and leave a healthy balance in their current account. And it would be a nice surprise for David. He would return from Paris to find everything organised and, hopefully, they would enjoy a peaceful weekend.

The Inner Temple always raised her spirits as she walked through the red-brick and stone archways admiring the beautifully tended gardens. David's chambers stood in one of the oldest buildings, dating back to the eighteenth century, the rooms reached by a winding staircase, the entrance adorned with a black wooden board on which the names of the barristers were hand-painted in gold copper-plate lettering. They appeared in order of seniority, Sir Richard Hibbert's at the top – but David's name was getting reassuringly high up the list: only ten or so before his and about twenty after. Towards the bottom she read 'Kitty Standing' and after it, at the very end, 'Arabella Clevely-Jones'. It looked as though the paint was still wet.

She breezed in, saw that the clerk's room was deserted and went straight to David's office. He kept it impeccably tidy. The desk was bare, just as it was at home, save for his computer and a copy of *Archbold's Criminal Practice*, the Bible on criminal law for all barristers. Rows of leather-bound law reports filled the shelves and in the corner stood the room's only ornament – an antique globe of the world, Victoria's present to him on their tenth wedding anniversary.

When Bob, David's clerk, turned up she would ask him for a cup of coffee – and the cheque – but for the time being she would concentrate on printing off what she needed before the morning turned even more humid. The computer started up and she switched on the printer. She was not sure how to find the CV. David had to use a computer these days – all the solicitors were getting e-mail and expected to be able to reach him that way – but, like many men of his generation, he had not embraced the new technology. She went into the word-processing function and saw that he

268

had not yet mastered the directory facility. What seemed like hundreds of file names appeared before her. He also didn't appear to know how to delete anything.

She began scrolling down: ashton-armstrong, sachers, farthing-littleton. All names of solicitors. But then stratford. These must be his personal files: stratfordcv. She opened it, saw it was indeed his CV, and printed it off. While she waited, she glanced idly at the file names still apparent behind the printing-in-progress message.

But before she had a chance to look more closely, Bob appeared. 'Mrs Stratford, what a nice surprise! I'll get that cheque for you.'

'Thanks, Bob. Just doing a spot of paperwork for David.'

'Right you are. Can I get you a coffee?'

'That would be wonderful.'

He retreated, and she collected the sheets from the printer, stapled them carefully and stashed them in her handbag. She turned back to the computer, about to switch it off, but as she did so, a file name caught her eye: electionspch.

She was taken aback. So, David was having a go at it himself! She would have to see how he was getting on. She was surprised to feel a little irritated. This was her territory, after all, and he had given her the impression that he had no time to do it himself.

She clicked on the file name. 'Access denied without password' flashed up in front of her, the words framed in a box on the centre of the screen. Now she was intrigued. He knew how to password documents, of course – lots of the material he dealt with was confidential – but she was surprised he had passworded this, unless he was afraid of a colleague's prying eyes. Perhaps he wasn't as confident in his own writing ability as he would like.

She tried his date of birth. 'Access denied without password.' The file stayed resolutely shut behind that annoying little box. She typed in 'stratford'. Then 'victoria'. Next 'alex' . . . and then 'emily'. Next she tried them all again using capital letters but it made no difference. Now she was getting frustrated. She must be able to crack this: passwords were notoriously easy if you knew the person. But before she could think any further Bob bustled in with a cup of coffee. 'Having problems?'

'Oh. No. Not at all. Just ... printing out some information David needs.'

He lingered. 'Can I help? I've been on quite a few IT courses.'

No. She just wanted to be left alone to think about this. 'Thanks, I'm fine. I'll come and ask you if I get stuck.'

Bob seemed reluctant to go: he stood around chatting about the Inner Temple cricket team of which he was honorary secretary, and then about the plans to redecorate the stairway. Victoria listened politely and eventually, after a prolonged pause, he was gone.

She went straight back to the keyboard. Now she wanted to crack this more than ever. So she started thinking laterally, about David's interests and hobbies. But, then, he didn't really have any pastimes outside politics. She tried 'summerston' and 'clement' and the surname of the Prime Minister, Edward Butler. All failed. She was about to give up when she thought about travel. David did enjoy that. And his favourite hotel was in Paris – the Bristol in the 8th *arrondissement*. They had gone there for a second honeymoon on their fifth wedding anniversary, just about bankrupting themselves in the process. She typed 'bristol'.

And, before her eyes, the file opened.

David wasn't as clever as he thought. She was elated, reading the first lines eagerly,

I am honoured this night to have been elected as the Conservative Member of Parliament for Wimbledon Village ...

So it *wasn't* a speech for the selection. It was a speech for the night of the general election. David knew he had the selection in the bag so he was looking beyond that to when he was elected to Parliament. It seemed a bit premature, but there had been speculation that the Prime Minister, with a small majority, might call a snap election at any time. Clearly David, ever meticulous, wanted to be prepared well in advance.

> ... And I shall endeavour to serve this seat with all the dutiful service so marvellously demonstrated by my esteemed predecessor Sir Reginald Summerston. I wish him a very happy retirement ...

Victoria knew he would – he had been anticipating that happy event for long enough.

> But I must thank my wonderful campaign team in Wimbledon. A special mention must go to Viscount Clement, whose wise counsel has been invaluable, and to Miss Hilda Rudge, without whose delicious refreshments I fear the campaign would have faltered ...

More boring tributes followed, covering everyone from the council returning officer to Major Bolton and the entire committee, name after tedious name.

> But I cannot leave this podium without a few personal reflections ...

At last, something to wake them all up. They would need it – the count would probably take until two in the morning. She was going to have to do some serious work on this speech if it was to do David and her justice. She hadn't even begun to think about election night. She thought idly of what she would wear, and then read on dutifully:

> The last year has not been an easy one for me. Political success has met with personal sorrow ...

What on earth was he talking about?

> As many of you will be aware, my wife Victoria decided last year to leave Wimbledon – and me – to seek a

*different life elsewhere. Many of you know Victoria and
I can imagine that her regrettable decision was as great
a shock to you as it was to me. But one cannot allow
personal distress to overcome one's commitment to
public service. And in this task I have been indebted to
Arabella Clevely-Jones, who has been a tower of
strength through these difficult months. I hope you will
not think me unduly sentimental if I add that Arabella
has become something more to me than a good friend.
And so, on this historic night. I hope you will join me in
sharing our joy at the news that she has graciously
accepted to become my wife . . .*

Victoria did not, could not, read any further. She was
shocked and utterly bewildered. For what seemed an age
she sat staring at the screen, seeing nothing, the words a
blur of lines and lights. And when eventually she did begin
to think she struggled to make sense of the document laid
out before her eyes.

Two explanations came to mind. One, this was some
particularly ridiculous male fantasy; two, David was
planning to leave her for another woman.

Was this some kind of mid-life crisis, confined to the
secrets of David's imagination? Or was it true?

It could not be true. It was unthinkable. They had a life
together, the children – what would she do? She certainly
wasn't planning to leave him, however he had presented it,
so he must be acting out some silly crush on Arabella.

But these were only her initial thoughts. Before she could
prevent them, other darker realisations filled her mind. All
the times he had been away. The new trips overseas.
Arabella at the party, seeming to help but jumping at the
chance to meet Emily. Clara in the garden at Marlow,
warning her about the implications of the house valuation.
She began to feel sick, a feeling of dread and awful
realisation taking her over. Instinctively, she needed to
know more. She recalled that Arabella's father was a judge.
She reached for David's copy of *Who's Who* and, thumbing

quickly through the pages, found his entry. He was His Honour Judge Clevely-Jones. Educated at Selchester and Trinity College, Cambridge. There followed a summary of his career. He had one son and one daughter. His address was listed in Beaconsfield. *Beaconsfield*. The scene of so many of David's recent trips. The place he had rushed to after the last selection meeting. The present he had gone to buy that had never materialised. She had begun to feel worse now, the blood draining from her face, and a coldness overtaking her.

How could she have been so stupid? So deluded and smug and sure of him. How could she have thought that such a betrayal, which happened to hundreds of women every week of every year, could never happen to her? Unless it *was* just a figment of David's imagination. But try as she might to be calm, level-headed and rational, it was difficult to avoid the worst interpretation. Put simply, she was being traded in for a younger model. No, worse than that, she was being discarded for a girl who was nearly half her age, stunningly beautiful and possessed of all the social connections that David had always craved. Arabella would become the wife of an MP, rich from the money Victoria had helped him accumulate and – who knows? – in time the wife of the Prime Minister, while she, Victoria, would languish forgotten and pitied in some cramped flat with Alex and Emily, having been presented by David as the guilty party . . .

But she had to be sure. She had to *know*. She printed out the speech. As she waited for the printer she heard a burst of laughter from the clerk's room where the barristers were returning after that morning's court session. Of course, everyone in chambers would be in on the secret. David often said that being part of a barristers' chambers was like being in a huge family – you could never keep a secret for long. She closed the file and shut down the computer, carefully folded the speech and hid it in her handbag. She felt giddy and wondered if she would be able to stand. As she sat gathering her strength, someone who looked vaguely familiar came into the room. One of the nice young barristers who had been so polite at David's party? It was impossible to think straight.

'Mrs Stratford, Bob said you were in . . .' She was smiling brightly but he read her well enough to introduce himself. 'Mark Crosbie . . . I was at your husband's party. Just thought I'd say hello.' He was looking at her now with some concern, running his hand uneasily through his thick blond hair. 'Are you all right? Would you like a glass of water?'

'Actually, I think I'd like a drink.'

He looked rather surprised at this but glanced at his watch. 'Well . . . there's the new wine bar round the corner. It'll be open now. I was going to get some lunch.'

'Thank you. I'll join you.' Leaning on the desk, Victoria got to her feet. Mark began chatting about some case he was working on. She followed him through the narrow lanes of the Temple, struggling to pay attention to his conversation, until they arrived at the chic wine bar, where Mark left her at a glass-topped table, slumped on some uncomfortable metal-weave chair, while he fetched her a brandy. Why had she asked for a brandy? She didn't even like it. Maybe it had seemed the appropriate drink in the circumstances.

And now she was caught with him. She could hardly ask him outright. But neither could she go quietly back to Marlow without knowing. There was no point in confronting David: he would deny everything, as he had on a couple of occasions when some unfamiliar scent on his shirt or the odd disappearance of a cuff link had caused her to ask him outright where he had been spending his time. She could predict exactly how the conversation would unfold: after David had, with growing irritation, articulated some perfectly sensible explanation, he would get angry, accuse her of paranoia and stupidity, deftly turn the tables on her so that *she* became the guilty one.

When Mark returned with her drink and an orange juice for himself, she had come to grasp, even in her shock and confusion, that he represented her best chance of uncovering the truth. If she was careful. 'I'm sorry about all this,' she said. 'I'm rather tired at the moment. I think the journey up may have been rather too hot for me.'

'Yes, it's awful, isn't it? Worse in a suit.' He gestured to his pinstripe, a cheaper version of David's usual style. They both looked up as the doors swung open and a gaggle of chattering young secretaries burst in, bare-legged in flimsy outfits and high heels, and began loud, flirtatious exchanges with the barman.

Victoria continued, 'And with David away such a lot, he relies on me for the paperwork.'

'Yes   ' There was a hesitation in his voice. And an undeniable keenness to change the subject. 'How's the house? It looked fantastic at the party.'

She told him, chatting blandly about the kitchen units, all the while considering how she could raise the subject. Like most flashes of inspiration it came on the spur of the moment. 'So you enjoyed the party? Of course, it was a surprise for me to see Arabella there. I hadn't been expecting her.'

He was caught in the headlights, uncertain how to react. She pressed on: 'Not that it's a problem.'

'No?' He sounded uncomfortable.

'No.'

'I can't really comment. I'm not married myself.' He turned his glass round and round nervously. A few lawyers had come into the bar now and the noise levels were rising.

'Well, as you get older you come to accept these things,' Victoria continued. Then she paused. She had opened the door.

He could not help walking through it. He spoke wonderingly: 'And you don't mind?'

'Of course I *mind*, but I have the children to think about.'

He wanted to ask more, she could feel it, but she knew that David's position in chambers held him back.

'Mark, I know it must seem strange to you. Our situation. But rest assured, I won't tell David about our lunch. I understand it's awkward for you . . .'

'It's just that . . . well, we all assumed you must know. After all this time. Still, it was a surprise to see Arabella at the party . . . But I suppose you don't want to discuss her.'

'Oh, David and I talk about her quite openly.'

'You do?' He was looking at her now with undisguised amazement. 'Wow. Very modern.'

'Just pragmatic. We have our separate lives – both of us.'

'Oh, I see.'

She could almost feel sorry for him – totally out of his depth, terrified of David and now wondering if the wife of a senior member of chambers was about to make a pass at him. More nervous still, he gabbled, 'I mean, I don't want you to think that we talk about you in chambers. David and Arabella – they're very discreet. I guess after two years it just becomes accepted in chambers, you don't notice it any more. I mean, she did her pupillage with us so she's part of the furniture now . . .'

Two years. Two years in which David had lived with her, had sex with her and planned in minute detail the future of their married life. Now she really had begun to feel sick, the brandy burning her stomach and the waves of cigarette smoke in the airless atmosphere wafting towards her. She needed some fresh air. She spoke abruptly: 'Well, it's been very nice talking to you but I must get on. Lots to do.'

He finished his drink. 'Mrs Stratford, are you sure you're OK? Do you want something to eat?' He gestured at the menu but she was already reaching for her handbag. 'Or can I get you a taxi?'

'No,' she snapped. Then she remembered that she was only supposed to be hot and tired, not recovering from the sudden news of her husband's prolonged infidelity. She made a determined effort to control herself. 'No . . . thank you. I'm going to walk for a while.' She got up, her head spinning, hoping to get away, but Mark got up too.

'I'll come with you.'

'It's really not necessary.'

'Yes, I think it is.' There was a new resolve in his voice and she did not argue. Clearly he wasn't as young and naïve as she had imagined. She should have remembered that David's chambers only took the best and brightest. He grasped her arm, led her out into the dazzling sunlight and, seeming to realise that chambers was best avoided, walked her along the Embankment towards the Temple tube station. In the small gardens dotted around, office-workers were eating lunch and sunbathing, the young men lying in their City shirts and ties, their suit jackets tossed on the ground beside them. Everyone looked so *young*.

They walked in silence until, pausing for Victoria to take some air by the river, Mark said, 'You didn't know, did you?'

She said nothing, looking out on to the dirty river and the unkempt tourist pleasure-boats that formed a straggled line along the river-bank moorings. She felt his hand on her arm. 'You didn't know, did you?' he repeated.

She sighed and glanced at him. 'No . . . And I'm sorry. I didn't want to involve you and as far as I'm concerned we never spoke.'

'Christ, I'm not worried about that.'

'But I had to know for sure.'

He joined her, leaning on the railings, and they stood together in a strangely comfortable silence. 'What are you going to do?'

How could she answer him? She had not the slightest idea. She could barely imagine undertaking the journey home, let alone planning what to do when she arrived there. 'I don't know – cut up his suits, maybe. Isn't that what wives do in these circumstances?'

Mark grinned. 'There are lots of things you could do. Actually, I had a client whose wife reported her husband to the Inland Revenue for fiddling his taxes. He got two years for tax evasion. Not one of my early successes at criminal defence, it has to be said.'

Victoria laughed. 'I'm sure you've got lots in front of you.' She felt a sudden pang. How wonderful to be young, with all your life – and all your mistakes – in front of you. To have time on your side so that you could get everything wrong, change direction and still have a chance to start all over again. Not to be thirty-eight – with two children and a failed marriage to show for your life. 'As for me, I don't know what I'm going to do. It doesn't appear that David wants me any more.'

'And do you want him?'

It was obvious, wasn't it? The answer had to be no. David had betrayed her, lied to her and humiliated her in the most public way. He was self-obsessed, intolerant and concerned only with his own advancement. She had supported him, encouraged him, and now she was to be ruthlessly discarded.

So why was it that, when she eventually replied to Mark's simple question, her voice faltered? 'I simply do not know,' she said.

It was fortunate that the Rib Room at the Carlton Tower Hotel, situated on the corner of Sloane Street and Cadogan Gardens, operated a relaxed dress code at lunch-time because Cal Doyle was wearing denim jeans and a black T-shirt teamed with a disintegrating pair of trainers. And no socks.

Annie had expected to be at Albert Road for half an hour, to choose the tiles, then catch the bus back to Cobham.

She had been determined to create a good impression. Cool, confident and, above all, *in control*. She had collected her pale yellow shift dress from the dry-cleaner's, added a white Thai silk scarf and put on a smart pair of navy suede shoes with a matching handbag. She had arrived at nine thirty a.m. and, clearly, the team had been at work for a couple of hours. Joe was building the new bedroom wall and Dave was plastering the sitting room. Cal had reverted to a supervisory role.

'Found it was all blown,' he explained, 'so we hacked it off and we're replastering. Easier in the long run than patching it up.'

There had been other, new jobs. The kitchen was now fitted but the ceiling had been taken down, reboarded and eight halogen down-lighters were being fixed in place by Little Dave. Cal had also, he explained, decided to lay new stones on the steps down to the flat to cover the chipped, stained concrete that had been there before.

She had chosen the tiles, endeavouring to guess the cheapest, and expected to leave after that. But Cal had announced that he was having problems with his new show house and would she come and have a look? He had brushed off the passenger seat and they had set off in his beaten-up white van – the footwell littered with empty cigarette packets, chocolate wrappers and polystyrene cups – and arrived twenty minutes later at The Meadows. Or what was to become The Meadows; eight six-bedroom houses in the usual Cal Doyle style, but now a building site on which JCBs manoeuvred around a clutch of white vans and men in hard hats.

One completed house rose up around its half-built neighbours. Cal strode in and issued instructions to the team of builders engaged in fitting it out. Annie stood aside as two workmen heaved a plastic-wrapped cooking range through the door – of a size she thought privately that would be better suited to a medium-sized restaurant. But Cal was already in the drawing room. 'You see, I want something stunning. Different. Not the usual country-house look. I'm bloody sick of swags and tails . . .'

Annie looked around her. The problem was the size of the windows: any curtains would have to be enormous if they were to suit the vast scale, which would add an unwanted heaviness to the room. 'You could use blinds,' she suggested.

'*Blinds*!'

She found herself laughing. 'I don't mean *Venetian* blinds. I mean panels of very thin muslin and then you could drape the curtains around them – using a light, flowing fabric. You could get the curtains made up so that they *look* draped, but the folds would actually be sewn in place. It's quite simple. That would give you the coverage you need without ending up with something too heavy. And then you pick up one of the colours – maybe a Provençal red – and use that to cover the chairs and sofas.'

He looked interested. 'Where would you get this stuff?'

'I know a shop in Knightsbridge that imports from all over the world.'

'OK. Let's have a look.'

It was only when they were back in the van and they had passed the turning for Albert Road that Annie had realised they were going, right now, to the shop. There didn't seem any point in arguing. Besides, Cal spent most of the journey taking endless calls on his mobile phone – mostly from his builders, wanting decisions on layout and finish and specification, but also one that she guessed was from Angus Campbell and another that sounded as if it was a journalist.

They had gone to the shop, chosen the fabric, and somehow she had found herself offering to bring round the portfolio of photographs of her curtains so he could see if there was anything he liked. Then Cal had announced he was hungry and that they were going for lunch.

If she had not seen it with her own eyes, she would not have believed it was possible to drive into the entrance of one of London's smartest hotels, climb out of a white builder's van, then coolly hand the keys to the liveried doorman for it to be valet-parked. But Cal did just that and no one batted an eyelid. They had gone in through the enormous revolving glass doors, passed through the lobby with its elegant sofas and black-skirted waitresses and headed down the corridor to the restaurant. The head waiter greeted Cal effusively, as did the barman and most of the waiters. Not only were they not turned away, they were seated in the middle of the restaurant, reached by a couple of steps down to a sunken area where tables were spaced discreetly apart.

She felt unaccountably nervous, almost gauche, to find herself in these elegant surroundings with such unexpected company. Fortunately, as they sat down she was saved from having to say anything by Cal's mobile ringing. While he sorted out some problems with the laying of the drains at The Meadows, she looked at the menu. It was not a question of what she wanted. It was a question of avoiding any foods that might in any conceivable way cause her difficulty. Fish was out – some stray bone would surely lodge in her gullet and Cal would be obliged to stick his fingers down her throat again. So were lobster, langoustine and any food that involved manual dexterity. Surely steak was safe? A small, medium-cooked steak could not pose any problems. She would choose that, a side salad, and eat very, very carefully having regard to the dangers of choking.

Cal ended his call and switched off his mobile. 'They'll just have to manage on their own for a while.'

They ordered – a large fillet steak for him, rare, a small one for Annie, medium. And a bottle of Château Margaux. She wondered how they had ended up having lunch together, but before she could ponder any further Cal had launched into a discussion of Albert Road. 'I want to apologise . . .'

'Apologise?'

'It's a bit behind schedule but we'll be out in two weeks. I had to take a couple of lads off the job last week to help out at The Meadows, but we'll be back on track soon enough.'

'You must let me know how much I owe you.'

He ignored this. 'Actually, I've really enjoyed it. It's been a long time since I've got my hands dirty.' He caught her look of surprise. 'Did you think I built the bloody houses single-handed?' And then she was laughing and he was telling her stories about walls falling down and impossible clients and his dreadful bank manager. 'You see, people think of me as a builder, but the real work is getting the money to buy the land and then build the houses. You've always got the bank on your back, worried they won't get repaid.'

'But they do in the end?'

'They have so far. But that doesn't stop the buggers pestering you all day long.'

Annie was realising that there was more to Cal Doyle's business than putting up houses. He had to find the land, wait months for planning permission and then spend a fortune building houses that he couldn't be sure anyone would buy. And at the end of it, no one seemed to have a good word to say about builders.

He went on, 'But, more importantly, are you OK at The Chapters?'

'Oh, yes, it's wonderful. Like a – a hotel. Elizabeth's getting really spoilt.'

'Good.'

'In fact, if I hear that Van Morrison CD one more time I think I'll go crazy.'

'Can't hear Van the Man too many times.'

'Actually, there was something about Elizabeth. She wanted to know – well, I was wondering – if it would be OK if she had a friend over. Just one, for the night . . .' She cantered on: 'It's her best friend Celine, and Elizabeth's stayed at her place so much it would be nice if we could invite her back.' Her voice drifted away: she was aware of Cal looking at her with bewilderment.

'Annie, you can have the whole bloody school round, if you want. You don't have to ask me. It's a house – not Buckingham Palace.'

Annie grinned. 'Well, it's almost as big. I don't think I've found all the rooms yet.'

'Aye, well, I guess you're a bit lost in there. I've got a flat in town myself, but you have to build to suit the market. And that's what people are buying.'

She wondered what his flat was like but didn't feel she could ask. Instead, they talked about houses and estate agents and the ups and downs of the property business. Annie managed to eat some of her steak without incident and when she had put down her knife and fork Cal reached across and took the rest for himself: 'Shame to waste it. You ought to eat a bit more. Put some meat on your bones.'

By now Annie had realised that with Cal you didn't have to worry about what you said to him because he didn't worry about it either. He was probably the most easy-going man she had ever met. Hugo had been laid-back but Cal was horizontal. Then she felt guilty for comparing them at all.

So she turned the tables and told him he ought to eat more healthily. Before she knew it he was telling her about his mother, who lived in Kilburn with his father who had worked all his life as a labourer and who was now crippled with arthritis, and his brothers who were still in Ireland. And although it was impossible not to wonder why he was unmarried, she was tactful enough not to press the point.

By the time they had finished dessert – fruit for her and crème brûlée for him – the conversation had moved from the realms of business and building to the personal. Maybe it was the wine, or the atmosphere, or the way that the waiters just let them sit and talk in the now empty restaurant, returning only to pour more coffee and bring Cal another packet of cigarettes that they shared companionably.

It was her name that had broken the ice: 'So, Annie, are you really Anne?' he had asked.

No matter how many times she had gone through this rite of passage with strangers, her heart still sank.

He went on, 'I think, from that silence, that you're not.'

He was eyeing her with amusement. 'Anna, Annabelle, Annette,' he guessed. 'I give up.'

'It's Anastasia.'

He struggled to swallow his coffee. He didn't even try not to laugh and then she ended up laughing too. 'How the hell did you end up with a fancy name like that?'

'Like most things, it was down to my mother. She's a fan of historical novels. When I was born she was really into the Russian Revolution.'

'I see. So you could have been Lenin.'

'And that's why Elizabeth is Elizabeth. I didn't have a clue what to call her.'

'Your mother was reading about Elizabeth the First?'

'Elizabeth Fry – the Victorian prison reformer.'

'Jesus, I thought my family were odd . . .'

'Until you met mine. Clara is named after some German revolutionary woman. And Victoria's the Queen.'

'And the dog's called Rasputin?'

'Actually, we had two hamsters, two boys, one was Albert and the other was Einstein.'

Soon everything was funny. And it was only when the waiters returned to start laying the tables for dinner that Annie looked at her watch and saw, with astonishment, that it was a quarter to six. He had dropped her back at the house and she had promised to go round to Albert Road with her portfolio of curtain photographs later that week, before she went away with Sam.

And after that there hadn't seemed to be anything more to say, and he had driven off into the early-evening sun.

Tom was conscious of his headache worsening as he sat in Jan's hot, airless living room. She did not have any ice so she had made do, as best she could, by rinsing a face flannel in cold water and applying it to his forehead.

'You ought to get it looked at,' she scolded him, but he could hear the soft note of worry in her voice as she took off the flannel to look at the angry, bloodied bruise beneath.

As she reached towards him, he caught her scent of suntan lotion and strong perfume and found it oddly reassuring. Jan's hours of sunbathing had paid off with the dark tan she now showed off in a white sleeveless T-shirt and cut-off jeans. 'I'll have to sit in Casualty for hours,' Tom sighed, 'and then they'll send me home with a box of aspirin.'

Jan did not look convinced. 'Little buggers. Are you going to tell the council? Get your boss involved?'

Tom looked up at her incredulously. 'I don't think I've got much choice. Most of the gym equipment's ruined. With a bit of luck the police needn't get involved. I'm not going to press charges.'

'You should!' exclaimed Jan. 'They can't get away with it.'

'Quite honestly, I don't think it was deliberate. Things got out of hand. Zareb took a swing at Sean and I was in the middle.'

'Stepping in to try to stop them, were you?' asked Jan sourly. 'I tell you, I wouldn't have taken a punch for Sean and he's my son.'

With that she bustled out of the room, and he heard the sound of the tap running and a glass of water being poured. He lay back on Jan's sofa, the soft velour rather comforting in the circumstances. When she returned his eyes followed her sleepily round the room as she put down the water by his side then drew the curtains to shade the room from the bright sunshine. The soft dimness was a relief – he had to admit that he did have an awful headache, and he wondered if he was concussed. Perhaps Jan might be right after all.

He had nearly not come in to the Southhead, but after Clara had left on Friday night he had wandered aimlessly around the house. He had considered popping over to see Annie, then remembered that she was in Devon with Sam.

He had even thought of going to Marlow to see Elizabeth, but David would be there for the weekend ... So he had read the papers, made a sandwich and when he had woken late on Saturday morning the estate seemed as good a place as any to spend the day.

He had done some paperwork – a memo to his boss suggesting an expansion of the gym-class timetable, then a proposal for a crackdown on loan sharks operating on the estate, next some expenses forms. The morning had passed and he was still in his office after lunch when he had heard shouting. Not the usual, occasional yell that could often be heard echoing round the walkways of the estate. Instead, a shouting that was more persistent and seemed to come from the direction of the gym. Which was odd because when he checked on the timetable he saw that there were no classes or training sessions scheduled – and the gym would be locked and bolted.

He had arrived to find an open door, the broken padlock and chain discarded on the pavement, and from within the shouting growing louder. Should he have hesitated, called for help, waited for others to arrive? Perhaps, but that had never been his style of work. He had strode in and a hush had fallen among the twenty or so youngsters who stood amid a vandalised and ruined gym – ripped punch-bags, broken weights, exercise bicycles and running machines turned over. Tom was too experienced, had seen too much, to register shock. Ever-professional, he took in the scene at a glance – but it was the boys he was concerned about. He had instinctively read their expressions: most of them were angry, a few, probably the culprits, defiant. Even one or two upset.

Seeing Tom, Ali had stepped forward. 'They've trashed it,' he shouted, his voice thick with accusations. 'They've trashed the gym.' He pointed at a group, Sean to the fore, who stood with cans of lager in their hands. 'Him and his stupid mates.' Ali spat out the words, his face twisted in anger, 'Because they're useless and they don't want it so they've trashed it.'

Ali's words aroused a murmur of agreement from his supporters. But Sean, stripped to the waist in a pair of football shorts, was defiant: 'Not us.'

'Bullshit,' yelled Ali. And beside him Zareb, always the hothead, took a step forward. Tom read the next move. He stepped between the two protagonists, as Zareb rushed Sean. But he failed to see the punch Sean threw in Ali's direction. It missed Ali, the full force hitting Tom on the forehead, sending him reeling to the ground.

Tom was too shocked to move, his head spinning, but conscious of the sudden tense silence that filled the room, and then the sound of footsteps rushing out, anxious to flee the scene – all except for Ali waiting with him until Jan, alerted by the noise and running, arrived and helped him to his feet.

Now, as he drifted off to sleep in the thick heat of Jan's flat, he was jolted by her voice. He opened his eyes to see her standing over him. She frowned. 'I don't like it – the state of your head. I'm calling an ambulance. Just to be on the safe side. Too bad if you don't like it.'

Tom raised a hand, acknowledging defeat. 'All right.' He knew when he was beaten.

But Jan had not finished: 'I'll need to call someone. Your *next-of-kin*,' she articulated officiously. 'They'll want to know at the hospital. That'll be your wife, won't it? What's her number?' she asked Tom, reaching for the telephone.

The terrace of the Café de Paris, furnished with elegant wicker chairs and small, *faux*-marble tables looked out on to the Place Morny. Expensive, Paris-registered cars cruised slowly round the cobbled town square, circling the sparkling central fountains. The midday heat did nothing to stem the tide of activity all around her: housewives returning from the market with baskets of ripe fruit, couples wandering arm in arm, French families greeting each other with extravagant embraces and kisses to the cheek.

It was a perfect scene on which to rest the eye. And, regarding it, Clara felt more irritable and discontented than ever. She tried to analyse, and thereby dispel, her undoubted exasperation with what had been such a long-awaited weekend. How could an event so long in the planning and anticipation be so different from how she had imagined it? Had it been the lengthy journey? Certainly, it had been a nightmare. They had arrived at Dover – Ben had booked a ferry crossing declaring it the most romantic way to travel – only to find that the ferries were behind schedule. They had been obliged to wait in Ben's TVR for two unexpected hours. Two hours in the merciless sun, no hope of shade, among harrassed families and crying children wedged into cars and people carriers lined up on the sweating Tarmac of the ferry port. But they had not quarrelled, they had remained harmonious, even during the bumpy crossing and the three-hour drive from Calais, which had become four hours on account of the queues at the autoroute tollbooths. Her spirits had lifted as they drove into Deauville, whizzing along the coast road past the fairy-tale castle of the Hôtel Normandy and into the town's most exclusive hotel, the Royal.

There was certainly nothing to fault at the hotel. More formal than anything Tom would have chosen, it was, none the less, luxurious without being stiff. Their room looked out on to the sea's white breakers, and, after they had explored it, they swam in the pool, then sat in the intimate panelled bar drinking chilled champagne with nothing more strenuous to do than choose dinner from the neatly typed menu. And it had not been their lovemaking – she had fallen asleep before that could happen.

No, if she were ruthlessly honest her doubts had surfaced before she had even left home. It had been when she had turned to say goodbye to Tom, utter the last of so many lies, and tell him that she would not work too hard and would be back on Sunday night. It had welled up in her when she had seen the forced cheerfulness of his smile and the sadness in his eyes. As she had slipped off to meet her lover, Tom had carried her case to the taxi, told her to enjoy herself and waved bravely as she headed off in the direction of Heathrow – until she had lost sight of the house and she had asked the taxi-driver to change the destination to Richmond Park.

Now Ben emerged from the interior of the café. He was smiling, as he had since the minute of their arrival, and that, too, had begun to unsettle her. She had not anticipated that he would know so many people here, speak the language so fluently or blend in so easily. 'Sorry, darling, just catching up with Nicolas. He's the barman here.'

He pronounced the name in the French way, without sounding the s, and Clara felt a stab of irrational annoyance. She knew she was being ridiculous, that any normal woman would sit back and enjoy herself, but somehow she could not dispel the persistent sense of unease that had descended on her from the moment of her departure from home. *Home.* The very word felt melancholy.

She summoned a small, brave smile. 'Fine.' She looked at the tables around her. Although it was lunch-time, few of the women were eating. Instead they sipped red wine and smoked menthol cigarettes. She knew that in England she would have looked slim and smart – but here, well, standards were rather higher. Most of the women favoured tight white trousers, high-heeled black sandals and clinging tops with thin straps that showed off golden tans. And they were slim in an altogether different way: their legs were longer, their arms too, and their bodies had a boyish quality to them that she knew, no matter how much she dieted, she could never attain.

Ben took her limp hand and massaged her fingers. He was bursting with enthusiasm. 'Darling, I thought we could go down to the beach next and then walk round the port. The fishing boats will be moored up. Then we could get some lunch – something really local like *moules*. Oysters are out of season, worse luck. Or maybe a salad. Or a crêpe.'

But she was starving now! And her feet hurt from her new sandals, which were chafing and forming blisters on her heels. And she was tired. But she raised another, tighter smile. 'Ben, why don't we have a bite now? We could go out later – when it's cooler.'

His face fell. 'I just want you to see everything. Really get to know the place. We've only got the weekend.'

She felt as though she had seen quite enough already. They had visited the market, walked along the seafront and window-shopped in every boutique from Hermès to Gucci. Ben went on, a note of hurt entering his voice, 'And you wanted to do some more shopping.'

That was the last straw. Vivid images of the earlier indignity in Ben's hotly recommended boutique flooded back. She had stood in the tiny changing room, the doorway scarcely covered by a too-small flapping curtain, trying to squeeze into a pair of white trousers in the biggest size stocked. Outside, as she had gazed at her red-faced reflection, she had heard Ben speaking fluent French to the giggling shop assistant who looked about twenty-one and had a figure the same as Clara's had once been – when she was twelve. As she had struggled to do up the zip the girl had pulled back the curtain and Clara had smarted under her disdainful stare.

Now she snapped at Ben, 'No. I do not want to go shopping! I'm tired, I'm hot and I want a rest.'

He was stung. 'Darling, I'm sorry, I didn't think . . .'

She got up. 'I'm going back to the hotel.'

'I'll come with you.'

'No.' She didn't want him to. She wanted to be alone. It was too much, too suffocating, being with Ben all the time. The attentiveness, which had been so flattering before, was fast becoming a cloying nuisance. In fact, Ben himself was beginning to irritate her.

He looked woebegone, and she softened. 'Look, I'm just a bit tired. Probably too much sun. I'll go back, have a rest, and you can catch up with your friends. We'll meet up in a couple of hours.'

He was reluctant. 'I want to come with you, look after you . . .'

She struggled to keep her voice even: 'No, you wait here and I'll go back.'

'Can't I sit with you? I love watching you sleep.'

'Ben. Really. *No.*'

She had walked off without a second glance, weaving her way through the crowds of visitors, ignoring the beautiful shop displays along the elegant roads. Walking as quickly as her aching feet would allow, she thought of what she and Tom would have done now. Undoubtedly have a lazy brasserie lunch – something filling like steak and *frites* with a bottle of Beaujolais – then wander slowly back to the hotel, while Tom poked fun at all the chic people around them, and then sink into bed for a nice afternoon nap. The thought of Tom provoked a pang and she scrabbled in her handbag for her new mobile phone. She dialled home, still not having mastered the memory function, but although she let it ring and ring there was no reply. It was probably wiser not to leave a message in case he tried to contact her at some inopportune moment, and instead she tried his office. No reply. She wondered where he was.

Reaching the hotel, she quickened her step up the elegant white driveway with its neatly tended borders and red-jacketed young men waiting to park cars and carry suitcases. She spun through the revolving doors with relief, the coolness of the lobby as welcome as the opportunity to be alone. She even managed to ask for her key in French, though all the staff appeared to speak English – and, indeed, even when she did stumble through some carefully rehearsed phrase they invariably replied to her in English too.

The lift was empty, and as it glided to the fourth floor she looked idly at the photographs lining its walls – posed shots of models pretending to be guests, their expressions always fixed in beatific smiles as they played the tables in the casino, breakfasted by the pool or dined as a couple with their eyes locked in mutual adoration. Looking at them, Clara felt that she was singly failing in the implied expectation that all guests must devote themselves to a blissful holiday.

She let herself into the room, closed the curtains to block out the sun, kicked off her shoes and slumped on to the carefully made double bed. Although she was ravenous she couldn't bring herself to take anything from the minibar: the prices were pretty steep – Tom would have had a fit – and she already felt guilty at how much this must be costing Ben. He had said he could afford it, and she accepted that, but it made her feel uncomfortable all the same. But she could hardly use her credit card, less still the joint account; likewise she couldn't risk drawing more French currency in Deauville. It all made her feel rather trapped.

She realised that she had been unable to relax since they arrived. Perhaps if they had been staying longer she would have unwound. Ben had told her half-jokingly to stop imagining that one of her students was going to pop up and say hello. He assured her that the British hardly came here, preferring to motor straight through Normandy to reach Brittany or the warmer south. But the possibility of encountering some stray student was the least of her concerns: she had agonised anew about Cameron's words of warning, the multiple ways they might be found out and the possibility of Tom needing to contact her in an emergency. And no matter how many times Ben reassured her, however often he reasoned patiently with her, the worries nagged at her ceaselessly.

She reached for the remote control and switched on the television. Perhaps if she could take her mind off everything then she could relax before dinner tonight. She flicked through a French chat show, some cartoons and a Nice–

Marseille football match until she found the English satellite channel. Twenty-four-hour news, better than nothing, but there was currently a break for the ads. She watched until the headlines came up and then sport, with interminable reports of the afternoon's soccer action by overexcited reporters whose shouts and exclamations at first stopped her hearing the ring of her mobile phone.

She leaped off the bed and scrabbled through her bag. It could only be Tom or Ben – they were the only people who knew the number. But unless she could find it quickly the damn thing would cut off – and because she was in France the number didn't show up so she wouldn't know who had called. At last she found it. And it was with astonishment, then shock, that she found herself talking to someone who didn't bother to introduce herself but said she was with Tom. The woman wasn't terribly clear in her explanation of what had happened, just that there had been a fight and Tom had been hit and he was a bit woozy right now and an ambulance was on its way. Clara asked to speak to him. His voice was fainter than she had ever heard it. 'I'm really OK.' he said. 'Jan's looking after me. It's only a headache. And probably a bit of shock . . .' His voice tailed off.

Clara, standing in her bare feet in the hotel bedroom, found herself shouting into the telephone, 'I'm on my way. I'm leaving now.'

'It's really not necessary . . .' Tom responded faintly.

She cut him off: 'I'm coming home.'

By the time Ben came in five minutes later she had finished throwing all her things into a bag. To all his questions she gave the same reply: go and find a taxi to the airport.

CHAPTER 10

Clara exchanged pleasantries with the two uniformed policemen, a sergeant and a young constable, before watching them retreat down the garden path into the night air. It was nearly midnight. She gently closed the front door and went softly upstairs, expecting Tom to have fallen asleep, but she found him sitting upright in bed. He smiled as she entered the room and held out a hand for her to come and lie beside him. She reached out, took it, and they lay close, side by side, on the squashy double bed, their Habitat 1980s three-drawer pine bedside tables on either side. Clara had been known to remark that if all the pine were removed from her home, she would be left with no furniture at all. A pile of social-work magazines and Sunday supplements stood on Tom's bedside table. On hers, a pile of legal journals was stacked alongside a clutch of slim modern literary novels. The room was dominated, if not overcome, by the heavy brown velvet curtains that had previously hung in the front room of their old house – and contrasted unsuccessfully with the pink sprigged Laura Ashley wallpaper. One day Clara planned to strip it off and paint the walls some exclusive shade of white . . .

Regarding it all, Clara couldn't help noticing the contrast it made with the opulence of the Hôtel Royal in Deauville – but she also had a sense that, right now, this was where she belonged, in the unglamorous, unfashionable, safe surroundings of home.

'I was really hoping I could avoid giving a statement,' Tom murmured. 'I think Jan may have phoned them.'

'The police?' asked Clara. 'Good thing, too! It could have been really nasty. You've got concussion, you know, it's not a trivial injury.'

Tom shrugged his shoulders. '*Mild* concussion. Medical-speak for a headache. I've seen worse.' His voice slowed. 'It's just a bloody mess. Once the director of Social Services finds out, there'll be a full-scale internal inquiry. Then the CPS will get involved, not to mention the press. They love anything that goes on at the Southhead – anything bad, that is. Try getting them to run a good news story, that's a different matter.'

Clara caught the bitterness in his last words. She had arrived home to find Tom giving his statement. For now she left unspoken the thought that had formed in her mind while she listened to him explain events to the solemn-faced officers: that Tom might be moved from his post at the Southhead. For the moment she was surprised, and proud, at how calmly he was reacting to events that – although he had tried to downplay them – she realised had been desperately volatile and potentially very dangerous.

'Tom,' she said firmly, 'you can't worry about that now. You have to think about yourself – get yourself well.'

'I know,' he said, sounding unconvinced. 'I just keep running through my mind whether I could have done anything differently. We were doing so well, really making some progress . . . changing something at last . . .' His voice tailed off. 'You know,' he said hopelessly, 'it feels so bloody pointless. I've tried for so long to change things and I finally thought I was getting somewhere. Then this happens. Maybe it is all a waste of time . . .'

Clara had never heard such a note of defeat in Tom's voice. Frustration sometimes, yes, and anger with the bureaucracy of the council or the attitude of the papers, but never this tone of depression. If anything, Tom's enthusiasm, his refusal to be put off by obstacles, his unerring ability to bounce back from adversity, had at times been a source of irritation to her. She had taken his earnestness as a sign of insensitivity. But now that she saw him sinking into self-doubt, she was filled with a warmth for him that she had not felt for so very long.

'No, that's not true!' she insisted. 'It's not a waste of time. You make a real difference to people's lives. And how many people can say that about their work?' She was determined to convince him. 'This is a setback, that's all. But the gym can be put back together and the equipment replaced. You can't let one or two bad elements ruin everything.'

'It's more than one or two,' said Tom morosely.

'Maybe,' interrupted Clara. 'But however many were involved, they're in the minority. You'll just have to get better security. You can't let them win.' Clara was surprised by the passion in her voice, the strength of her defence of Tom's work and her determination not to allow him to give up. It was almost as though she was being taken back to their years at university, when Tom's idealism had been a source of inspiration to her.

She had forgotten she had once felt that way.

'Yep,' said Tom. 'I suppose so. Maybe I should just be grateful that they didn't torch the gym – and the estate with it. Mind you, might be an improvement . . .' he concluded, but she caught, with relief, the lightness in his tone. He shifted beside her, his arm reaching over to hold her waist. He rested his head on the pillow and turned to her, his voice apologetic and regretful. 'And you. I feel so bad about your weekend, dragging you back. What did you tell them?'

Clara had anticipated that question, but she still felt a twinge of anxiety run through her. She avoided meeting Tom's eye. Her voice, bright and casual, sounded to her own ears horribly false. 'Just that I'd had a message you were unwell and I needed to come back. He was fine about it . . .'

Keep it simple. No unnecessary details to remember, confuse or contradict. And nothing that even hinted at the truth, which was that she was lucky to be there at all. The Deauville charter flight leaving that Saturday evening had been full, but at the last minute one passenger had failed to materialise and she had run across the Tarmac of the tiny airport to board a plane full of carefree British tourists.

'Still, he'll miss you . . .' Tom sounded thoughtful.

He. For a split second Clara assumed Tom was referring to Ben. She felt her stomach lurch, and her heart began to race.

'. . . seeing his best member of staff disappear,' continued Tom. 'Did Julian take you to the airport?'

'Oh, no. I got a taxi.' Clara, listening ever more acutely to her own voice, now wondered if it betrayed her relief.

'I would have thought he'd give you a lift,' said Tom, surprised, 'How far away is the airport from his place?'

Clara felt a growing discomfort with Tom's line of enquiry. She felt caught off guard, struggling to make up convincing replies to his unexpectedly detailed questions. She needed to change the subject. 'Not far,' she said vaguely. 'I wasn't concentrating on the journey. I was thinking about you.'

That part, at least, was true. She *had* been thinking about Tom. Jan's call had raised more questions than it had answered: Clara had had no idea whether she would arrive to find Tom in intensive care or safely back at home. Thank God it was back at home. Gratitude seeped through her – and with it guilt. Because if she hadn't gone to France, if she hadn't left Tom on his own, he wouldn't have been at the Southhead and none of this would have happened. Perhaps it was some sort of sign, some punishment. No, at least she could put that thought out of her mind. She had never been superstitious. She didn't even read her horoscope.

Beside her, she listened to Tom's breathing slow. She sat motionless, careful not to wake him, only moving to glance at the time on her bedside clock. A quarter to one in the morning – a quarter to two in France. Now she allowed

Ben to enter her thoughts. She wondered where he was, whether he had returned to England, when she would see him again. And what she would say to him when she did. She thought about the mobile phone in her handbag – the ease with which she could slip downstairs to call him. To say . . . what exactly? That she loved him? That she wanted to be with him? That she was sorry the weekend had ended? Would she utter all those words now? She knew that once she would have. But after today it seemed to Clara that the time for easy answers was over – and the future looked far from certain.

Clearly Lucretia was a regular at Bluebird. She was waiting for Victoria at a window table, which looked out on to the bustle of the King's Road below. Victoria was late: she had been delayed at Lady Charlesworth's interminable ball committee meeting, and by the time she arrived Lucretia was already halfway through a kir royale. Lucretia waved aside her apologies. 'Don't mention it. I'm at home here – in fact it's almost a second home.'

Victoria could believe it: the cool white airy room, with its smart diners and even smarter young waiters, suited Lucretia's style. Lucretia waved to a waiter, whom she appeared to know quite well, and playfully asked him to bring her friend a kir. 'I can thoroughly recommend it after a day on your feet – although the shop was dead today. Everyone's still on holiday.'

Victoria grimaced. 'Please don't remind me about holidays. We spent an hour discussing them at the ball committee. It's been a nightmare selling the tickets because everyone's away, and now Lady Charlesworth is panicking about numbers.' She sighed. 'I've had to go right through my address book to get a table together – finally.'

'Who have you got coming?'

'Nancy and Hayden Masters, the Texans.'

'I met them at your party. She's been into the shop, actually. Quite a big spender.'

'I can imagine. Then Philly and Algy.' Lucretia rolled her eyes. Victoria smiled ruefully. 'Yes, I know they're not the most exciting company, but they are reliable – and, most importantly, they're available. Then there's Annie, and I've invited Sam Swinburne for her. He was Hugo's art teacher.'

'He must be ancient.'

'That's his saving grace – no wandering hands. It's only a few months since Hugo died and it might be a bit too soon. But she needs to get out. I wish you could have come on our table.'

'So do I. But you try saying no to Hilda Rudge. She invited me ages ago. God knows who I'll get stuck with. She's dragooned poor Viscount Clement to take her.'

'As if things weren't bad enough with his wife running off . . .'

As the waiter arrived to take their order, Victoria reflected on what good, easy company Lucretia was. All in all it had been an awful August, first uncovering David's affair, then everything that had happened to Tom and through it all the ball to help organise. She had come to dread the fortnightly committee meeting: two hours in Lady Charlesworth's drawing room, with nothing more to keep her going than a lukewarm cup of coffee, listening to a group of women discussing tombola prizes and the raffle. She had found herself growing more impatient with every meeting, longing to tell them just to shut up, make a decision and stick to it. But instead they debated and quibbled and quarrelled about every tedious detail – right down to the colour of the ribbon to be tied round the bouquet of flowers to be presented to the Prime Minister's wife. They were jolly lucky to have the Prime Minister coming at all and Victoria could only imagine, judging by the committee meetings, that he would spend the evening bored out of his mind.

At least tonight would be entertaining. Victoria had no intention of discussing David or anything else distasteful – not that she had buried her head in the sand. Rather the opposite. She had combed through David's pockets, his credit-card statements and his mobile-phone bills. The last two had been tricky. She had had to go back into chambers and pick the lock on his filing cabinet – he always had them sent there for his clerks to deal with. She had done other research too. Arabella's mother, Pamela Clevely-Jones, was a regular on the London social circuit. Victoria had thumbed through her old society magazines, seeking out her poised, confident figure. She was a great attender of charity balls, and Victoria had seen, in her attendance at the Action Against Alcohol ball, that she was an unlikely candidate for David's supposed – or was the word *fictitious* – drunk driver. And the final confirmation had come, as if she had needed it, when she had telephoned the Hôtel Bristol in Paris to be told that Mr and Mrs David Stratford were out. Which was odd, considering that David was supposed to be staying with a colleague and Victoria had been told she could only call him on his mobile.

Lucretia's light-hearted conversation was just what she needed. But after they had ordered, Lucretia flirting happily with the young, tanned Australian waiter, she leaned forward conspiratorially. 'Actually, I've got some news.'

Something in Lucretia's eyes told Victoria that this was serious. She fervently hoped it would not involve David.

'I've left him,' said Lucretia firmly.

'You've left him?'

'Yes – my married man. Ended it. A couple of weeks ago.'

Victoria was unsure what to say. Was this cause for commiseration or congratulation? She settled for extracting further information. 'How did he react?'

'Oh,' Lucretia said breezily, 'he was distraught. Sent flowers, hounded me with messages, turned up unannounced at my place. But it's over. Done. Final.'

'And . . . what brought this on?'

'That's the funny thing. It was so trivial. You see, I was expecting him on the Saturday. I had tickets for the Royal

Opera House. And then, about half an hour before he was due, he called to say he couldn't make it. His daughter had called round unexpectedly with her new husband and they were all going out to dinner.' Lucretia laughed.

'You must have been furious, though,' exclaimed Victoria.

'Not really. It's happened so many times before. You grow to expect it – you *expect* them to cancel and it's a bonus if they can make it. And I've had a lot worse than that.'

'How?'

'Well, take my op two years ago. I had a lump removed from my breast. Fortunately it was benign – but that's not the point. He didn't once come to see me in hospital – and I was in for two days – because his wife had relatives staying and he was required at home. You see, he always said that he was there for me – *said* that we were a couple. It's just that he really meant he was at the other end of the telephone, if it was convenient.'

'So why now?'

'Because I went to the opera on my own. They were bloody expensive tickets and I was dolled up, ready to go, and damned if I was going to waste them. And the thing is . . . it was fine. I thought I'd feel stupid and self-conscious, but actually, if you take the time to look, there are quite a few people on their own. It's just that when you're in a couple you never notice them.'

Victoria thought. 'No, I suppose not. But it's been a long time with him. Doesn't it feel . . . strange being on your own?'

'I think you mean is it lonely? Lonely is such a sad word. And, yes, sometimes it is. But for a while now I've known, deep down, that he was never going to leave. Or, even if he did, it would only be because I'd forced him to and then he'd resent me for pushing him. We'd probably have ended up hating each other. Not to mention that he'd get cleaned out by his wife in the divorce so we'd end up living at my place on my money. And there's another side to loneliness, you know.'

'Is there?' Victoria could think of nothing worse.

'Yes. It's called independence. Being able to do what you want when you want. Not having to cook endless meals or collect their dry-cleaning or buy the newspaper they want. Lying around at the weekend, having a bath at midnight, eating Marmite sandwiches in bed.'

'I think you're incredibly brave.'

'No. It's only like that at the beginning. It was the same when I opened the shop. I was terrified, I thought no one would come. But they did. And I did make mistakes. But I recovered and slowly it got easier. By the way, I'm thinking of opening another. Anyway, the point is, I'm on the market. I want you to find me a nice, eligible man.'

Victoria was saved from thinking of likely candidates by the arrival of their starters – inevitably two salads – accompanied by a bottle of chilled Sauvignon. She was hardly in the mood for matchmaking. There was more than enough of that going on in her own marriage at the moment.

But fortunately, Lucretia chatted on. 'You see, by the end I was only with him because I was afraid of the alternative. But if you stay in something bad because you're afraid of the alternative, you'll never find anything better.'

Victoria considered this. What if you left and never found anyone else? It was all very well if you were eighteen or twenty-five, but surely it was a different game when you were nearly forty. It was a depressing thought, a wave of misery overcame her. Of course, she couldn't admit any of this to Lucretia so she settled for another question. 'But how do you meet people?'

'Oh, it's not meeting them that's the problem. It's sifting them out. I meet people in the shop and the gym and, well, everywhere, really. I don't understand why everyone thinks it's so terrifying. Surely the scary thought is spending your whole life with someone you don't love. Wasting all your love on a man who doesn't love you.'

That was too much for Victoria. She felt her resolution, and her composure, slipping away. Feeling tears spring to her eyes, she reached into her handbag for a tissue. Lucretia looked mortified and the waiter clearing their plates endeavoured to react as though weeping women were a normal part of the job. 'God, Vicky, what did I say?'

How could she reply? Lucretia, after all, was on the selection committee. And Victoria had sworn herself to silence. Even with David. There were to be no sordid scenes, no recriminations, just a period of cool assessment of the options until after the selection meeting. She would bide her time and if at the moment they were hardly speaking to each other that was no different from normal. Then, after the selection she would confront him, make it clear that getting the seat had been a joint achievement, and that that was how life would continue. She would have gathered her strength by then and she would be firm. Whatever stupid fling he had enjoyed with Arabella she would forgive, provided he promised never to see her again. And if he refused . . . Well, she had not quite worked that one out. Call his bluff, she supposed, threaten to throw him out, then wait for him to realise he had too much to lose by leaving.

What, after all, was the alternative? For a start, there were the children. Everyone knew that children from broken homes grew up to be at best screwed-up and at worst delinquent. Then there was the house, destined to be sold in any divorce, and she could imagine the split David would negotiate. Divorce wasn't just a question of losing a husband, you lost a whole way of life – friends drifted away, couples shunned you, Christmas Day was a meal of ready-basted turkey breast and an afternoon on your own while the children went off with their father.

Love did not enter the equation. Love was for the young, the irresponsible, and the childless. So why was she crying?

She looked up through streaming eyes, reached for her handbag, where David's speech was still carefully hidden, and gazed blearily at Lucretia. She was, she understood, at a defining moment, the point at which she could say nothing – and continue to live the lie. Or tell the truth, end the pretence and confront the possibility of change with all the frightening implications that held for her. She looked at Lucretia's face, saw in her eyes compassion and friendship, and felt a sense of calm inevitability descend. It was if in that instant all the noise and rush of the restaurant fell away so that she and Lucretia were alone. And then she heard herself speak. 'Actually, I've got some news too. Things aren't the way they seem. Far from it.' She looked into Lucretia's eyes. 'David's having an affair. And most of what he's going to tell the selection meeting is a lie . . .'

Annie was folding muslin panels carefully over the kitchen table. She was regretting her choice of fabric for the curtains at Cal's show house at The Meadows. Not only did she need a great deal of it – it was also difficult to cut accurately and liberally interspersed with natural imperfections in the weave. She wasn't at all sure that Cal would be amenable to the idea of any imperfection in one of his houses, natural or not.

'Are you still doing that?' Elizabeth called, as she sauntered into the kitchen, in the skimpiest of white vest tops and a blue-printed sarong. She made straight for the refrigerator ice-dispenser, which was to her one of the kitchen's most attractive gadgets.

'I want to get it right,' murmured Annie, holding two pins between her teeth.

'You could swallow those,' said Elizabeth. 'Very gruesome.'

Annie took them out of her mouth. 'If you haven't got anything to do, you can help me.'

'No can do. Celine's still here,' Elizabeth said breezily.

'Still!' exclaimed Annie. 'But it's nearly lunch-time. Since when did a sleepover mean moving in? What on earth do you find to do in your room?'

But her tone was light-hearted. She had feared that Elizabeth would no longer trust her or, worse, blame herself for Annie's actions, until Dr Gove had pointed out that the best way she could prove to Elizabeth and herself that the past was behind them was to live in the present, a day at a time. So she had embarked on Cal's curtains, gone on Sam's painting trip to Devon and had appointments later that afternoon to quote for kitchen blinds at a very large house in Weybridge, then to measure up for bedroom curtains in Oxshott. And Elizabeth had seemed to take her cue from Annie: she was as moody and argumentative as ever but also more relaxed and carefree than she had been during those last few weeks at Railway Villas.

'We've run out of Coke,' said Elizabeth, peering into the fridge.

'But I only bought some a couple of days ago. Can't you drink tap water?'

Predictably, this brought no response. Annie had never known anyone drink as much as her daughter – the ice-dispenser seemed to encourage her: cartons of orange juice and bottles of Coke seemed to disappear as soon as they entered the fridge. At least they had some money coming in: she had done two paid jobs now, both swags-and-tails curtains, and she had found that at Surrey prices she could undercut the competition and still make a healthy profit. Not enough yet for a car, though. Thank goodness Sam was coming later on that afternoon to drive her to Sainsbury's and on to her appointments. Then they were off to see Helen who, in pulling off some of the Boston ivy that was obliterating her upstairs windows and those of the complaining Stimpsons, had fallen off a ladder and was nursing a broken leg.

Elizabeth wandered over to the kitchen table.

'Shouldn't you be looking after Celine?' enquired Annie, not looking up from her careful pinning.

'She doesn't need *looking after*,' said Elizabeth. 'Anyway, she's in the bath.'

Annie did not need to ask more. Elizabeth could only be referring to the whirlpool bath in the master bedroom, which all her friends were desperate to try.

'Are these for Cal's house?' asked Elizabeth.

'One of his show houses, yes,' answered Annie, distractedly.

'He's in *Hello!* magazine,' Elizabeth had the tone of someone who was excited but trying not to appear so. 'There's a photo of him. Celine brought it over to show me – her dad knows him. When am I going to meet him?'

For a second, Annie stopped pinning the delicate fabric. '*Hello!* magazine?' she asked, confused.

'Mum, even you must of heard of *Hello!*' Elizabeth groaned.

Annie had never bought it, but she had, on visits to the hairdresser, had a good look through the salon's copies. Surely they couldn't be doing one of those features on Cal that went on for pages and pages? He was a property developer – hardly of interest to the average reader of *Hello!* 'Meet him?' she said. 'I've no idea. Maybe not at all. He's just lending us the house.'

'Hopefully for loads longer,' said Elizabeth.

Annie wanted to ask more about the photograph – but something held her back. And before she could enquire any further, Elizabeth disappeared upstairs with a packet of chocolate digestives snatched from the cupboard. Her departure did not remove the photograph from Annie's mind. Perhaps it was one of those charity dos, Cal supporting some good cause with the added – or was it essential? – aim of keeping his name in the press. From what he had told her over lunch, he spent more time selling his houses than building them. Or perhaps it had been a private party. A film première seemed unlikely. And she certainly couldn't imagine him at an art exhibition.

She was seized by a desire to know, to see the

photograph. As she pinned the fabric, careful not to let it pull out of shape, she listened for sounds from upstairs. She could not simply go up to Elizabeth's room and ask for the magazine. That would seem too obvious, ridiculous even, and, besides, for some reason she wanted to look at it alone. At last she heard doors slamming, the thudding of feet on the stairs, laughter, then Elizabeth shouting from the hallway, 'I'm just going with Celine to the bus-stop.'

Neither girl came to say goodbye, and ordinarily this would have annoyed her, but now she found herself shooting upstairs, feeling slightly ludicrous yet unable to contain her curiosity. For some damn reason she had to see that picture. She found *Hello!* on Elizabeth's bedroom floor. It seemed logical to start at the beginning, but there were pages and pages about some fresh-faced pop star, whom she didn't recognise, pictured with his fiancée in their newly acquired Brighton seafront home – a rather elegant Georgian town house, which Annie thought they had comprehensively ruined with their luxury refurbishment. Then, more of the same sort of thing with some American actress on holiday, a few pages on that grey-haired man from breakfast television and then the *Blue Peter* presenter with her new baby . . . Until she got to the final page, a gazpacho recipe, and asked herself if this was the right magazine. She began rifling through the clutter on Elizabeth's floor – teenage magazines but no other *Hello!* So she started again, this time from the back, for no better reason than that she couldn't bear looking at what the pop star had done to the interior of the Brighton town house again.

And then she found it, tucked away at the bottom of a page of photographs headed 'Diary of the Week', which was made up of lots of pictures of different parties. She had missed it because it was a small photograph – and because on her first skip through she had only noticed the girl. A sultry dark-haired girl in a gold sequined dress, cut high on the thigh and low on the breasts. Even Annie knew who she was: Tania von Stein, the new star of *Stretton Surgery*. Now Annie saw that she was holding Cal's arm. Tania was looking at the camera and Cal was looking at Tania. She tried to read his expression. It was difficult, she concluded, to judge that he looked anything other than perfectly happy.

Hello!'s party columnist had written a piece at the side of the photograph:

> *Wednesday saw me at the launch of the Guy's Hospital Campaign – 'A Perfect Ten' – set up to raise funds for the purchase of ten new scanners. Among the celebrities present were Tania von Stein, who plays barmaid Carol in Stretton Surgery*. Tania has sent the top soap's ratings soaring as viewers tune in to watch her seduce her boss . . . and his son! With Tania was Cal Doyle, whose latest premier development, The Meadows in Surrey, is already nearly sold out. Also attending were . . .

Annie didn't bother to read on. She continued to look at Cal's face in the photograph. She had never seen someone she knew well in a magazine before – a familiar face now somehow set apart. It felt confusing, almost disorientating and not altogether comfortable. In her mind he belonged at Albert Road, not in some glossy magazine. She wondered why he hadn't mentioned Tania over lunch. They had talked for so long and with such ease . . . But, then, why should he? Lunch was just another part of his damage-limitation campaign in the wake of the Barbara de Longden débâcle. Only, at the time, it hadn't felt like that.

She closed the magazine. As she did so, she felt rather foolish because she had allowed herself to thaw in her feelings towards Cal. Not so that she felt anything romantic towards him – she could never imagine feeling like that ever again – but to allow herself to like him. And to imagine that he liked her, too. But now, as she replaced *Hello!* where she had found it on the floor, she realised she didn't really know him at all. And that allowing herself to develop even the faint stirrings of friendship left her vulnerable to feeling . . . if not hurt, exactly, then more disappointed at the sight of some silly photograph than she would have imagined possible. She would have to be careful not to allow that to happen again. To be more guarded, to take a casual invitation to lunch at face value, and not under any circumstances to put herself in a situation where she might get hurt again. The safest course of action, she decided, was to put Cal right out of her mind.

Victoria was not sure whether to offer Clara coffee or a glass of wine, even if it was only eleven o'clock in the morning. She had known from the tone of her sister's voice on the telephone that this was not going to be a casual visit. She wanted to come round straight away. it was urgent and it couldn't wait. Clara was at the office and she would be in Wimbledon in ten minutes. As she had put down the telephone, Victoria's best guess was that it was about Tom. She knew he was on extended sick leave while the council investigated the incident in the gym – perhaps they had decided they needed a scapegoat and had sacked him.

But now, as she made coffee, she glanced furtively at Clara – pale and anxious, her head in her hands – sitting at the kitchen table, and had the certain instinct that this was not about Tom but about Clara. And it was serious.

'I don't know what to do,' said Clara, looking up at her with an expression of dull despair. 'I can't carry on like this. It's impossible. Work . . . Tom at home on sick leave . . . Trying to juggle everything . . . All the lies and excuses . . .'

Victoria murmured sympathetically, not at all sure what Clara was talking about. She took over a mug of coffee. 'I'm sure it's not so bad. You've been working very hard and doing so much for Annie. Perhaps you're tired – run down.'

But Clara, usually so positive and no-nonsense, did not

respond. Instead she stared at her coffee and began to speak in a voice filled with misery. 'There's someone at the university. A final-year student. His name's Ben.'

Victoria nodded. She thought it best not to say anything.

Clara hesitated, then spoke. 'It's got, well, let's just say it's got rather complicated. For a while things were fine. But now . . .' Her voice cracked. 'Now everything's changed. I thought I could manage it – I thought I had the situation under control – but I can't cope any more.' She began to weep softly, her head bowed, as she reached into her handbag for a tissue.

Victoria was struggling to make sense of her words. Was it a crush? Some sort of student–teacher relationship that had grown into a friendship? Who on earth was Ben? Clara had never mentioned him. Surely Clara wasn't saying it was serious? Victoria cleared her throat. 'I'm sure it can all be sorted out. Students get crushes on their tutors all the time, don't they? I'm sure if you make it clear to this boy, Ben, that you're married—'

'But I'm having an affair with Ben! It's been going on for months!' Clara burst out.

Victoria, in stunned disbelief, watched as Clara cried uncontrollably, tears streaming down her face, her fingers shredding the tissue she held into tiny pieces that fell into her lap. She was struggling to speak through her tears. 'God knows what I thought would happen. I didn't think – I wanted him so much – but I can't carry on. I'm leading a double life – lying to Tom – and then when Tom got hurt at the weekend I so, *so* nearly got caught out.'

'But you were with your boss in France, weren't you?' said Victoria guilelessly.

Clara gave a hollow laugh. 'I was in France but not with Julian. I was with Ben. In a hotel for the weekend.'

Victoria, who was thinking furiously, fought to keep the shock she felt from showing in her expression. Of all the people she would never have believed capable of having *an affair*, Clara was at the top of the list. 'And Tom?' she ventured.

'He doesn't know. But I feel so bad. It's as if Tom getting hurt somehow brought everything to a head. I've realised that it's only a matter of time before I get caught out. I can *feel* it,' she emphasised. 'I can feel my luck running out. Maybe there are women who thrive on this sort of thing – all the deceit and the double-dealing – but I'm not cut out for it.'

Victoria began to see that Clara's complaints about Tom over the last few months had been more serious than she had appreciated. She felt a stab of annoyance at her own lack of perception. Bitterly she considered the evidence: not only was she a poor judge of her own marriage, she had also failed to notice that her sister was having an affair. So she was not about to give advice.

'I've got to end it,' said Clara wearily. She looked up at Victoria. 'I've been avoiding Ben since I got back from Deauville,' she confessed. 'I know I'm being a coward. I just haven't been ready . . . to face him.'

'Is that,' Victoria asked tentatively, 'because you love him?'

Clara sat motionless. At last she spoke. 'I thought I did. I could never have done this if I hadn't. Ben . . . inspires me. He makes me feel young again. Attractive and alive. I know I'm talking in clichés but that's the way it is. The excitement when I know – when I *knew*,' she corrected herself, 'I was going to see him.' She paused. 'But it isn't enough. Oh, it's passionate and intoxicating and . . . addictive, almost. That need to be with him. But I need something more. That's what I began to realise when we were in France. It felt like I was playing a part. And the person who I belong with – who knows me inside out – is Tom. It's the history we have, the years we've been together, the way I can anticipate what he will do or say or think. I had begun to find that so *ordinary*, but now I know how important it is. Companionship, shared interests –

God, I sound like a vicar!' She managed a rueful laugh. 'But it's true. It's the difference between an affair and a marriage. It doesn't mean you always agree, it means . . . looking at the world through the same eyes. And, of course, Tom drives me mad sometimes – but who's to say that Ben wouldn't annoy me at times, too? Believe me,' she looked up at Victoria, 'all that youthful enthusiasm can be very wearing . . .' Clara stopped, and took a sip of cooling coffee. 'You see, I had forgotten the most important thing – that I can tell Tom exactly how I feel and know he'll understand. But I stopped talking to him and then I blamed him for the way I felt.'

'So you definitely want to end this . . . *relationship* with Ben?' Victoria asked tactfully.

'I have to,' said Clara firmly. 'Before Tom finds out. While I still have a chance to make things work.' She paused, then added bluntly, 'I don't think I've got any choice.'

Victoria reached out and held Clara's hand as tears overtook her sister. In the silence that followed she felt her shock dissipate. Like so much that had happened recently, the past was falling into place to form a different picture from the one she had imagined. She felt as though she were living in a film – a film in which the final scene revealed all that had gone before as a sham, a trick played in which nothing was as it first appeared, the whole story constructed on scenes of half-truth and ambiguity, a film in which the truth was very different from that imagined by the viewer.

Victoria found herself filled with a kind of admiration for Clara. Not for her betrayal of Tom – desperately Victoria hoped that he would not suffer the pain of discovering infidelity as she had. But now was not the time to talk about herself. That could wait for another day. For the moment, though, she could not deny that in some sense Clara had . . . courage. The courage to tear up the script, rewrite it and create a different ending. Clara was going back to Tom because she wanted to – because she had looked at the alternative and said no. And whatever pain she endured, she was living in a way that was true. Clara lived by looking for the truth, then accepting it.

Whereas she herself had so wanted to believe. Wanted to believe that David loved her, that their marriage was strong, that their life was perfect. She had ignored every sign that told her otherwise. She had done more than ignore the signs – she had wilfully denied them. And all the while she had told herself that it was for the good of the children, and was nothing unusual because every marriage went through difficult times. David had lied – but so had she. She had lied to herself for years until she could lie no more, when the weight of all the pretence bore down so that it was unbearable, and late into the night she had confessed everything to Lucretia, knowing as she did so that she could never go back.

Now the truth had been revealed: fear had kept her in her marriage. Fear of being alone, humiliated and pitied, stripped of the money and security that marriage for women like her still carried with it. Fear of admitting that David's love for her was dead – and hers for him was dying now that she had seen him for what he was: a man who loved life's prizes more than he loved her. A man who would probably never find happiness because it would always lie for him in the next achievement or conquest, never in the present. A man who was, at heart, painfully unhappy.

She could not change David but she could decide to change herself – taking care not to make any rushed decisions. Now was not the time to tell Clara. Or any of her family, come to that. And, above all, not David, if she was to have any chance to emerge from his shadow and into the light, to a place where her fears could be faced and even overcome.

The day of the Wimbledon Village Conservative Association ball was not going as Victoria had planned. The last-minute committee meeting had overrun by an hour. They had been through the guest list, with many tedious anecdotes from Lady Charlesworth, and, worst of all, Victoria had discovered that the whole Clevely-Jones family was coming. Mrs Bolton had been euphoric: her husband and Judge Clevely-Jones had, it turned out, been in the Army together. And since, Victoria guessed, the Boltons hardly knew anyone else, their children Arabella and Charles were coming too to make up the numbers.

Then the whole committee had trooped off to the Grosvenor House Hotel – only a *London* hotel would do for the highlight of their social calendar – to fuss over place settings and tie rolled napkins with bright blue ribbon. Lady Charlesworth, relishing her power as chairwoman, had been very particular about the bows and made Victoria redo all of hers on the grounds that they were not of exactly the same size. If Lady Charlesworth weren't on the selection committee, Victoria would have been tempted to tell her where to put her bows, her ball programmes and her tombola rota.

Running late, she had got home to receive a garbled message from Consuela that Spam had phoned. Spam? No matter how many times Victoria tactfully asked Consuela to let the telephone ring and switch to the answering machine when she wasn't there, the wretched woman insisted on dashing to the telephone and confusing any caller. So Victoria called Sam who told her apologetically that he couldn't come that evening after all. It was every ball hostess's worst nightmare – one man down. She had barely listened while he had droned on about his mother's fall, her suspected broken hip and ended by sighing and asking resignedly what else he could do.

Personally, Victoria thought he could leave his mother to it and make up the numbers as planned. But she had commiserated politely before phoning David. She had run out of options, short of inviting Jean-Pierre, who was coming round after work.

She reached David in chambers. It was their first proper conversation for four days. He had gone into a titanic sulk after she had arrived back from Lucretia's at four a.m., rather the worse for wear after most of a bottle of Baileys' Irish Cream liqueur. Normally she would coax him out of his silence, ask him attentively a hundred times what was wrong, before he would eventually speak, accuse her of some misdemeanour and wait for her profuse apologies. But she wasn't coaxing him this time and the silences, which in the past had been unbearable, were now rather pleasant.

'Sam's not coming,' she told him. 'His mother's broken her hip.'

'Bloody hell!' exclaimed David, wasting no time on Sam or his mother. 'That means we're down to *seven*. You should have got more people! Some tables have got *twelve*. We're going to look like a load of refugees.'

'I *tried*. Can you think of anyone?'

David came back instantly. 'Cal Doyle! I've got his card. It'll be a great chance to impress him.'

'You can't possibly foist him on Annie,' Victoria objected. 'It's her first proper night out since Hugo, and Cal Doyle's hardly the most appropriate company.'

'I think he'll be fine,' retorted David.

'No.' Victoria was firm. 'You'll have to think of someone else.'

From the silence at the other end of the telephone, David appeared to be doing that. 'Chambers is deserted, all in court . . . I know – Mark Crosbie's in. I'll ask him. He's a nice young man – he'll do.'

Victoria was panic-stricken. It was far too risky. Either Mark would think this was her latest ploy to extract information from him – and sit all night like a terrified mute – or he would get blind drunk to cover his nerves then blurt out their wine-bar conversation, which she now wanted more firmly buried than ever.

'Isn't he a bit young?' she said frantically. 'And inexperienced? You don't want him letting you down. Not with the Prime Minister there.' This was good – David always jumped at the mention of the PM. 'Maybe you're right, darling, suggesting Cal Doyle. First instincts are the best – that's what you always say. And he would add a bit of excitement to the table.'

David snorted. 'It's his cash we want, not his personality. If I could reel him in as a Party donor . . .'

'It would be a triumph for you, darling. I think it's a brilliant idea. Inspired. Give me his number and I'll call him right away.'

It had been short notice, Cal Doyle had sounded surprised – and she had had little choice but to be honest about Sam dropping out – but he had accepted.

He was a man, he wasn't Mark Crosbie, and that was all that mattered. All that remained was to tell Annie, who was due at any moment.

It was now five o'clock and they had to be at the Grosvenor House at eight. David, pleading a heavy case, had taken his dinner suit to chambers to change there. Thinking about the number of times he had done that before, she wondered why. Arabella must have a flat in town and perhaps he found it more congenial to shower in her bathroom – and linger in her bedroom. She had picked up other clues that, before, she might have missed. David had started talking ominously about making economies. Once he was elected to Parliament, his salary as a backbench MP would be a fraction of his earnings as a top barrister. He had made it clear that she would need to get a job, then gone on to suggest that she did a secretarial refresher course. But when Victoria had suggested that she could work as his secretary, in the House of Commons, he had accused her of planning too far ahead. She had let it go – and now she was glad she had.

Annie and Jean-Pierre arrived together, in a bustle of activity, Jean-Pierre laden with brushes and bottles, Annie carrying a holdall and attempting to prevent her wrapped ball gown dragging on the floor.

In Victoria's bedroom, Jean-Pierre tore off the dry-cleaner's plastic and surveyed Annie's dress with disdain. 'What is this? You go to charity shop to get it?'

Annie looked dumbstruck – even before Victoria had a chance to tell her it would be Cal Doyle who would be scrutinising her in just a couple of hours.

'No, no, no!' tutted Jean-Pierre. 'This black is all *wrong*. Why do English women always wear black? It is not glamorous. It is boring, boring, boring! And you,' he pointed at Annie, 'you have white skin and pale hair. You will look like Dracula in black dress.'

Victoria and Annie sat on the bed in silence as Jean-Pierre threw open Victoria's wardrobe doors and rifled through her evening dresses. She had heaps, thanks to all those dull black-tie legal and political functions she went to with David. 'You should have a good clear-out,' said Jean-Pierre. 'It is like Oxfam in this wardrobe.'

'What about the blue?' suggested Victoria.

Jean-Pierre tugged it out and curled his lip. 'These frills – you want your sister to look like powder-puff?'

Victoria sat back and said nothing as every dress was pulled out and returned with a loud sigh. Finally Jean-Pierre was tugging at a dress in its shop wrapping. 'I never wore that,' she said. 'David thought it was too low-cut.'

Jean-Pierre gave her a withering glance. 'So, your husband is now Yves Saint-Laurent? I am *so* sorry, I did not know.' He held the dress up to the light. It was a pale pink Valentino, cut in a simple sheath shape, the silk draped over one shoulder to fall across the bust in a low scoop. Victoria remembered the night two years ago when she had put it on for the Conservative Party conference ball in Bournemouth. David had taken one look at it, asked her if she was coming as his *whore*, and demanded that she change. She had been obliged to go in the black trouser suit she had been wearing all day.

'I think this is good. You two are same size – though your sister Antoinette has bigger breasts. Good. Try this on.' Annie gave Victoria a startled look before she was herded by Jean-Pierre into the guest bedroom.

'Now, we will do your hair.' He took the towel off Victoria's head, peered at her wet hair with faint interest and took out his hair dryer.

Jean-Pierre was in fine form, gossiping outrageously about his Wimbledon clients. Lady Charlesworth, he claimed, had given birth to a love-child by her butler thirty years ago. Victoria found this and most of his other stories hard to credit, but they passed the time. The first she knew of Annie coming back into her bedroom was Jean-Pierre's exclamation: '*Très bien!* Excellent! This is good.'

It *was* good – more than that, it was breathtakingly alluring. The dress fitted as if it had been made for her, creating an hourglass silhouette and a look of effortless, sexy glamour. 'But it's so low,' wailed Annie.

'And you are not boy. You are woman. It is fine. I am not interested in *décolletage* myself – but if I was I would like it,' chirped Jean-Pierre, who had now abandoned Victoria with a multitude of plastic clips in her hair and gone to fuss round Annie.

'Hey, I have some shoes, too,' remembered Victoria. 'Bottom of the wardrobe . . . And I've got the perfect necklace.'

Annie went to bend down and then realised that the fit of the dress made it impossible. So Jean-Pierre rooted through Victoria's collection of shoes, occasionally holding one up to ask what kind of a woman would wear a *clog* like this, and finally found them tucked away at the back. Meanwhile Victoria was shuffling through her jewellery. Eventually she extracted a velvet box. She opened it and held up an intricate necklace of pearls interwoven with tiny rubies: David's present to her on their tenth wedding anniversary, five years ago. It seemed an age away, before Emily was born, when they had still taken care in choosing presents for each other, before everything ... Victoria's thoughts were interrupted by Annie protesting that it was far too good for her to borrow but Victoria assured her, in a voice which was unusually resolute, that it was fine and please would she stand still while Victoria fastened the clasp.

'Perfect,' she announced, but before Annie had a chance to look at her own reflection, Jean-Pierre advanced with the shoes.

'They're a bit big,' said Annie, as she slipped them on.

Jean-Pierre grabbed some tissue paper and stuffed it into the toes. '*Magnifique*!' he proclaimed. 'Now, I cannot stand here talking to you. Take off the dress, have a shower and we will try to rescue your hair. I can see the condition is terrible ...'

In the end Jean-Pierre cut, coaxed and ordered Annie's hair into an elegant wave, sweeping round and falling over her bare shoulder. Her usual frizzy blonde hair had been dried into submission so that it was sleek and shining – 'Like TV advert', in the self-satisfied words of Jean-Pierre.

Victoria still hadn't told Annie about Cal, and just when she thought Jean-Pierre would push off he took it upon himself to do Annie's make-up. 'Where's Simon?' she asked.

'He is making TV commercial. For sanitary towels. He is man who is parachute instructor while girl jumps in her period.'

Victoria exchanged a glance with Annie.

Jean-Pierre went on, 'Of course, he does not do jump. This is for stunt man. He is man who takes off helmet on ground when they have landed. Then he drives off in sports car with girl. He thinks this is big break for him.' He was applying foundation to Annie's face. 'The trick is not too dark. Just a little, to add glow. You have small suntan.'

'Holiday in Devon,' gulped Annie.

'I do not know this place,' he said, and changed the

conversation back to Simon and their most recent trip to St Tropez.

It all took so long. Consuela was late arriving to babysit, then Jean-Pierre insisted on changing Victoria's dress from the black she had planned to wear to a red chiffon dress she had long since discarded as being too *young*. Eventually it was only in the taxi on their way to the ball that Victoria was able to speak to Annie. And, worse, it was Annie who raised the subject. 'I hope Sam's got there all right. Maybe we should have met him at your house and all gone together.'

Victoria took a deep breath. They were hurtling in a black cab along the south side of Hyde Park and she was just about staying on her seat. 'Actually, he hasn't. I mean he won't. He's not coming.'

'Sam's not coming?' Annie sounded devastated.

'Yes. No. He's not. He did try to call you but you were out. So he called me. His mother's broken her hip. But it's all right.'

'His mother's all right?'

'No. Well, yes – probably. I mean it's all right because I found someone else. Or, rather, David did.'

Annie looked hardly less anxious. 'But it's someone I know?'

'Yes. Actually, it's Cal Doyle.'

Annie let out a shriek, which caused the taxi-driver to swerve maniacally. '*Cal Doyle*!' She looked down at her bulging cleavage and ran her hands over the sides of her dress, which clung determinedly to every curve. She wailed, 'I only agreed to wear this because it was Sam. Oh, God.'

'It'll be fine. You had lunch with Cal, didn't you? You're like . . . old friends.'

'*Old friends*! I've just about got to the stage of looking him in the eye. Have you any idea how . . .' Annie wasn't quite sure of the word. Not embarrassed any longer, certainly. Nor ill at ease. But unsure of what, if anything, their relationship was supposed to be. '. . . Uncomfortable I feel every time I see him?' she concluded lamely.

Even that wasn't the right word but it was the best she could come up with. And then that wretched *Hello!* photograph entered her mind. She let out an anguished groan. 'Not to mention the girls he normally goes out with – from what I've read in the papers I'm old enough to be their mother. And now I'm going to have to sit next to him.'

'And dance with him,' added Victoria. 'It's a ball, remember. And from what *I*'ve heard he's quite a raver.'

Annie would have buried her head in her hands if she hadn't remembered just in time not to smudge her make-up. 'I want to go home,' Annie begged.

'Too late,' said Victoria. 'We're here. And I'm not losing any more guests today.'

They walked through the lobby of the Grosvenor House to its elegant ballroom, down a sweep of stairs above which a balcony was laid out with all manner of temptations designed to entice guests to part with their money. Lady Charlesworth's daughters were selling ball programmes and the tombola stall was piled high with prizes – if you were unlucky you might win a tired basket of bath salts or a remaindered cookery book. A more fortunate ticket could yield a bottle of House of Commons whisky signed by the Prime Minister, two tickets to the ballet or best of all, thought Victoria, a case of Krug champagne. Victoria was down on Lady Charlesworth's rota to do an hour at the tombola later, but for now she led Annie to a black-suited waiter holding a huge tray with glasses of champagne and orange juice.

'Just orange juice for me,' said Annie, but Victoria handed her a fizzing flute of champagne.

A trickle of guests had begun to arrive, Tory MPs and Tory hopefuls, aged members of the Wimbledon Village Conservative Association and a sprinkling of celebrities. Victoria recognised Mike Sawyer, the Cockney comedian, and Linda Richardson, who presented *Holiday Swaps* on daytime television. She was not surprised to see Philly and Algy arrive first, anxious to extract every moment of enjoyment from their tickets.

Philly was breathless with excitement, her ancient floral cotton ball gown stretched tight around her tubby midriff. 'Victoria.' She kissed her on both cheeks leaving Victoria anxious that she was now daubed with Philly's bright red lipstick. 'Isn't this exciting? So glamorous! Is that Linda Richardson?' she gasped.

'Yes,' said Victoria, 'and this is my sister Annie.'

Philly tried to look interested, all the while peering over Annie's shoulder at Linda Richardson, who was holding court surrounded by a gaggle of Wimbledon ladies.

'Hi-dee!' Nancy and Hayden descended. Hayden had clearly been dressed up for the occasion – much as his son, Connor, was expensively turned out for birthday parties. He wore a dinner suit like all the other men, but Nancy had teamed it with a yellow brocade waistcoat and a matching yellow bow-tie, which gave him the air of a circus ringmaster. Nancy herself had surpassed all of Victoria's expectations, metamorphosing from Midwest housewife to all-American glamour girl. Her hair had achieved new heights and was topped with a large pink bow of the same material as her taffeta ball gown, a strapless creation that flared dangerously at the waist and prevented anyone getting within two feet of her. The effect was clearly intended to be *Gone With the Wind*, but Victoria was unconsciously reminded of a crocheted loo-roll cover.

Nancy took control. 'Victoria, I sure hope you're gonna introduce us to the Prime Minister.'

Victoria could hardly admit she barely knew the man.

Philly cut in, 'Oh, I shouldn't get your hopes up. He'll probably talk to the MPs – and the celebrities.'

Nancy balked. 'I'm sure he'll want to talk to Hayden.'

Victoria was saved from further exchanges by the appearance of Lucretia. Hayden looked impressed. She was breathtaking in a silver sequined dress, cut low to reveal her bronzed cleavage.

'Let's look at the stalls.' Nancy took him by the arm and dragged him towards the raffle.

'You'll never believe who Hilda Rudge has put me next to,' exclaimed Lucretia. 'Viscount Clement's uncle! He must be mummified by now. Last year they had to wheel him in.'

Victoria laughed. 'Well, after dinner you can escape to our table.' She left Lucretia chatting to Annie about Afghan cashmere and wandered off in search of David. He was late, naturally, and as she scanned the room she saw Arabella arrive. Her heart missed a beat. No matter that she had been forewarned, it was still a shock to see the girl. And the dress. She recognised it immediately. It had hung in the Versace window in Sloane Street for a week earlier in the summer: pale blue, strapless and suitable only for a tall, beautiful, young girl who could carry it off.

Arabella did much more than that: she looked sensational and as she walked to the balcony, heads turned to stare. Victoria marched towards the raffle stall. She had decided to avoid Arabella. There were, after all, limits even to her self-control. She had calculated that with hundreds of guests present she could easily evade Arabella. And she couldn't imagine that Arabella would seek her out.

David found her taking an encyclopedic interest in the raffle prizes. They were in public so he kissed her dutifully before hissing, 'Shouldn't you be with our guests? They're fanning out like lost bloody sheep.'

'I'll round them up,' Victoria sighed, 'and you can help me.' Before he had a chance to protest she had taken his arm, clenched it with an iron grip, and set off in search of their guests. Now they were only waiting for Cal Doyle.

Annie was waiting too, leaning over the balcony and looking at the tables below, where waiters scurried around laying out plates of poached salmon. Alone, she half wanted to be rescued from her solitary state – and half dreaded acting as a couple with Cal. Try as she might she could not get that photograph of Tania von Stein out of her mind. *She* would have carried this dress off. *She* would have mingled expertly, danced elegantly and, however much alcohol she consumed, would have managed to stay upright on her feet all evening. And even if, as seemed doubtful, Annie passed all those tests tonight, she could never be like Tania. Tania von Stein was young.

'Hey, who's the belle of the ball?'

The Irish voice was unmistakable. How long had he been standing there? Annie steeled herself and looked round. Men, she had realised long ago, fell into two categories: those who looked smart in black tie, and those who looked absolutely fantastic. Cal was in the second category. As he leaned forward to kiss her cheek, she smelt the same faint aroma of expensive aftershave that she had first detected all those months ago in very different circumstances. He stood back, the gleaming white of his shirt setting off his tanned face and black hair, which was as unruly as ever. 'I'm only sorry I'm second fiddle to Sam,' he said wryly.

Annie laughed. 'I can't imagine you playing second fiddle to anyone.'

'Pretty necklace,' he said casually. But before either of them could say more Philly arrived breathlessly, with Victoria and David in tow. 'Have you seen the raffle prize? It's a Richard Webster.'

Cal looked blank.

'England's leading modern watercolourist,' explained Annie.

'I thought that was Sam,' remarked Cal, with more than a hint of sarcasm.

Annie ignored him. 'Richard Webster is a genius. He exhibits everywhere – the Royal Academy, all over the world. His paintings sell for a fortune.'

'And he's a Tory,' gushed Philly, 'which is even better. Most of these artist types are socialists.'

'Does he get big tax bills, then?' asked Cal, but this went

over Philly's head and she began counting out change for as many raffle tickets as she could stretch to.

'It's the *Thames by Moonlight*,' Philly continued. 'Terribly valuable.'

Worried that Cal was going to make some other Philistine remark, Annie turned to kiss David. Then David shook Cal's hand. 'Good to see you.' He was at his most effusively charming, and soon he was chatting to Cal about the new law on green-belt planning controls – and, more particularly, on how it could best be circumvented.

From the corner of her eye, Victoria could see that the Prime Minister had arrived. Or, rather, she could see the crowd of people who surrounded him and convulsed themselves with laughter at his every light-hearted aside. No wonder these politicians got an inflated idea of their own importance. Then Edward Butler was heading in their direction. Philly looked as though she would faint with excitement, Nancy had adopted her most toothy smile, and David stood poised with an attempted expression of statesman-like brevity. But when he reached them, and David held out his hand expectantly, the PM slapped Cal on the back and greeted him heartily. 'Cal, good to see you.'

David's expression froze in a sickly smile and he attempted discreetly to withdraw his outstretched hand. But Cal was unmoved. 'What are you going to do about this bloody planning law?'

The PM looked suddenly serious and drew Cal to one side. Victoria was left with her open-mouthed guests staring in astonishment at Cal, who was clearly giving the PM a piece of his mind. Fortunately, at that moment the master of ceremonies boomed, 'Dinner is served!' A tide of dinner suits and taffeta edged towards the steps of the ballroom. Victoria herded her flock down the stairs, looking over her shoulder at Cal, who appeared to be writing his telephone number on the back of an old till receipt for the PM. Then he was caught by a raffle-ticket girl and had to sprint after them to take Annie's hand at the foot of the stairs. At the table, Victoria marshalled them into their seats. Earlier she had written their names on gilt-edged cards. She knew from long experience that the seating arrangements could make or break the evening – on no account could guests be allowed to sit where they wanted.

Annie was placed safely between David and Cal. Meanwhile, as the hostess, it was Victoria's duty to occupy the most boring men so she had Algy on one side and Hayden on the other. Nancy sat to the other side of Cal – they could talk about skyscrapers or something like that – with Algy to Nancy's left. Maybe he could sell her a painting. Philly was tricky. David had specifically said that he didn't want to be anywhere near that boring woman. So Victoria had been pleased to put Philly next to him. As they sat down, she leaned over to her: 'I wanted you to sit next to David. He *so* wants to learn more about Selchester and I know you're the expert . . .'

David gave his wife a filthy look but there was nothing he could do. Of course he wanted Alex to go to Selchester but he was uninterested in any aspect of the school beyond its famous name. In all honesty, Victoria thought, he was pretty uninterested in his children.

They waited, sipping wine, while the other tables assembled themselves. A hubbub of chatter, laughter and braying greetings sent the noise levels soaring as the ballroom filled. All around them, in the centre of a modern city, men and women wore evening dress that had hardly changed in a hundred years. In some cases, the dresses looked as though they had been around even longer: silk and taffeta and even the occasional fur stole on the shoulders of some teetering old dowager. Dresses that their owners had long ago outgrown but into which they steadfastly clambered year after year. Long-sleeved and strapless, clinging or plain matronly, the styles bore little relation to the age of the flesh on display. Victoria wondered, for the umpteenth time, why fat women with sagging arms always chose strapless dresses. Only the young girls, the daughters of the committee ladies, could carry off such an unforgiving style. They were still wandering round the room, beneath the glittering crystal chandeliers, flirtatiously selling raffle tickets to overweight, balding men strapped into their dinner jackets with black silk cummerbunds. The old-money wore black bow-ties they tied themselves. The younger, flashier types favoured wing collars, ready-made bow-ties and flashes of colour on decorated waistcoats.

David followed the old-fashioned look. Of course, he always tied his bow-tie. She remembered his first efforts – she had had to hold a yellowing library book for him, *The Young Man's Guide to Etiquette*, while he struggled with increasing irritation to follow the page of step-by-step diagrams.

At last grace was said and they tucked into their salmon – to be followed, of course, by chicken. Victoria had attempted to get the committee to change the menu they had stuck to loyally for the last twenty years, but to no avail: it was safe, inoffensive and everyone liked it. She fell into her usual pattern, conversing with equal attention to the men on each side of her while attempting to monitor the conversations around the rest of the table. Cal was discussing his new development, The Meadows, with Nancy. 'So,' Nancy commented, 'these are at the lower end of the real-estate market?'

As Cal struggled for a reply, Victoria heard Philly launch into a description of the Selchester house system. 'You see, it's terribly important that you get the uniform colour right. They need their house colours on all their PE kit. That's how the teachers know what house they're in. There are eight houses but I think the best is . . .'

Victoria turned to Hayden. 'How's Ute?'

He looked confused, 'Ute?'

'Your au pair.'

'Oh, yeah. She took over from Marlene, right? I can't really say. Nancy handles all of that.' He lapsed into silence.

Clearly, conversation was not one of Hayden's talents. Victoria had another go, asking him with feigned interest what he thought would happen to the US economy in the next year. Hayden revved up and launched into some convoluted explanation of interest rates and economic indicators. Half listening, Victoria could see Annie laughing with Cal. That, at least, was going well. Sam's mother had done them all a favour. Pondering this she realised Algy was asking her about the Wimbledon selection meeting.

'Yes,' she replied, 'it's in a couple of weeks' time. I'm surprised Janet Williamson isn't here, actually.'

They talked politely about houses and children, and the evening meandered on. Victoria managed a glance at her watch. It was only ten o'clock. Then there would be speeches, the raffle draw and dancing. Lady Charlesworth had been lucky to get the 'in' society band of the moment, Lord Arro and the Cats, after they had had a late cancellation. Apparently a wedding had been called off after the bride-to-be had found the groom in bed with the man who was putting up the marquee. Of course, Lord Arro wasn't a real lord: he was the musician son of a Church of England bishop. But the Cats knew what their audience wanted and churned out cover versions of old favourites, carefully avoiding rap, soul or anything that had been in the charts much after 1985.

Victoria stole a look at David. Annie was occupied with Cal so he was well and truly stuck. Philly seemed to be on the subject of the Selchester Garden Party. 'Everyone goes. The mothers wear hats and lots of the daddies wear striped blazers. Like Henley. You take a picnic and then you sit on the grass. Like Glyndebourne. Then the school band plays and the boys walk around in their formal uniforms with their hats. The hats are a bit like bowlers and you can only buy them in the school shop. They've been made by the same firm for two hundred years. It's wonderful, so traditional, such a marvellous memory for the boys to take away of their schooldays.'

David was now ploughing determinedly through his dessert, nodding politely, too scared to offend anyone before his selection meeting. He was saved any more of Philly's lecture by Lady Charlesworth, in red velvet, walking up to the microphone stationed on the dance floor in front of the band. After exhaustive thank-yous and a couple of tedious anecdotes – during which Victoria could hear whispers of conversation – she uttered the magic words, 'I give you the Prime Minister.'

A great bellow of applause, cheers and foot-stomping broke out. Edward Butler had been Prime Minister for one term and, with luck, he would scrape in for a second. But Victoria could quickly tell that his success was not down to his oratory. It wasn't that he was a bad speaker, it was simply that his speech had been so badly written. No cliché was left unturned. Facing the Future. Building a Better Britain. Citizens in Partnership. And when he attempted a joke it was wordy, so laboured, that even this most loyal audience scarcely managed more than polite laughter.

At last it was over. But no: Lady Charlesworth was setting sail again across the floor. 'We will now draw the raffle, and Mrs Butler has most kindly agreed to select the winning tickets.'

Mrs Butler stepped forward. Victoria tried to imagine what it must be like to be in her place. No power but plenty of responsibility. She must look good, dress well and at all times retain a fixed smile, otherwise the lady columnists of the tabloids would tear her to pieces for her dire dress sense or sourpuss expression. One slip-up, one mistaken outfit, and she was liable to be plastered all over the newspapers and ruthlessly analysed by fashion editors on daytime television. No wonder she looked drawn and tired.

Lady Charlesworth was ordering her about. 'As is the custom, Mrs Butler will announce the results *in reverse order.*'

God, they said that every year. Mrs Butler made a great show of rummaging around in Lady Charlesworth's picnic basket into which the tickets had been decanted. The third prize, a television set donated by Match-Point TV and Audio was won by a young man in what had to be a hired dinner suit. There was more interest in the second prize, a holiday for two at a tennis resort outside Nice. There was a pause after Mrs Butler disclosed the winning number. Everyone was searching through their tickets. Then a cheer went up. Victoria saw that the clapping was coming from Major Bolton's table.

And then, like a film star, Arabella emerged. Victoria, her hands clenched, willed her to fall over, but Arabella strode, purposefully but with consummate elegance, across the dance floor. The pale blue dress hugged her full breasts, the light silk skimming each curve of her perfect figure, drawn tight round her tiny waist and across her flat stomach. Every eye was upon her. Victoria looked at David just as Nancy fixed Hayden with an authoritarian glare. But David's face betrayed no emotion. Arabella gave her most gorgeous smile to Mrs Butler and spun gracefully to return to her table, tickets in hand. This time the applause took longer to die down, as if the audience knew that this girl was perfectly suited to run gracefully across a Nice tennis court before stretching out her amazing body in the afternoon sun.

'And now the first prize . . .' Once again Mrs Butler rummaged and the audience held its breath. Victoria looked at her five tickets without much hope – she never won at raffles – and Philly fanned out her ten before her on the table.

'The winning number is two, five, one,' announced Lady Charlesworth.

Clearly Mrs Butler could not be trusted to read it out.

'Two, five, one,' she repeated.

Victoria looked expectantly round the room. She wouldn't have been in the least surprised if Arabella had won again. That sort of girl usually did. But then she saw

Cal rise to his feet and, without a word to any of them, amble off to the microphone.

Whatever inspired Cal, it was not paintings. With as much interest as he would size up a building brick, possibly less, he stood in front of his prize receiving precise instructions from Lady Charlesworth on where he should collect it at the end of the evening.

As he came back to their table, Lady Charlesworth ushered Mrs Butler away, then turned to Lord Arro and, with a curt nod, indicated that it was time for him to begin. Lord Arro responded with 'Lady in Red'. The irony in his choice was clearly lost on Lady Charlesworth, who waved back at him with a coquettish flourish. As the band played, a few brave couples took to the dance floor. Hilda Rudge led Viscount Clement round in a sedate waltz, his not unhandsome features set in an expression of aristocratic duty. Philly jumped up and grabbed Algy's hand. Soon he was doing a dance, or jogging on the spot it was difficult to tell, while Philly was swaying her broad hips in a manner clearly designed to be seductive. It failed but they looked happy enough. And then a few of the youngsters joined in.

'Luck of the Irish! Congratulations!' Annie was shouting at Cal – to be heard above the music.

He leaned close to her, so that their heads just touched, and bellowed back, 'No luck. It's easy . . .'

'How?' she shouted.

'You just buy half of the tickets. Then it's odds-on you'll win. I fancied the holiday, actually.' He pulled a huge wad of tickets from his suit pocket. Annie looked amazed, but he carried on, 'Anyway, if my art expert's right – that's you, by the way – it should make a tidy profit.'

'You're not going to sell it?' asked Annie.

'No. There's someone I know who'd like it.'

Tania von Stein, no doubt. Annie knew all about her new house in Hampstead. So did the other million or so readers of *Hello!* for whom Tania had appeared just that week, promoted to an exclusive eight-page photo-spread, leading the readership through kitchen, living rooms and bedroom, where she lay draped on a zebra-skin bedspread. Annie hadn't been able to resist buying the magazine – in much the same spirit of self-torture by which she had of late become a regular viewer of *Stretton Surgery*.

More conversation was exhausting so Cal settled for lighting a cigarette and filling her glass. He must be driving. Annie saw that David had disappeared. By now, after a couple of songs, the dance floor was still only sparsely populated. Many of the dancers probably required oxygen. Evidently Lord Arro had decided to take action: the band was belting out a sure-fire winner and Annie had recognised Abba's 'Dancing Queen' from the first few bars.

The next thing she knew, Cal was stubbing out his cigarette and hauling her to her feet. She tried to make an excuse but he couldn't hear her, leading her determinedly towards the dance floor. Of all the potentially toe-curling situations she had calculated that the evening had in store for her, dancing with Cal was at the top of the list. She felt acutely self-conscious, like some fourteen-year-old at her first school disco. Worse still, he was pretty good, moving amazingly well for such a big man while she was giving a great impersonation of a lamppost. He grinned at her, grabbed her waist and began to twirl her round. 'Just follow me,' he shouted.

And she did. Guided by his touch, spinning and swaying to the music, she felt herself relax. And, suddenly, she was the Dancing Queen, singing along to the words, infected by his enthusiasm. And when the music stopped it was too soon – so they stayed put for 'You Can't Hurry Love'.

'One of my favourites,' hollered Cal. Now they were really getting into their stride. Steps from long-ago gym classes – jazz and something she had done for a few months called funky-fit – came back to her. She noticed a few admiring glances in their direction and soon they were attempting ever more complex moves, often unsuccessfully, but that didn't seem to matter. Poor old Sam would have been completely out of his depth.

'Enough,' called Cal, eventually. 'I need to sit down.' They went back to the table and sat in companionable silence, catching their breath with the help of a cigarette. No sooner had they lit up than Nancy moved away. Annie thought she was miming 'Passive smoking', but couldn't be sure. At any rate she and Hayden were heading for the dance floor. And the table was in for a shock. As they looked on, Nancy and Hayden began a rock-and-roll routine to 'Greased Lightnin''. Hayden picked Nancy up and swung her round with startling expertise. Soon people noticed them and the space around them grew wider, lined with gawping onlookers. Even Mike Sawyer broke off from groping Linda Richardson to take a look.

When the music finished they got a spontaneous round of applause. Nancy came back to the table, Philly regarding her with an expression of distaste overlaid with a dollop of envy, but Nancy was oblivious to it. 'Actually, we were the school prom champions. Then Houston junior swing dance champions. At one time we thought about going professional, but I figured banking was more reliable.'

As Lord Arro launched into 'I Will Survive', the Wimbledon ladies stomping defiantly around the dance floor, Lucretia came over to their table and sat down next to Annie. Victoria got up and yelled into her friend's ear, 'I've got to do this bloody tombola. Come and talk to me later.'

As she made her way up the stairs she stole a glance at the Boltons' table. Judge Clevely-Jones and his wife were in deep conversation with the Major. There was no sign of Arabella. She arrived at the tombola table, which was deserted, and resigned herself to a tedious hour. In fact, the whole balcony was deserted, enlivened only by the boom and echo of the music in the ballroom below. After five minutes even that died out: Lord Arro and the Cats were taking a break. The handful of couples who wandered over to her were unimpressed by the scattering of leftover tombola prizes – a tacky silver-plated photograph frame in a battered box, an electric whisk and two copies of some forgotten cabinet minister's autobiography. After three-quarters of an hour she gave up and went downstairs.

The table was deserted, all of them dancing, so she sat alone, listening to the music until she checked her watch for the umpteenth time and was relieved to see that it was five to one. Only five more minutes. On cue, Lord Arro invited them to take the floor for the last dance. It was packed now and she could hardly make them out. She peered through the crush of dancers, searching for the pale pink dress, and it was then that she saw the blue. Arabella was in David's arms. Lord Arro crooned, 'Once, twice, three times a lady . . .' They were dancing very slowly, very close, hardly moving. However hard Victoria tried, she found it impossible to look away. She could not see David's face, but she could see Arabella's and she knew that Arabella's adoring expression was mirrored in his.

At last, Victoria sat back and closed her eyes in silent contemplation of her disintegrating life.

For Annie, heady with champagne and carefree in her mood, it would have been easy to press closer to Cal. The night, the music and the evening they had spent together seemed to invite it. But just in time she pulled herself together – and away. The fact was that Cal had not invited her: he had come as a favour, to cover for Sam, in order to help Victoria. He was virtually a professional playboy to whom dancing the night away was second nature. And all that would happen, if she moved any closer, would be an embarrassed clinch and later some humiliating talk in which he would stutter through a handful of clichés ending with the inevitable 'I hope we'll always be friends'. So she stiffened, avoided his eye and, at the end of the dance, turned neatly on her heel, leaving the couples around them to kiss and embrace.

CHAPTER II

Tom was waving from the sitting-room window and Clara waved back, feeling the falseness of her smile, distracted from summoning all her concentration to manoeuvre the car out of the tight parking space outside their house. She was conscious of her hands shaking as she pulled away to commence the short, familiar journey she had made so many times in the past months. The journey from home to Ben's cottage. But the elation with which she had previously been consumed was now forgotten in her dread of what was to come. She had not seen Ben since Deauville, their only communication his disconsolate messages on her mobile phone. She knew she had behaved appallingly. She had made her decision, after all, and it was surely only cowardice that had stopped her facing the inevitable with Ben. Somehow, though, she had not been ready to say goodbye, unable to say it was over . . . until the days had stretched into nearly two weeks and she had forced herself to act.

And then she must go to the university. She hadn't been in for over a month – first the holidays, then Julian had forbidden her to go in until Tom was well – so she had missed the examination meeting and the posting-up of the results. She knew the scene, had observed it in so many years of teaching, as the gaggle of students waited for Julian to emerge from the meeting and pin them up. They would crowd round anxiously, and then there would be jubilant cries from those who had done well and tears from those who were disappointed.

But now she *had* to get back to work. Her second Tellium action meeting was taking place in a week and she needed to prepare an agenda for James Agnew. Then she had all her teaching preparation to do for the coming term – hand-outs, reading lists and seminar questions to write and photocopy. She had left Tom to sit in a deck-chair in the garden, happily ploughing through a month's worth of *Social Work Weekly* and Sunday newspapers.

His convalescence had been surprisingly rapid, not that the council had taken any notice of that. Officially, he was still signed off on sick leave. Unofficially, Tom knew, they were buying time until some subcommittee inquiry team had decided whether he could go back to the Southhead. She knew he was anxious, fearing the pronouncement of failure on his part by the team, desperate to go back and continue the work he had started, but until then he could only sit at home and wait. But being Tom he couldn't do nothing for long. Clara could only admire the way in which he had thrown himself into a whirling social round. And she had been taken aback to be reminded of how very popular he was. Every day brought invitations and visitors – Annie and Elizabeth, Victoria and even David, who had gone so far as to congratulate him on taking on that *bloody rabble*. The argument had started soon after.

But there had been plenty of other more agreeable company. Brendan, whose boxing classes on the estate had also been suspended – much to his vocal disgust – had taken it upon himself to draw up and supervise a fitness regime for Tom, whom he had pronounced in need of a bloody good shape-up. Cal Doyle had come too, several times, and sat deep in conversation with him for hours on end. She couldn't imagine what they found to talk about. Everyone from Tom's office had visited, and even Jan had turned up one afternoon with a bottle of some rum and cream liqueur. Clara, seeing the discomfiture in her eyes, had popped out to do some shopping and left them to it.

Clara drove past Ben's cottage, observed his TVR

outside and parked four streets away. His expression, when he had opened the door, had gone from startled surprise to enraptured joy. He had thrown his arms around her, smothering her in kisses until she broke away. 'Ben, we need to talk.'

'Yes, darling, of course we do . . .' He had gone to the foot of the stairs, then reluctantly followed her into his front room where she sat down abruptly in the leather armchair. Looking at him standing there, so anxious and dishevelled, she was conscious of how young he was – and how old she suddenly felt. He made to come to her but she forestalled him, crossing her arms, so that he had no choice but to sit on the edge of the sofa.

Seeing that he was about to speak, she lost no time in beginning her prepared speech. 'Ben, the last few weeks have been wonderful. *You* are wonderful. You have so much ahead of you—'

'*We* have so much ahead of us.'

Clara ignored him and stuck to the script. 'And I don't regret meeting you. But we have to stop. We can't carry on seeing each other. I'm not going to disappear out of your life – if you need me I'll be there for you. But as a friend.'

He looked stunned. Poor, sweet Ben had not been expecting this. He ran his hands through his uncombed hair and regarded her with bewilderment. 'This is about Tom, isn't it? About him getting injured. And I understand that you have to look after him. I'll wait for as long as you want.'

'It *is* about Tom, but not in that way. It's about Tom as my husband—'

'But that can change! You can get a divorce when he's better. We can live here.'

He really wasn't getting it. She ploughed on, 'I'm not going to get a divorce. I'm going to stay with Tom.' God, this was awful. She had known it would be difficult, she had anticipated his every objection, but she could never have foreseen the depth of the pain in his face.

She looked away but still the hurt in his voice rang out.

'But you can't! We love each other. We're perfect for each other. You can't stay with him because you pity him.'

Maybe she should let him think that, imagine her as some sort of martyr, spare him from her love for Tom. But she had resolved, in the weeks before, to be honest. It just wasn't so easy in practice. 'Ben, Tom and I have been together for a long time. We have a life together.'

'But—'

'Please, Ben, let me finish.' God, she sounded like his tutor. She *was* his tutor. 'We have a life together. We understand each other. And it's not a perfect marriage, but a perfect marriage doesn't exist – I've realised that now. You change together. The passion goes and what replaces it isn't exciting or heart-stopping but it's *real* . . . Ben, the time we had together, it was very special. But it wasn't real life. It was a fantasy, a sweet, lovely . . . fantasy.'

'But we could have a proper life, too.' An older, more cynical lover would have let her go, but Ben was suddenly animated and determined to fight. 'We can have a life. I'll be working, you'd carry on at the university . . . We could have a baby.'

She had not anticipated that and he had caught her off guard.

He rushed on, 'I know this is about Deauville. I didn't include you, I made you feel left out. But that will never happen again, I promise. I'll change, I'll do anything . . .'

It was pointless to carry on. And her resolve was slipping. She reached for her handbag and rose to her feet. 'Ben, I'm sorry. It's over.'

Now that the purpose of her visit had become undeniably clear, he sat motionless. Clara could almost have gone over to him. Not only had she endangered her job, her marriage and her professional reputation, she had encouraged Ben, allowed his love to grow, only to abandon him in a world where he was already too much alone. And she had allowed her love to grow, a love that was reckless, foolish and flawed – a love which, for all that, she had been powerless to stop. She knew now that you could love someone with whom there was no future, delude yourself that there would be no consequences and still, at the end of it, not quite bring yourself to regret that it had ever happened. But it would not, *could not* continue.

'Ben. I'm sorry. I'm so, so sorry.'

She heard him break down. Unable to stop herself she took a step back towards him to hold him just one more time . . . But then she turned, ran to the front door and let herself out. She had no choice – it *must* end now, the whole mistaken affair. All that remained was to forget it had happened and remove all traces that remained of it from her life. She closed the front door softly behind her.

It was over.

Sam had brought round a couple of her paintings – seascapes of Salcombe Mouth – which he had framed for her, and now he sat with Annie in the enormous back garden of the show house at The Chapters enjoying the last few days there before her move to Albert Road. Elizabeth sat with them. Bored rigid with her summer holidays she was now reduced to sitting with her mother and Sam in an effort to fill the tedious days.

An uneasy calm prevailed. Before Sam's unexpected and welcome arrival, Annie and Elizabeth had been arguing furiously in the kitchen.

'You're just being ridiculous!' shouted Elizabeth. 'Stupid and old-fashioned and – and ridiculous.'

Annie had endeavoured to keep cool. 'You're too young. You need to do your schoolwork. You've got your GCSEs next year.'

' "You need to do your schoolwork," ' mimicked Elizabeth, in a singsong catcall. 'I can do my work *and* do the modelling. It's my only chance – and you're going to ruin it.'

'You'll have plenty of other chances. You're only fourteen—'

'Nearly fifteen. And look at Jessica-Anne. She's done heaps.'

'Yes, and look at her results!'

'Results! That's all you care about. Exams. *Fucking* exams.'

This last expletive had been designed to wind Annie up. And it did. But just as they were set for another round Sam had arrived.

Now they sat drinking iced tea. The house had fantastic garden furniture – all cast iron with cushions the size of pillows – and Elizabeth was reclining on a bed-sized sun-lounger. Sam was chatting happily about his next trip – to Norway – and asking Annie if she wanted to come.

Annie hesitated. 'I'll have to see. It depends how the money goes.'

There was a melodramatic sigh from Elizabeth, who raised herself on one elbow and peered at them over the top of her Versace sunglasses. 'If I did the modelling we'd have heaps of money.'

Annie sighed. 'Even if you did do the modelling, that would be for you. To go into a trust for your education. Not to spend.'

With a disgusted look at her mother, Elizabeth got up and stomped into the house.

'I'm sorry,' said Annie to Sam.

He shrugged his shoulders. 'I'm afraid I'm not much help. Selchester was all boys in my day, still is, so I'm not much good with girls. Always heard boys were more straightforward.'

'Definitely,' agreed Annie, who had no experience of teenage boys but couldn't believe they might be worse than a fourteen-year-old girl in possession of a modelling offer from one of London's top agencies. The letter had arrived two weeks after Elizabeth's Oxford trip, where she had been *spotted*, and life had been hell ever since. The money

340

was amazing – and it would be useful – but Annie, who had no qualifications, regarded exams as a Holy Grail to be pursued with single-minded devotion.

All this talk of money put her in mind of Cal. She hadn't seen him for two weeks now. Not since the argument. If they had been lovers it would have been their first row. But they were not, and so it seemed destined to be their first and last argument – following which he had disappeared from sight.

It had blown up out of nowhere. After the ball she had gone back with David and Victoria, and Cal had gone back . . . well, presumably, to his flat or wherever else he was currently bedding down. There hadn't seemed much to say. The music had stopped, Cal had looked awkward, and David and Victoria were clearly on the verge of the most monumental row. Anyway, they had parted, and she had spent the next week frantically designing, cutting and making up the curtains for The Meadows. It was fortunate that The Chapters' show house had such a big kitchen table. But she had finished them and met up with Dave at The Meadows to hang them. She had half-hoped that Cal would be there. It had taken most of the morning, the pelmets had been a total nightmare and halfway through they had had to start again when one toppled off the wall. But Dave had refixed the pelmet, she had rehung the curtains and the end result had been pretty good. The muslin panels were a masterstroke. And the curtains, if she said it herself, were the best she had ever made. But there had been no sign of Cal.

When he did appear, it was unannounced that evening at The Chapters. In fact, he passed a tearful Elizabeth – who had stormed out after yet another rerun of the modelling row, having announced that she was going to live with Celine.

It was all, Annie could see in retrospect, most unfortunate timing. She had been upset, he had been nonplussed, and they had ended up sitting over a bottle of wine in the garden. He had seemed on edge – and soon she was on edge too, assuming he was disappointed with the curtains. Her nerves frayed, she summoned up the courage to ask him. He looked surprised. 'The curtains? No, I think they're bloody classy.'

Annie gave him a relieved smile. 'Really? I'm just pleased you like them. And I'm glad to be able to do something for you. I enjoyed it . . .' She had no intention of charging him. He'd paid for the fabric in any case and her time was hardly that valuable.

He put down his glass. 'Actually, it *was* something about the curtains but I didn't want to say anything straight away. You see, I've got this contact, a woman who's editor of some fancy magazine – *Interior Inspiration*.'

One of many such female contacts, no doubt, thought Annie.

'And when I saw them I thought, well, I thought she might want to come down and photograph them. Do a piece in the magazine about you. So I called her this afternoon and she's keen.'

Annie was astounded. *Interior Inspiration* was the top-selling magazine for house and garden design. A mention in that – let alone a photoshoot – was worth thousands in advertising. Every chic interior designer, not to mention every rich Surrey housewife, read the magazine cover to cover. 'I'm stunned,' she stuttered. 'I'm . . . I'm . . . very grateful. It's just what I needed to get the curtain-making off the ground.'

He looked happy. If only she had left it at that. But circumstances conspired against her. She had just had the row with Elizabeth. An unexpected bill had arrived that morning from The Maltings for next term's extras. She was worried about the mortgage and all the other bills that would descend on her when she moved into Albert Road. Not to mention paying Cal – whatever Tom had said, she wasn't going to take charity from him. And there had been no one to talk to: Dr Gove was away on holiday and she couldn't bother Tom – he had enough to deal with.

Unfortunately, she had ended up confiding in Cal: 'It's fantastic. Thank you. The publicity will be priceless – and I can't pretend I don't need the money. In fact, it's all I can do to stop Elizabeth taking on this modelling job to help me out. And I'm not having her do that.'

He had looked thoughtful. 'Annie . . . you know, if you ever need anything, anything at all, you can always come to me. If I can help you . . .'

An innocent enough remark – so what had caused her to bridle at 'anything at all'? He was only offering help. But, then, that was exactly the point. She didn't want his help. Or, at least, she did. So why did she feel so ridiculously annoyed?

Whatever the reason, in the confused emotions of the moment she had reacted badly. In retrospect, perhaps overreacted. She had regarded him stonily, speaking with an edge to her voice she had never used with him before. 'Thank you. I appreciate your help. All of it. But in a week I'll be out of here. And I can manage very well on my own after that.'

He had looked astonished. 'I'm only trying to help you with anything you need.'

So, now he was patronising her. He thought she was *needy* – some lunatic woman he had been unlucky enough to stumble upon. She was damned sure he didn't think of Tania von Stein like that. But, then, he didn't put her in the same category – for starters she was past it.

'I know you must think I'm some sort of idiot,' she had snapped, 'some hopeless charity case. Well, I'm not.' She had stood up, hands defiantly on her hips, trying to look authoritative. 'Whatever mess I've got myself into, I can get myself out. I've been very grateful for your help. And I intend to pay you back – every penny. But I don't intend to be patronised, or worse, by you.'

At that point Cal had stood up. But she had to hand it to

him: while she had been shaking with emotion, he was cool. 'Annie, I don't need you to tell me what I think. I came here to help. Maybe I'm not good with words . . . but I think a lot of you. I don't want your money – I know it must be tough being a woman on your own . . .'

The very words Martin Hollis had used. Memories of him mauling and insulting her flooded back. That had done it. Annie had completely flipped. 'Oh, yes . . . Listen to yourself! You don't want my money – well, what do you want? We all know what happens to women on their own. I know, at any rate. Is that what this is all about?'

Now he was angry – and bemused. 'What the hell are you talking about?'

His fury was infectious. Now she was shouting at him: 'I'm not going to spell it out for you. You, of all people, seem to be something of an expert—'

'What the fuck are you going on about?'

So, now he thought he could swear at her. Well, she would show him: 'I think you ought to go. Now. Get out!'

At this point Annie realised belatedly that she was ordering Cal out of his own house. But it was too late to get into technicalities. In any case, he had left – without another word – striding through the house and slamming the front door behind him. It was a wonder that it was still on its hinges. The whole scene had started and finished in a few minutes. And that had been the last time she had seen him.

Now, two weeks later, she sat in the same place with Sam. She could hear Elizabeth banging around upstairs, then some dreadful CD blaring out. She got up and shut the patio doors. Calm descended. Sam gave her a sympathetic look. 'Annie, this is only a suggestion, but have you thought about asking the agency if they would postpone the offer for a year? Then Elizabeth could take her exams and if they went OK she could do some modelling. Maybe over the summer.'

Annie pondered this. 'Do you think they would?'

Sam laughed. 'Annie, you're asking the wrong person. It wouldn't hurt to try.'

It was so typical of Sam. He never rushed in, never imposed his advice, views or opinions, but every so often he would quietly make a suggestion – and in such a relaxed way that it carried no pressure to accept it. He really was a terribly nice man – even regarding her less successful paintings, she really wasn't very good at drawing people, he had always somehow contrived to find something positive to say. Now he was chatting on: 'Of course, we never had children so I hesitate to give advice. Not to mention being over the hill. I suppose one should be grateful for the happy memories.'

'Yes,' said Annie, and then found herself adding, 'But I don't think you can ever rule out falling in love – again.'

It was the most astonishing thing for her to say. Not because of Sam, simply because she could never, in the aftermath of Hugo's death, have even faintly contemplated the prospect of finding love again. Dr Gove had been the catalyst for change. In their last session before he went on his three-week break they had talked about love. He had brought up the subject. And she had endeavoured to cut him off. She had been married to Hugo for nearly five years, and he had been dead barely six months. That was when Dr Gove had pointed out another number to her. Or, rather, a fraction. That at a conservative estimate she still had half of her life ahead of her. Did she intend to live without love for the remainder of her days? It had proved a thought-provoking comment.

Now she went on, 'I don't think it's got anything to do with age, actually. Or past relationships. I think it's about an attitude, being open to love and prepared to change.'

He looked pleased. 'So you don't think one can become . . . too set in one's ways? Unable to adapt to living with another person again?'

'I'm sure it must be more difficult when you're older but, then, I know plenty of impossible younger people.' She raised her eyes to Elizabeth's bedroom window, and Sam grinned. 'The point is being in love, truly in love, with the other person. And being willing to discuss any problems that arise.' She couldn't imagine anyone having difficulty discussing anything with Sam. They really did have the most interesting conversations: a discussion on art would lead to religion and into the realms of spirituality or the universe or goodness knows where. Or they could just sit and talk about gardening. There was only one topic they both shied away from: sex.

Sam got up and began clearing away the glasses. 'Well, I must be off. Dinner with Mother tonight.'

Oh, God. She hadn't even asked him about her. 'How is her hip?'

He looked nonplussed. Then, 'Oh – yes. Coming along nicely.' He trotted off towards the kitchen door. Annie watched him retreat. That reply was so characteristic of Sam, too. He had never once burdened her with his problems. And from the way he had brushed aside her question, she suspected that his mother might be much worse than he was letting on.

Clara knew that she would have to tell Tom. She couldn't sit in Richmond Park for ever. And it was hardly the quiet refuge she had envisaged, what with the deer, the joggers, the dog-walkers and the cars, not to mention the planes skimming overhead into Heathrow – it had to be the busiest park in England. But now that she was barred from the university she had taken to coming here in the morning, occasionally going for a walk but more often just sitting in the car and contemplating how the concoction of lies and betrayal that she had constructed was about to come tumbling down on her head. And all for the most unlikely reason.

It was hard to believe that it was only a week since she had fled from Ben's cottage. It seemed so much longer. Leaving Ben, driving to the refuge of the university, she had

346

believed the worst was over and, however badly she had
behaved, whatever misery she had created, neither Tom nor
anyone else need ever discover any different.

She had arrived at the law school and gone into the
office. Her postbox was bulging and the overspill had been
decanted by Julian's secretary into a cardboard box. She
gathered her mail together, and paused to look at the
results sheet. Ben had got a first – she had known that,
Cameron had mentioned it when he last called. Belinda
Weaver had got a second, undoubtedly the right classifica-
tion but she would have been disappointed. Francine Lewis
got a third, which was no surprise. She reached the staff-
room door just as Julian opened it. 'Ah, Clara, I heard you
were in.'

She realised immediately: she saw it in his expression,
heard it in his voice, felt it in herself.

'Perhaps you could come into my office.'

There was no 'perhaps' about it. Julian knew. They were
both too experienced, understood each other too well, to
play games. Clara followed him into the room where he
gestured her, appropriately enough, to the low chair at the
side of his desk. He began to shuffle papers.

'Please, Julian, let's just get on with it.'

He looked relieved: Clara, ever the professional, wasn't
going to make this more difficult than it already was.

He reached for a file on his desk. She could predict the
form: a rumour had circulated and could she comment on
it? Yes, she could – and then the careful, evasive replies.
They would be tricky – and, in her present state, hard to
sustain. She braced herself.

Julian sighed and put on his trademark gold-rimmed
round spectacles. 'There has been a complaint. A formal
complaint. In essence the substance of the matter is that
you, in contravention of university regulations, have con-
ducted over a period of time,' he looked over his glasses at
her, 'which includes the period of university examinations,
an improper relationship with a final-year student – namely

Ben Ford. The complaint goes on to allege that you showed undue favouritism towards him to the detriment of other students. Detriment that has affected final-examination gradings. It also alleges that you seriously neglected your teaching duties and your pastoral work on account of this relationship.'

Clara was horrified. A formal complaint. That took the matter into the arena of sexual misconduct. *Serious misconduct.* But surely those regulations were designed to stop old male lecturers, or rather lechers, seducing young impressionable female students? Not a situation like hers, which was utterly different.

'Julian, this is ludicrous,' she protested. 'This is a completely inappropriate response . . .'

Julian surveyed her coolly. 'I think you will have to let the university decide on what is an appropriate response.'

That stung. He had slapped her down like a recalcitrant child.

'As I was saying. The complaint is one of serious *sexual* misconduct.' The word, coming from Julian, was charged with an air of sordid misdemeanour. 'I take it from your reaction that there is some truth in this.' He took off his glasses and moved to face her directly. She was a prisoner under inquisition.

'Yes . . . No.' She faltered. 'I mean, the situation is not as simple as that.'

'No?'

'No. I did have a relationship with Ben Ford, but it is over. And it has never interfered with my teaching commitments. I never showed him any favouritism what-soever.'

Julian said nothing. The silence was worse than any condemnation. He consulted his papers.

If only to break the awful atmosphere, Clara said, 'Who has lodged this complaint?'

'Belinda Weaver. And I have to tell you she has done

rather more than lodge a complaint. She seems intent on pursuing the matter with some vigour.'

'But this has nothing to do with her.'

'Not in Miss Weaver's view. She says that some weeks ago she asked you to supply a reference for her – which has still not been received by her potential employers. She also notes that whereas you awarded her,' he leafed through his file, 'sixty-nine per cent for her medical-law paper, Ben received seventy-two.'

'Which were correct marks!'

'Maybe . . . but it made the difference in her case between a first and a second.'

Clara sat back. If only she had got that wretched reference finished. If only she had been to the exam meeting – ever-generous she would have argued in favour of a first for any candidate poised so narrowly on the margins. And she knew exactly how Belinda felt because, nearly twenty years ago, she too had narrowly missed a first. And it had taken her years to forgive the anonymous examiners who had robbed her of the success she had believed to be her due.

'In any case,' continued Julian, 'I'm not here to act as judge and jury. On the surface there is a case to answer. And that will need to be heard before a university disciplinary hearing.'

'But how long will that take? I need to get on – I've got a Tellium meeting next week.' At least that would mollify Julian. But from his stony reaction Clara realised she had misjudged his mood still further.

'Clara, I'm not sure you understand the severity of this. I have no choice but to suspend you until the outcome of the hearing. You may wish to get legal representation.'

A suspension? Legal representation? How on earth would she explain this to Tom? Tom, who was mentally shattered, physically weak and more dependent on her than ever, telling her every day that she was his support and inspiration to get well.

Julian was continuing, 'Of course, it may all come to nothing. Or just a formal reprimand.'

'And at worst?'

'Clara, I can't mislead you. Sexual misconduct is a touchy issue, these days. The university has to think of the publicity. You should at least consider the possibility that you will face dismissal.'

How had it come to this? It wasn't possible. An affair, something people did all the time . . . She was stunned and unable to respond. She caught Julian's closing words. 'I suggest you go home. I'll call and let you know the date of the hearing and the procedure to be followed.'

'But my preparation – the Tellium meeting?'

His reply hung in the air: 'You should have thought of that before'. But instead of voicing those words, Julian rose to his feet. 'All in good time.'

He was cutting her loose, she could sense it. His distaste, and disappointment in her actions, were almost palpable. It had taken so long for her to build up a reputation – and so little to destroy it. And if she lost her job it would be difficult to find another. She had lost Ben and now she would lose Tom, too.

She went to the door. 'I'll just go to my office and get a few things.'

'No.' His response was decisive. 'I'm afraid I must ask you to leave the university premises straight away.'

Shocked, distraught and nauseous she had stumbled to her car.

And now to the park, where for days, pretending she was going to work, she had agonised as to how she would tell Tom the whole, awful, sordid truth. She still was no clearer in her thinking. But how could she continue to conceal the loss of her job? And, more significantly, the reasons for it. However much she ran it through her mind, it just wasn't possible.

Finally, she started the engine and prepared to drive

home – where she would have with Tom the conversation she had most hoped to avoid.

The day of the Wimbledon Village Conservative Association final selection meeting had at last dawned. After years of planning, months of preparation and days spent rehearsing David's speech, everything would be settled today. Everything. Victoria stood in the guest bathroom, David having banned her from theirs, applying her make-up. Jean-Pierre had not been available so she had washed her hair, tied it back in a severe ponytail and was currently daubing on grey eye-shadow.

She knew she looked terrible, which, in all the circumstances, was hardly surprising. The selection meeting had all but taken over her life in the last month. Clothes, speeches, constituency research had all been painstakingly assembled. And in between times she had been dashing over to Richmond. Tom was making a breathtaking recovery but Clara looked dreadful – the suspension and the waiting. Tom, of course, was livid.

From their bedroom, she heard David's voice in yet another recitation of his speech. In truth, it wasn't one of her best. But, then, she was only human, as she had latterly discovered. It was difficult to feel inspired by a husband who danced with his mistress at the ball she had spent so many tedious hours helping to organise. But she had taken some small immediate revenge, casually asking David over dinner when they would receive some fees from his Beaconsfield drunk driver because the final payment for the garden was due to Earthly Pleasures. Caught off guard he had stalled, before retaliating with the exasperated explanation that his client was the wife of a judge, he was carrying out a professional favour, and naturally he could not charge for his assistance. He had gone on to remind her that she had forgotten to collect the Dubai cheque, which he had been obliged to bank himself, and with half of the filing cabinets in chambers broken into by some petty thief it was a wonder he had accomplished anything at all.

Victoria knew that that had been a masterstroke – she had levered open Kitty Standing's desk drawers into the bargain with her nail scissors.

But at least David had been out most of the time – whether at Arabella's or smooching the committee Victoria didn't care. He had, she knew, called in on all its members, listened to their woes and offered his services at any hour of day or night. Lady Charlesworth had taken him literally and he had been obliged to cancel a lunch engagement to drive her to her chiropodist. She had then booked him for the return appointment in a fortnight. Between the round of drinks and dinners he had also found time to nip furtively into Village Sunbeds to top up his tan – worried that with everyone else newly returned from their holidays he would look pale and, therefore, poverty-stricken.

Now, as they arrived at the constituency offices, David looked rightly confident. True, he had complained about Victoria's suit – an old black number that had put in sterling service over the years – but he had no reason to feel anything other than perfectly prepared. He looked frankly gorgeous, hair swept back, white shirt gleaming, red tie immaculately knotted. The red tie had been touch and go, but she had persuaded him to wow them with a bit of glamour.

Once more, she took his arm and they stepped gracefully into the familiar drab committee room. There were more people this time – the final selection vote was open to all the Association's members, not solely the committee, but barely thirty had bothered to attend. As Victoria had told Philly, always a fan of David, the result was a foregone conclusion – and, yes, Philly must go to Rufus's speech and drama lesson that same morning. She would not be missed – Victoria would be sure to give her apologies personally to Viscount Clement.

In the crowded room the committee circled each of the

two candidates, like vultures round wounded animals. Lady Charlesworth was looking particularly dark and feathery in a fur-trimmed black wool suit. Victoria had discovered that it was Lady Charlesworth herself who had returned Janet's application for a ball ticket, with a curt note to the effect that all the tickets were sold. She would be a problem. So would Hilda Rudge. Victoria had realised that Hilda had only a handful of hobbies, few interests and absolutely no friends. She could find no one who would admit to having been taught by her in her thirty years as a headmistress – maybe girls under her tutelage blotted out the experience in some kind of post-traumatic stress reaction.

David walked straight past Janet Williamson, not through any desire to snub her, at least not openly, but because he did not recognise her. Janet was chatting happily to Viscount Clement in a trim-waisted cream suit, her auburn hair falling to her shoulders in much the same style that Jean-Pierre had created for Annie. Somehow, she had contrived to lose nearly two stone in just over a month. She looked radiant. The more romantic members of the committee would be enchanted to ascribe this to her recent engagement – proof of which was the sparkling engagement ring that graced her left hand, drawing more interest than her last speech ever had.

The radiance was in fact down to a new regime of intensive moisturising, exfoliating and toning. Simon had proclaimed her skin dehydrated while Jean-Pierre said it reminded him of *peasant woman*. An appointment with a dermatologist had followed. Then laser work on her broken veins. A beauty therapist, manicurist, and an octogenarian lady who taught deportment – inevitably a client of Jean-Pierre – had been engaged and put to work. Victoria had dragged Janet to and fro, all the while monitoring her daily intake of four grapefruit and three ghastly slimming milk shakes, but Janet, whatever her initial bewilderment, had been a trouper.

Jean-Pierre had been tempestuous, irascible and brilliant.

He had described Janet as his greatest ever challenge. And afterwards his most triumphant creation. He had even chipped in with the speech – the first draft of which had been discussed between Victoria and Janet during the interminable day it took to do her hair extensions, the appointment extended even further by Jean-Pierre rushing off every five minutes to field yet another personal telephone call. Though in the end Victoria had been obliged to drop Jean-Pierre's suggestion as to a new bank holiday to mark London Fashion Week.

As for Simon, his main part was still to come. He stood gallantly to Janet's side, the epitome of Tory manhood. Clean-cut, short-haired – although that had been something of a battle – and encased in a sober suit of near black. His City shoes gleamed. Victoria had had to do the polishing – shoe cream gave Simon atrocious eczema.

As David continued his progress round the room, Victoria spoke discreetly to Janet. 'Best of luck! You look marvellous. It's yours for the taking.'

Janet replied, in her newly acquired Home Counties accent, 'Thank you so much, Mrs Stratford. You've been awfully kind. I do appreciate all your help.' The elocution teacher had not only straightened out her vowels: she had provided her with a whole new *super* vocabulary. And forbidden her to indulge in any northern ideas about first names or affectionate greetings. *Darling* was in, *pet* was out.

At five to eleven Viscount Clement called them to order. It was not expected that the meeting would take more than a couple of hours: with only two candidates required to give a ten-minute speech and answer questions, everyone expected to be out, after a short deliberation, in time for lunch. Victoria looked across to where David and Janet were standing with Viscount Clement. David had clearly recognised Janet now and Victoria could see that he had been caught off guard, smiling charmingly, of course, but not quite succeeding in banishing the faint trace of bewilderment at her transformation that Victoria, if no one else, could read in his eyes. Victoria continued to watch him closely and caught his further look of surprise when Janet volunteered to go first. David rapidly accepted her offer, presumably before she had time to change her mind. This seemed to restore his equilibrium and he gave Victoria a light-hearted wave as he left the room. She settled herself next to Lucretia. This time spouses were not only allowed to attend, they were expected to sit next to their partner and be prepared to answer questions from the audience.

As Janet stepped up to the speaker's table, Simon sat to her side, his features fixed in manly love. Both aspects were important. He must be strong but supportive, loving but not cloying. He had been a willing student, sitting with Victoria through hour after hour of videos – *Love Story*, *Butch Cassidy and the Sundance Kid*, *Rocky I* and *II*, though Victoria had given up after that. Then they had watched David's old tapes of the Conservative Party conference. The end result had emerged as a cross between Brad Pitt and Winston Churchill, Simon excelling in his expression of smouldering statesmanship. He had thrown himself into the part – it had been Janet who had taken some persuading. Reinventing herself, she had argued, was one thing: inventing a wholly fictitious other person was something else entirely. Until eventually Victoria had asked her bluntly if she wanted to win or settle for second – for the umpteenth time? Did she actually want to be an MP or carry on in the useful but not terribly fulfilling role of the token woman drafted in to make the short list of every safe constituency in the country look respectable? And what about all those girlfriends and fiancées of bachelor, or rather confirmed-bachelor, candidates, who somehow never made it to the altar? At that Janet had buckled. Janet wanted to win.

And now all eyes were upon her. The room was full, plastic chairs crammed into every corner. Victoria estimated there were thirty-five people. Janet gave the room her most elegant smile, like the Queen's when she was receiving a posy from a young child – which indeed it had been modelled on. Gone was the warm northern bluster. In its place, a sober reflectiveness.

'Today our minds are turned towards Wimbledon Village – our strongest and most traditional Tory constituency. Our hopes lie in the continuation of our marvellous Conservative government. But our souls remain steadfast in our loyalty to Britain and the Queen . . . and for me, there is another more personal thought. The joy and honour that I have in presenting to you my fiancé – Charles.'

Charles. A princely name. There was a pause as the audience gawped at Simon, his head slightly inclined in majestic patronage.

Janet had made a superb start. She had flattered the constituency, the government, and got the Queen into the first paragraph. Victoria settled back and listened to her own words. Janet was talking about the family, the foundation of a law-abiding society, and dropping in a bit about her non-existent wedding plans. Then the economy and heaps about Wimbledon. They liked it, but more than her words they liked *her*. The suit was perfect, the make-up subtle and the one-inch heels on her navy court shoes just the right height – ladylike, not tarty. She hadn't got the vowels quite right, but no matter: most of them needed hearing-aids anyway. The room was getting increasingly hot, and Hilda Rudge chose a moment halfway through Janet's speech to bang around opening a window, with the result that Victoria's sentence on juvenile crime was all but drowned out by a passing police siren. But Janet coped. She paused and repeated the line: 'Young offenders must learn – the hard way – that crime will never pay.'

Major Bolton gave a loud 'Hear, hear,' at that point, earning himself a filthy look from Hilda. But he was looking adoringly at Janet. He would be. Tom, master-minding the entire operation from his deck-chair, had roped in Cal Doyle. Victoria wasn't sure why – though Cal appeared to be under the mistaken impression that Janet had been born in Liverpool, the daughter of an Irish brickie. But he had been happy enough to put in a call to the PM, who had in turn spoken to his private secretary, who had in turn telephoned Major Bolton to tell him that the PM was currently working on the New Year Honours List. He had been most impressed to hear of Major Bolton's work with the Heritage in Architecture Association. And did Major Bolton agree that it was vital to get more women into Parliament? Major Bolton did agree, emphatically and absolutely. And now he sat contemplating Janet, the key to his anticipated peerage no less, willing the filly on to the finish line.

The ten minutes passed in a flash. Then the questions. Victoria was suddenly nervous and looked to Lucretia for moral support. But Lucretia was too busy getting her question in first. Viscount Clement ignored the hands that had gone up before hers: 'Lu – Miss Stanley.'

'Thank you, Lord Clement. Miss Williamson, congratulations on your engagement!'

Victoria began clapping and soon they had all joined in, except Hilda Rudge.

'Can you tell us if you have any plans to start a family?'

Good. Get it out of the way with a sympathetic question.

Janet smiled. 'I believe – perhaps I'm old-fashioned – that a baby is a gift from God. If Charles and I are so blessed then I will greet the Lord's decision with humble gratitude, while drawing strength from Him to carry out my parliamentary and motherly duties to my utmost ability. And if it is ordained that we are not given the gift of a child, then I will accept that also.'

That would stump them. The matter was now in God's hands – and even Lady Charlesworth would hesitate before ordering Him about. It was all going swimmingly. Monarchy – yes. Socialism – no.

Then Hilda Rudge. Victoria held her breath.

'*Miss* Williamson, how do you expect to combine the

work of an MP *if* you are selected,' Hilda made this sound as likely as Janet flying to Mars, 'with your championing of the cause of single mothers?'

Easy. They had worked on that one for hours.

'Miss Rudge, I think you are wholly right to ask that question.' Janet smiled.

Hilda looked confused.

'*Wholly* right,' repeated Janet. 'Which is why I am leaving my present post to join my fiancé,' she exchanged a simpering glance with Simon, 'in his business. Which, I am delighted to inform you, is a film-production company currently planning a Dickens adaptation to be filmed in this very constituency.'

Whispers broke out. Who would star in it? Would they need extras? Most of them could supply their own original costumes, thought Victoria. She had calculated that however stuck-up they were, everyone loved the glamour of movies – and nearly everyone had a child, niece or godchild with theatrical ambitions.

Hilda sat back, defeated. There were no more questions. Janet took Simon's arm and sedately left the room. They passed David on his way in. He didn't give Simon a second look – he never noticed staff.

As he took his place, Lucretia leaned over and whispered to Victoria, 'That tie – how on earth did you persuade him to wear it?'

Victoria, making her way to David's side, had no chance to respond beyond a conspiratorial smile.

Viscount Clement also appeared to be regarding David's garish red tie with bemusement. He was key to the entire operation. Victoria had enlisted Lucretia or, more accurately, her cleavage to deal with him. Lucretia had started gently with an invitation to a small drinks party she was holding. Then dinner for two. And then . . . Viscount Clement had found himself pursued by a beautiful woman who appeared to wear less and less on each of his successive, and ever more frequent, visits. He found her intoxicating. Overpowering. And very persuasive. The feminist cause had never been close to his heart, but Lucretia had given him quite another perspective on the matter. If she was your average feminist, then put him down as a convert.

David didn't know it – thank goodness – but he was starting from behind. That explained the laid-back way in which he regarded the committee. Victoria knew he should be looking more respectful so she gave him a broad smile, their code to indicate that Janet's speech had fallen flat. David visibly relaxed still further. Then he was off: 'I would first like to thank you for inviting me here today. My particular thanks go to Lord Clement, your esteemed chairman. The issues that confront our constituency . . .'

Good. By singling out Viscount Clement for thanks, David would have offended the rest of the committee who had not been mentioned – he had pointed this out but Victoria had countered successfully that Viscount Clement was the single most important figure in the room and must be accorded due respect. Sure enough Hilda Rudge, who normally gazed at David with unalloyed devotion, wore a distinctly peeved expression. Then he was off through family policy, defence policy and the future of the monarchy. Victoria had added a bit about careful reform, hoping that any mention of change would upset them. Next came the drains: 'Our Victorian drainage system is in danger of collapse – with all the problems of insanitary conditions and rat infestation that come with a disintegrating network of sewers and pipework . . .'

This had been the hardest part, but Victoria had assured him that it was the issue dearest to the committee's hearts: he just hadn't picked up on it because, quite rightly, he had been bogged down in listening to all their anecdotes and ailments. And, sure enough, when David had popped in to see Lucretia a couple of days later, the silly woman had seemed obsessed with the subject.

Now he was running through an explanation of water-table movements over the past hundred years, flood-assessment risk, and a detailed overview of the infrastructure spending that would be needed to replace all the manhole covers in the constituency over the next ten years. The audience shifted, bored and somewhat bewildered by this latest prolonged topic.

But then their attention was caught by the door of the committee room swinging open. Jean-Pierre stood in designer black, two shuffling pensioners to either side. 'I am taxi-driver,' he shouted. 'This is Mr Stratford's parents. Mother and father.' He pushed them into the room, then bolted before anyone had a chance to recognise him. In any case, all eyes were on the two newcomers, while in the background David finished his explanation of the pros and cons of water-metering.

Mr Stratford shuffled forward, his shapeless trousers teamed with a patterned grey cardigan worn over a faded shirt. David's mother, contrary to Victoria's precise instructions, had made more of an effort. She had squeezed herself into a 1970s viscose trouser suit, navy blue, to which she had added a corsage of pale blue artificial flowers.

For a second, Victoria felt a pang of conscience. As David's parents, neglected and all but forgotten by their son, they had arguably suffered enough. But she had needed them if she, as well as Janet, was going to win. She needed them because of what they represented – by their mere presence, for the doubt they would plant in the committee's minds. She needed the reaction of unpleasant snobbishness which they would provoke among the more stupid members. And she wanted the questions they would raise among those who were more intelligent. As if on cue, she caught Viscount Clement flick through the papers in front of him until he reached David's CV. A CV on which he would find a date of birth, but no place name. A CV careful to detail David's qualifications, but not his school. David had never been so stupid as to lie about his past. He had simply buried it and replaced it with a façade that no one – at least until now – had thought to question. Why should they? All the pieces fitted so perfectly – a flourishing practice at the bar, a son down for Selchester, a smart London club. A country house, beautiful wife and parties at which all the right people drank flowing champagne amid antique furniture. She could go on. After all, she had participated in constructing the illusion for long enough. But now she had come to her senses and realised – as the committee were doing – that David was not what he appeared. That he was a fake, a fraud, a man who was not at all what they had imagined him to be.

Lucretia got up and took two chairs to the front. David was paralysed, beads of sweat forming on his brow. But no sooner had the Stratfords, amid much fussing, strewths and blimeys, sat down, than Mr Stratford reached into his cardigan pocket, pulled out a tin of tobacco and a sheaf of cigarette papers, and rolled himself a cigarette. David was now labouring against a tide of tobacco smoke, his father's hacking cough and the astonished muttering of most of the room. His final section, including an impassioned plea against the addition of chlorine to drinking water, passed over his audience in a haze of confusion.

A flurry of chatter broke out as soon as he sat down, the members craning to gain a better view of the surprise newcomers. Evidently David's mother judged that this was the right time to follow Victoria's suggestions: she heaved herself up, trotted over to a horrified David and patted his hair. 'How's my boy, then?'

Maternal devotion was called for – and maternal devotion she would provide. Victoria had made everything clear. David, she had explained gently, was ashamed. *Ashamed* that he had not proved himself worthy of the upbringing his parents had sacrificed themselves to provide. But, at last, he felt he might be good enough to stand before them. More than that, he needed them to will him on. Admittedly all this had taken an inordinate amount of time over several visits. She had been obliged to sit for hours in their stuffy flat, thick with smoke, half-deafened by the television that was never switched off. She had assured them that they were wonderful people, salt of the earth, and they mustn't change a thing about themselves. David didn't want to hide his origins – wherever had they got that idea from? He revelled in his working-class roots. As would the committee. So, they could help David by dressing just as they always did, acting as they did at home, and mixing with as many members of the committee as possible.

David appeared to be in some sort of trance. To each question he gave the briefest reply, grateful to sink back into his seat. Victoria was conscious, as surely David was too, of the room regarding them with a shared expression of bewilderment. She knew she looked terrible. Simon's white theatrical make-up, teamed with the grey eye-shadow she had liberally applied to the sockets of her eyes, lent her the air of a Victorian heroine about to succumb to consumption. There followed two more questions. Hilda Rudge, in an obviously planted one, asked David what qualities he could bring to the constituency. In the minds of the committee the answer was clear: two God-awful parents and a wife on the verge of keeling over. But David rallied, waffled on about character and commitment, only to be floored by a question from a hitherto unknown member asking him for his views on the latest round of Anglo–Cuban trade talks.

Finally Viscount Clement leaned forward and, in the tone he would use to an imbecile, gently asked Victoria if she would like to add anything. Victoria spoke haltingly, apparently attempting a tone of forced ebullience. 'My husband David has said all there is to say. My role is behind the scenes, where I know I will be ably supported at every turn by David's parents – Ron and Jean.' Only in her last sentence did she sound genuinely enthusiastic: 'They're *so* keen to get involved!'

As Victoria nodded to them, Ron and Jean gave a hesitant wave to the room. The room did not wave back.

David closed his eyes. As the meeting broke up, in some disarray, Victoria leaned over to him. 'I think that went rather well.'

He appeared unable to speak.

'I'm off, things to do,' she continued brightly.

'You can't . . . leave!' David stammered.

'Yes. I can. Besides . . . I have a feeling this will take longer than we imagined. And you'll be occupied with your parents.'

David, seeing his father advancing towards Hilda Rudge, had no chance to reply before he leaped into action and diverted Ron off course to the relative safety of Lucretia Stanley – then darted over to his mother, who was taking out his childhood photograph album. Victoria marched towards the door, paused to take one last look at the scene, and observed, among the mêlée of the shell shocked committee, Lucretia purposefully steering Ron towards Lady Charlesworth.

She only had a limited amount of time. As soon as she got outside the constituency office, she began to run as fast as she could in her black pumps – chosen for the purpose – down the deserted pavement to the house. *Her house.* She was relieved to see a van parked outside. Mr Brandon, his portly, white-haired figure smartly turned out in white overalls, was kneeling by the open front door. 'Ah, Mrs Stratford, so sorry to hear about your trouble. Been a couple of burglaries round here this week. Terrible business. Not that the police ever catch . . .'

She had no time to stand and talk. Instead, she sped upstairs to find Consuela, shoved a wad of banknotes into her hand and told her to take the children out – anywhere. The cinema, a museum, the zoo, it really didn't matter. But on no account should she bring them back before six o'clock.

While Consuela dealt with the children, Victoria locked herself in David's study to telephone the bank. How betrayed wives had managed before they brought in twenty-four-hour telephone banking she really couldn't imagine. She gave precise instructions for the *entire* contents of the joint account to be transferred to the personal account she had opened two weeks earlier. Immediately. And she confirmed that the Dubai cheque had cleared – only just – which was terribly convenient because it could now go straight out again along with all of the rest.

When she heard the children disappear out of the still-open front door she ran downstairs to the kitchen and pulled out the two rolls of black bin-liners she had bought earlier that week. Stopping only to pay nice Mr Brandon – for the new locks and bolts – she began to pile David's clothing into them. It took fifteen – incredible, although if she had bothered to fold his clothes they might have taken up less space. Too bad. She heaved the bags downstairs and stacked them in the small front garden. Then she started on his study. In went his laptop, his current casework, and the pile of filing and bills he had left for her to deal with. All a bit mixed-up, but he could sort it out later. Maybe Arabella could do it for him. Dashing into the hallway she paused by the drawing room – and, as an afterthought, added their wedding photograph.

God, where had all her energy come from? She hadn't felt so inspired and enlivened – so free – for years. She hurled the last bag on to the pile – presumably the laptop made that cracking sound – shut the door and drew the bolts.

Now it was only a matter of waiting.

In the event it took four hours. She had more than enough time to shower – Simon's white make-up rinsed from her face in white rivulets mixed with grey splodges of eye-shadow. And even time to remove David's surprisingly large collection of expensive toiletries, which up to then had covered all available shelf-space in their en suite bathroom. So bottles of cologne and aftershave, canisters of shaving cream and deodorant, razors, tweezers, and nasal-hair clippers all went into a seventeenth bin-bag accompanied by a host of male moisturisers, exfoliants and David's new bottle of Californian aloe aftersun lotion. Unwilling to go to the trouble of unlocking the front door, she threw the bag out of the bedroom window, from which it fell lopsidedly on top of the others. Then she made several trips to and from the guest bathroom with her things. It really was extraordinary how much space David took up – and how quickly his presence could be obliterated.

In the meantime Tom telephoned once, anxious to hear that she was all right, and she promised to call him back as soon as anything happened. She asked to speak to Clara – privately worried that Ben was still calling her mobile umpteen times a day – but Tom explained that Clara had complained of a headache and was asleep.

The she changed into a pair of tight jeans and a clinging purple Lycra body, which she knew David particularly detested. And sat down to wait.

The first sign – or sound – was the noise of David's key scraping unsuccessfully in the lock. Then a long silence – he must be pressing the bell, unaware that she had disconnected it earlier. Then the banging began: his fist pounding on the front door. 'Victoria! Open this bloody door!' Victoria got up from the drawing-room sofa and walked leisurely upstairs to their – or rather her – first-floor bedroom. Taking her time, she drew up the sash window and looked down at him.

He was livid. 'What the hell are you doing up there? Come down and open this door!'

She gave him her sweetest smile. 'How did the selection meeting go?'

'Janet . . . Janet . . . fucking . . .' He could not say her name. 'Of all the halfwitted *women* in the world, that group of idiot geriatrics had to choose her! I can't believe it! Instead of *me*!'

'Never mind, darling,' Victoria smiled at him. 'It's not the winning that matters, it's the taking part.'

David looked up at her, his face reddened with frustration, the red tie falling loosely over his shirt, the top button of which was unfastened.

'And my *parents*. What the hell were you playing at getting them along?'

Victoria looked innocently confused. 'I thought it would help, darling. Emphasise the importance of family.'

'Family?' he choked. 'They're not family – they're my worst nightmare. Have you any idea of the impression they made on the committee?'

'Oh, I can imagine,' replied Victoria airily. 'But I can't stand here all day talking to you—'

'Let me in,' David yelled. 'I can't open the door!'

Victoria surveyed him coolly. 'No, you can't. That's because the locks have been changed.'

'The locks have been changed,' David repeated, bewildered. 'Why?'

Oh dear, he really was very slow on the uptake. 'Because,' she continued, 'you don't live here any more. Oh, it's all right. All your things are over there.' Victoria gestured to the heap of black bin-bags lying haphazardly around the garden. 'Everything except your books. But I'll get some boxes and send them on.'

David began poking around in the bags as if to confirm this ridiculous statement. A bottle of cologne slid out of the uppermost bag and smashed on the paving stones. He turned back to her, astonished. 'Is this some kind of joke? Because if it is it's in very bad taste.'

Victoria sighed. 'David, I can assure you I'm utterly serious. And since you seem determined to be particularly dense today I shall spell it out. You–do–not–live–here–any–more. Is that clear enough?'

David ran his hands through his hair. Then, in his most commanding voice, he shouted, 'Victoria, I order you to open the front door!'

'No.'

At that point, Major Bolton appeared, alerted by the commotion.

David turned to him. 'And you can fuck off too, you old windbag.'

Major Bolton looked highly offended. 'Young man, state your business.'

David squared up to him. 'My business, not that it's any concern of yours, is to enter my own property.'

'No,' called Victoria, 'actually he's trying to break in. He doesn't live here any more.'

Major Bolton looked nonplussed. 'Right-oh.' He lingered, fiddling with his tweed tie, still dressed in the dark brown worsted suit and brogues he had donned for the crucial meeting.

'So you can bugger off,' snarled David.

Major Bolton bridled. 'Look here, there's no need for that sort of language. Not in front of a lady—'

David moved to within an inch of him. 'She is not a *lady*. She is my *wife*. And this is my property. So I would thank you to remove your – your antiquated self back to your antiquated house before they both fall down.'

Major Bolton, even more offended, nevertheless retreated.

David turned back to glare at Victoria, 'Let me in!'

Victoria sighed. 'This is getting very tedious, darling. No.'

David regarded her anew. Seeing his expression change she knew that he knew that she knew. He looked at her now with a calculated wariness, adopting a tone of cloying persuasion. 'Victoria – darling. Let's be reasonable. I assume you have . . . jumped to some silly conclusion. And I'm sure I can put your mind at rest.'

'My mind is perfectly at rest. And I haven't jumped to any conclusions. I know everything. Which is why you are leaving, with your things, to join Arabella. I'm sure she'll be delighted – if surprised – to let you in. Then she can unpack your clothes – some of them may need ironing by the way –

cook your dinner and do the other hundred tasks you require performed each and every bloody day!'

'But – but—'

'Yes, I know, the plan was that *I* was supposed to leave. The plan has changed. So has everything else. But we can discuss that another time – when we work out the divorce. And don't worry about the children. Not that you would. You'll see them next weekend – they can come and stay with you and Arabella.'

David, stunned, tried another tack. 'Let me in! You have no *legal* right to do this. I am the owner of this house!'

Victoria retaliated, 'And I am its occupier. If you want to get some legal advice, good. While you're about it, do some research on the law on adultery. Arabella can help you. And her father – he's a judge, isn't he? I'm sure he'll be most concerned when he finds out that his precious daughter is about to be *named* in some very unpleasant divorce proceedings.'

And with that Victoria slammed the sash window. For a few seconds David stood still, apparently stunned. Then he resumed banging on the front door – until Major Bolton reappeared, escorted by the local policeman, who informed David in no uncertain terms that if he continued he would be arrested for a breach of the peace. Victoria, from the bedroom window, watched as David was faced with no alternative but to find a taxi, lug seventeen black bin-bags inside it, amid much moaning from the cabbie who made no move to help him, and – surrounded by a sea of black plastic – disappear in what seemed to be an easterly direction.

CHAPTER 12

'I just couldn't do it. When the time came, I just couldn't.'
Clara looked shattered, her face pale, dark shadows under
her eyes. She was slumped on a rattan sofa in the
conservatory of The Chapters' show house, the blinds half-
drawn against the autumn sun. The house was quiet,
Elizabeth at school, only a few days remaining before
Annie's move to Albert Road.

Victoria and Annie exchanged a glance. Annie was still
wearing the look of bewilderment with which she had
reacted to the news of Clara's affair. What had, to that
point, been a quiet morning packing her belongings at The
Chapters – with the capable assistance of Victoria – had
been transformed into some sort of crisis meeting with the
arrival of Clara, distraught and tearful, an hour before.

Clara turned to Annie. 'I'm sorry, I never wanted you to
get involved . . . I know how difficult it still is for you, and
now the move.'

'You should have told me,' said Annie.

When Clara had haltingly related the story of the affair,
Ben, Deauville, and the events at the university, she had felt
at first uncomprehending, then shocked and eventually hurt
that Clara had confided only in Victoria. To Annie it had
felt as though they were all children again and she was cast
back in the role of baby of the family, excluded from the
whispered bedroom conversations of her elder sisters.

'And I know how much you think of Tom,' continued
Clara imploringly, 'how close you are. I thought you'd
think I was such a terrible person to have done this.'

Annie sighed. 'Of course I don't think that. You're my sister, for goodness' sake! I'm not a baby, you know.'

Too late, Annie realised that this was exactly the phrase – *I'm not a baby, you know* – that she had spent much of her childhood shouting in frustrated rage at her two sisters. Clara and Victoria began to laugh, incapable of stopping themselves despite the seriousness of the moment. And then Annie was joining in.

'I'll make some more coffee,' she said, rising to her feet. 'Then, it seems to me, we need to talk about what you're going to do.'

Clara looked up, caught between laughter and tears, catching the strength in Annie's voice.

'You can't live in the past,' Annie continued. 'Whatever has happened has happened. The important thing is not to live in the problem. You have to live in the solution.'

Now Clara and Victoria exchanged a glance.

'One of Dr Gove's phrases,' explained Annie, with a small smile.

'Pity he's not here now,' muttered Clara, as Annie took the tray into the kitchen.

Clara turned to Victoria. 'It was impossible. I had decided to tell him, I really had.' She looked at Victoria as if for confirmation of her words and then, seeing Victoria nod her understanding, continued, 'But when I got home it all went wrong. Tom was in the garden and, of course, he knew something awful had happened as soon as he saw me, and I started telling him about going into the office to work on Tellium and then meeting Julian and how I had been suspended. And then he jumped in and got *completely* the wrong end of the stick and said that Landward couldn't be allowed to get away with it.'

'Landward?' interrupted Victoria, confused.

'Yes. As soon as I said I'd been suspended he assumed it had something to do with Landward Pharmaceuticals, who make Tellium – that they had somehow engineered things so that I would lose my job because of my involvement in the court case.' Clara sat back, her face despairing. 'And then, well, I didn't know what to do. Tom was ranting about how outrageous it all was and how I must fight it, and I began to think that maybe I didn't need to tell him about Ben, after all. It seemed like an escape route. I had told him the truth about being suspended – but not the real reason.'

Annie wandered back in. 'Kettle's on.' She perched on the edge of the sofa next to Clara.

'But now all he does is go on and on about the best way to fight Landward,' continued Clara exasperatedly. 'I've told him that Cameron – I work with him, he's a lecturer – is helping me with it, but every minute I spend at home he wants to talk about it. I just don't know if I can keep it going.'

'Well, speaking from experience of keeping plans secret,' Victoria said wryly, 'you haven't got much longer to hold out. The hearing's next week, isn't it? As long as you can keep Tom away from the university, there's no reason why he would find out. You'll just have to bite your lip and keep going. Think about what's at stake. I would have thought it was worth a go.'

Victoria was so much better at this sort of thing than I am, Clara thought. She had the ability to keep thinking straight, even in the most fraught situations. Watching her in action over the last few weeks had been a humbling experience. Privately, Clara had always considered herself the calm, cool, confident sister of the three, but at the moment she didn't feel any of the assured composure that she had hitherto taken for granted. Victoria might have been slow in admitting the reality of her marriage to David, but she hadn't wasted any time in taking action once she had.

Annie looked thoughtful. 'Are you sure – absolutely sure – that you want to keep this a secret? That you want to stay with Tom? You didn't have an affair for the hell of it –

you're not that sort of person. Things can't have been right with your marriage.'

'I'm sure,' said Clara, definitely. 'I love Tom. I know that now. And I don't want to hurt him. And . . .' she hesitated, almost embarrassed '. . . I was thinking . . . I know this sounds ridiculous . . . I was thinking that we could have a baby. Not to patch things up – I know that's the oldest mistake in the book – but because I really want one. I want to be with Tom and have a baby and be a family. Just an ordinary family.'

'Bloody hell,' said Annie, half laughing, 'but you're the career girl.'

'Yes, I know,' said Clara, caught in the uncomfortable position of executing a public volte-face, 'and I know I've always said I wasn't interested in children, but whatever it is . . .'

'Biological clock ticking,' interrupted Victoria.

'Oh, give me a break,' retorted Clara, but affectionately. 'Maybe it's this Tellium thing. The woman I've been helping, Laura Turner, I've seen a lot of her recently and her little boy, and it's changed the way I feel.'

'Well, I think Tom would make a fantastic father,' said Annie firmly. For just a second Annie paused – and she could not conceal the sadness from her voice: 'Clara, you never know what's around the corner. Don't assume there's plenty of time.'

A silence fell between them, Hugo's name in their minds but left unspoken, until Annie got up and said brightly, 'I'll make that coffee.'

Clara watched her. Annie had a calmness about her now. Her grief was still there, but it was no longer the brittle, angry, hopeless emotion that had once consumed her – and nearly destroyed her.

But Annie had got one thing wrong. It was not some idea of Annie as the baby of the family that had stopped Clara confiding in her. It was guilt. That she, Clara, had everything Annie had lost – a husband, a home and a future. But she had gambled with it, rolled the dice with excitement, only to discover that the game was far more dangerous than she had ever stopped to appreciate.

The basement flat of 18 Albert Road had been transformed. Cal was much more than just a builder, Annie could see. He had a feel for buildings – for the way the light fell, the use of space, and the numerous tricks of the trade that could turn a damp, dingy basement into an uplifting home. Throughout the flat the replastered walls were an expanse of smoothly gleaming antique-white. The stripped-wood floors set off her Persian rugs to perfection, and light shone from the halogen downlighters that peppered the new ceilings. At night they could be dimmed to glow, illuminating her books, paintings and photographs. And her mother's postcards, which now numbered six, the latest from Thailand.

The living space had swallowed up both the red sofas from Railway Villas, the walnut writing-desk and even the glass-fronted yew bookcase. In the kitchen, the cream-painted units, offset by shining stainless-steel appliances, led on to the conservatory, where she had placed not only the antique oak dining-table but even found room for the two high-backed Queen Anne armchairs that had stood before in the bedroom. And her bedroom here – which, like Elizabeth's, seemed miraculously to have increased in size – had somehow contrived to take her new French cherry-wood bed, a present from Victoria, and the pale blue hand-painted bedside tables. All her clothes hung in the new fitted wardrobes. It was like a much smaller, cosier version of the house at The Chapters. Even the white marble bathroom looked identical – and, try as she might, she could find no sign of dents or chips. The entire flat was empty – Elizabeth mercifully back at school and her neighbours, whom Annie had yet to meet, presumably out at work.

She sat waiting for the afternoon repeat of *Stretton*

Surgery, having missed last night's episode on account of another curtain quotation. Since the October edition of *Interior Inspiration* had appeared she had been rushed off her feet. But *Stretton Surgery* could not be missed. Tania von Stein seemed to occupy most of the screentime, wearing very few clothes, on account of the current headline-grabbing storyline, which had Tania's character now set on seducing the married owner of the local betting shop. Annie knew she should switch it off – just as she should stop thumbing through the tabloids in the news-agent's – but she couldn't stop herself. This was one secret she couldn't confess even to Dr Gove.

She knew it was all because of Cal. Cal who had disappeared from sight. She had hoped to see him on so many occasions – the day of the move, for example, which had been masterminded by Tom – but Dave and Little Dave had turned up instead. The weeks had passed. She had thought of writing to him, but every time she tried to compose a letter she stalled. It was too complicated to try to explain awful Martin Hollis, the touchy subject of money and the confused mixture of gratitude and discomfiture that characterised her own feelings towards Cal's help. Her own feelings towards him she could never hope to articulate – she barely understood them herself. All she could be sure of was her compelling need to see him again. And she had a permanent reminder of him every time she entered the flat: the Richard Webster watercolour, *Thames by Moonlight*, had greeted her on the day she moved in, hung on the living-room wall.

There were five minutes to go. Unable to bear the same old advertisements for washing-powder and nappies, she thumbed through the local paper, the *Cobham Chronicle*. She reread the front-page story – police feared that a new wave of designer robberies was set to sweep Cobham again after local businessman, Martin Hollis, had been held up by two masked men on his way home. The paper reported that he had been ordered from his car, robbed of his watch, wallet and clothes, and left in Oxshott woods while the thieves took off in his red Jaguar sports car. Police were looking for two men wearing balaclavas – which, thought Annie, hardly narrowed the field. Scouring the report for the tenth time, Annie concluded that at least there was some justice in the world.

She looked up as the announcer declared the afternoon repeat of *Stretton Surgery*. As the theme music started she sank back and took in the room a second time. And it felt fine. More than fine, it felt good. True, it wasn't Railway Villas, or married life, or any of the things she had imagined her life to be not so very long ago. That was the frightening thing. You could be so content, happy and settled – and then one day something terrible happened that you could never have predicted. And you knew, with absolute certainty, that from that moment nothing would ever be the same again.

Nothing would ever be the same again. Hugo was dead, Railway Villas sold, and Elizabeth was slipping into her own life. But Annie had been given a second chance, a second life, and she was going to live every minute of it with courage and passion and hope.

Hunched over the kitchen table, Tom was formulating his plan. Clara was trying to be kind – he understood that – but it was unnecessary. He was in perfect health and his mind was as sharp and alert as ever. Best of all, he was going back to the Southhead next week. He felt elated, vindicated by the inquiry which, although three weeks late in reporting, had judged him blameless. Predictably the director had expressed doubts about sending him back. Then Jan had arrived, local newspaper photographer in tow, to present a petition at the council offices: over a hundred signatures calling for his return. Tom had decided to presume they were all genuine.

But the present challenge lay in Clara's disciplinary hearing the next day. Whatever she said, he was going to be there: companies like Landward Pharmaceuticals had to learn that they could not throw their weight and money around to persecute people like Clara who dared to stand up to them.

He thought back to the day last month when she had arrived home, white-faced and shaking, to tell him that she had been suspended. She had looked dreadful. He had known straight away, without her needing to tell him, that Landward was behind the whole trumped-up suspension. Landward was behind the university's decision to suspend her for writing an honest, truthful and decent article about Tellium. Of course, Clara wanted to play the whole thing down, but it was obvious she couldn't cope. She was permanently exhausted, constantly taking to her bed, throwing back aspirin to quell her headaches.

It was clear that he really did know better in this case. She was an academic, unsuited to standing up for herself, and relying on that Cameron person for advice – but he was just another lawyer. Tom understood that she was trying to protect him from the stress and strain of it all, indulging in whispered telephone calls to Cameron when she thought he was asleep, but it was all unnecessary. Clara might have forbidden him to come to the university, but tomorrow he would be there, come hell or high water.

Drops of silvery rain fell on Bluebird's windows, blurring the outlines of red buses and huddled shoppers below. The lunch-time crowd sat around Victoria: Chelsea ladies in their autumn outfits – tight, tailored trouser suits in browns and beige – lunching *à deux* amid piles of crisp designer shopping-bags. David had demanded to meet her. The situation, he had shouted at her over the telephone, could not continue. It was unreasonable of her to expect him to live like this: his life was a chaotic mess and his work was suffering – only last week he had failed to attend an extremely important chambers drinks party because it wasn't noted in his diary. After several increasingly desperate telephone calls, she had agreed to meet him at Bluebird.

Now she sat waiting, watching the Chelsea ladies at lunch. It was an appropriate choice. The same table, in the same restaurant, where, under Lucretia's sympathetic gaze, she had begun the terrifying and exhilarating process of changing her life. Allen, the Australian waiter, brought her a glass of kir. He knew her regular drink now – just as she knew his name, where he lived and all sorts of interesting facts about his life. Somehow they were on first-name terms now.

David, inevitably, was late. Bluebird, come to think of it, was probably inconvenient for him: he would have preferred to lunch in the vicinity of the Law Courts. But she was conscious that, relieved just to get a date out of her, he would have agreed to meet her anywhere.

'Fucking traffic. No cabs either.' He appeared at her table from nowhere, slightly out of breath, definitely more dishevelled than normal. His shirt cuffs were not as crisply starched as usual. His silver cufflinks failed to gleam. His suit needed pressing. He had cut himself shaving. And his expression was of uncharacteristic agitation. He fingered his tie nervously, at least that looked up to standard, and looked across at Allen, who sprinted over.

'Double Scotch. No ice,' he barked.

To compensate for his curtness, Victoria flashed Allen her most winning smile. 'Allen another kir for me, please. Oh, and a packet of cigarettes.'

'No worries!' Allen hurtled off.

David stared at her, bewildered, 'You don't drink *kir*. You don't *smoke*. And who's *Allen*?'

'Oh, just a waiter.'

David looked distinctly peeved. But before he had a chance to continue Allen zipped back, tray in hand from which he dispensed their drinks with a theatrical flourish.

'Allen's an actor,' explained Victoria, 'and before that he was a championship surfer.'

'Really.' David seemed impatient for him to depart, only to be interrupted when he returned bearing Victoria's cigarettes and a box of Bluebird matches. Then he proceeded to unwrap the packet, offered it to Victoria and then stood so close that his thigh brushed her arm while he struck a match for her. David watched, drumming his fingers on the table. Victoria was aware that he was surreptitiously surveying her new clothes – the tight black polo-neck sweater and clinging brown suede skirt over knee-high black leather boots. A look Allen had proclaimed *ravishing*.

And a look David had paid for – along with the mortgage and all the other bills, under threat of being hauled into court for failing to support his wife and children. Eventually Allen departed, returned with menus, then departed again. David leaned forward, took a gulp of whisky and, not quite managing to look her in the eye, adopted his most reasonable tone. 'Now, Victoria, we must resolve this situation, if only for the sake of the children.'

Victoria said nothing: she was concentrating on blowing smoke rings at him.

'Victoria!'

'Sorry.'

'As I was saying, we must move forward. This state of affairs is quite unsustainable. I cannot be expected to support two households while living like – like – some homeless refugee!'

'Oh – I didn't realise there was a problem.'

'Problem? There are multiple – innumerable problems. Starting with the children. I can't be expected to have them every weekend. I have my work to do, papers to pre-pare . . .'

Arabella to screw, thought Victoria. She was anticipating that this would be first. 'But can't you get some help?'

David threw his hands into the air. 'I *did* organise some help. Consuela. Until the wretched woman failed to turn up. Didn't even have the courtesy to call.'

'How inconvenient,' commiserated Victoria.

'It was. As I say, I can't be expected to take them every weekend. It's far too much. I'll have them once a month – that's all I can manage.'

Victoria looked astounded. 'But how will I get my work done?'

'Work? You don't work.'

'I do now. Why don't you ask your parents to lend you a hand? No? Well, how about Arabella's parents? Or Arabella herself. She got on well enough with Emily at your birthday party.'

'Emily is hardly being co-operative. Neither is Alex, come to that. If they're not eating like pigs and breaking everything in sight, they're parroting on about how bored they are.'

It was astounding, Victoria reflected, that his spirit had been broken so soon. As she had belatedly realised, David didn't want custody: he had wanted her to be frightened that he wanted custody. Oh, he was happy enough to turn up at the nativity play or sports day and would run to watching the odd Disney video while reading the Sunday papers, but hands-on, twenty-four-hour, unassisted, unrelenting childcare was a different matter.

Which was why she had been intent on foisting them on him at every opportunity. But she had not expected him to be so easily crushed. She had calculated on David and Arabella holding out for at least another month even after she had relocated Consuela. How adept she was becoming at salvaging triumph from disaster! Emily and Alex had returned from their first weekend with David and Arabella to announce that Consuela had looked after them while Daddy and Bella had gone out a lot. There had been other unwelcome revelations. 'Bella has big boobies,' reported Emily, while Alex chimed in that she had only fed them chocolate ice-cream.

It had been the most amazing stroke of luck that Victoria, on her way to the gym, had encountered a chuffed-looking Ute loading her battered suitcase into a minicab outside the Masters' house. Ute, it turned out, had been poached by another mother in a deal that guaranteed her better pay, shorter hours and – this was the clincher – driving lessons. Victoria had seized the moment. Nancy had been livid – and all too ready to take Victoria's advice on the quaint English ways that ensured the finding and keeping of domestic staff. Victoria had named some extortionate salary for Consuela, inspected Ute's old room and ended by advising Nancy that weekend working was the key to maintaining a long-term working relationship.

'Anyway, what has happened to Consuela?'

'Oh,' said Victoria vaguely, 'she left. Got another job. With Nancy Masters, actually. Terribly good terms – live in, which she's always wanted, and Nancy's paying heaps more than we did but she insists that Consuela must work weekends so she and Hayden can go jogging.'

'Jogging!' spat David. 'Well, I think it's bloody disloyal. Years with us and she walks out with barely a thank-you. Anyway, the situation is intolerable.'

Victoria knew it was. She had neglected to tell David that Consuela would not be coming after all and as a result he had unexpectedly found himself landed with two tired and fractious children for the entire weekend. Victoria, to the delight of Emily and Alex, had allowed them to go to bed exceedingly late the night before, and had spent the morning filling Emily with orange squash but omitting to remind her to go to the lavatory before David's arrival in his new sports car. From Alex's description, Victoria discovered that David had disappeared only a few hours later, pleading paperwork in chambers, leaving both children with Arabella. One could almost – but not quite – feel sorry for the girl.

She had tried reading them stories but after half an hour suggested they go and play together. Which they did, until one of Arabella's Chinese vases had crashed to the floor. David had returned that evening to find all three of them in tears, Arabella weeping on her designer futon amid a scene of carnage. Her pristine white bed linen was now matted with breakfast cereal, crisps and chocolate ice-cream. Felt-tip pens had smudged over her silk-trimmed pillows, and her Japanese rug was giving off a decidedly lavatorial aroma. Alex said that some sort of argument had followed . . . and Daddy and Bella had ended up staying in all evening watching *Scooby-Doo* videos, instead of going to her brother's party.

David looked at Victoria beseechingly. 'Please, darling. Please take the children.'

Victoria lit another cigarette. 'I think, before we decide anything, we need to look at the situation as a whole. The divorce. And money . . .'

David regarded her warily. Clearly he had hoped to limit this conversation to securing freedom at the weekends.

'As I see it,' continued Victoria coolly, 'the first question is housing. Mine, of course. You have a home with Arabella—'

'A home?' squawked David. 'It's not a *home*. It's a *room* – it's all open-plan. When the children are there it's like sleeping in some bloody village hall. And there are no curtains – Emily wakes up at midnight and four o'clock, and every bloody hour in between, asking if it's time to get up yet. And there's no space. All my things are there, and now I've got the boxes of books, too.'

Victoria could imagine – twelve packing cases had been dispatched to Arabella's elegant loft last weekend, which she guessed had now lost its minimalist look amid the deluge of black plastic bags and splintered crates.

She spoke smoothly. 'Well, if you'll let me continue, the answer is to sell the house.'

'I agree! Sell Wimbledon and Marlow. Then you can get yourself something more practical, more manageable.'

'Smaller?' snapped Victoria. 'Is that the word you're looking for? Well, actually I agree . . .'

A look of relief came over David's face.

'. . . In part.'

David slumped back in his seat.

'We'll sell Wimbledon. I never liked it much anyway. But not Marlow. I want to live there, full time, once the renovation works have been done.'

'Renovation works?'

'Yes. I've drawn up a plan and I'm getting quotes. Don't worry, it's all in hand. We sell Wimbledon and we split the proceeds. Say twenty–eighty.'

David looked as if he couldn't believe his good fortune. 'Fine. Excellent idea.'

'And with your twenty per cent you can get a place with Arabella.'

'Twenty per cent!' David was horrified. 'But I worked for that house! For years. Blood, sweat and tears. All hours of the day and night.'

'Hardly that. You were shagging Arabella for plenty of the time too.' Victoria lowered her voice and regarded David menacingly. 'I worked for that house, too. For years. I supported you, sacrificed my own career, and raised two children. I thought we were a team. If you want to go off and play on your own, fine, but don't expect me to suffer the consequences. You've made your bed, you can lie in it.'

David rallied, thumping the table with his fist, causing two matronly ladies to look askance in their direction, until David fixed them with a particularly long and icy stare. He snarled at Victoria, 'No. This is totally unreasonable. Let's go through the figures . . .'

'Yes. But not here. You can write to my lawyer.'

'Lawyer?'

'Yes, *lawyer*. You do know what a lawyer is. Mine is Daniel Parnell. Of *Parnell's*.'

She paused to give this information ample time to sink in. David sat as if winded by a devastating punch, which in a sense it was. Parnell's were London's most aggressive firm of solicitors with an infamous reputation for extracting huge amounts of money from errant husbands.

'Daniel,' continued Victoria, 'also says I should start divorce proceedings as soon as possible. On the grounds of your adultery, naturally. If you don't want that, well, you'll have to pay more. But I assume you want to get this over with as soon as possible, before the election, as you planned. How's the hunt for a seat going?'

'Seat! I haven't got time to look for a *seat*. It's all I can manage to find a clean shirt in the morning.' David's head sank into his hands.

Victoria breezed on: 'OK. Let's just get the Wimbledon house on the market. We'll meet the estate agent together.' She had no intention of giving him scope for any dirty tricks. 'You can organise that – you've met him before, haven't you?'

'Next week, then?' asked David weakly.

Victoria took out her diary. 'Hmm. No. I can't make next week. Too busy. I'm having dinner with the Prime Minister's wife.'

'Victoria,' stormed David, 'this is no time for silly jokes!'

Victoria put down her glass and leaned across the table. She held his eye and spoke very deliberately. 'But I'm not joking. Janet introduced me to her. The poor woman's sick and tired of being criticised by the papers so she's decided to launch a charm offensive. New hairdo, new clothes and new interest in charity work. She's taken on three new charities in the last month.'

'Well, I don't see how you can be any use with that,' interrupted David irritably.

'Oh, but I can,' countered Victoria smoothly. 'I'm writing her speeches. Last week I did 'Plant a Tree Week' and now I'm working on one about premature-baby units. Don't worry, it's terribly easy – she only chooses popular causes.' She paused. 'So you see, David, I have got a job. I'm officially a speech-writer.'

Tom stood in the University of Thames law school car park, surrounded by a gaggle of students and lecturers.

Arriving with a safe margin of time, half an hour before Clara's hearing was due to start, he had been amazed to find a real demonstration in progress. Current and past students, at least a hundred, held a variety of placards – *Law Not War* and *Save the Law School One*. Although some seemed distinctly inappropriate – Cameron Hawes was clutching a banner proclaiming *Love Not War*, which was all very 1960s but hardly relevant to Landward. Cameron had been most odd, urging Tom to go home and monopolising him thereafter in some inconsequential conversation when Tom had made it quite clear that he wasn't going anywhere. Goodness knows what Clara had told them about his state of health – they all seemed to regard his arrival with astonished horror.

Breaking away from Cameron, Tom escaped to talk to Anthony Chang. But Anthony, too, looked distinctly uncomfortable when Tom appeared at his shoulder. It only confirmed Tom's view of academics: perfectly at home in their cloistered libraries but unsuited to fighting real battles in the real world.

'So,' said Anthony nervously, 'you decided to come?'

Tom was ebullient. 'Wild horses wouldn't have kept me away. You have to stand up to these people – show them you can't be beaten.'

'Oh.' Anthony had sounded uninspired. 'Yes . . .'

He made to move away but Tom grabbed his arm. 'You see, people get intimidated in these situations. Ordinary people think they don't stand a chance against money and power. But you have to take power back – that's what demonstrating is all about. Who organised all this by the way?'

Anthony looked dumbstruck. 'Um . . . some of the students.'

'Good for them,' exclaimed Tom. 'Good to see a bit of radicalism coming back. I think it's great.' He looked over to where Ben was chatting to some first-years. 'Ben seems to be the leader. Good for him.'

'Good for him?' repeated Anthony wonderingly.

'Yes! I must go and speak to him.'

'Speak to him? To Ben?'

Tom was bewildered. God, these academics were hopeless. Like rabbits caught in the glare of headlights. They had no conception of group action and the necessity of fostering camaraderie among the protesters. Or maybe they regarded him as some sort of incompetent invalid. Tom was suddenly irritated. 'Well, why on earth shouldn't I? I'm not ill, you know. Admittedly it's all been rather traumatic, and some of the scars take time to heal. But I'm not going to see myself as a victim.'

Anthony looked at him anxiously. 'All the same I mean, we have to concentrate on the protest. Might it . . . stir things up a bit?'

'That's what we want!' enthused Tom. 'Some passion, fire . . .' Tom was aware that the group of lecturers around him were staring at him with undisguised amazement.

At that moment, Belinda Weaver pulled up in a taxi. She emerged, clad in a black suit, clutching a brand-new briefcase. All around a murmur of disapproval went up and even some hissing. Belinda regarded them all with defiance, and strode down the driveway towards them.

'Trouble-maker,' shouted a shrill female voice.

Belinda stopped and sought out the perpetrator. Then her eye fell on Tom. 'My God,' she hissed. 'She's even got you here. You really are . . . *sad*,' she concluded venomously, before escaping inside.

Tom turned to Anthony 'What on earth is she doing here?'

'She's . . . giving evidence. As the person bringing the complaint . . .' he faltered.

'*Bringing the complaint!* Jesus, you're not telling me Landward have given her a job? Is there nothing they won't stoop to?'

Anthony, like all those around him, said nothing. Tom could sense their unease – and that, more than anything, they did not want him there. In the silence he looked anew at the placards they were holding – *Freedom of Expression . . . Love Is Not Illegal* . . . A faint, but unstoppable feeling of disquiet overcame him . . .

An hour later Clara emerged. The hearing had been close. Kate – on this committee as she was on virtually every university committee – had been particularly obstructive, but Clara, rallying every argument and piece of evidence more forcefully than she had ever done in her life, had saved herself. And, in the end, she had been honest, discarding Cameron's carefully prepared arguments to say boldly that she was guilty of a love affair but nothing more. And if a love affair was unacceptable to them then they must take whatever action they wanted . . .

A loyal cheer went up from the crowd. She looked worn, tired but relieved. Cameron ran over to her.

'I got a formal warning,' breathed Clara, 'and a very stern lecture from Julian not to do it again.' She lowered her voice. 'As if I would. I'm thinking of becoming a nun.' As Clara saw, with amazement, the cheering demonstration all around, she felt the heady elation that can only follow escape from disaster.

Cameron embraced her and whispered discreetly in her ear, 'Tom's here.'

The relief that had filled her was replaced with dread. She stared at Cameron beseechingly. 'Does he know?'

'I don't think so, but it's been touch and go. I managed to get him talking about the Southhead.'

Clara looked at the crowd which, seeing the look of happiness in Clara's face, had judged the result positive. Shouting and applause rang out. But Clara barely heard it as her eyes desperately sought out Tom. Then she spotted him: he had broken away from the crowd and was walking away from her, heading directly towards Ben. She tore free of Cameron's grasp and began to run in Tom's direction. But it was too late. Before she reached Tom's side she glimpsed – it was all so quick – the right-hand hook that sent Ben spinning into a crowd of startled students. Tom drew back his left hand ready for the follow-up punch as Ben lay dazed on the floor. Clara reached him, just as two rugby-playing students took hold of him.

'Stand up!' Tom yelled at Ben. 'There's more where that came from!'

Clara pushed her way to Tom's shoulder. 'Tom! Please! This isn't the way to deal with it.'

Tom, still restrained, struggled round to face her. 'And you! You lying, conniving . . .' He could not say it. Instead he spat out, 'It's over. We're over. And I never want to see you again.'

'Tom, *please*, we have to talk about this – give me a chance to explain.'

Tom had wrestled himself free of his two student bodyguards. Ben was struggling to his feet, his nose bleeding. 'Explain! There's nothing to explain. It's all fallen into place. The days in the library, the late nights in the office. And there never was a staff meeting with Julian, was there? Just out of interest, where were you?'

Clara was aware of the fascinated silence around them. The crowd of students and lecturers had now been joined by the office staff, who had come out to see what all the fuss was about. She lowered her voice discreetly. 'It doesn't matter. Let's go and talk about it somewhere—'

'Oh, yes,' yelled Tom. 'That's fine now. It's OK for me to stand here like a bloody halfwit, demonstrating in favour of my wife's right to shag her students.' He waved his free arm at the ogling crowd. 'But when it gets awkward for you, you want to retreat behind closed doors.'

Ben stepped forward only to retreat as Tom aimed a surprisingly fast left-hook in his direction. As half the university rugby squad moved to take hold of him once more, he advanced on Ben. 'And as for you, you little shit, the fun's over. If anyone should be launching a complaint it's me, the bloody fool who stood by, thinking his wife was at work while all the time she was bonking you. What did you call it? Private tuition? Extra coaching? *Examination practice?*'

Ben, squaring up to Tom on the driveway, stood his ground. 'I'm sorry – I'm sorry you've found out like this. But I love Clara. And if you don't want her, I do.'

Clara rushed up. 'Ben. Stop. This is madness. It's over, you must accept that.'

'Yes, shut up!' added Tom.

'Clara doesn't want it to be over.' An edge of pleading had entered Ben's voice. 'She's just a prisoner – of you and of her job.'

Before Clara could respond Belinda Weaver, hotly pursued by Cameron and Anthony, marched through the crowd. 'You see? I was right,' she proclaimed. 'I was right. Of course, *you*,' she glared at Clara, 'covered it all up. You've probably slept with the whole committee.'

'Not with me, my dear.' Clara was astonished to hear Kate's voice. Kate had confronted Belinda on the driveway, which now formed an impromptu stage: Tom, Clara and Ben, with Cameron and Anthony, were posed alongside Belinda and Kate. From the corner of her eye, Clara could see that even the kitchen staff had joined the swelling crowd of spectators.

Kate was lecturing Belinda: 'Now, listen to me, young lady. The university has heard your complaint. All the procedures were followed – to the letter. I should know – I was in charge. And at the end of the day there was no evidence, absolutely none, that Ben in any way benefited from his relationship with Clara.' She could not resist a pause. 'Not academically at any rate. I can't comment on his other skills . . .'

There was a titter from the crowd. This sent Belinda into a monumental tantrum. Hands on hips she advanced, tank-like, towards Clara. 'It's not fair,' she shrieked. 'It's not fair. I should have got a first.'

'So, now we find out what this was all about,' Cameron snarled. 'It was never about Clara, it was about Ben – and

388

the simple fact that you were jealous of his success.'
Cameron regarded her searchingly. 'Fancy him, did you?
Did you ever make a pass at him – only to be rebuffed?'

Clara, seeing Ben shift uncomfortably, knew that
Cameron had guessed right. She looked at Belinda. But
Belinda did not reply. And Clara, who could not help but
feel a trace of pity for her, saw that in that moment Belinda
admitted defeat. Not by words, but in her whole appearance. She stood somehow diminished, as if all her energy
and animosity had been forced from her, and all that
remained was a young girl dressed in an incongruous
business suit whose expression could not conceal her hurt
and disappointment. In the exhausted silence that had
fallen among them – Ben and Cameron, Belinda and Clara,
grouped against their will in the drizzle that had begun to
fall – an uneasy calm descended.

Belinda looked up and caught Clara's eye, her voice
defensive, 'You can't blame me. You were sleeping with
him. What did you think would happen? *Plenty* of students
didn't come today,' she said desperately. 'Lots of us don't
trust you any more – it's not just me. Some of the others
were talking about how you must be helping Ben . . .' Her
voice faltered. 'I just wanted to do well. I've worked so
hard. Not just the studying, all the other things I've done,
like the Law Society and the library committee. And I've
done summer placements every year – I've *never* been on
holiday.' Clara watched wordlessly as tears welled in
Belinda's eyes and fell down her reddened cheeks. 'I wanted
a first so badly. I deserved one. And him,' she pointed at
Ben, 'he didn't do half the work I did and he got one. It's
just not *fair*.'

The easy response for Clara at that moment would have
been to tell Belinda the truth. That what separated her from
Ben was not hard work. It was the difference between those
who come first and the second-placed in every walk of life.
It was talent, the ability to look at a problem in a different
way from all the others, to use the same facts but with

imagination, flair and intelligence to find a solution that was not just good but brilliant. The truth was that Ben had never needed Clara's help. Clara stepped forward. 'Belinda, you have a fantastic career ahead of you. You're clever and brilliantly well-organised, and you can go on and achieve anything you want to.'

Belinda sniffed. She could not bring herself even to look at Clara but neither could she throw Clara's words back at her. She needed the praise too badly.

Clara went on, 'And I'm sorry if my actions have upset you or made you suspicious of my motives and . . .' Clara summoned every inch of professionalism to utter the words she didn't quite believe but knew must be said '. . . and if we needed an inquiry to clear the air then I'm glad it happened.'

She knew that Belinda would not answer: she was too young to summon gracious words in response. It was Julian who broke the silence. Clara had not noticed him until he stepped forward, did not know how long he had been standing in the crowd, but had never been so grateful to hear him speak.

'I think,' he said decisively, 'that it's time for all of us to go inside . . . All of us,' he repeated commandingly, turning to the crowd of onlookers who, sensing that the drama was concluded, began reluctantly to wander away. 'And, Clara,' he continued, 'we'll expect you back at your desk on Monday. Business as usual.'

Abruptly he walked away. And she knew that, as far as her job was concerned, that was it: Julian would never refer to the matter again. It was now her task to re-establish her standing and her reputation within the law school.

Only she, Tom and Ben remained standing in the rain, now falling more heavily, each waiting for the others to speak. She saw Tom regarding Ben, read the pain and suspicion in Tom's eyes, and understood that it fell to her to break the deadlocked silence. Not by saying what she felt – how could she in front of Tom? – but by accepting that the end of a love affair is always the same. There are no truly mutual decisions, no amicable partings, no best of friends. There is an end, and it is always met with grief, regret and pain.

She turned to Ben. 'Ben, I'm going home now. I'm leaving . . .'

He looked into her eyes. His face bore an expression that fell something short of acceptance, something closer to resignation in the sadness of his downcast eyes. His voice was weary. 'I know.'

And that, more than any other, was the worst moment. To hear his detachment and recognise the finality. That now, for both of them, it was over. She felt his pain – and, for the first time, his courage.

Ben picked up the damp poster that lay at his feet. 'I'll leave you to it.' And slowly but purposefully he walked away from them to the shelter of the law-school building.

As he disappeared through the heavy double doors, Tom took a set of car keys from his pocket. He looked away, towards the trees of the landscaped grounds, speaking as if to no one in particular: 'I'll take you home.'

She was caught unawares, had expected Tom to leave without her. 'I can get the bus,' she stuttered.

'I'll take you home.'

David's books were an absolute nightmare. It had been bad enough clearing them out of Wimbledon but there seemed to be twice as many in his study at Marlow. Victoria began filling another cardboard box, retrieved from the Marlow branch of Oddbins. She had become quite friendly with the manager there – not that she had gone into details as to why the boxes were required – and this morning he had been happy to give her another half-dozen. Wine boxes, she had discovered, were the strongest and small enough that even when loaded to the top she could still just about lift them. Books were so incredibly heavy.

But she had to crack on. The furniture from Wimbledon

was arriving in barely a week and all the Marlow clutter – David's clutter, that was – had to be removed to accommodate it. In old jeans and a fleecy Boden sweatshirt, she mounted the stepladder and began to clear the top shelf. It seemed to be full of old school textbooks. At the end of the shelf there was a stack of school exercise books. She took the top one and looked at the dull blue cover. DAVID STRATFORD was written in thick blue felt-tip. How typical that he had used such large capitals. She thumbed through it, recognising David's elegant handwriting of today as it had evolved from the childish script. Neat, even then. She closed it. She had learned the hard way not to live in the past.

This was to be her study now, in her home with her children around her. The sale had been agreed on Wimbledon, the house snapped up after the first weekend of viewings, and she had been free to move. There had seemed no good reason to linger and the autumn half-term had been as good a time as any for the children to start at their new schools. That change, like so much else, had been accomplished with surprising ease. Not that Marlow was as comfortable as Wimbledon, but once the money came through she could start the building work. She thought definitely a new kitchen, some redecoration, maybe new bathrooms. But she did not feel in any rush. October, with the rain beating down on the study window-panes, felt like a time to retreat indoors, whatever the unfashionable décor and odd patch of damp. None of that seemed important any more – builders and plans could wait until the spring.

And there was no one to tell her any different. For the first time in years she could do as she wanted. She could spend time with her children and with her family, and not go to a single party, function or event that she did not wish to attend. She could laze on a Saturday morning with no cries for breakfast, clothing or help in finding whatever article – car keys usually – David had mislaid. She never, ever had to speak to Lady Charlesworth again. She could cut her hair short. Or grow it long. She could eat cheesecake from the fridge at midnight. Or watch *The Simpsons* with the children and a pizza, then leave all the clearing up until the morning.

And she could hold a party – a house-warming party – with all the people she wanted to see, organised in exactly the way she liked, in two weeks' time to celebrate her house move and her new job and – why not? – her impending divorce.

Clara was not sure if Tom was asleep or merely pretending. She slipped into bed, pulling the duvet over her as gently as she could, aware of Tom lying with his back to her, as close to the edge of the bed as it was possible to be.

She had hoped tonight would be different. Their first session at the Kingston-upon-Thames branch of Relate had taken place that morning, both of them quelling their embarrassment at ringing the doorbell of the discreetly signed office hidden in a side-street of tatty shops and takeaway restaurants. How had it come to this? To be brought to this small room, with posters for workshops, helplines and courses, to sit with a stranger and discuss the very thing she had hoped never to reveal. And if she had hoped for some sign of reconciliation, then Clara had been brutally disappointed. Tom, the great believer in therapy, appeared to have abandoned all faith in talking where their own problems were concerned. His anger had been bitter, and the calm woman counsellor in the beige suit – forty-something, slightly too prim for Clara to warm to her but deserving every ounce of credit for staying so calm under fire – had tried vainly to turn Tom's words to something more positive.

Tom was raging: 'It's the *lies* I can't stand. How she lied to me.'

'Perhaps you could talk to Clara,' the woman had suggested. 'Tell her how you feel.'

Clara's stomach had turned at that. But Tom hadn't told her how he felt. He hadn't even been able to look at her.

'I want to know everything. I want to know *exactly* what has been going on behind my back.' Tom stared fixedly at the carpet beneath his feet. 'You've taken me for a bloody fool. I trusted you and you've betrayed that.'

The woman – what was her name? Marion! Marion had interrupted: 'I understand why you're asking that, Tom but we need also to look at why this situation between you came about.'

That had really set him off. Clara had never seen Tom so angry. Ranting on about how he could never trust her again, barking at Marion that it was all pointless and they should just get divorced, then detailing all the times she had said she was at work and what she was really up to. Until Marion intervened to ask Clara what her thoughts were and Clara found herself incoherently trying to avoid saying anything that would further provoke Tom. Then the hour had been up and Marion had said encouragingly that it was often like this at the start, and would they like to come again next week? Clara had looked at Tom who, with a grudging shrug, had said he didn't see any harm in it. And they had left without a word to each other, remained silent in the car, and arrived home, where Tom had retreated into the kitchen and she had gathered her papers and gone to work.

She lay in bed, with Tom, feeling miserably alone. The silence, the awful, sullen distance that Tom had put between them since their return home, continued. Apart from the odd barbed comment from Tom – older women and younger men a favourite theme – they had barely communicated at all.

As she lay in the darkness she ran the session of that morning through her mind, trying to recall each question and response, searching for some way to break the bitter deadlock. If Tom was really so angry, so utterly unforgiving as he appeared, why didn't he just leave? Because, she instinctively understood, Tom didn't want to end this marriage any more than she did. Something told her that Tom, deep down, wanted to give them a second chance. That the affair itself was not fatal.

It was almost as if, for some strange reason that she could not quite fathom, Tom could forgive her the affair. And his anger, although provoked by betrayal, was now fuelled by another, still stronger emotion. She lay listening to Tom's breathing, deeper now, genuinely asleep. Could it be fear? she asked herself. Fear of moving beyond the lingering but ultimately irrelevant details of who, what and where, which Tom seemed to be determined to pursue? To pursue ... only then to dwell on each new piece of information – the name of the hotel, the secret lunch, a freshly uncovered lie – in such a way that his anger, far from being assuaged, appeared only to intensify. It was a futile, masochistic exercise and Tom was intelligent enough to know it. Which, as she thought about it more deeply, led her to wonder if perhaps Tom's anger was a smokescreen, a defence, something he could hide behind lest one day the blaming might stop and the talking begin ... until eventually it might be Tom answering the questions, not Clara. And, in particular, asking the question that both of them had a responsibility to consider: why had her affair happened at all?

Victoria considered that her house-warming party was going brilliantly. The drawing room, which looked on to the autumn night and the reflected lights on the river, was nearly full. Her guests were relaxed in a way they never had been at her old drinks parties – or were they really David's? She had decided that this party was going to be *very* different from David's fortieth. For a start, David wasn't going to be there. Neither were any caterers or waitresses. Having helped themselves to platefuls of food from the buffet, downed large glasses of wine and smoked wherever, and whatever, they wanted to, her guests were now settled comfortably around the house, chatting perched on the stairs or packed amiably into what had been David's study or slumped on the drawing-room sofas. At the time her parties always used to end, this one was just getting going – and Victoria wouldn't be at all surprised if they all staggered off at dawn.

There was one member of David's chambers present: Mark was currently standing in the kitchen opening bottles of wine. Annie, enveloped in a huge white apron, was refilling a cut-glass dish with warm potato salad.

'Vicky, how many people have you got here? They're going through the buffet like locusts.'

'Not sure. Fifty? Sixty? You see,' she lowered her voice, 'I wasn't sure anyone would come so I invited everyone, and then they all accepted. Well, nearly all . . .'

Philly and Algy, for example. Philly had pleaded some unspecified prior engagement. Victoria hadn't been surprised – now that Alex had left the school, and Victoria had left David, and David wasn't going to be the new MP, Philly had no need to be friends with either of them. But the fair-weather – or was the word illusory? – friends had proved surprisingly few. The Masters had jumped at the chance of visiting *a real old English town* and promptly booked themselves into the most expensive suite of the Compleat Angler hotel. Connor had come with them – Consuela, it appeared, did get some time off – and he was now happily ensconced with Emily and Tom and a bowl of cheese footballs watching the latest *Scooby-Doo* video. Tom was content enough – though rather confused that the children had decided to start addressing him as Shaggy.

Then Lucretia and Viscount Clement – or Peter, as Victoria had learned to call him – had arrived, now apparently an item. He looked ten years younger and several pounds lighter. Lucretia had clearly teased him out of his trademark tweed and he had arrived at the party in a stylish black suit and, inevitably, a black cashmere poloneck. The Boltons had turned up, and so had Janet –

though without Simon who was regrettably, she had explained to the Boltons, away in Hollywood fixing a deal. Major Bolton hardly let Janet out of his sight, these days, marshalling her around Wimbledon, all the while happily, if over-ambitiously, contemplating his New Year Honours List peerage and practising his new lordly signature.

And then there had been old friends she had newly got in touch with, many of them hitherto banned from the house by David, and new friends she had made in Marlow. But not her mother, of course: she was in Australia now, headed for Ayers Rock.

Mark disappeared to top up glasses.

Annie looked impressed. 'He's keen, isn't he? And very attentive.'

Victoria, checking that the kitchen was now empty, replied nonchalantly, 'Yes. He is.'

'Too keen?' asked Annie, picking up the hesitation in Victoria's voice.

Victoria looked serious. 'I don't want to rush into anything. Anything serious, that is. I've made one bloody big mistake in my life and I'm not about to make another . . .' She tailed off. When she spoke again it was with studied thoughtfulness. 'Not that it was all bad. Whenever I think of David I always think of the children too and that's why I can't ever say that I totally regret it.'

'Marrying him?' said Annie.

'Yes. And there were some good times, but they didn't last. That's what I couldn't see for so long. That David had changed. I kept holding on to this idea that underneath he was the same person I'd met all those years ago. And he wasn't. People *do* change, and it isn't always for the best.'

Victoria began stacking plates in the dishwasher, but Annie wasn't quite ready to let the subject drop.

'But that wasn't the question,' she persisted teasingly. 'What about Mark?'

'Maybe,' admitted Victoria, 'but not now. The children

have been through too much. I've told them he's just a friend who's helping me with the move.'

Annie unconsciously looked at her watch.

'Relax,' said Victoria astutely. 'He'll be here. He's probably just—'

'Bonking Tania von Stein.'

'Caught in the traffic,' concluded Victoria firmly.

Annie finished topping up the half-empty salad bowls and took off her apron. She knew she looked good – she had spent most of the day getting ready – but now her nerves were frayed beyond measure. She attempted to catch her reflection in the door of the cooker – her hair cut and blow-dried at Victoria's favourite Marlow salon, and the clinging cornflower-blue silk dress Victoria had lent her looked pretty good too.

'Come on,' said Victoria, grabbing her hand. 'You can't stand here moping.' She dragged her into the hall where Sam and Helen had just arrived.

Helen was rearranging her crutches and Sam was fussing around with gloves, keys and a present for Victoria. 'Sorry we're a bit late – problems getting the car started. I detect a nasty chill in the air these evenings.'

They began to peel off layers of scarves and jumpers. Annie supposed that at sixty-odd she would be like that. But, thankfully, not quite yet. Sam looked at her hesitatingly. 'You look . . . very nice. We must have a quiet word in a minute.'

But before Sam could drag her off, Clara appeared and shunted her back into the kitchen, shutting the door behind them. She leaned against the kitchen table and began miserably chewing a piece of ciabatta. 'This is awful. I wish we hadn't come.'

'But I thought it was getting better?'

'It does – until the next argument. We have a day when everything seems quite normal, then the following day there's some monumental row over something ridiculously trivial.'

Annie put her arm round Clara's shoulder. 'Look, it's been barely a month. You've only just started with the marriage-guidance counsellor.'

'Please, don't talk to me about that wretched woman. It's torture. Ever since she lectured us on being completely honest. Tom took that as an open invitation to grill me on every detail – and I mean every detail – about Ben. It's horrendous. I can't keep track of what I've said or not said and I keep tripping myself up.'

'Well,' said Annie, 'maybe you should be completely open?'

'Oh, yes,' said Clara morosely. 'I can just hear myself. "I had an affair, Tom, because I was bored in bed and I fancied the pants off Ben." No. I just have to keep repeating how it was all a silly mistake and I was flattered by the attention, which is true by the way, and how I wish it had never happened. But the whole point is it did happen. And now it's over. I do love Tom, I see that now, but he's so intent on dwelling on the past that we never move on.'

Annie squeezed her hand. 'It will work out. Even the biggest problems have a solution. You just have to find it – and sometimes that takes time.'

Clara roused herself and clearly decided to change the subject. 'I hear Cal's coming.'

'He's said he was,' Annie sighed, 'but if he is, he's leaving it pretty late.'

'But he's an entrepreneur, wheeling and dealing. He's probably just tied up somewhere making a million.'

'I wouldn't know. I haven't seen him for weeks. And if he does come I'll probably put my foot in it, say the wrong thing, start some ghastly row.'

Annie was interrupted by Sam walking in. His face fell when he saw Clara and, taking the hint, she made her excuses. 'Sam! I'm sorry to rush off, but I really must rescue Tom from the third showing of *Scooby-Doo*.'

Sam raised a smile, but as soon as Clara had disappeared

he came to Annie's side. 'Can we talk somewhere that we won't be disturbed?'

Annie, vaguely surprised, could only think of the conservatory. As Sam followed her in he closed the doors. 'Don't want to be interrupted. Something . . . well, something private I need to say to you.'

Annie had a distinctly uneasy feeling. This was clearly going to be a personal conversation – and she was not at all sure that was the type she wanted to have with Sam. He cleared his throat. 'I – I – Well. You probably think that I'm a bit old to be saying this. An old has-been. But . . .' He paused.

Annie wished fervently that he would get on with it – while simultaneously worrying about what the *it* was going to entail.

'When you get to my age, well, you tend to think that love . . . and romance have passed you by. You get accustomed to your own ways, set in them, maybe, and . . .' Inevitably there was another pause. 'But, you see, since I met you I've started to see things differently. It was something you said, actually. About love being a state of mind.'

Annie felt a rising tide of panic. Sam, sweet, reliable Sam, appeared to have got totally the wrong idea about their relationship. Or, rather, that there was no relationship. But it would be hopeless to try to forestall him. He had clearly been working his way towards this for some time.

'And that's why I've decided that the time has come for me to get married again. And I wanted you to know first because, well, you sort of brought it all about. You see, I've asked Helen to become my wife and she, very graciously, has accepted.'

Annie could not have been more happy – or grateful. She threw her arms around Sam. 'That's wonderful news! Congratulations!'

Sam looked relieved. 'I was so worried that you might . . . disapprove. I mean, she and I haven't known each other for that long but we have become close. And – well, I've got a confession to make. I didn't come to the ball because of Helen, her accident. And I felt truly dreadful about telling . . . an untruth to you – and Victoria, but I just didn't feel the time was right to say something.'

'Sam, forget it. I'm delighted. And I don't think one is ever too old to fall in love! And as for disapproving, well, all I can say is that you should announce it tonight!'

Sam looked elated, and Annie rushed out of the conservatory to forewarn Victoria. She found her sister engrossed in conversation with Mrs Bolton, catching the end of the older woman's words to Victoria: '. . . as I say, we never liked him much. You're far better off without him.'

Victoria reflected on the surprisingly large number of people who had said exactly the same thing to her.

Annie butted in, 'Sorry, but Sam's going to announce something.' She whispered in Victoria's ear, 'He's getting engaged to Helen!'

Victoria greeted this news with a flash of inspiration. 'Champagne! David's got a whole load – he was storing it here ready for election night. It's in the cellar so it should be pretty cold.' She called Tom over. 'How do you feel about opening some of my soon-to-be-ex-husband's vintage champagne?'

'I could manage that,' replied Tom, with undisguised enthusiasm. Victoria dispatched him and Mark to the cellar while Sam, shying away from making a formal announcement, spread the word discreetly, Helen standing proudly at his side. By now the party was in full swing. Alex had appointed himself DJ for the evening and had started churning out the latest teen bands until Hayden came over and insisted that he try some of the Masters' country-and-western CDs brought in from their car. As Alex finished his last track, at full volume, Victoria caught the sound of the telephone ringing. She rushed into the kitchen and grabbed the receiver. 'Hi! . . . Cal! I can hardly hear you.' He must be on his mobile – from the sound of it underwater. She could only catch every third word. 'Where are you? . . . *Where* in the town? Easy. You just need to turn round and head back over the bridge – the *bridge* . . . There's only one, it's white . . . And head towards Bisham. Our road's on the right . . .'

At that moment Tom opened a bottle of champagne with a racing-driver flourish, sending waves of foam all over the floor and Victoria's shoes. She shrieked down the telephone, 'Sorry. It's a madhouse here. Tom's just opening champagne. We're celebrating Sam getting engaged to—'

But at that moment all further conversation was drowned out by the yee-hahs blaring out of the speakers as Hayden put on his first CD. 'I'm sorry, Cal. I can't hear a thing. The Masters are here – you met them at the ball. I think they're starting a barn dance,' she yelled, unable to hear Cal's reply. 'We'll see you in a minute, then.'

She put down the phone and started mopping her shoes with kitchen towel. Tom had thrown himself into the task of dispensing David's champagne, and soon the party was divided into two camps: those taking a country-and-western lesson in the drawing room, where mercifully the music had been turned down, and the rest of the party chatting animatedly just about everywhere. Victoria hurried off to tell Annie and found her chatting to Tom. 'Cal's just called. He's on his way. He'll be here any minute.'

Tom, who had just been reassuring Annie that Cal would arrive, looked insufferably smug. 'Told you so.'

Annie wasn't listening. She dived upstairs to check her hair and make-up for the umpteenth time that evening, leaving Tom to go and find Clara.

He discovered her alone, in the dining room, thumbing through one of David's old legal magazines. He leaned on the doorframe. 'Fancy a dance?'

Clara looked up – but warily. 'Are you sure you want me as your partner?'

Tom closed the door, dulling the music, and sat down

402

next to her. 'Of course I want you as my partner . . . I just . . .'

'Can't forgive me?'

Tom looked around the room, then sat with his head in his hands. He knew at that moment that he should be honest – totally honest. Instead, he took Clara's hand. 'I just want things to be the way they were. To have it all back again – the closeness, the trust . . .'

Clara let out a sigh. 'Tom, they can't ever go back to that. I lied to you. And, yes, I was unfaithful. But that doesn't mean it will ever happen again. Because now I can see what I had to lose – what a stupid risk I took. But we have to forget it, you know.'

And Tom *could* nearly forget it. It was the unease it had provoked in him that was more difficult to tackle. Because, at the end of the day, Clara had wanted something he could not provide. Excitement, romance, sex – and probably all three. 'Maybe – maybe I'm not the man for you. Perhaps you want something different. I mean in bed.'

Clara sat totally still. This was the closest they had ever come to really talking about the affair. Talking – as opposed to arguing, bickering and point-scoring. 'Tom, that can change. Perhaps I haven't been very good in the past at telling you what I want. But . . .' her voice broke '. . . we don't make love any more. Please, Tom, just give me one more chance . . .'

Clara wanted so desperately to be close to Tom again. To feel his familiar body, for all its faults, next to hers. And she wanted a baby to take away the emptiness inside her. She might not have felt guilty before, but now she felt empty, bereft and forlorn. She yearned so much for a baby that she saw Laura Turner twice a week now, ostensibly to report on Tellium and Landward's ever more generous offers of an out-of-court settlement, but really to see Jamie, whom she now helped bath, dress and feed as she talked to him in his own private language.

Tom reached over to her, his hand tracing the outline of

her face, watching the tears well in her eyes. 'Come on. We'll go upstairs. We won't be missed.'

He took Clara's hand, and then her body into his arms, holding her tightly as he had longed to do for so many weeks, then broke away and led her upstairs. And as they reached the bedroom and he saw her sit on the bed and look expectantly up into his eyes, he knew that he would for ever be a hypocrite. Whatever had happened, on those long, sultry afternoons in Jan's double bed, it would always be his dark secret. And if Jan had a past – and he suspected from the things she had taught him that she probably did – it hadn't stopped him loving her, if only for a few short weeks. He began to undress slowly. He might be a liberal – and he did, in almost everything, believe in equality – but when it came to affairs it was different for men . . . wasn't it?

Emerging after an eternity spent retouching her make-up in the bathroom, Annie saw Tom and Clara slip into the bedroom. Downstairs she could hear Sam talking to Viscount Clement – no *Peter* – about weddings, and the sound of dancing from the drawing room. She felt wretched. Cal must have called at least a quarter of an hour ago. How could he possibly take so long to drive less than a mile? She wondered if he was lost, but no one had phoned, and then she began worrying that he had had an accident. Realising that she could not stand for ever on the landing she wandered downstairs.

Lucretia was having a girls' chat with Victoria.

'I can't believe it. Peter's a new man. He's adorable.'

Victoria laughed. 'You sound like you're in love.'

And Lucretia did not hesitate: 'Yes. Yes, I am. And I hope you are too.'

It was to be expected, Victoria supposed. Everyone wanted her paired off, a neat and happy ending, no loose ends left to be tied. But she found herself resisting the easy option. Mark was great company, fun and exciting, but just at the moment she didn't know that she wanted to be part of a couple again. She was in control of her own life – and her children's. She actually talked to Alex and Emily, these days, over dinner in the kitchen – she had so much more time for them now without David around. She found out about their friends and their worries, she heard about Daddy's arguments with Bella, she discovered how much Alex had dreaded going to Selchester – and knew how happy he was at his local Marlow school, a school where none of the children went away to country houses at the weekend. Now most weekends saw their house occupied by whoever were their current friends – and as they charged round the garden or yelled about the house, in a way never permitted by David, she did the cleaning or the ironing or whatever chore she had been surprised to find herself enjoying. And the evenings, which she had feared would be so lonely, were taken up with the heady exhilaration of writing speeches.

And as for David, it was over. Whatever idea she might once have had of taking him back had long since evaporated. It was ironic that he was the one holding up the divorce – telephoning almost every day, dropping innumerable hints about the house-warming. Not a chance, though, of going back. And if things weren't quite as rosy with Arabella – or in chambers – as he had envisaged, then that was no concern of hers. Mark had suddenly become much less bothered about David's opinions, too. Maybe it was the way Sir Richard Hibbert had reacted to the news. Or Judge Clevely-Brown. Neither of them approved of David's ungentlemanly behaviour. There was talk in chambers of an atmosphere – maybe even David leaving: he would have to be the one to go. After all, Arabella was the daughter of a judge.

From the drawing room the sound of country-and-western music was blaring out. To the strains of 'Eatin' Right, Drinkin' Bad', Hayden and Nancy demonstrated the Texas two-step to their bewildered class. Hayden had announced that, for one evening only, they formed the

Honky Tonk Marlow Stompers and everyone was going to enjoy a *good ole hoedown* . . .

Three hours had passed since Cal had called. It would soon be midnight. Unable to bear the sound of the party any longer Annie slipped out of the kitchen door. The chill November air hit her and she wrapped her coat closer round her. She wandered down the garden, careless of her shoes, feeling the wet leaves beneath her feet. As she reached the river-bank she looked out to the dark river where now only a few lights lit up the black water.

She had lost him. She knew that now. He was in another woman's arms, and whatever faint, ridiculous chance she had ever had of knowing him she had thrown away. Two of Juliet's lines came back to her:

> *My only love sprung from my only hate,*
> *Too early seen, unknown, and known too late . . .*

If only she had truly learned those lines. Oh, she had prattled on to Sam about the importance of talking, revealing one's feelings, but she had never had the courage to do so herself. Too afraid of looking foolish. She stood mesmerised by the water, listening to the faint music from the house. She heard an animal move across the lawn – a rabbit, maybe, or a fox – but as the sound grew louder and closer she realised it was a person. She turned and tried to make out the figure coming towards her in the dark. He was almost next to her when she realised it was Cal.

She had learned her lesson. She turned to him and made no effort to disguise the elation in her voice. 'You're here! I thought you weren't coming.'

Instantly she regretted it. His voice was distant, cold, even, and he stood, arms folded, looking out across the river. 'Well . . . I got delayed.' He made no effort to turn towards her. 'Victoria said you were out here. I came straight out. I won't stay.'

She said nothing. This was worse than if he had never

come at all. She had the ominous feeling that he was about to discard her without ever having truly embraced her.

He shrugged. 'I ought to say congratulations.'

'To Sam. Yes. They're inside.'

He sounded surprised. 'They?'

She detected some confusion in his voice. Was he drunk? 'Yes.'

Without any interest he asked, 'When's the wedding?'

'Oh, no idea. Probably next year, I guess. I haven't been told.'

'*You haven't been told?*'

He sounded mystified. At least he had turned to look at her. Now she had started to feel alarmed. He really seemed most odd. She decided to prattle on in the vain hope he might get back to normal. 'Sam and Helen haven't told me.'

'Helen? Well, what the hell has she got to do with it?'

Now it was Annie's turn to look bewildered. 'Sam. And Helen. They'll decide it together. And then I daresay they'll tell me and all the other guests.'

He stood utterly still. 'Are you telling me that Sam . . . is marrying Helen?'

Annie lost patience. 'Well, yes, you bloody fool, who else would he be marrying?'

And then he began to laugh, recklessly and hopelessly, looking at her with an expression that was something more than affectionate until he came over and stood with her beneath the willow, his hand resting on the tree. 'Jesus! I thought he was marrying *you*. I thought he was marrying you, Annie. Christ, I've been sitting in some pub trying to work out what to say to you. How to talk you out of it.'

Whether through relief or happiness, Annie began to laugh too. 'I'm not marrying Sam! And I thought you weren't coming because—'

'Why?'

She turned away. 'No, it's too stupid.'

He stood still. 'Tell me. Tell me everything.'

She steeled herself. This was the test. Did she really

believe in truth and courage and honesty – or was she as empty as her words?

She took a deep breath. 'I thought you were with Tania von Stein. I saw it in a magazine and I thought you were just . . . being kind to me. Salving your conscience. And then I thought that if I threw myself at you I'd end up—'

'Getting hurt? Annie, let me tell you two things. First, builders don't have a conscience, and second, Tania Smith – that's her real name by the way – is not with me. She never has been.' He evidently caught an appraising look in her eyes. 'We have an arrangement. A *business* arrangement. I take her out, pay for the evening, and we both get our faces in the papers. The glamour couple – the readers love it. And the journalists make it all up – all of it. And the only, *only* reason I spent any time with that boring girl is to get my properties mentioned in the paper. I need the publicity. It's work, nothing else. They wrote about The Meadows, didn't they?'

Annie nodded.

'And everything I've ever done for you wasn't about conscience. If you had been anyone else, I'd have walked away, called it business and forgotten the whole thing.' He stopped abruptly and moved away from her, uncomfortable and restless, unable to stand still but with nowhere to go, reduced to pacing the lawn around the willow tree. 'Look, Annie, I can't keep this up any longer. It's time I put my cards on the table. Everything I've done, it's been for you. I've wanted you since I first saw you on bloody Cobham high street. I did it all for you. As an excuse to see you.'

She felt impossibly reprieved. 'So, there was never anything with Tania?'

'I swear to you. No. Christ, Annie – I haven't had *time* to do anything else. You've taken over my life. I wanted Albert Road to be perfect for you – I spent bloody days finding the kitchen and the bathroom and—'

'But you said—'

'I said a lot of things because I knew you'd never take money from me. So I bought it all and made up umpteen bloody stupid stories about women who didn't like their kitchens and dockers dropping bathrooms. And that was after I had the house at The Chapters furnished for you.'

Could this really be true? 'But you said it was the show house . . .'

'Was it hell! That got sold ages ago. So I started again with that one. Meanwhile I was spending hours with your brother-in-law trying to find out more about you – and all he ever talked about was that gym of his. And when I wasn't doing that I was working out how to get you to have lunch with me. So in the end I just decided to take you. I've been on a bloody roller coaster. I even had Martin Hollis . . . Well, never mind . . .' He hurried on, 'Then at the ball, when you wouldn't let me hold you, Jesus, girl, you were breaking my heart. And then, that day when you told me to get out, I came so close to giving up. But . . .'

His words faded. They were standing perfectly still now, almost touching, the only sound faint music from the house and the lapping of the water against the river-bank. 'Annie, I can't play games any more. I want you in my life. And I know . . . I know it may not be what you want.' A hint of uncertainty entered his voice, which she had never heard before. 'It may be too soon, but that's fine. I'll wait.'

She made to speak but he rushed on, 'Maybe I've been wrong . . . because I've never asked you about Hugo. Not about him . . . dying. God, I could see it was bad for you. And I didn't know what to say. So I did what I could, with the flat and all, to make things easier. I should have said something before . . . asked you about Hugo.'

'No. You haven't done anything wrong,' said Annie firmly. 'And there was nothing you could have said. Nothing at all.'

Her mind ran on. Now was not the time to talk about loss and grief and the awful pain she had endured. Nor to talk about disloyalty. Was it wrong to live, to laugh – to love again? She had believed it was. Until she had realised that living in a morass of pain was to condemn herself to a life in which she might as well be dead, turning her back on all the good and happy and wonderful things that could happen, existing in a past that could never be reclaimed.

'Cal, there was nothing you could have said because I wouldn't have listened. I had to do it my own way – the hard way. I had to accept that Hugo was dead. And I had to decide to live without him . . .'

A still silence fell between them. He picked up a stray stone from the lawn and sent it skimming across the water. Then he turned to her. 'Annie, I'm not asking for anything, just a chance to be with you. And maybe it'll be great. Or maybe you'll decide I'm just some thick Irish builder. But I think it's worth a try.'

It was all so simple. There was no need to hesitate or question or feel afraid. She caught his eye and held his gaze. 'I think it's worth a try, too.'

And with nothing left to say he took her hand and they walked slowly back to the lights of the house and the party.